VALHALLA BURNING

VALHALLA BURNING

MICHAEL POGACH

DIVERSION
BOOKS

Diversion Books
A division of Diversion Publishing Corp.
www.diversionbooks.com

For more information, email info@diversionbooks.com

First Diversion Books Edition: July 2026
Trade Paperback ISBN: 979-8-89515-146-4
e-ISBN: 979-8-89515-144-0

Design by Westchester Publishing Services
Cover design by Alan Dingman

Printed in the United States of America
1 3 5 7 9 10 8 6 4 2

For all those who fear it's too late to start . . .
It's not.

PROLOGUE

There is a moment at the start of a raid that exists between sounds. A moment when the cracks and pops of nighttime fires and the snores of goats and the moans of sex all stop. A moment before the screams of first blood and the song of the spear-din.

It's a moment Rúnr knows well, an interlude to ask the gods for their favor, to prepare for making slaughter and pillaging gold. It's a moment he often enjoys.

On this night, however, he's not the one asking the gods' favor. He's the one waking, the feeling of something wrong in his gut. He's the one in danger.

I must rise. I must fight. I must defend.

But he's still drunk. Last night was Vetrnætr, the Winter Nights festival honoring the end of summer and the coming of winter. Such festivals are cherished by gods and men. Celebrations deemed safe from enemies and fear and regret. The ale horns and mead cups and beer skins are passed around the mead hall, endlessly refilled like Thor trying to drain the sea from his giant horn.

Rúnr remembers the first drinks. He remembers empty barrels being replaced with full ones. He remembers Torstyn, his friend and brother, helping him up the hill to his home, to his wife and daughter. The hill that now sounds with heavy boots and the promise of murder. He tries to sit up, only to find he's already sitting. His mind is slow, as so much drink makes it. His arms and legs are heavy. He staggers from bed.

Fight. Defend.

Instructions from the gods. From Odin, for Rúnr is his champion.

"Berthe," he says, meaning to wake his wife, but she's already up. Ever quick to action. Shield in hand before he can even find his axe.

"Protect Yrsa," she says. She charges from their home into the night, shouting to rouse the people of Skyjavík. A leader. A hero. A shield-maiden.

"Papa?"

Yrsa, standing there, four years old, pink cheeks, bright coppery hair and blue eyes like her mother.

My Little Bear.

And like her mother she's armed and ready. In her hands, his axe seems overlarge.

"Stay inside," he tells her. "Be brave. It'll be okay."

"I will, Papa," she says without a tremble in her voice.

As if in answer, the gruff shouts of invaders announce that nothing will be okay. Shirtless, bootless, shieldless, Rúnr takes the only weapon left, a long dagger, and means to follow his wife, but there's no need. The enemies step into his house, three of them, Fenns clearly by their shield markings, led by a large warrior, his tattooed face bearing the twisting form of Jörmungandr, the Midgard Serpent who encircles the world.

Rúnr tries to position himself before his daughter, but she won't have it, standing at his side. The painted one orders the others to dispatch Rúnr, but father and daughter are not so easily dealt with. The two Fenns come with spear and axe. Rúnr goes low and high and low again. One Fenn has lost his testicles and is screaming out his life's blood. The other does well to avoid his strikes but not Yrsa's. She lands a clumsy blow on the back of the Fenn's knee. He turns, an instinct. A mistake. Rúnr separates his head from his neck, then faces the Painted Fenn.

There's no hurry in this brutal-faced warrior. There will be no mistakes made by his practiced hands and the broad-bladed sword he holds. Here stands a warrior who's surely heard his name in songs.

"Run," Rúnr tells his daughter.

"But, Papa," she says.

He turns his head, just a little, just enough to meet her eye and make her know he means it. The Painted Fenn doesn't miss his opportunity, swinging a tight arc that almost decapitates Rúnr, who can only duck the sword and shove Yrsa toward the bed.

Crawl under, he wants to yell at her, but he can't spare the breath. The Painted Fenn is advancing with fury while the clash of the sword-storm rises outside. Two more Fenns enter the house, and behind them the flames of war burn as more Fenns approach.

Quickly Rúnr is overmatched, but he feels something coming, rising from within and falling from above at the same time. The god trance. It begins in his teeth, like how they sweat at the smell of meat on a fire. His vision next, blurring at the edges. His heart last, beating like a war drum, faster than a heart should. Then he's gone. Lost. A memory in another's mind.

A Berserkr.

* * *

The one who rushes from Berthe's house has the look of a brutal warrior indeed. Broad shoulders. Large sword. The Midgard Serpent tattooed across his face. Snakes coil in her belly at first, the fear that he's emerging victorious from her home, but she's heard the roar of the Berserkr. She knows her husband will protect Yrsa.

"Die!" she shouts, running up the path.

The Fenn looks right at her, eyes wild with fear. Only now does she perceive his limp and the ferocious wound across his shoulder and chest. He's lucky to be alive and knows it—as do any who face a Berserkr in battle and live—and chooses to flee. Likely to die of his wounds. Or not. That's the gods' concern, not hers. Now that the short-lived battle is won and the invading Fenns have been driven back to their ships, all she cares for is her family.

She charges inside, her daughter's name on her lips, to find Rúnr sitting on the floor, cradling Yrsa in his arms, her body limp. No breath in her lungs. No light in her eyes. Only blood and her throat gouged open to the bone. And his axe still in her tiny hand.

"What happened?" she says, her own voice sounding far away.

"The Painted Fenn . . . I wasn't strong enough," he says, rocking Yrsa like when she was a babe.

Only now does Berthe see the enemies her husband cut down by the grace of Odin's gift, strewn in pieces. Heads, hands, legs, fingers, eyes, an ear—they'll not go to Valhalla whole, but it wasn't enough to save Yrsa. The gods be damned it wasn't enough. She has no consoling words for Rúnr. All she wants is to hold her little girl to her breast.

"The Valkyries will come," he says as she takes her daughter. "They'll come for you, Little Bear."

But they do not come.

PART ONE

"Thralls alone avenge themselves at once; cowards never."
—*The Saga of Grettir the Strong*

CHAPTER 1

Rúnr is awake, though he doesn't want to be. He keeps his eyes screwed shut, thinking maybe sleep will find him again, but someone is coming.

"Of all the places you could choose," Torstyn Helvigson says, his voice unmistakable.

Rúnr opens his gummy eyes to the blurry night. How did he end up out here, behind the mead hall where the rubbish is tossed?

He starts to ask, but his stomach clenches. He fights the need to retch, belching loudly.

"Nice," Torstyn says.

"Fuck you," Rúnr manages.

"You're supposed to be inside."

"The Assembly?"

"By Odin's fucking eye, the Assembly isn't for a week."

"Then what difference does it make where I am?" Rúnr looks up at his adoptive brother, the jarl's blood son, his vision swimming in the moonlight.

Torstyn grins within his red beard, always happy. Easy to be happy when no one expects anything of you. When you have nothing to risk but your life and your father's disappointment. He comes closer, the moonlight casting his face pale. Growing paler, graying, wrinkling, withering before Rúnr's eyes, his red beard lengthening and turning bone white until he's a desiccated corpse, then a hoary skeleton, eye sockets empty pits, then this too begins to decompose, bones flaking away to dust until there's nothing left and Rúnr is choking on his own breath and fear, vomiting until he's heaving empty.

"You saw it again?" Torstyn says. He's moved around Rúnr and stands beside the simple black chair, the *nithstóll*, upon which only dishonorable criminals are meant to sit, bound so they can't escape while awaiting punishment for their crimes. His face is whole. His beard is bright. He's smiling again.

"I did." Relief mingles with disappointment—would it be better, just once, to find these visions of decay are real, rather than seen and gone? He clutches the bear's tooth that hangs around his neck, always cool to the touch, always calming.

"You should speak with the seeress."

The same argument. The visions are nothing new. An effect of Odin's touch, surely, for they began the day Rúnr received his gift, the day of the black bear. And what price is it really, to see such things, in comparison to that gift? What could the old seeress, Olga, tell him other than that? Better to keep it between himself and his brother.

"I'm fine."

"Nothing about this looks fine," Torstyn says, kicking the snow and ice coated chair. "What would the people say if they saw you passed out beside this?"

"Nobody cares a seal's asshole what I do so long as I stand at your father's side when necessary, and fight when called upon."

"Our father." A correction Torstyn only makes when he's annoyed.

"Lucky me."

"If this is what luck looks like, the gods can ignore me for a while."

Rúnr leans against the chair. The night is cold, the ground covered in a thin layer of iced-over snow, the spring thaw still a week or two away. He shivers. "What do you want? Is it just disapproval of where I sleep?"

"You're calling this sleep?"

"Not since you woke me up."

"Did you have the dream?" Torstyn asks. Another secret between brothers.

"I'll dream somewhere else tomorrow if it pleases you," Rúnr says.

"Somewhere else, indeed."

That tone, Rúnr knows well. Mischief and determination. Whatever Torstyn says next is going to get the brothers into trouble.

"It's time to do something," Torstyn says.

"Do I need to be sober for it? Give me a minute and an ale."

"No, something else. Something right, that should have been done months ago."

"Father has agreed to send us north?" Rúnr begins to stand, hopeful for the first time since his daughter's death, these long months of storm and blizzard during which the jarl has refused to allow anyone to travel north. What an unfamiliar feeling hope is, that he may soon free her from the black mist where she wanders, denied Valhalla. Because he's been denied vengeance.

"Jarl Helvig," Torstyn says, "is a stubborn old man. You know he has not agreed."

Rúnr drops back onto his ass. "I can't go against him. I have to stand by my jarl."

"You're not standing by him now. He's speaking to the people in there right now"—he points at the mead hall—"making plans for the Assembly while you sit here in your own filth."

"Until he changes his orders—"

"Fuck his orders."

Rúnr rubs his fists into his eyes. If anyone else spoke like this, they would be brought before the jarl to face his wrath. If Rúnr—the champion of Skyjavík, largest town in the Opplands—were heard speaking like this, insulting the jarl like this, it could be the wound that one of Helvig's rivals has been waiting to exploit.

"I have to stand by my jarl," Rúnr says again. "It's the law."

"I can't believe in all the Opplands, only Berthe had the courage to act."

"And look what happened to my wife," Rúnr spits.

"Ex-wife."

Rúnr gets to his feet as quickly as he can and punches Torstyn in the mouth. Or tries to. He barely manages to keep his balance long enough to aim the blow. Throwing it sends him spinning. Torstyn moves easily aside and lets him fall. Rúnr's face smashes off the chair's seat, making the night flash bright as the sun.

Next thing he knows, he's on a knee beside the punishment chair, rubbing his jaw. Nothing broken, though his head feels as if a thousand oarsmen are slapping his skull from the inside.

"She was the bravest of us, I would wager," Torstyn says. He offers his brother a hand.

Rúnr takes it and comes to his feet. He spits blood and tries not to think of Berthe, which only leads him to a hundred other thoughts. The coming Assembly. Summer raids. Has the roof fallen in on his house in the weeks since he's been home? What will he drink tonight? The need to piss. The need to shout at the moon just because. Everything. Anything. Except Berthe. And in trying not to think of her, he does. Which leads his thoughts to Yrsa. Their daughter.

"It's time to do something about it," Torstyn says.

"We could be exiled. We—I could lose Odin's favor. What then?"

Torstyn puts a hand on Rúnr's shoulder. "The Allfather chose you to protect and to fight, not to follow orders."

"And I failed the first. I should not fail the last now."

"You sound like Father. Or Leif, when he actually speaks. What if ignoring orders can right the first wrong?"

Rúnr drops onto the chair.

"Brother!" Torstyn says, horrified that any honorable man, let alone the jarl's son, would sit on the *nithstóll.*

"Might as well see how it feels now," Rúnr says, enjoying this rare moment of seriousness, of joylessness, in his brother.

Torstyn pries Rúnr from the chair. "Come, away from this place."

Rúnr lets himself be led around the mead hall and down the way to the stables, boots crunching the ice, where two horses wait already laden with gear.

"You're serious," Rúnr says, more surprised that Torstyn has thought ahead enough to make preparations than he is at his brother defying the jarl.

"Father's two best."

"Because if you're going to be a jackass, might as well insult him too?"

Torstyn shrugs, his grin, his joy, returned. "I spoke with one of the fur traders who came by way of the Kattegat the other day. Says he's been north, all the way to the Fennvold. He knows the village we want. He's seen the man with his own eyes."

"The Painted Fenn," Rúnr says, his blood cold, his flesh pimpling.

"Who's there?" a voice calls.

"Hide," Torstyn tells Rúnr, gesturing to the shadows behind the horses.

Rúnr doesn't move as a man comes into the stables.

"By Thor's beard, Brondulf," Torstyn says. "What are you doing here?"

Brondulf, the cattle-butcher, looks over the two of them and then the horses. "The jarl sent me to find you," he says. "Rúnr," he adds with a nod.

Rúnr returns the gesture. It's been some time since the three of them have been together, since the summer raids at least. He wonders how well their long friendship will hold up in the face of insubordination.

"No point in telling a lie, is there?" Torstyn moves closer to one of the horses. Where a sword hangs.

"No point," Brondulf says. "Pretty clear you two are leaving Skyjavík."

"But Father wants to see us."

"He does."

Torstyn moves even closer to the horse, within reach. Brondulf raises his hands, unarmed.

"Are you going north?" Brondulf asks.

"Depends on him," Torstyn says of Rúnr.

"To do what should have been done?"

"Are you going to stop us?" Torstyn asks, petting the horse's flank, hand inches from the sword.

"I would go with you," Brondulf says. "But then who would convince the jarl that his sons must be somewhere on the South Mountain, hunting night hares or bathing in the hot springs?"

Torstyn turns to Rúnr and waits. It's the right thing to do, Rúnr knows, even as it's the wrong thing. Perhaps it's a test. The gods are not above such trials, such games pitting desires against oaths. It's been months without action. Without vengeance. Without sober sleep or unhaunted dreams.

The dream.

"They cannot find me, Papa," Yrsa says in those dreams.

"Who cannot find you, Little Bear?" he asks.

"The Valkyries—they cannot find me in this black mist. They cannot bring me to Valhalla until you free me from it."

"How?"

"Kill it."

"Kill the mist?"

"The brute, Papa. The one who murdered me lives on unpunished. Are you not ashamed?"

Soon, I will no longer be, Little Bear, Rúnr thinks.

"Let's go," he says, mounting one of the horses. "To do what should have been done."

Torstyn smiles the way he does when a pretty serving girl brings him an ale. He and Brondulf embrace before Torstyn climbs atop the other horse.

The cattle-butcher stands aside and says, "Bring us our honor back."

CHAPTER 2

"Bathing?" Jarl Helvig says.

The cattle-butcher bows his head and confirms it.

"Bathing!"

The cattle-butcher looks around, probably wishing he'd delivered this news in the mead hall's central hall before his friends and kin rather than here in the jarl's chambers. As if an audience would lessen Helvig's rage. Let one man tremble, or a hundred—all that matters to Helvig is for the people to know who's in charge.

"And you're still standing here why?" he roars.

"With all respect, my jarl, the South Mountain is treacherous in daylight. To go climbing now, at night, just to find them—"

"Is exactly what I ordered you to do. What would it look like if the meat didn't slice under your blade? Or if the cattle didn't come when you herded them? Could you be a butcher then?" Helvig enjoys the way the man squirms.

"No, of course not."

"Then how do I look when my sons don't appear in the hall when I call them?"

"It doesn't make you look weak, my jarl."

"Weak?" Helvig shouts. "Who said weak?"

A thrall sticks his head into the room and waits. Helvig leaves both butcher and slave lost in silence until he can't stand it himself.

"What do you want?" the jarl says.

The thrall flinches. Good. "The Lady Thyri asks a moment of your time, my lord."

"Of course she does. Are you married, butcher?"

"Yes, my jarl. Ljufu is my wife."

"Gorvark's daughter." Helvig can't help a smile. A pretty girl. The kind he might have once invited to this room, married or not. He coughs and begins to pace. The fire's smoke is thick tonight. "Good warrior, her father was. Raided the Saxons with me twice. Does she interrupt you when you're butchering?"

"No," the butcher says, more like a question.

Helvig is suddenly tired of tormenting this man. He's a good Opplander. A great butcher. A friend of Torstyn's. Always hanging around when they were boys, the three of them—Torstyn, Rúnr, and Brondulf.

Friends of three, like the old days. He thinks of Njal and Leif and himself. Then doesn't want to think of that anymore.

"That's a good wife, then." To the thrall, Helvig says, "Tell the lady I'm on my way."

The thrall nods and exits. Helvig pulls up his belt and makes a show of adjusting his groin. Winks at the butcher, who smiles back. A man who understands, or thinks he does. Good. Let the people know their jarl still takes what a husband needs from his wife.

"Give them until morning, then," Helvig says. "But if you can't find their faces by sunrise, go climb that mountain and tell them their father, their jarl, demands to see them before I finish the morning's first cup of ale."

"Of course," the butcher says. "It's my honor to do as you ask."

When the jarl is alone, he exhales and yanks up his belt again. Whatever Thyri wants, it's bound to be a thorn in Helvig's ass, even more so if she actually desires him in her bed. He tries thinking of her bare breasts, but his mind keeps slipping to the butcher's wife. It's enough to get him started on his way to Thyri's bedchamber down the hall from his, but halfway there he's thinking of Torstyn and Rúnr again. Bathing in the hot springs on the South Mountain at night? It feels wrong.

The cattle-butcher wouldn't lie to me, would he?

But of course he would. The friendship of boys holds together even under the withering gaze of a jarl, no matter the fear he saw in the man. No matter that Helvig still commands Skyjavík with strength and respect. For childhood friends, he knows, lies and theft and murder are no more than rain off a sailor's seal-oiled cloak.

Helvig sighs. Whatever the boys are up to, it can wait until morning. If only his wife could wait too.

He sucks in his gut and knocks on Thyri's door the way he used to when they were young. When he knew she was waiting inside in nothing more than the silk-lined marten-fur shawl he gave her on their wedding night.

She opens the door fully clothed, mouth turned down in a frown. An argument, then, it'll be. Helvig closes the door behind him, letting his gut sag over his belt, filled with more relief than disappointment.

CHAPTER 3

The snow is deep and heavy, forcing the horses to a high-stepping trudge over the mountain pass. The brothers have ridden all night and into the morning by the barest glow of the splinter moon, and though they're not yet halfway to the Fennvold, they're far enough from Skyjavík to feel safe from pursuit.

It's the first night in a long time Rúnr has passed the darkness without the dream. *Maybe*, he thinks, *I should sleep in the day like a bat.*

But he knows better. The dream will come whenever he closes his eyes. And he wouldn't deny it, either. It's all he has left of Yrsa, like a knife stuck in his ribs, the steel keeping him from bleeding out. And thinking of bleeding brings his thoughts to her body on the floor of their home.

No, not this. He forces his mind elsewhere. The way north. The mountains. The horses. They need rest. Food and water too. Maybe there's a spring nearby. He scans the landscape. A mist clings to some of the slopes. Mist brings memory. Why? He doesn't ask, just remembers. Yrsa holding his thumb as they walked the fence, checking for places chickens could get out or wolves could get in.

"But the wolves won't get in, will they, Papa?" she said, all four of her fingers not enough to fully cover his thumb.

"No," he had told her. "I'll keep the chickens safe."

"And Mama and me too?"

"I'll keep us all safe, Little Bear."

"Rúnr!"

"What?" He's lost his thoughts again, like a child distracted by every cloud, coin, or cow.

"I said, we should take that road." Torstyn is pointing to where the pass forks, one way bending toward the midnight-colored sea.

"If there's this much snow when we get there, we'll look like mounds of dung against the drifts. They'll see us coming half a day off."

Torstyn combs his fingers through his beard and laughs. *He'll die laughing*, Rúnr thinks, and isn't comforted by it.

"Open your eyes, brother," Torstyn says. "Wide like you want to see more than just vengeance."

I'll keep us all safe, Little Bear.

"There's only vengeance."

"If that was true, you wouldn't have waited all winter."

"I didn't wait. I—"

"Then, you waited," Torstyn says. "And now you don't."

They ride on, with Torstyn looking side glances at Rúnr. "Is there more you want to tell me?" Rúnr finally asks.

"A question."

"Ask it."

"Why will the Valkyries not take her?"

Rúnr wants to sigh. Or scream. He wants to tell his brother to ask the seeress since the old woman has refused to say any more than Rúnr must heed the dream. He wants not to answer at all, not think on any aspect of it but seeking the vengeance that will resolve the matter. But Torstyn is not often one to worry about *why*, so Rúnr admits, "I don't know. The gods don't tell me. All I know is what she says when I see her in my dreams—I must kill the Painted Fenn. Then the Valkyries will find her."

Torstyn doesn't ask more. Rúnr both loves and hates that about him.

Sometime later, Torstyn says, "Look."

Rúnr follows his pointing finger out to sea where a ship cuts the waves close to the rocky shore. "Danes," he says, recognizing the sail. "Must be lost to sail north of the Nordfjord in winter."

"Maybe we can wave them down. Hire them."

"Nobody sails to the Fennvold before the thaw."

"If they're crazy enough to come this far, a little gold might be enough to prompt them farther."

Rúnr considers the snow. It'll take two more days to reach the Fennvold. Three even, if the snow deepens or a storm comes. Half that by ship.

"We won't have to come over the mountain like dung, either," Torstyn says.

"You've brought that much gold?"

"Enough to take us and wait for our return."

"And to pay for the return?"

"There'll be coin enough to take from the Fenns."

It's at least as bad a plan as riding the rest of the way. Sailing north in winter is as smart as sticking your head into a hungry wolf's maw. Then again, two warriors against a village is no smarter.

"If we survive," Rúnr says.

"The god trance will come, and we'll do more than survive."

Torstyn's confidence makes Rúnr feel unmoored. What if it doesn't come? It hasn't since that night.

I've not fought a battle since that night.

But still, it's always been there, since the choosing—the day of the black bear—under his skin like a smoldering fire.

What if it never comes again? What worth can I have without it?

Rúnr's horse gets skittish. He calms her with a pat and whisper.

"Did you know they'd be here?" he asks his brother about the ship.

"Danes are crazy fuckers," Torstyn says with a shrug. "Never know where you might find them. Besides, think about Father's face when we sail into the harbor on a Danish ship, singing our victory and vengeance."

Rúnr wants to think about it. He wants to grin the way his brother does. But he sees her face out there in the sea. Yrsa, four years old, throat cut wide by the Painted Fenn's blade, deep to the bone. How could one little girl, his beautiful daughter, bleed so much?

Which takes his thoughts, like a diverted creek, back to Berthe, the only Opplander to deny Helvig's order and go north seeking vengeance, until now. To the blizzard that came the night she left, and the one that followed that, and the next after. To the waiting for her return, which never came. To her fate, surely frozen to death and buried in the snow—maybe just over there beside the road—gnawed upon by ravens and mountain cats.

Better than drowned, maybe. Either way, this is Yrsa's vengeance. It is Rúnr's vengeance. It's Berthe's and Torstyn's and Skyjavík's vengeance. It belongs not to the Danes.

"We'll continue on our own," he says.

Torstyn smiles, his beard as red as the morning sun, and draws from the pack strapped to his horse's rump two gray cloaks made of wolf pelts. "Now we won't look like dung coming over the mountain." He whoops loud at his own humor and rides north.

Rúnr looks back the way they've come, their tracks dark in the snow, like corpses, and then follows his brother. As hope sits uncomfortably in his chest, Rúnr knows that it rests entirely on him. On the god trance taking him. On Odin's favor, which he hasn't felt since the night the Fenns came. Which wasn't enough to protect his daughter.

Maybe it will be enough to avenge her.

CHAPTER 4

The Fennvold is the true North. Rúnr would never say such a thing aloud. He's barely comfortable thinking it. But the cold here is biting in a way the Opplands only knows a few nights a year, and the snow is a different kind of heavy, soaking through leather like water through a fishing net.

It's also not a singular territory like the Opplands. Sprawling for a day's ride in every direction, the Fennvold is a loose confederacy of villages across frozen wetlands, meadows, fjords, and farmlands. So Torstyn has taught Rúnr during their ride north. Jarl Dagfinn, the Gray, is the first to unite the people of the Fennvold, though if it was on his order that the warriors of this village should raid Skyjavík during the Winter Nights festival, Helvig's son doesn't know.

It's night now, as the brothers, cloaked in their wolf pelts, watch the village from the southwest, counting torches as they're extinguished. Their horses remain nearly a half day's trudge south, tied and hidden in a gully, hopefully able to withstand the cold long enough to carry the brothers home.

Torstyn nudges Rúnr. "I said, does it come for you?"

Rúnr breathes deep. The night air is sharp with the flavor of wet snow. Above, the moon is barely a sliver, but the Bifröst lights the sky green and violet, reflecting the shields of the Valkyries as they prepare to collect the dead. And there will surely be dead tonight. More if the god trance comes.

If it doesn't, we've come here to die.

"Not yet," he says.

"You're certain?" Torstyn looks disappointed.

Rúnr rolls his shoulders and flexes his arms. His muscles are tense with anticipation and his heart drums an eager beat, but that's all. For now.

"Not yet," he tells his brother again.

"Can you make it happen?"

A part of the plan they probably should have discussed—what to do when the fickle gods refuse to look their way. "Can you make Freyja lift her skirt?"

Torstyn smiles wide as if he'd like to try. "Two against a hundred is a glorious way to die, but I'd prefer not to see the Valkyries' faces tonight."

Rúnr isn't certain he wouldn't want to meet a Valkyrie, to grab her by the wings and scream at her: *Find my daughter, curse you! Bring her to Valhalla!* But no, he doesn't want to die tonight either. At least not until he knows Yrsa's vengeance is made.

"We can do it quiet," he says.

"Like assassins afraid of honor."

"They came as assassins, creeping by night into Skyjavík. We don't lose honor in revisiting that upon them."

Torstyn nods his agreement. "You want to do it quiet, then?"

Rúnr considers the village. Its mead hall is short and squat, half the size of Helvig's. There's no watch set. Its buildings, houses and fishmonger huts and butcheries, are clustered here and there across uneven terrain. He imagines one of those houses holding the only man he needs to kill. The Painted Fenn, with the Midgard Serpent, Jörmungandr, tattooed on his face. He remembers that face looking at him as he emerged from the god trance. That face, twisted in battle-lust and speckled with blood.

Yrsa's blood.

And now she wanders, trapped in the black mist between Valhalla and the realm of the lost dead, that one named for its queen: Hel.

Torstyn's hand on Rúnr's shoulder ends the memory like an axe cleaving cabbage. By the gods, how Rúnr hates the way his mind flows in many streams rather than a single, purposeful river. It has set him apart since his earliest days. His father—his blood father, Njal—treated him like a cracked bowl, one tap likely to shatter it. His mother, Alina, knew it, hugging him more than other mothers did their boys.

Eyes that seek only one river are blind to all others, she would say, trying to hide his flaw in foreign proverbs. *But the man who sees all the rivers of the world can know all its truths.*

Whatever people Njal took her from didn't understand the North. Good Northerners, men like Torstyn, give themselves to their tasks, fully in body and mind. When Torstyn chops wood, he chops wood. With complete focus. Each strike perfect.

When Rúnr chops wood, his mind seeks the way he'll build tomorrow's fire. Or the large halibut that escaped his hook yesterday. Or the shape of a boar's snout within the log's grain. Or Yrsa, murdered by the Painted Fenn.

This is why we're here.

"Yes," Rúnr says. "We'll do it quiet, one house at a time until we find him."

Torstyn grins wide and joyous, always the same whether for battle, for drinking, or for fucking. It's the grin of a happy man. A man who has only one mind to tend.

"The Painted Fenn will die tonight," Torstyn says. "On Odin's eye, I swear it."

"On Odin's eye."

The brothers make their way into the village, choosing a cluster of wattle-and-daub huts. Torstyn leads the way to one with a door made of bound reeds. Carefully, he opens the door so Rúnr can enter. A low fire illuminates a man and a woman sleeping fitfully with two children beneath wool blankets. A pleasant scene. Until the man's face rots, and the woman's eyes ooze, and the children wither and flake to dust as if the years of their lives have run their course in seconds. Rúnr's breath catches in his throat. He can't help coughing on it.

"Rúnr," Torstyn hisses.

The family sleeps sound now, whole and unblemished, chests rising softly. The only death in the house is what the brothers have brought.

Rúnr hurries outside, heart hammering within his rib cage.

"You look—is it coming?" Torstyn asks.

Rúnr shakes his head.

"Maybe we should split up," Torstyn says. "Search more houses."

"Good idea."

"I wouldn't want to be caught inside somewhere with you if it does come."

"No, you wouldn't."

The brothers choose their next houses. Inside Rúnr's is another family, faces free of tattoos. He leaves as quietly as he entered. Outside, Torstyn emerges from a house and shakes his head. On to the next two, but the man they seek doesn't sleep in these either.

"This way," Torstyn says.

A dog barks somewhere as they slip into another pair of houses and emerge again disappointed. When Rúnr exits the next house, rain is falling and more dogs are barking. The sound of boots pounding the frozen ground is unmistakable.

"We're discovered," Torstyn says.

Rúnr pushes back his wet hair. Long has he wished to enter battle at his brother's side, but it's never come to pass. Rúnr was chosen as Odin's champion on the day they were bonded men, before they could go on their first raid. And though he's the first in generations, the stories were never forgotten of the champion's gift to slay all foes. When the shield wall forms and the god trance takes hold, Rúnr stands in the front. Alone. Always.

And now here he is, tightening his wooden shield's leather straps and drawing his steel sword—a gift from Jarl Helvig to replace the axe he buried with Yrsa—beside his brother. The moment is less than he'd hoped. There is no shield wall on either side. No war drums beating. No skalds watching to record and sing the glories of battle. There is only a slow silence, a few seconds that stretches far longer than they should. A pre-battle moment of beat-held hearts and peace being made with the gods. Of fear and the fear of showing fear. A moment all warriors know well.

Torstyn draws his sword and rises to his full height as five men come from the center of the village. They're armed but not well armored, with only two shields among them. A quick preparation. The first wave. More will come.

Rúnr grips the bear's tooth around his neck and commits himself as one of the Fenns points a spear and shouts. Like beacons being lit, cries go up across the village. Torstyn answers with a savage growl. The spearman charges. A mistake. Torstyn meets him, splintering the weapon and gutting the man with two quick slashes. The remaining four hold their ground as more Fenns arrive.

Too many more.

Torstyn retreats to his brother's side. Though they've not fought together, they know the ways to neutralize an enemy's numbers. Rúnr prepares to dig in for the next charge, but his vision blurs at the edges, like rain slipping down a sail. His chest becomes heavy. The many streams of his thoughts converge into a tumultuous river. Odin's favor is filling him.

Yes, the god trance. Yes, vengeance!

Until he remembers Torstyn, trapped beside him within a growing circle of Fenns—what is about to become an arena of death.

"Wait," he says, as if Odin would heed his words.

Two of the Fenns advance, growing somehow smaller as they do.

I am growing larger.

Somewhere, the crash of thunder and the roar of a monster.

"Berserkr," one of the Fenns cries, pointing in terror.

"Brother," Rúnr tries to say, to warn Torstyn, tell him to run, but his voice is no longer his own. His muscles clench as if wanting to burst free and fight on their own. Some impulse makes him bite the iron rim of his shield. Thor's lightning charges through his jaw, igniting his shoulders and rippling down his spine until there's nothing left of him but the need to kill.

CHAPTER 5

Thyri watches her husband pace behind the jarl's chair, the rune-engraved symbol of his power. Though he is thinner these days, he's still a commanding presence. Especially when he puts on shows of disfavor and anger. Especially when such shows have a full mead hall for an audience. Another outburst is coming, these good people know. They wait for it, cups held motionless halfway to their mouths. Outside, the rain shoots down like arrows. The wind shrieks. Thunder breaks the sky.

"Not one goat-fucking coward saw them ride out on my best horses?" Helvig shouts. As he paces, long strides like a man hurrying to war, he slaps away a cup from the arm of his chair, sending it into the fire. "The reddest beard and the blackest beard and not one person saw them? Not one traitor will admit to helping them go?"

Traitor is too far, Thyri knows. He's put on shows like this before, there was even shouting earlier today when he was first told his horses were gone, but this is the first time he's ever called anyone a traitor. Her eyes find Ubbein, famed hero of the Battle of Mjøsa, watching thoughtfully from deep in the hall. With his shaved head and crooked nose, broken too many times to count, he looks the way Baldr, son of Odin, might, she thinks. Of all men in Skyjavík, that one she doesn't trust. He sees what she sees. The pacing. The shouting. The accusations. They're not born of strength but of fear. Helvig is terrified for his place on the jarl's chair and for the life of his son.

Sons, she reminds herself. A familiar twisting, like a fist, grips her gut. Though she'll never accept Rúnr as her own—no matter that she once would have borne Njal's child proudly—he's Helvig's son, has been since Njal was killed seven summers back. Another fact Ubbein sees, she knows.

When did heroes become such schemers?

"I should set every man here—"

"Husband," Thyri says, saving him from himself.

Saving myself, she thinks. There isn't a weakness Ubbein won't try to exploit. No ambition he would set too high. Hero already, then what? She doesn't dare think it. If he becomes jarl, it will mean her end.

Unless . . .

"Do you have something to say?" Helvig demands.

He hates being interrupted, especially by his wife. Always willing to take her counsel in private, he fears having the look of a man who can't lead without a woman. Thyri wonders, not for the first time, if he's aware of these facts about himself, of how regulated by fear he's become.

"Our son is headstrong, and his love for his brother"—she forces the word—"is like oak. Neither needs the aid of others to run off like this."

Helvig stares at her, eyes half threatening, half pleading for her to keep going, to save him from the corner he's backed himself into.

"And the two of them, Torstyn and Rúnr together," she says for all to hear, knowing what she knows: Torstyn is well beloved, and Rúnr is well feared, and all here want vengeance against the Fenns. What man wouldn't want to stand by his brother? "Yes, together they can, perhaps, collect the price we are owed. Imagine it, two men against all the Fennvold. They came because we took our trade to the Rogaland instead of the Fennvold last summer. They came and whipped us like sleeping dogs." The mead hall is filled with boos and hisses and whistles like the thickest smoke. "Oh yes, they did. And they sing of it now even though we rose up and sent them fleeing in their ships with more dead than stolen gold. Well, think of what Torstyn and Rúnr might revisit upon them. Think of Skyjavík's renown when stories are told of what two of our warriors have done against the false-hearted Fenns!"

The mead hall is all cheering now. Drinks are drunk once more. Helvig has calmed. Only Ubbein appears darkened by ill thoughts.

Outside, the wind calls like a thousand wolves.

"Think of our reputation, husband," Thyri goes on, unable to stop herself. "Our family. No greater songs will be sung in the Opplands than those of our son."

She lets it hang in the air like mist—our *son*. Will he argue, insist she include Rúnr, as he often does? He says nothing for a time. Over his shoulder, Thyri watches one of Ubbein's camp whisper to the hero. When did his following grow so large, and with so many strangers among them? Ubbein barks at the man, then finds Thyri's eye. Yes, let him know what she knows. Let him wonder if Helvig knows it too. If he wants an easy road to a jarldom, he can go find a chair in some other land.

Helvig grips Thyri's shoulders and kisses her on the cheek. On the forehead. On the mouth. It's been a long time since her lips tasted his, their bedding duties performed for each other, so often as they are anymore, usually without talking or kissing. Without patience for the act itself, so different from the intimacy they used to share.

"I have the wisest wife," Helvig declares.

The mead hall could not be happier, the cheers rolling like waves. Outside, thunder rumbles as if in agreement.

"I have the bravest sons," the jarl says.

The people of Skyjavík love to hear it and voice their support. But Thyri watches Ubbein as he shoves open the doors, letting in the storm, and strides out followed by his band. In their wake, others hurry to close the doors. To keep the illusion of safety within the hall. Helvig releases her and returns to his chair, slumping into it like a man with too much drink in him. The cost of rule and of the fear of losing that rule, Thyri knows. It has made her husband gray and suspicious. It has left his once-strong arms and breast saggy.

"Another cup," Helvig says, his words quieter, for his wife alone.

She could order her handmaiden, Hrodny, or any other thrall, to bring it, but she likes to serve her husband. To remind him how much he needs her. Hrodny, always attentive, is there for her with a full horn of ale. She takes it and brings it to her husband. He raises it sloppily and speaks their son's name to a chorus of cheers. When he opens his mouth wide to say more, to add the name of Njal's son to his salute toward honor and victory, however, the doors of the mead hall are thrown open once more with a crash. Rangvald, the carpenter, hurries to stand before the fire, dripping wet from the storm.

"My sons?" Helvig asks. "Is there news?"

There's that twisting again in Thyri's gut. She remembers how simple things were once, before Helvig became jarl. When he and Leif and Njal were young warriors building their names, and she, though a poor farmer's daughter, was a prize just become old enough for any one of them to earn. That summer, so full of hope. Then the three sailed south and east and farther than their fathers ever had and returned changed. Helvig came with the belief in his right to the jarl's chair. Leif came with scars and a new stoicism. And Njal came with a dark-haired girl who spoke only foreign words.

By winter, Thyri was Helvig's. The summer after that, Helvig was jarl, and Torstyn was born, then Rúnr just two weeks after to Njal's foreign bitch.

"No, my jarl," Rangvald says, nearly out of breath. "The storm."

"Yes, yes," Helvig says. "A wild storm it is."

But Rangvald is rocking foot to foot, worried. Incongruous with the bravado of the hall. The people quiet. Whispers begin. A death? A flood? An invasion?

"My jarl," says the carpenter. "There's been an accident."

Thyri's heart catches in her throat. But no, Rangvald said there's no news of Torstyn. It's someone else's child who's had an accident. She doesn't even try to hide her relief.

CHAPTER 6

"Tell me again," Rúnr says.

They ride their horses along the ridge above the fjord. Many times Rúnr has sailed this way through the fjord's ice-blue waters, the mountains rising on either side like the comforting hands of giants funneling them home.

"He was not there," Torstyn says.

"You looked upon each body?"

"You remember nothing, truly?"

This is the way of the god trance. Rúnr is himself and then he isn't. In between is haze and smoke and blood and little else. Sometimes he wakes moments after the killing ends but sometimes later. The waking is like being pulled from the sea seconds before drowning. Wheezing for air, lungs burning, vision pocked and streaked. Less a person than a desire, an endless need, to just keep breathing. Later, memories like lone snowflakes, quick to melt, fall through his mind. A screaming face. A severed hand falling. The pumping of blood from a belly. No more than that. No threads connecting the sights or sounds. Or tastes.

"I drank blood?" Rúnr says, the metallic flavor suddenly on his tongue.

"Not that I saw."

They ride on. Rúnr marks a familiar crag. "What of Berthe?"

Torstyn asks, "What of her?"

"Did you find her body?"

"You think she made it all the way to the Fennvold?"

"If any warrior could."

"Brother, even if she had survived the worst blizzards seen in our lifetime and found her way to the Fennvold and died in glorious battle against them, they would not have made for her a cairn. Did we make cairns for the Fenns killed during their invasion of Skyjavík? No, we dragged their corpses far off and left them for the animals and the gods."

"Of course," Rúnr admits. He thinks for her an apology—for letting her go off alone, for not loving her like a husband should, for not thinking of her often enough since she left—and a prayer that she died in battle so that she may dine with Yrsa one day.

When I've found the Painted Fenn and finally had our vengeance.

"Look," Torstyn says, pointing ahead. "The fjord bends."

And where it bends it will come together with two others to make Skyjavík's harbor. And in that harbor, riding low in the high tide, will be Thor's Island, that sacred place where the god of thunder first rode the Bifröst to Midgard.

"Almost home." The realization does not bring the joy Rúnr had hoped. He looks back the way they've come, as if he can see all the way to the Fennvold. Will the Fenns come for war again to repay what Rúnr and Torstyn have done? This question brings another, and another again, until he is considering the dangers ahead, not from Fenns but from Skyjavík.

There will be alarm at unexpected riders coming along the ridge. Will Helvig order his Hersir, Leif, the general of his army, to stand a watch or to send a volley of arrows? Will the brothers be in more danger as strangers or as the known sons of Helvig, returning after defying the jarl's word and stealing his horses?

"They'll welcome us," Torstyn says, as if hearing Rúnr's thoughts.

It's not enough to calm Rúnr's mind. "You're certain he wasn't there?" he asks again.

"Brother," Torstyn says. "We've been riding for days, and you've asked me this question more times than I have fingers. It's not my memory that's broken."

Rúnr flinches. Being Odin's champion is not just a great honor. It's an enormous burden. None of the old stories talk about that, though, or the cutting stigma—the fear friends can't hide from their eyes. It wasn't like this at first, of course. Being the Berserkr was glory upon glory for Rúnr, barely sixteen winters old at the time and just weeks removed from his father's death. It was respect. Envy from those who wanted what he'd been gifted. And he enjoyed it all for those first few years.

Long dimmed is that glory now, though, like a fire left untended in winter.

"I didn't mean it like that," says Torstyn. "After you . . . did what you do, while you slept, I turned over every corpse and sought his face. I went house to house killing those who remained. There's not a man left alive in that village. He wasn't there."

"He could have fled."

"Don't you trust me?"

And Rúnr does. Suddenly. Completely. Confidently. "Of course I trust you."

What he doesn't say is that he remembers their oath, on Odin's eye, that the Painted Fenn would die that night. A broken oath is no small thing. Broken oaths have taken down more warriors, heroes, and jarls than songs can remember.

"He lies dead somewhere," Torstyn says. "You cut him that night during the raid, right?"

This Rúnr cannot forget. Returning to himself on the floor of his home. The Painted Fenn limping away, wild-eyed, blood pumping from countless wounds, the sword that cut open Yrsa's throat in his hand. Rúnr wanting to give chase. His muscles did not respond.

"I cut him, yes."

"Maybe he bled out on their sail home, and they dropped him into the sea," Torstyn says. "Or his wounds betrayed him on a hunt and his flesh litters a wolf den. His bones have been shit out and already rot."

"No," Rúnr says. If his daughter's killer were dead, she would no longer haunt his dreams. "He's still out there."

Torstyn looks as if he'll argue, but he merely nods. "Then we will find him."

It's a comfort, if a small one. Below, the joining of the fjord with two more whale ways marks the opening to the deep blue waters of Skyjavík's harbor.

"Do you think they see us?" Rúnr asks as the brothers turn down the path that will take them to the north end of the beach. Though they've been gone only days, the thaw appears to have begun. And Skyjavík seems to have grown, a new building having risen at the far end of the beach.

"They see us," Torstyn says.

The people are gathering already, perhaps coming as one from the mead hall on the word of a watcher who caught early sight of the brothers. By the time their horses have carried them halfway down the path, the crowd gathering on the beach has grown to contain more than half of Skyjavík's numbers.

"They've come to cheer us," says Torstyn, despite the number of warriors down there, armed and grim, among the waiting crowd.

He laughs, a comforting sound that always reminds Rúnr of what a focused mind, a proper mind, can do to make enjoyment out of all life's storms. But Rúnr's mind is neither focused nor proper. He squints at the new building, seeking its purpose, only to realize it's no building at all. It's a pyre standing ready for flame. A recent death.

Torstyn says, "Bad omen."

Before Rúnr can reply, his brother kicks his horse into a gallop, careening dangerously down the path. "Ho, Skyjavík!" he cries.

At the sight of the jarl's son, the crowd lets off a great cheer. Even from this distance, Rúnr can see Leif, broad as a beer barrel, stoic as ever, order his warriors to stay their weapons. Another cheer goes up from the crowd as Torstyn shouts of victory and glory. Rúnr, however, makes no hurry to follow his brother, his many minds running the many roads of Skyjavík. To his house, where his daughter is buried. To the mead hall, where Helvig will shout down their disobedience. To the seeress's dark home . . .

"Victory," Torstyn shouts again.

His name the people call in answer.

"Vengeance!" he replies, master of all popularity in this moment.

They bellow Torstyn's name once more as Rúnr finally arrives among them, but no one looks for him. No one clamors to be near him. Women, meanwhile, press for Torstyn as he climbs from his horse, daughters and wives who care nothing for their duties and oaths now. They're in the moment. This is the secret to happiness, how the Opplanders are always laughing as they go about their daily chores. Gutting fish, fucking wives, fighting battles—all with a smile and a joke in the next breath. Because they think only what they do.

And I think only the hundreds of things I have done, could have done, or have yet to do.

Brondulf pushes his way through the crowd to Rúnr and takes the reins of his horse.

"My friend," the cattle-butcher says. "We have all worried for you."

"All?" asks Rúnr, climbing down from his horse.

Brondulf clasps him on the shoulder, laughing. "Worry. Shout about. Even curse and threaten. All the same from your father, eh?"

Together they approach Leif, his stance strong and commanding as always, his long, pointed beard beginning to show gray.

"At least you brought the horses back," he says.

"And news of victory," Brondulf says. "Can you not hear Torstyn telling of it?"

"The Rus in their lands can hear Torstyn telling of it."

At this, even Rúnr laughs.

"Is it true you've made the Fenns pay the blood price?" Leif asks.

"It is," says Rúnr.

"That's good. Your father is in a mood."

Torstyn, standing atop a fish barrel, is holding the crowd with his words, telling of the blood he's spilled, each killing more glorious than the last. All eyes follow him. He is the jarl's son, after all. Beloved. Everyone's friend. Many women's desire. A good fighter. The expected jarl when, one day, his father no longer wishes to sit in the chair. Or dies.

"The threat from the Fennvold is no more," Torstyn shouts. The people cheer. Many of Leif's warriors join the acclaim. "The criminal Fenns are no more!"

"He knows how to play a crowd," Brondulf says.

It's like a feast day now. Cups and horns of ale in every hand. From where they came, Rúnr doesn't know. All around is embracing, kissing, groping without shame. The docks, the beach, the town is a celebration. From the throes of it, Torstyn emerges, spreading his arms over each of Rúnr's and Brondulf's shoulders.

"Get the horses," Leif orders Brondulf. To Rúnr, he says, "Gather your brother. The jarl will speak with you."

The Hersir nods to Torstyn, then shoves his way through the crowd.

"You'd think it was his horses we took," Torstyn says, the crowd still adoring him.

"The pyre?" Rúnr asks Brondulf.

Before an answer can come, Torstyn says, "Let's see our father punish us now."

A pair of ravens scoop low over the docks. They separate and come together once more, angling toward the mead hall at the center of town.

"See her? Sifgrid?" Torstyn points at a young woman with blushed cheeks and a full bosom. "The smith's youngest daughter."

"The smith cut off Sverre's finger when he took his oldest daughter," Rúnr says.

"She was promised to someone. Totally different situation. Come, we'll find you a willing daughter too!"

One day, Torstyn will find himself at the mercy of an angry father or a jealous husband, Rúnr thinks, but not today. Today, his brother is a hero.

And Yrsa still walks in the black mist.

Rúnr wants to scream. To fight. To kill. He wants to get away from all this celebrating. "I need to do something first," he says, intending to go . . . where? Certainly not home. He can't breathe the air there. Hasn't spent a night under that roof since Yrsa's death, not even while his wife, Berthe, still lived.

Ex-wife, he admits, though the label feels disrespectful of the dead. Then again, what's more disrespectful, more shameful, than how seldom he thinks of Berthe and honors her bravery? Theirs may not have been a marriage of passion, instead arranged and adhered to with a sense of duty, but they did enjoy each other as companions, partners, lovers at times. They did laugh and comfort each other and love their Little Bear with unquestioned devotion, like a ship's crew or warriors within a shield wall.

"Do you think she's waiting for you somewhere," Torstyn says, "since she's not here to welcome you, I mean?"

"Who?"

I know who.

"You know who."

"She's a friend," Rúnr says.

"How long has it been since you've spoken with her?"

Rúnr doesn't want to hear it. Not the truth of Torstyn knowing his desires, nor his words on the nature of his relationship with Velaug, daughter of the seeress.

Torstyn pulls at his arm. "Come, let's go see Father now. Then the night is yours for whatever, or whoever, you wish."

Rúnr lets himself be led through the crowd, the occasional congratulatory touch meant for Torstyn finding his shoulder instead. Louder, his brother tells the story again as they march the way to the mead hall, Rúnr's mind growing scattered and distant once more, seeking peace, finding the past, and the ill-omened pyre on the beach.

CHAPTER 7

The mead hall stands on a large rise that juts like a ship's hull in the middle of the valley. Here, the people of Skyjavík have lined the way to the hall like the mountains flanking the fjord. And standing at the end in the evening sun is Jarl Helvig with his wife by his side.

"My sons," the jarl says.

Sons, Rúnr notes. Had they returned in defeat, Helvig would not claim their kinship aloud or in private. But in victory, even the Berserkr may be embraced.

"Torstyn, of my blood," Helvig continues. "And Rúnr, of my best mate's blood, my son by love and law. Your departure gave the people of Skyjavík a scare, but you have returned both unharmed and victorious, having punished the Fenn cowards for their attack on our peaceful town."

The cheering is deafening. Torstyn's name is on the lips of all who are gathered. Rúnr's name is not. Above, the sky is turning shades of orange and red atop the mountains.

"Come, let us celebrate."

The doors of the mead hall are thrown wide, and the feast begins. Helvig sits proud upon his chair, in need of its annual spring repainting to bright crimson, while Thyri calls for those gathered to take their seats. All do, save for Torstyn who stands beside the jarl's chair. Rúnr finds his familiar place in the corner, far from the fire.

"A cup for victory," Thyri says, raising a gold goblet. "A cup for family. A cup for the gods and fate. Skyjavík's sons are returned, and we are avenged."

Skyjavík's sons, but not her own, Rúnr observes, as she hands the cup to Helvig, who drinks deeply. When the vessel is empty, he gives it back so that Thyri can upturn it to show no drop remains.

"Let us eat and drink, ever mindful of our luck and our strength."

The words and the ceremony complete, Thyri sits in her chair beside her husband. Those gathered cheer, and the serving girls bring the feast. It is hastily put together, of course, as little warning had been offered of their return, but there is plenty for all, and joy at each table.

Torstyn tells the tale of the slaughtered Fenns once for every bite of mutton he takes and every gulp of ale he drinks. As he does, the story is repeated by others, so that by Rúnr's third cup, there are a dozen versions being told at the same time in the hall, each different. And each featuring the mindless beast, the Berserkr killing without thought or honor. A bear set loose that only Torstyn can control, according to his tale.

All the while Rúnr hears these words, not a single man or woman comes to share his usual table in the corner, his self-imposed exile within the mead hall, never comfortable in the center near the fire with his brother. Even Brondulf is nowhere to be seen. It's more than fear of the Berserkr, he knows. It's the price of being different. His black beard, braided the way his mother's hair was. His distractions and inability to stay in the moment. His lack of effusive humor like Torstyn. Few have ever truly accepted him, even before the black bear came. Only Torstyn and Brondulf.

And Velaug.

He seeks her face in the hall, but she's absent. She'll be home, of course, preparing for the role she will someday take—her mother's role: seeress—easy to find, but difficult to approach. He tries to put her from his mind, but memories pile on memories in a manner out of order with the way they happened. The Saxon witch killing his blood father, Njal. The time he and Torstyn braved the wilderness against Helvig's word and had to be saved by Leif when Torstyn fell through a frozen lake. His mother's funeral. His first raid west the following summer. His marriage. His adoption ceremony. The black bear.

He knows the facts of the day, though he's never been able to recall it. Everyone in Skyjavík knows the story. The adoption ceremony was nearing its end. Helvig was bolstered, perhaps by Odin, perhaps by Loki, to demand a champion. Some tell that Helvig simply asked. Some tell that he demanded the champion be his son. Did he mean Torstyn? The brothers never speak of it. The jarl never speaks of it. The story continues. The black bear, blacker than night, burst into the mead hall. Only one warrior didn't hesitate. Rúnr charged. The bear took him in its great maw and bounded from the hall. Helvig and Torstyn led the charge after it, finding it in the marketplace, Rúnr standing over it, eyes wild and unseeing, eating its heart.

His hand finds the bear's tooth where it hangs around his neck on a rope.

Around him there is dancing and shouting and joy in the moment, as always. Not for him, though. When he eats, he thinks of a fight to come or one already won. When he cuts down an enemy, his mind is on the hot springs, or a slice of meat, or a barrel of ale. When he chooses a shield or a path in a crowded wood, his mind finds Berthe's smile on their wedding day, or Velaug's the day they first undressed each other.

Gods, how I envy these people.

The only single-mindedness he knows is in the god trance or at the bottom of a barrel of ale.

"Girl," he shouts at a passing thrall.

She brings ale. He downs it at once and demands another. The thrall offers a long horn. He takes it.

"Tell me," he says to her. "The pyre. Who died?"

The girl makes a sign with her free hand, warding off ill omens. "The boy Ivar, Hrist's son."

Rúnr knows the boy, born the same spring as Yrsa. "What happened?"

"There was a storm. Tossed their fishing boat. Hrist came to shore, but the boy was taken out into the harbor. They found him on Thor's Island after the storm passed."

The girl looks as if she might cry. Rúnr dismisses her, his thoughts on Ivar. On Hrist and the agony he knows she feels for surviving. On the way he survived when his mother drowned. On his mother's funeral pyre. On Yrsa. On the failure to find her killer.

Stop! his mind shouts at the vision of Yrsa dying in his arms.

He drains his ale, but he's not drunk enough yet.

I should speak with the seeress.

But that would mean seeing Velaug. What will he say to her? How will she reply? Will they talk of old days when they were young, days before she committed herself to her mother's training? Days when they played and kissed and fucked in her home while her mother was out gathering herbs?

I will tell her I miss her. No, that she is pretty. Or that she appears fierce? Strong?

"You stink."

Torstyn stands before Rúnr, grinning like a fool. It must be late for Torstyn to have finally made it to this corner, the congratulations running thin as the crowd disperses. Surely, he has a woman in mind for the rest of the night, but for now he's here.

"Do you hear me, Rúnr? You smell like a chicken's asshole after it drops eggs. And the lice—your hair is like a hive."

"You smell like a sow after it's been mounted." Rúnr's throat is raw, his voice broken.

Torstyn grins. "Time for a bath," he says.

"So go jump in the fjord."

"Not me, you pig's ear. Your beard looks like a goat's after it's been drinking from the mud."

There's laughter from those who remain in the mead hall. Rúnr wonders if it's still night, or if morning has come. He tries to stand, to deliver a brilliant retort, but his thoughts are slow, like walking underwater, and his legs are unsteady. He manages only to fall back onto the bench and belch. It tastes of vomit. For a moment he fears he'll be sick.

"I'm fine," he says.

Torstyn sits. "The smell is even worse down here. When was the last time you took those clothes off?"

"It'll take more than such sweet talk to get me out of them."

"Okay, when was the last time someone else took them off for you?"

"You need more ale." Rúnr calls for a serving girl.

She comes quickly enough, looking like a young Velaug. Rúnr grabs for the cup, managing instead to make the girl spill. Torstyn laughs so hard he almost falls off the bench.

"She's a thrall, you know," a deep voice calls. "You don't have to propose marriage to fuck her."

"Eat shit, Eilif," Torstyn says.

Rúnr looks up. Way up. Eilif is the tallest man in the world, so far as Rúnr knows. Tall as a spruce, they say, yet almost as thin as a sapling.

"Skyjavík's mighty hero," Rúnr says. "Oh wait, it's not Ubbein."

"No. It's Ubbein's bitch of a slave girl. More ale, slave Eilif!" Torstyn says, raising a cup in mock salute.

Eilif slaps the cup from Torstyn's hand. Those left in the hall quiet. Rúnr looks to the fire, beyond it to the jarl's chair. Empty. How long ago did Helvig leave?

Torstyn gets slowly to his feet. Rúnr does the same, trying to keep his balance as if aboard a storm-tossed ship. Fighting in the mead hall is not allowed. During a holiday or an Assembly, it's punished by a fine, a loss of lands, or even banishment as an outlaw. That will not be the case today, but it's still not a good idea.

"Crawl back to your hero's taint, you dungpile," Rúnr says.

"Brave words," Eilif says, "coming from Torstyn's penis cleaner."

Torstyn flexes from shoulder to fist. "Jealous?"

Behind Eilif, Ubbein approaches with scar-faced Gellir at his side, snarling like a dog beside its master. This night may have been in honor of Rúnr and Torstyn's victory, but that is merely one song. Ubbein's song would take many nights to sing. His victory at Mjøsa alone—outnumbered ten to one, the last survivor of his shield wall, and somehow, he alone stood upon the battlefield when the Valkyries came to claim the dead—is legend throughout the North. His accomplishments and victories are without peer, even compared to a Berserkr. Winner of seven Challenges, he has won battles on both land and sea. He's a hero like in the old stories. And his hatred of the sons of Helvig is palpable as he nears.

"The heroes of the Battle of the Fennvold," Ubbein says. His eyes are always cunning. His voice always confident. He bows his head in a mockery of deference.

Rúnr's head is clearing, as it must. A fight is coming, though if it will continue with words or become something more—if it will happen tonight or in the future—he does not know.

"Come to drink with us?" Torstyn asks, his voice full of mirth, though his stance says he sees what is coming as well as Rúnr does.

Ubbein remains a step behind Eilif and doesn't respond. Rúnr thinks, best as he can this far into his drink, that this is a test. A setup. But for what?

"A drink with you would taste of piss," Eilif says.

"What do you want?" Rúnr demands. His blood is running hot now, but the longer they continue with words, the sooner the ale in his gut will remind him how close he is to passing out.

Eilif speaks more to the crowd than to Rúnr and Torstyn. "The hero Ubbein wants to know if you're going to raid with us this summer."

This is it, then. Ubbein understands Rúnr's vengeance is not yet found. He's going to use it to chip away at Helvig's popularity as jarl. The summer raids will surely seek treasure in the Saxon lands across the Western Sea. The Painted Fenn is surely not there, however, and Ubbein has worked out that Rúnr means to find the killer of his daughter no matter what. But if he refuses Ubbein's request, he opens himself to accusations of cowardice, which would shame the jarl. And Ubbein, whose own desire for the jarl's chair is hardly a secret, will gain strength.

"The summer raids are not yet named," Torstyn says, coming to Rúnr's aid as always.

I can do this myself, Rúnr thinks, though it's plain even to himself that he can barely stand.

"And yet, we all know what our honored jarl will declare, do we not?" Ubbein says.

"Do you have the courage to sail with us, or do you lack it?" Eilif demands.

"Big words from a big man," Rúnr blurts. *I sound like a child.*

Torstyn adds, "If only your penis could match your height."

Eilif is fast for a big man, his open palm hitting Rúnr's chest like a charging boar, sending him over the corner table. The pain is not much, but the spinning doesn't stop once Rúnr lands. There's shouting and crashing. He needs to get to his feet before Torstyn does something stupid and forces Helvig to punish them.

Torstyn stands to his full height, his eyes barely reaching Eilif's collarbone. Around them, as Rúnr finally gets back into the mess, the crowd gathers. Brondulf is there, looking eager to join.

"Always fighting your lover's fights," Eilif says.

"Only ever choosing to fight drunk men," Torstyn replies.

"I've been waiting for him to sober up first, but I'm beginning to wonder if he ever will."

"Fuck you," Rúnr tries to say. It comes out more like a grunt.

"Maybe if you drank less, your daughter would—"

Rage, grief, guilt, like Surtr's flame engulfing all in Ragnarök, ignites in Rúnr, vaulting him past Torstyn to get at Eilif's throat. He knows he's being played like a *talharpa* and doesn't give a goat's testicle. He rips at the tall man's beard until Torstyn grabs him by the shoulders and Ubbein and Gellir take Eilif's arms. Shouting rises all around.

"Calm your brother," Ubbein says.

"Heel your dog," is Torstyn's reply.

"I'll cut your heart out, you seal's cunt," Rúnr screams at Eilif.

The combatants are dragged apart, leaving the mead hall in a slowly calming uproar.

"There is mess to be cleaned," Ubbein says, motioning for Eilif to go. "We didn't get your answer, Rúnr. Will you be raiding with us this summer?"

"I told you," Torstyn says. "The jarl has made no announcement of the summer raids."

Ubbein smiles. "And yet I hear whispers of his plans."

"Then listen for my answer in those same whispers," Rúnr says.

"I look forward to counting you among my oarsmen, Berserkr."

Gellir makes his first sound of the encounter, a snort that reminds Rúnr of a sneeze. Ubbein spins on a heel and leaves, Eilif and Gellir following like small boats tied behind a longship.

"You shouldn't let him goad you like that," Torstyn says as conversation returns to the hall around them.

"I was going to say the same to you."

"We should tell Father of what happened here."

"I'm sure he'll hear."

"Ubbein has never come after one of us before," Torstyn says.

"Have you heard about Hrist's son?"

Torstyn bows his head. "The funeral was to be today, but Father delayed it until tomorrow when our ship appeared."

They sit beside each other in silence a moment.

"You still stink," Torstyn says. "Tomorrow is also *laugardagur*, did you know?"

Rúnr has kept little track these past months, with the weekly bathing day of the smallest concern.

"Go find a girl," Rúnr tells his brother.

"What will you do?"

"Drink. And sleep."

Torstyn gathers a full cup and hands it to Rúnr. "Sleep well, then."

Rúnr drinks once more, then twice more, then lays his head on the table, meaning to do just that.

CHAPTER 8

The fire is out. The hall is quiet. The tables cleared. No servants. No thralls. Just Rúnr wiping drool from the side of his face and blinking crusty sleep from his eyes. Just Rúnr and the memory of a dream—of Yrsa, her tiny hands slicing a salmon anus to neck.

This is how I died, Papa, she says over the gutted fish, *and you let my killer live!*

He runs his fingers through the tangles of his beard. His tongue tastes like wet leather. His head thrums as if filled with bees. Bowls of water sit on some of the tables. Not his table, of course. He groans as he stands. His joints pop. Muscles ache. When he reaches the next table, he slumps onto a stool, nearly falling off the edge of it. He belches fire. For a moment, he worries he might shit himself. Deep breaths. Dry swallows. He drags the bowl closer.

Specs and flakes float within like tiny translucent ships in a still sea. Not early morning, then. Where is everybody?

He cups water from the bowl and splashes it on his face. It's not cold, but he shivers, his flesh pimpling. He rubs his eyes again, then digs some dried snot from one nostril, a little bloody, and rinses his hands and face again. He tries to remember last night. It's like attempting to pick up a single snowflake from a drift.

He grabs the bowl and dumps all its contents over his head and howls at the chill. Two serving girls emerge from the rooms behind the jarl's chair. Rúnr waves them off, and they flee back from where they came.

You stink.

That's what Torstyn said, he remembers. Today is bathing day. That must be why the hall is empty. Most in Skyjavík like the cool waters of the harbor for cleansing. Some like the hot springs of the North Mountain. These are too crowded, too close to town, for Rúnr. He prefers the steaming springs of the South Mountain, near the ravine that dives so deep, the stories go, that if anyone could brave the journey, it would bring them to Yggdrasill's most distant roots.

Then there are other stories that say the ravine is an entrance to Hel itself.

Rúnr isn't interested in stories. A bath, however, does seem a good idea. He gets to his feet, waiting for the unsteadiness to pass, and throws open the mead hall doors. The sun, at midday height, is relentless, driving him back inside, hands to his eyes.

"By the gods!"

Keeping his head bowed and his eyes squinted, he makes his way outside. The streets of Skyjavík are as empty as the mead hall. Too empty even for bathing day. Reflex brings Rúnr's hand to his belt, but there is no battle waiting and no weapon upon him in any case. Swords and axes are not worn in the mead hall. They're stacked on racks just inside the door. He could go back for his, but when he turns to consider it, he sees smoke rising in dark columns from the beach: Ivar's funeral.

All are expected to attend such an event, yet none have woken him. Anger comes as he turns his back on the beach, on the people of Skyjavík, on Ivar and Hrist, as he remembers the pyre built for Yrsa, the one upon which he refused to lay his daughter.

He remembers the pain in his ribs, in his muscles, in the very blood in his veins. He remembers Berthe's tears, the only ones he'd ever seen her shed.

He remembers late one night Yrsa couldn't sleep because of a storm. Berthe snored contentedly beside him.

"It's just the sound of Thor's chariot as he rides across the sky," he told Yrsa of the thunder.

"What if Thor crashes into our house?" she asked with the earnestness of childhood. "What about the Valkyries?"

"What do you mean?"

"The Valkyries come for those who die in battle, to bring them to Valhalla, right?"

"That's right."

"Papa?"

"What is it, Little Bear?"

"Can I hold your axe tonight?"

"I tell you what. I'll keep it right here, and if we hear death coming, we'll grab my axe together so the Valkyries can find us."

"Thank you, Papa."

The memory makes a fist in Rúnr's chest. He coughs and wipes his eyes and goes to the beach. For Ivar, he tells himself, and for Hrist. He goes for duty and for the gods. But each of these reasons is less than the whole truth. He goes mostly for the hope of seeing one person, and she is neither the dead nor the grieving.

All of Skyjavík is indeed there, gathered before the pyre, with nine burning fires surrounding the space and the harbor calm and bright. Rúnr doesn't join the crowd. He stands apart, finding a small hill where the grass encroaches on the beach's sand and stones. From here, he can see everything. And everyone.

There are the fishermen, the warriors, the farmers, the horse tenders. There is the smith and the butchers. There is Brondulf and his wife, Ljufu. There is Ubbein, in a place of honor, flanked by Eilif and Gellir and a fistful of unfamiliar faces, some wearing the topknot hairstyle of Sogn, pressing close like lambs for their mother's teats. There is Helvig sitting in his chair, as it's always brought to where it's needed within Skyjavík's bounds. There are Torstyn and Thyri standing at the jarl's shoulders, a show of authority necessary after last night. There is Leif just behind the chair, a show of power. And behind them stands a tent erected for this day. Inside waits the seeress, unseen until it's time for her role in the ceremony.

Hrist, Ivar's mother, kneels, head bowed, shoulders shaking with grief. Before her Ivar lies upon the pyre, so small compared to the timbers that hold his child's weight. A small axe on his chest, his hands gripping the handle. A carving of a longship and some other objects surround him. A wooden shield at his feet.

Helvig rises silently. A thrall brings a torch to the jarl. He takes it carefully and the ceremony begins.

"For Ivar," he says, holding the torch high. "For Odin."

"For Odin," the people of Skyjavík chant.

"For Ivar," Helvig says. "For Freyja."

"For Freyja!"

"For Ivar. For Hel."

"For Hel." This final intonation comes more subdued.

The naming of the gods who rule the afterlives complete, Helvig approaches Hrist and offers the torch. She looks up at her jarl, and for a moment Rúnr sees her taking the torch and setting it to her own breast, where surely—as Rúnr knows—the pain is unbearable. She does no such thing, however, instead shaking her head. Placing the burden on Helvig. He does not shrink from the moment, again holding the torch high.

"For Ivar," he says one last time. "For Hrist."

This, the people do not repeat.

Rúnr is suddenly thirsty. He licks dry lips. Helvig approaches the pyre. This is what Rúnr was meant to do for Yrsa, but he could not bring himself to offer her body like that, reducing it to ash.

Helvig lights the pyre. The flames scream, audible even at this distance. Now, too, Hrist screams, her pain grinding into a wail of anger and loss. Rúnr turns away, only to find his eyes on the tent as the seeress comes forth, tall and painted, her face shades of white and black. The crowd parts. She moves among them with purpose and grace so that Rúnr is unable to look away, even as she approaches Hrist and the pyre. Here, she spreads her arms wide and speaks the words the gods long ago prescribed, telling of the joys Ivar will know now that he's left this realm.

It takes some time for Rúnr to know the voice, and that knowing comes like a hammer blow because it's not the voice of the old seeress but her daughter.

"Velaug," he says, only now recognizing her through the paint.

Where is Olga, the seeress who is meant to speak the words and lead the funerary ritual and act as *kjósa*—as chooser of the dead to usher Ivar from life into death? He must be mistaken. It must be the paint confusing his mind. Surely it is Olga speaking. He seeks Velaug in the crowd once more, only to find Torstyn staring at him. Even from this distance, he can see his brother's face well—the knowing there.

Velaug speaks with the authority of the gods, like her mother, who is not present. And for that, there can be only one explanation. While Rúnr and Torstyn clashed with the enemy in Fennvold, Olga went to meet the gods, and her daughter took her role.

Velaug finishes quickly, as the ritual for a child who did not die in battle is brief. She disappears back into the tent. Helvig speaks once more, and Hrist is taken by strong men to her home to mourn. The ceremony is complete. The people of Skyjavík disperse. It will be a solemn day today. The baths and springs will be for silent reflection. Rúnr tells his legs to carry him down the beach, to the tent, before it's too late. The *kjósa* must cleanse after a funeral. It can be hours, or even days, before she is seen again. Already, she'll be gone from the tent. No one knows the secrets of where.

But he cannot move.

Torstyn comes, face grim. “There’s an Assembly tonight,” he says. “Father expects us to be there in proper attitude.”

Without causing trouble, he means. Without being drunk and ready for a fight.

“Did you know?” Rúnr asks, motioning to the tent.

“I only found out this morning.”

“You didn’t tell me.” Rúnr doesn’t intend to sound so insulted.

“I shook you till you nearly fell off the bench. You wouldn’t wake.”

Rúnr tries to remember this attempt, but there’s nothing in his mind between Ubbein’s departure last night and waking up today.

“It’s a long time since you’ve seen her,” Torstyn says.

“What do you know of it?”

“Enough.”

Rúnr’s hands become fists.

“Go ahead,” Torstyn says.

Rúnr wants to hit him. To hit anyone. Anything. A tree. A rock. Himself.

“I need to go,” he says instead.

“Don’t be late,” Torstyn calls after him. “The Assembly.”

Rúnr follows the beach toward the South Mountain without looking back.

CHAPTER 9

The South Mountain is no easy climb. It's where warriors go to test their mettle. It's where fathers take sons and leave them for a night with no food or weapons, to learn self-reliance. Where Rúnr's first father brought him to face the bite of winter to prove he could be a man. Where Helvig taught him and Torstyn how to descend the most treacherous cliffs to gather bird eggs, auks and terns being Rúnr's favorite.

More than midway to the summit, west of the ravine, Rúnr sits in one of the hot springs, his naked ass on the smooth rocks, arms out in the sun. There are seven hot springs on this mountain, and this one—deeper and hotter than the others—is the most difficult to reach. It's the least used and, therefore, Rúnr's favorite.

Inhaling the humid air, Rúnr slides under the water, curling his toes and holding his breath and fighting the heat as long as he can before surfacing. Torstyn may have been right in suggesting he come here, but he'll never admit it to his brother's face.

"I may just kick your balls for joking about lice, though," he mutters, as he brushes his beard with his fingers. Or maybe he'll leave some stew beneath his brother's pillow like when they were young. That'll teach him.

Thinking of their childhood turns his memory back, this way and that, from his wedding ceremony to the Saxon witch rupturing Njal's spine with her axe. From the adoption ritual with Helvig beaming proudly, to his mother singing him night songs when he was younger, sometimes in her native tongue, to Berthe's horror when she discovered Yrsa bled out in Rúnr's arms. More and then more again. Too fast they come. Too potent. Down into the spring again, he tries to escape beneath the surface where the water is almost hot enough to make soup, deserving the burn on his face and in his lungs before he comes up gulping air.

He remembers Velaug as a little girl wearing a brown dress made from a grain sack. Then she's tall, able to beat all the boys—all of them, even Ubbein—in an arm wrestle. Soon she's a young woman inviting Rúnr into the hills where none would find them, each of them new to the pleasures of another's body. Velaug telling him on the beach beneath a moonless night that she'll walk the path of the seeress one day, taking no husband, knowing no lover any longer.

The next day, hurt and angry and afraid others would see the stain of tears on his cheeks, Rúnr demanded Helvig find him a wife. Less than a week after, Helvig announced Jarl Harald, of the Hordalands along the sea, had promised his daughter, the famed shield-maiden Berthe, to wed Rúnr.

"The only woman in all the world," Helvig said, "who might tame such a man as my son Rúnr."

My son.

The words echo in Rúnr's head even as he remembers more. Velaug's absence from the announcement. Ubbein's words of support, tainted with envy obvious as Odin's beard. Torstyn's words of joy.

"A fierce woman for my brother," he said. "Strong, too." At this, his hands mimicked the "strength" of her rumored large breasts.

She was twice her reputation in ferocity and valor, and half it in breast size. Which brings Rúnr's thoughts back to Velaug and the feel of her body against his. The smell of her hair. The way she—

The sound of approach banishes the past, like goats scattering at the scent of a wolf.

"This spring is in use," he calls out, seeking a familiar voice in return.

Silence hangs heavy until it's broken by the slide of loose stone. Not a man coming, then, but an animal. He listens closer, thinking what he hears is smaller than a bear but larger than a rabbit. Rúnr glances to where his clothes are piled on the other side of the spring, his sword still far away in the mead hall. Careless. Foolish enough to get a man killed.

A growl calls his attention to a wolf loping into view from the brush alongside the path. Gray and black and hearty, it quickly begins to wither, its flanks sinking in, its fur matting and dropping off in clumps until it stands on legs of bone, what's left of its flesh dripping like thick gruel. Its head seeks Rúnr, but it has no eyes, only black pits from which outpour even blacker insects to stream over the ichor-matted fur of its skull. Its breath, even from this distance, is rancid and makes Rúnr's belly clench and roil.

He begins to climb from the spring, but something grabs his leg. He looks down into the steaming water and sees a boy panicking, eyes wild, slamming his fists against the surface as if trapped under ice.

"Boy," Rúnr blurts. He reaches for the boy but cannot grasp him.

The boy stops thrashing and looks up. It's Ivar. Rúnr's throat knots. Ivar's mouth opens. He breathes deep from underneath and begins to convulse.

"No, hold your breath, Ivar! I'm coming."

But Rúnr can't reach him. He can only watch as Ivar drowns, his arms and legs flailing in thick murky ripples.

And then the boy is gone.

Rúnr calls his name again, but the water of the spring is calm and clear. The white fog is gone. There's no one but himself.

The wolf-thing!

He turns back to find the creature gone as well. The mountain is quiet. He climbs from the water, vomiting all over the ground and himself, more and more coming out until he's exhausted, his throat raw. When there's nothing left, he rolls onto his back on the warm stones around the spring.

"No more," he says, to both the vomiting and the remembering.

But memory will not be tamed. It brings a story of old. The Raumsdair Berserkr. A champion to sing of. Until he began having difficulty returning from the god trance. Each time, he was less the man he was before the trance took him until his mind was finally lost and he became like a mad beast, unable to think or speak. He forgot how to walk on two legs. In this way, he fled into the wilderness, driven away by the people of his village.

I must speak with the seeress, he thinks.

Until he remembers that the seeress is now Velaug.

His stomach heaves again.

"Odin Allfather," he says, "have you sent madness upon me?"

The gods rarely speak directly to mortals, and this moment is no exception.

The scrape of a boot breaks Rúnr's peace once more. He looks up at the sky. The sun is growing tired of the day. It must be Torstyn coming to make certain he doesn't miss the Assembly.

"There was no lice," Rúnr says, only to find himself giggling like a boy.

He rolls to his knees, ready to stand, when a man comes from the path, followed by another, both armed and armored. Not an easy climb so encumbered, Rúnr knows. They've come with purpose. Aware of his nakedness, Rúnr holds up a hand in greeting to the strangers. They each regard him, however, as if he's familiar to their eyes. And to this, the pair seem familiar to Rúnr as well. The taller one grins.

"Have you come to bathe?" Rúnr asks, noting his clothes still on the far side of the spring.

"That's him," the grinning man says. He's almost as dark as Rúnr and holds an axe with a broad head. His voice says he's not from the Opplands. Sogn or Morer to the west, perhaps.

The other one, shorter and with a longer beard and armed with a spear and shield, edges around the spring the other way, cutting Rúnr off from his clothes. "Doesn't look so dangerous," he says.

Rúnr opens his mouth to speak but belches instead, the taste of old ale and vomit churning his stomach. The men have flanked him quickly, leaving no way to escape. The smell of sweat and excitement fills the air. Pre-battle. No denying it.

Now might be a good time, Odin, he thinks. There is no tightening of focus, however. No hint of the god trance coming.

A fight, then. So be it. Rúnr can be quick when he needs to be, but he's not faster than a spear at this distance. With the wet rocks around the spring, however, he doesn't need to be fast. He only needs to be determined and sure of foot.

He stands and makes as if to grab for the spear. His intention is a feint, but instead he falls prey to the wet rocks and nearly tumbles into the spring. The tall one, perhaps thinking it a ploy, doesn't strike, wasting an opportunity.

The gods do not wish me in Valhalla yet.

Such realization gives strength and daring. Rúnr regains his balance and charges in the other direction, but doesn't close in enough, and takes a hard blow from the axe's knob for his trouble, driving him to a knee. He hears the spearman closing behind him. The axeman is raising his weapon. Rúnr is in a bad place.

"Too easy," the one says.

"He said it would be a good fight," the other replies.

"Barely worth the coin."

Rúnr spins on his kneecap, shredding the flesh, and launches straight up at the axeman, inside his reach, slamming his shoulder in the man's chin. He takes a grazing blow on the arm but forces the axeman back. He's made distance between himself and the two enemies, but they're still coming. Until the spearman slips.

"Gudbrand," the axeman shouts.

Rúnr doesn't hesitate, throwing himself at the spear. Getting a hand on the shaft while slamming a shoulder into the spearman, knocking him into the spring. Keeping the spear, Rúnr turns to press his new advantage only to have the weapon split in half by the axe, the blow nearly taking off his hand. Rúnr reverses his swing, catching the axeman's jaw with the spear's butt end. Down that one goes. Rúnr checks his flank to find Gudbrand pulling himself from the spring, a long knife in hand.

"You die now," Gudbrand says, beard dripping wet, angling his approach to allow his companion to regain his feet.

The next moments are furious and fatal, leaving the spearman sprawled on the path, half his own blade lodged in his chest. But the axeman is still coming, swinging his weapon savagely. Rúnr, with only the butt half of the spear, does his best to keep alive, searching for any way to turn the tide. The axeman is relentless, swinging, slashing, using his weapon like a sword to make quick jabs so that Rúnr loses his balance. His feet tangle. His heel smashes a stone. Down he goes at the edge of the spring, losing his spear into the water, the breath driven from his lungs. Behind and above him, he hears the axeman position for the killing blow.

"Double the coin for me," the man says.

Rúnr braces for the pain. His hand, dangling in the water, searches desperately for a weapon—stone, stick, anything. He finds a hunk of timber, a handle—an axe! He grips it and rolls as the enemy's weapon strikes stone where his head was. He comes to a crouch and kicks out, catching the axeman's ankle, bringing the man down. He swings his newfound weapon, severing the man's leg above the knee. The axeman cries out in pain. Rúnr rises and cuts his enemy's spine in half. Silence descends. The fight is over. Rúnr slumps to his knees, eyes on the familiar axe he holds.

Impossible!

But there's no mistaking this weapon. It was his first raid, his and Torstyn's, barely men, sailing to the Saxon Isles with their fathers. The victory was already complete, the song already being sung, when Rúnr followed his father into the witch's hut. Njal checked the front, Rúnr the back, which smelled of spice and rot like an inversion of Velaug's home, but neither saw the witch. To this day, Rúnr doesn't know where she hid. She appeared, axe in hand, no warning, and split Njal's spine with it. Rúnr screamed. The witch blew dust into his eyes and slithering words into his ears, but he fought, pulled the axe free, and cut down the witch with three strong blows—the first opened her throat, the second removed her head, and the last cleaved her heart.

That axe, its beard shorter than an Oppland axe, its blade sharper, its handle of a blackened wood for which there is no name and etched with unfamiliar runes that seem to twist if Rúnr looks at them too long, came home with him as both memorial and trophy. That axe he'd wielded since to great victories both in and out of the god trance. That axe he handed to Yrsa to protect her the night the Fenns came.

That axe he buried with her this past winter.

CHAPTER 10

He must speak with his brother and his father. He must declare what has happened.

But what has happened? Assassins he can explain, but what of the wolf-thing, Ivar, the axe?

Phantoms, he tells himself as he bounds down the mountain. The way is still laid with snow and slick stone, and he nearly loses his balance more than once. Then into the trees, whipping branches hungry for the flesh of his face. Then into Skyjavík, along the beach, past the fishmongers, the stables, the smith, Brondulf's butchery, weaving through and around the familiar faces of his home, all giving him a wide berth, for he is the Berserkr and he's covered in blood.

The sun is dipping. The Assembly will begin soon. Rúnr knows where he should go. What he must do.

He does not do it.

Instead, he continues to the hollow between the North and East Mountains where the seeress lives, seeking the words he needs to speak, but they flee like fireflies from a child's hand. He wants to tell. To ask. To demand. What? *The axe!*

That's it. The axe in his hand is no phantom. It's as real as it is impossible. This he clings to as he winds his way up the path, the house coming into view. He stops. It's been years since he walked this way. Flowers surround the house, yellows and reds mostly, different from what he remembers. Yet similar to the way his own house was garnished in those first years of his marriage.

Berthe loved flowers almost as much as she loved battle. Purple ones were her favorite, but yellows and reds and whites and more kept their home as bright as the Bifröst. Until Yrsa died.

Berthe did no gardening after that, no preparing the land for winter's frost. So Rúnr tried. He gathered winter flowers from where they grow around the East Mountain. Poppies and daisies. Nothing purple, but he brought them to her, to cheer her, in the marketplace.

"Do you think I want flowers?" she had asked.

"I want to see you happy again," he told her, offering the gift.

She swatted them away. "Do you even—"

She wiped at her eyes. It wasn't until that moment he understood how she blamed him for Yrsa's death. For not protecting their daughter.

"Rúnr Njalson," she said, her words loud and vicious and violent. "You're a drunk, and a coward, and you're worthless in bed. I divorce you!"

The marketplace went silent as it had never been before. Even the birds above seemed to stop flying, awaiting his response.

"You cannot," he said meekly. The worst defense—the weakest defense—any man has ever offered within sight of the gods.

"By law, I can." She looked at those gathered—half of Skyjavík, it seemed—each in turn. "And I do."

Not one could hold her eye. Not one spoke in Rúnr's defense. Not one called for reconciliation or counsel before the jarl. A heartbeat passed, then five, and ten, and twenty. A few more, and it was decided. They were divorced.

She turned as swiftly as he'd seen her spin in battle, and she never looked back. The whispers began immediately. Would the

Berserkr emerge in grief or in rage? Should they gather the warriors and drive him into the wilderness?

"Rúnr Njalson."

The memory is lost. The door stands open. Velaug, red hair dancing in the breeze, looks over him without surprise.

"You knew I would come?" he asks. *Do you know of whom I was thinking?*

She laughs. It's been a long time, and he's surprised to find he misses her laughter even more than the sight of her.

"You sound like a bear chuffing up a tree," she says, her eyes daring him to laugh. "I could hear you over Thor's thunder."

He wants to find the banter they once shared, the comfort they knew around each other, but his mouth won't form those words. He says the only thing he can.

"I need to speak with you."

She doesn't answer. He wonders if she's deciding. If she's looking into his mind. If she's seeking the words to turn him away.

"Do you seek the seeress?" she says, before adding quietly: "Or Velaug?"

Rúnr doesn't know. He wants Velaug, but he needs the seeress.

"Come in," she says when he doesn't answer and stands aside.

Familiar smells embrace him as he enters. Spices and smoldering candles and Velaug herself, like all the aromas of springtime and death rolled into one. On a table beside the door, a bloodstained knife sits like an offering.

"You should not be here," she says. "The Assembly will begin soon, and you have a tale to tell."

"A tale to tell, that's why I've come."

"Am I the first person you've met?"

He doesn't understand the question. "Today?"

"You've spilled blood." She points at him, at his weapon. "Put that away in this house."

Again, he's confronted with the obvious. The blood on himself. The weight of what he's done by coming here first, bypassing so many houses on his way. Rushing by so many people in silence.

"It is man's blood, yes?" she asks.

"It is."

"Was it in defense?"

The law is clear and without pity. A lawful killing, such as one in defense, must be declared to the first person met after the deed. If the killer passes more than two houses without declaring the act, he may be found guilty of murder.

"I've killed two men in defense," he says, knowing it's too late to speak these words. He holds forth the axe so she may see it. So she may understand the ways law cannot apply to what's happened. So she can see that she must come with him to the Assembly to explain. To defend him. "They attacked me at the hot spring. This is why I've come."

She doesn't look at him or the axe. "No, it's not."

Velaug wasn't like this when they were young. She was warm. Caring. Quick of mind and quicker with her words, and mischievous as Loki himself—all aspects Rúnr used to like in her, maybe even love in her—but never so . . .

So much like her mother.

The old seeress, Olga, spoke only in riddles and half statements. She stood as apart within her home as her home was from the town. The way Velaug feels apart from Rúnr now. He can't help remembering her words on that moonless night when she told him she would one day become the seeress.

"We were never for real, Rúnr," she whispered, lips to his ear, naked body across his. "We were never more than a dog chasing a squirrel it knew it couldn't catch."

Only later, after she'd gone, did he wonder which of them was the squirrel and which was the dog.

"Why did I come, then, seeress?" he asks.

She points at the three-legged stool where those who want to hear her words sit. Impersonal. Business. He drops onto the stool, the axe still in his hand. She kneels before him, and he's filled suddenly with anger. He wants to tell her to piss off. He wants to slap the probing look from her face.

He wants to kiss her.

She betrays no similar desires. Shows no hint of the past. Of any recognition at all. "Tell me," she begins, but she stops abruptly, her eyes finally on the axe.

He turns it so the candlelight gleams off its blade. So she can be sure. The change in the small house is palpable, the way a storm can be felt before it crests the mountains. He realizes how rare it must be for the seeress to be surprised.

"What have you done?" she asks, tense, as if trying not to recoil.

"I told you. This is why I've come."

She eyes him like he's mad. "You've desecrated her grave."

"You think—I did no such thing!" These words he can barely stammer. That she would accuse him, that she of all people would think he would—that he *could*—do such a thing to his daughter. He stands, almost knocking the stool over. "You're right. I should not have come."

Velaug is on her feet, grabbing his arm. It's the first time he's felt her touch in years. If she'd put her hand on him when he first arrived, he might have forgotten himself and picked her up and taken her like he used to. Now, however, the only heat he feels at her touch is a growing rage, as if he's too close to a forge and blaming the fire for his own foolishness.

"How did you get that axe?" she asks.

"I thought the seeress knew all."

He might as well have hit her for the way she shrinks from him, like a sail suddenly absent the wind. That fast, however, the wind returns. She stands confident, her eyes to his.

"Tell me first of those you killed," she says, motioning for him to sit once more.

"Strangers," he says, sitting, the axe across his knees. But were they strangers? He's now unsure. Could he have seen their faces somewhere?

"They happened upon you?"

"I was bathing in the hot spring on the South Mountain where we used to—" He stops himself saying more. "They came seeking me and spoke of payment from another for their actions."

Velaug, still standing, watches him as he speaks, betraying no emotion. No nostalgia. He imagines she's waiting for him to find an answer in his own words rather than offering one herself. He asked her once, when they were still young, why a seeress could not just tell what she knows. She laughed the way one does when they need time to find the right answer.

"Mortals know nothing, not even the seeress," she told him then. "We're vessels, ships, that's all. Some are overladen. Some await a crew. Some twist in the wind without a helmsman while others sink beneath the waves. And some know best, because the gods whisper to them when the winds will blow and from where."

He thinks of this, of the assassins as empty ships, filled with coin and captained by a scheming coward.

"They didn't speak the name of their employer," he says. "If they had, I would've come to his door, not yours."

Velaug remains silent.

"I don't understand why someone would pay for my death," he says.

"Many fear the Berserkr. He is both more than a man and less. An animal and a weapon. But a weapon from a fallen hand is still deadly."

Rúnr looks at the axe again. "You're saying I'm a piece of someone's strategy, not the goal?"

"You are more than a piece on a battlefield, Rúnr. You underestimate yourself. You always have."

He has no words to this, the kindest thing a woman has said to him in a long time.

"Show me the axe," she says.

When he holds it out, she kneels once more, leaning close to inspect the weapon but not touching it.

She says, "The path of our conversation is not cut by—"

"I'm in no mood for riddles," he snaps, surprising himself.

A bird caws from somewhere inside the house, up in the rafters.

"The gods speak as they will," Velaug says.

A darkness crosses her face like a shadow passing over the moon. She places her hands on his knees, a neutral gesture. Benign. Comforting. But there is no mistaking the stirring Rúnr feels.

"You have broken the law," she says.

"I've come to you first. Right or wrong, it's the choice I made."

"And that choice has placed the jarl in danger."

"Now? At the Assembly?" Rúnr tries to stand, but Velaug's hands on his knees keep him on the stool.

"Not the danger of the blade."

"The chair," he says, understanding. "If the jarl's son breaks the law, it breaks the strength of his claim on the jarl's chair. But who could know I would survive the assassins? Who could know I would not announce the killings by the law?"

"The wrong questions."

He means to ask the right ones, but he can't find them. For all the currents his thoughts travel, for the breadth of the netting they cast into the sea, what he seeks slips through the holes down into the depths. Lost.

"Tell me, seeress," he says, knowing no other way, "what am I meant to do?"

Like a crash of lightning, Velaug becomes the seeress. All color drains from her blue eyes until they are like ice. Her hands become claws gripping his knees with ferocity. Her body tightens.

"Three times the god trance will take you," the seeress says, her voice no longer her own. "Three times on your journey as you seek the killer in the red house, the Temple of the Hanged God. There, Yrsa will have her vengeance."

She slumps so that her hands on his knees are all that keep her from falling. He drops the axe with a clattering and takes hold of her wrists. A seeress must be allowed to return from her trance without interference, he knows, much as a Berserkr must return from his, but he cannot help himself. After a few breaths, she raises her head. Her eyes are Velaug's eyes, blue as the fjords. She seems older now than she did moments ago. The bird in the rafters caws once more.

She rises. Turns her back. The gods have spoken through her. The visit is finished.

Rúnr retrieves his axe and stands. He has questions, so many that he can hardly think on one before three more take its place, but he knows his role here. The gods will have their way.

"Thank you, seeress," he says, speaking the necessary words. "Your sight is my sight. Your voice is my voice. Fate is and always will be."

There's only one thing left to do. He goes to the table by the door and takes the knife. Pauses, hopeful. For what? Answers? A word to prove who she once was is not lost? A kiss?

Candles flicker though there's no wind, prompting him. Dutifully, he draws the knife across his hand. His blood runs freely. He places the knife on the table, then presses his palm to the doorpost, where the dark stains of countless bloodied hands paint the wood. This done, he makes a fist and opens the door.

"Wait," Velaug says.

He turns. She grabs his injured hand. Opens it and kisses the wound. Then she pulls him close and kisses him on the mouth, his own blood, warm and salty, mingling between them.

She breaks off the kiss, her wet lips moving to his ear. "Survive," she whispers.

Then he's pushed outside and the door closes behind him. It's night. The Assembly must be underway. He knows he should make haste to the mead hall, but he also knows something else now, as if that knowledge was given to him by Velaug's lips.

He knows who paid the assassins.

He just needs to prove it.

CHAPTER 11

"Where is the stupid boy?" Helvig slams his fist on the chair's arm.

Thyri places her hand on his, supportive as a jarl's wife should be. Helvig knows he's lucky to have such a woman by his side. Many jarls have lost their chairs, and their lives, to the schemes of overly ambitious, or simply bored, wives. His own grandfather, the first of his line to sit in this chair, met such a fate.

"He'll come," Thyri says. "His dark corner will not sit empty long."

It takes Helvig a moment to understand she means Rúnr.

"Not him," Helvig says. "Torstyn. Where is your son?"

He speaks hastily when angry. He knows this of himself, but it's no longer a thing he apologizes for. Jarls have more important tasks before them than apologies.

By the gods I have to piss, he thinks. It's a constant pressure, almost a pain, but even if he pulled out his prick right here, there would be little more than a spatter. He shifts in the chair, thinking he should have one of his wife's attendants make a cushion.

"He'll arrive," Thyri says, withdrawing her hand.

"You're looking for me, Father?" Torstyn says, coming from behind Helvig's chair as if summoned, tall and strong and beaming. Giving Helvig strength. And hope. He may not have the temperament for the chair yet, but it lives in him.

"You should've been here from the start," Helvig says.

The Assembly has moved beyond trappings and ritual, past the obligations of the jarl to settle simple grudges and hear minor requests. The lawspeaker is present, drinking wine near Ubbein, who, Helvig finds, is watching him like a wolf, his pack grown now that he's added warriors from Sogn to his entourage, a necessary bolstering of Skyjavík's forces after the losses they suffered to the Fenns over the winter. But to whom are they loyal, the jarl or the hero?

"I was looking for my brother," Torstyn says.

"Drunk," says Thyri.

Helvig glares. The jarl is speaking to his son of his other son. Neither the jarl's wife nor anyone else in the hall has the privilege to join such a conversation.

"He should be here," Helvig says.

Smiling as ever, Torstyn says, "He will be."

Helvig lowers his voice. "I hope your faith isn't misplaced this night or any in the future."

A voice from the back of the mead hall calls out: "Torstyn, avenger!"

Another follows: "Fennslayer!"

More join until the hall is thicker with praise than it is with smoke. Helvig dabs the corner of his eye and shifts once more in his chair, nearly crushing a testicle as he does so. It's a politic set of movements, at odds with comfort, being jarl. He raises a hand to call for silence when Ubbein steps before the fire.

"The Opplands stand above all others in the Northlands," the hero says, turning his back on Helvig to address the hall. "Blood came to our beaches, and the sons of Jarl Helvig visited that blood back upon our attackers tenfold!"

Bold fucker.

Ubbein continues, "But I've heard talk of further vengeance. I've heard talk there's one in Skyjavík who would destroy the balance struck by the taking of our owed blood price from the Fenns."

The cheers of the people turn to murmuring, even the clamor of dissatisfaction. Helvig sees it happening like a storm rolling in on a ship caught listless without wind. There's nothing he can do.

"The Fenns got what they deserve, but that is a village claimed by Jarl Dagfinn. If we allow others to disobey our great jarl and draw more blood, will that not bring Dagfinn himself to our harbor?"

Though Ubbein hasn't spoken Rúnr's name, his intention is clear enough. Everyone knows of Rúnr's daughter's fate, and of his wife's—gone off into the depths of winter for vengeance, never to return. But to what end?

And where is the fool boy?

Helvig grinds his jaw, furious and impressed with Ubbein's machinations.

"We do not want war, do we?" Ubbein asks.

The people answer clearly and loudly: They want gold, not war. They want raids, not one man's vengeance. Helvig cannot blame them.

"The Allfather granted us his champion," Ubbein says. "We are his favorite people, are we not? And yes, there's gold to be had from Jarl Dagfinn, but not like what waits elsewhere. Not like what hides in the Christian temples of the Saxon Isles."

"Why not have both?" someone shouts.

There's laughter and cheers and pounding on tables and many mouths drinking, but Helvig knows it's a dangerous road he's being forced down. He looks to the lawspeaker, to see if he can end this speech, but the bald and fat little bastard has his eyes on Ubbein like a girl ready to spread her legs. Ubbein will continue until he's achieved his aim, and then, soon enough, this chair, this uncomfortable fucking chair, will be his.

The only way for Helvig to hold on is to find new riches, new lands, and new titles to offer his warriors. West is the answer. Only west lies what Helvig needs most: glory.

And fuck him if he doesn't want to go just for the adventure. And the summers there, so warm. No snow. Few mosquitos. How he loved sweating like that when he and Njal and Leif were raiding those Saxon fuckers. Yes, one summer west and Helvig's name will be such that he can demand Torstyn follow him upon the chair and even Ubbein will not be able to deny it. And then Helvig can take a kingdom in the west and live out his days in comfort, with Thyri by his side, waking up each morning without the pain of frost in his knees.

"Yes," Ubbein says, playing the crowd like a skald with his poem. "West is the way!"

Thyri stands and calls for wine. A thrall brings her a large jug, and Ubbein is forced to pause and watch as she fills Helvig's cup. Torstyn's cup. Ubbein's cup next. Then as many more as she can fill before the jug runs empty. The serving girls take over then so that Thyri can return to her place beside her husband. Helvig tries to hide his smile. His wife is wise and as calculating as Ubbein could ever hope to be.

"For the treasure hoards that await us," she says, her voice commanding. "For the victories that deserve us. For the fates the gods choose for us. With Jarl Helvig to lead us, and heroes like my son Torstyn and the great Ubbein, son of Sigurd, to support him, the future of the Opplands is blessed. Let it ever be so. Let us ever share drinks such as these as kin."

Whatever adoration Ubbein had gathered is lavished now on Thyri. There was a time when Helvig was suspicious of such shows by his wife. She's younger by two fistfuls of winters, after all, and the less he can piss without discomfort the less he can pleasure her. Such is the makings of trouble, his father told him—and he does not miss the way she refuses to name Rúnr—but look at her, wielding the adoration of the people the way the greatest warriors wield swords.

"Thank you, my lady," Ubbein says. "If I may, Jarl Helvig is as wise and brave as his wife, no doubt. And almost as pretty!" Great laughter and joy fill the hall. Even Helvig grins. "And a wise jarl such as he knows the Saxon Isles is our future. West we must go!"

The mead hall erupts. If Helvig didn't know better, he might look up to be sure the roof wasn't about to be shuddered loose and fall in on all of them. Despite Thyri's best effort, Ubbein is carrying the Assembly and choosing Skyjavík's future. And why not? West is the way, Helvig cannot argue. But it's the way that denies Rúnr, that denies Yrsa. And Ubbein is too astute not to know this.

Cursed be any moment Helvig considers actions other than vengeance for Yrsa, his own granddaughter by law. He held her the day she was born with as much pride as held Torstyn upon his birth. He bounced her on his knee and rode her on his back and lavished upon her more love than he thought he had in his old bones.

Poor Yrsa, lying cold in the ground.

Sweet Yrsa, unavenged.

What kind of jarl am I—what kind of man am I—if I don't gain her vengeance?

But he cannot give his Berserkr leave to abandon the summer raids. And now he cannot call a raid south or east or north or to wherever the Painted Fenn might be hiding. This, then, is Ubbein's plan, he sees too late. He must choose between the jarl's chair and his adopted son, between his duty and his granddaughter.

Thyri huffs but doesn't speak. He can imagine her thoughts, always coming back to those two decisions he made that both solidified his jarldom and cut a wedge in his marriage. The first, taking the son of his closest mate as his own when he adopted Rúnr. The second asking—*who am I fooling; I demanded*—Odin for a champion. What had not been done in generations. But for him, the gift had been granted. The black bear came, sent by Odin Allfather, who does not work the way of sane men.

How he remembers the smell of blood that day, as if rusted iron fell on the rain, and Rúnr standing over the bear, its heart in his hands, still beating, his eyes blazed vacant as he ate of it and became Odin's champion: Berserkr.

Be wary of receiving that which you ask from the gods, the old seeress, Olga, told him when he asked how to call on Odin for a champion. Wise words, they proved.

Thinking of Olga brings her daughter to mind, the new seeress. The girl Rúnr once ran around with. Perhaps he will seek her out in these next days, see if she offers advice as wise as her mother's. Maybe this time, he'll listen.

"I have a suggestion," Torstyn says.

"By all means, Torstyn son of Helvig, let us hear your wisdom," Ubbein says as if it's his Assembly.

"I think we should raid north and west," Torstyn says.

The crowd is full of talk. Support. Dissent.

"Divide our warriors?" Ubbein says as if Torstyn has suggested going into battle naked and unarmed.

"With you leading our warriors west, how can they find anything but victory? Meanwhile, there are more Fenns who have yet to pay in blood for their cowardly raid."

Thyri's hand finds Helvig's once more. She squeezes, the pride of a mother. It's a bold suggestion, to split their numbers. Perhaps Helvig should have thought of it himself. Perhaps Torstyn has the makings of a wise jarl after all.

Ubbein asks, "And who will lead north?"

"I will," says Torstyn without pause.

"With what ships? We'll need almost all we have to go west."

"Almost. But I only need a ship or two. A single warrior from Skyjavík is worth a dozen men from the Fennvold, is that not so?"

The mead hall is now abuzz for Torstyn. Even Helvig finds the desire to shout his approval, and with that comes fear. Has he traded one usurper for another? Ubbein for his own son?

Torstyn wouldn't be the first son to come for a jarl's chair before his father was ready to abandon it.

"And which expedition will the Berserkr join?" asks Ubbein.

Torstyn doesn't respond quickly. He's not considered this question yet, Helvig sees.

"It's time to make a statement," Thyri says to Helvig.

Yes, but his mind is suddenly empty. What can he say? How can he support his son without offending the hero?

How am I struck so mute?

"We should allow Rúnr to choose," Torstyn says.

"Fool," utters Thyri, too quiet for any but Helvig to hear.

"Choice is the jarl's domain," Ubbein says.

The mead hall goes silent. All eyes seek the jarl. He stands, his knees creaking, the weight of expectation heavier than that of fear.

"No warrior sails a crew without voice and vote," he says. "This is our way."

Before he can continue, the doors are thrown open. Helvig flinches, expecting Odin himself to finally relieve him of the burden of his chair and his life, but it's not the god of hosts and of burdens who enters the hall. It's Rúnr, covered in blood, a dark bag hanging at his belt, heavy by the way it falls. The blood, again, brings the black bear to Helvig's mind. His heart thunders in his chest. A pain rises in his head. For a moment, he thinks he must cry out, but the fit passes.

"Brother," Torstyn says, hurrying forward.

For a moment, the two brothers, Helvig's two sons, stand shoulder to shoulder. Same height. Torstyn the greater girth around the chest, his hair and beard red as the setting sun. Rúnr the longer arms, his hair and braided beard black as pitch. Oh, how Helvig wants to feel the pride he knows he should, the pride that fills him in the quiet hours of the night. But here, before all in the mead hall, he knows only fear.

Would it be the same if Odin had granted his gift upon Torstyn, and not Rúnr, like I wanted?

Rúnr waves his brother off and makes his way through the crowd to the fire where he stands beside Ubbein and looks the hero in the eyes without blinking.

"What is this?" Ubbein says as if offended.

"Helvig," Thyri demands, her voice like spurs in a horse's flank.

"My son," Helvig says. "What's happened? Have you been attacked?"

"Attacked," says Rúnr. "Yes, at the hot springs."

Torstyn snatches a horn from a serving girl and gives it to his brother, who drinks with great thirst.

"Are you injured?" Ubbein asks, he too finding a cup and bringing it to Rúnr.

"I'm unhurt."

Helvig notes the way Rúnr's hand finds the handle of an axe at his belt, patting it as if to be sure, but not grasping it. Not threatening to wield it. No one should have such a weapon in the hall before the jarl, but he doesn't call attention to it.

"Who attacked you?" Torstyn asks.

"I have an accusation to speak," Rúnr says.

Helvig knows as plainly as he knows his own name that he must stop Rúnr from speaking, but fear is a cold drink, filling his limbs from the core, freezing his tongue.

"Tell it to me," Torstyn says. "Privately first, brother."

"I cannot," Rúnr says. "I've broken the law, and I must explain before our jarl and the gods."

"What law?" asks Ubbein hungrily.

I've put my foot in a snare, Helvig thinks, though he cannot yet see the rope or the tree it's tied to.

"I sought peace in the hot springs of the South Mountain where few bathe. Two men, strangers, came for me there."

"You fought?" Ubbein says. "A disagreement?"

"Fenns!" Torstyn says. "We must strike them again, strike Jarl Dagfinn himself if need be."

The mead hall is a raucous place again. Ubbein appears uncomfortable. If blame can be placed on the Fenns, the raids will have to go north. A trap avoided, but another ahead.

If we sail north, Helvig knows, *I cannot strengthen my hold on the chair.*

"Not Fenns," Rúnr shouts. "Men from Sogn. Men who spoke of coin paid for my head. Assassins."

The word hangs in the mead hall. The only other sound is the popping of the fire and the restlessness of Thyri in her chair.

Rúnr takes the sack from his belt and dumps it at Ubbein's feet. Someone gasps. A serving girl screams. All others are silent as the severed head rolls to a stop, its topknot touching Ubbein's boot.

The hero nudges it aside. "What's this?"

"One of the assassins. The rest of him, and the other one, remain at the hot spring for any who wish to look upon them."

"This is not a matter for the Assembly."

"But it is," Rúnr says.

The feeling of something coming, a tide rising unstoppable, fills Helvig. Fate. Though Thyri is tense for him to act, he knows he cannot speak against what the gods desire.

"This man, I saw with you at Ivar's funeral," Rúnr says, indicating the severed head. He then points at the remaining three of Ubbein's new allies. "A friend of yours, yes?"

Thyri is to her feet. "Helvig," she says. "You must do something."

What, woman? he wants to yell at her. The lawspeaker is present. The accusation is implied if not yet spoken. The tide becomes a wave and will drown them all if it wishes.

"Sit down," he tells her.

She tilts her head that way she does when they're alone and she's angry, but she sits. All around them, there's arguing. Jostling. Even shoving. The people are already taking sides.

"You admit killing this man?" Ubbein shouts to be heard.

"Him and his fellow assassin," says Rúnr.

"Is there anyone who witnessed your defense?"

"No."

The need to piss is suddenly all Helvig can think of.

"Did you speak this murder to the first person you passed afterward?"

"I committed no murder," Rúnr says calmly. "I merely defended myself."

Odin, help me.

Ubbein doesn't take his eyes from Rúnr. "Did you speak this murder to the second person you passed afterward?"

"He said it was defense," Torstyn says.

"Not even to the tenth person," Rúnr says. "Nor the first or second or fifth houses I passed either."

"Idiot," says Thyri as Helvig squirms in his chair.

"Did these bandits you claim as assassins name their patron?" Ubbein asks, casting eyes about.

He's frightened, Helvig thinks. He's never seen the hero flinch on the battlefield, but the mead hall is unlike any fight with sword and shield. The great Ubbein, about to be taken down by the unraveling of his own foolishness: sending assassins to kill a Berserkr.

That's it! All Rúnr needs to do is tell how the god trance came to him, to defend him from the assassins. That will place Odin's approval on killing them. It will allow him to accuse Ubbein of hiring them. There's relief in Helvig's groin. His hold on the chair tightens. He'll step from it when he's ready, not one day before. He is jarl of Skyjavík!

"They did not," Rúnr says. "They came for me as men. I fought them as a man. They're dead. I live."

No, foolish boy! Say you did so in the god trance. Speak it, true or not.

"I accuse Rúnr, son of Helvig, of murder!" Ubbein's voice cracks with the force he screams the words.

"You sack of pig's piss," Torstyn shouts, reaching for Ubbein.

The lackeys come. Gellir and Eilif and grim men from Sogn. The mead hall is afire with shoving and grabbing and shouting. A thrall is knocked down. Cups spill. A few punches are thrown. And there stands Rúnr, watching it all like a fisherman eyeing his line in the water, waiting for the moment to pull.

Perhaps I've been preparing the wrong son for this chair.

"Enough, Helvig," pleads Thyri.

Strength returns from somewhere. Rúnr, he sees, is doing exactly what he means to do, and by the gods Helvig will help him.

"Silence, Skyjavík!" he shouts.

The mead hall quiets. Torstyn lets go of Gellir. Ubbein straightens his beard. The lawspeaker, pressed cowardly into a corner, peers out like a rat against the light.

"An accusation has been spoken," Helvig says. "It must be answered. Rúnr, son of"—he pauses; there is only one way forward, just in case—"Njal, speak your defense."

"Father," Torstyn protests.

"I killed assassins," says Rúnr. "Assassins hired by Ubbein. Of this, I accuse him."

Finally, the lawspeaker waddles to the fire. Not for the first time, Helvig wonders how much stronger his rule might be if not for this soft bastard's presence.

"Competing accusations," the lawspeaker says. "Rúnr, son of Njal, adopted by Jarl Helvig, has committed two murders without legally declaring them." Careful words, but do they lean for

Ubbein or Helvig? "However, if the dead men were hired assassins, hired by one of us in this hall, then the crime of murder is moot, and the crime of assassination is to be punished. What say you, Ubbein, son of Sigurd, hero of Skyjavík and all the Opplands?"

Ubbein, his swagger back, says, "I say this accusation is a lie told by a liar, a man everyone here knows cannot be trusted behind our backs, for he can become an animal at any moment."

There is only one solution now, Helvig knows. *I hope you've thought this through, boy.*

"Speak, Rúnr," the lawspeaker prompts.

"One accusation for another," Rúnr says. "Let us then settle this as men must, beneath the eyes of the gods. I make the Challenge, Ubbein. Will you accept?"

"I am no coward," says Ubbein. "I accept."

Thyri stands and departs, followed by her servants. Helvig has no stomach for her dissatisfaction or theatrics tonight and lets her go.

"The Challenge is made and accepted," says the lawspeaker. He then slips back to the shadows.

The mead hall is a maelstrom. Helvig clings to his chair the way drowning men do. With Thyri gone, Leif comes near, lending strength with his presence.

Helvig closes his mind to the noise. "Ubbein and Rúnr," he says, the words like tar in his mouth. "You will meet tomorrow on Thor's Island when the sun is highest, where men fight men and even the gods cannot interfere."

He can do no more. Leif offers his hand, and Helvig takes it.

"What will you have me do, my lord?" Leif asks.

Helvig looks at Torstyn, strong and foolish. He looks at Rúnr, morose and unpredictable. He looks at Ubbein, above all things a threat. And he doesn't know how to answer his Hersir, his friend. The gods help him, he doesn't know.

CHAPTER 12

Thyri dismisses all the servants from her bedchamber, save for Hrodny.

"How may I serve you, my lady?" her handmaiden says, smoothing a place on the bed for Thyri to sit.

This is Thyri's conundrum. There is not a servant in her husband's hall whose allegiance is sworn to her. She comes from plain people. Free, yes, but in all her life, her father owned one thrall. Before her marriage, she knew more of barley and chickens than she did of a jarl's duty or a jarl's wife's place. The first gift she received as Helvig's intended was a maidservant from his mother. An insult, really. A way of calling attention to Thyri's unworthiness.

Hrodny was that handmaiden, only a winter older than Thyri herself. But more than two decades she's served the jarl's wife now, and Thyri feels a kinship there. Of all her servants, Hrodny is the one she treats best. The one she rewards. The one whose loyalty she's been cultivating all these years. For now.

For tonight.

Thyri looks about the room to be certain they're alone. Her bedchambers are remote enough from the benches of the mead hall that the noise here is lessened. She imagines Helvig and Leif conspiring beside the jarl's chair, their heads together, seeking a way to draw advantage from what's just transpired. Like trying to draw wine from a stone, she thinks. Rúnr has brought misfortune and set in motion ill events with his carelessness.

Assassins? What does it matter? The jarl's son—the jarl's fucking adopted son—cannot be allowed such a foolish act as not declaring the murder he's done. And this Challenge? Thyri almost laughs in some strange combination of fear and glee. Whatever comes next, the Challenge tomorrow will set fate.

If Ubbein wins—when Ubbein wins, for the god trance cannot influence a Challenge on Thor's Island, such is Odin's law—Helvig's hold on Skyjavík will be loosened. The end, her end, will be in motion.

Oh, Ubbein will not reach for it just yet, she knows. He's too smart to be so overt so soon. It will be a slow process, but not so slow as to allow Thyri and Helvig to wait it out. And what of Torstyn? What is his fate once Ubbein has the chair within his reach?

There is only one outcome for a jarl's son when the chair is lost, she knows.

And if Rúnr defeats Ubbein?

Unlikely. Impossible. But if? Then Helvig's hold on Skyjavík will be iron. Ubbein will likely leave to seek his fortune elsewhere. And Rúnr will be both champion and hero. He'll be lauded like in the stories of old. He will be the choice of the people for Skyjavík's next jarl.

A Berserkr as jarl.

Odin must be enraged at the thought. Or engorged on laughter.

Rúnr as jarl over Torstyn?

Not while I breathe.

"Hrodny," she says, decision made, knowing she's placing her life in her maidservant's hands. "I need you to deliver a message, word for word. Will you do this for me?"

"Of course, my lady."

"No one, not even my husband, can know you carry it. And no one can know to whom you bring it. Will you do this for me?"

Hrodny bows her head. "My lady, you are wise and kind, and I am yours."

Thyri knows both the weight and strength of promises, and that even the best of them is worth no more than a sword upon a sinking ship. But for Torstyn, she will—she must—take this risk.

"Very well," she says. "Bring what I tell you next, my exact words, to Ubbein before the sun rises."

CHAPTER 13

Home.

Bleak. Sagging roof. Rotting timbers. The land unkempt. Though still night, dawn is coming, and the East Mountain lays its shadow here as if trying to hide what happened.

Rúnr has not set foot inside since the night Yrsa died. Berthe continued to live here for the few days she remained in Skyjavík, sleeping in the same bed all three of them used to cuddle in on cold nights. Not Rúnr. He spent his nights in the mead hall, table beneath his face rather than a pillow. Ale in his belly rather than the warmth of his home.

He has a large skin full of mead with him as he takes in what's become of his home. Only one winter abandoned, it feels like no one has lived here for years. Like no one has been loved here for lifetimes.

To the side of the house, where carrots once grew, there is a low mound of earth, seemingly as fresh as the day he laid it. Here he sits and pats the cold dirt.

"I should've done it right," he says. But he couldn't bring himself to commit his Little Bear to the fire as Hrist did for Ivar. He needed her near. He needed this visible grave to remind him.

And now he has this axe to remind him.

He holds the axe and drinks his mead and thinks of the night he handed it to Yrsa.

"Stay inside," he told her. "Be brave."

"I will, Papa," she said without a tremble in her voice.

Rúnr drinks deep. The mead pours down his beard and over his chest. He belches and drinks more. Needs more to do what must be done. He measures the mound by eye, knowing the spot where her chest must lie. The spot where he wrapped her fingers around the axe months ago. He sets aside the skin and the axe and digs with his hands, careful not to go too deep. Disturbing the dead is a heinous crime.

So how has the axe come to me? he thinks as he digs, his fingers bleeding from the rocks of the earth. *How am I burying what was already buried?*

He stops digging before he reaches her. The hole is deep enough. Has to be, for he cannot force himself to dig deeper. He takes the axe in hand.

"It's cursed," Torstyn told him at the burial. He meant the Saxon witch. He meant how the axe drank Njal's blood and refused to protect Yrsa's. "You must break it."

It was only the two of them, with Berthe refusing to look upon her daughter's body after it was cleaned and prepared. The ground was cold and hard as the summer had faded then. Snow was piled all around except where Rúnr had cleared it, where he had dug.

"I will," he said. "Alone."

Torstyn understood. "Rest well, brave Yrsa," he said to the wrapped body—his niece—that Rúnr had already placed in the hole. "Live well in Valhalla."

When he was gone, Rúnr tried to snap the axe's handle. To dent the blade. To separate steel from wood. He could not injure it. He found a wood cutting axe and swung it with all his strength. He threw it against stone. Smashed it against shield. Called for Thor to blast it with his lightning. The axe remained unblemished.

As it is now.

Rúnr runs his fingers over the alien runes on its face. He considers trying to break the weapon once more. He thinks of taking it to the harbor and throwing it into the water. He considers opening his own throat the way Yrsa's lay open as she died.

"What should I do, Little Bear?" he says.

The answer is obvious. To enter Valhalla, Yrsa needs the weapon she died with as much as she needs Rúnr to kill the Painted Fenn. He places the axe inside, gently, like a mother placing a baby to sleep. Exactly as he did when he laid Yrsa within.

As he pushes the dirt back over the grave, a bird comes, landing on the roof. A black kite with a red-streaked body ticking its head this way and that. Watching. When Rúnr has finished his labor, he drinks. The bird *chwirks*.

"Do you want a taste?" he asks it, offering the skin.

"What is this?"

The bird flies off in a huff as Rúnr turns. Torstyn stands there, eyes wide.

"Something was digging up the dirt here," Rúnr says, the lie coming quickly.

"We should bring some eagles out here, then, to keep the place free of vermin."

"There are birds," Rúnr says.

Torstyn grunts, eyes on the grave. Then on Rúnr's hands. "That was a memorable display tonight," he says. "Why didn't you declare the killing?"

"I wasn't in my right mind."

"The god trance?"

Rúnr shakes his head. "I went to see the seeress."

Torstyn sits. Rúnr offers him the mead. They pass it back and forth for a time.

"Did Velaug tell you to accuse Ubbein?"

"She's like her mother now, more riddles than answers."

"How do you know it was him?"

"I didn't at first," Rúnr says. "Until I remembered seeing them with Ubbein at Ivar's funeral."

"You're certain? It could be taken as an accusation against Sogn as well."

"You saw his face when I tossed the head."

"You can't fight him," Torstyn says.

"I have to."

"Not in a Challenge. Not on the island. Odin can't help you there."

Though his words echo Rúnr's own fears, hearing them aloud make him bristle. He'd hoped for support not a lecture. "The Challenge is made."

"And how does losing that Challenge help? Ubbein will be claiming the jarl's chair within two winters if this happens."

"It is happening," Rúnr says. "It must happen. Did you see him when I entered the mead hall? He never expected to see me again, except as a corpse. But if all he wanted was me dead, he could have done that himself. Found an excuse. Or challenged me outright. Why the assassins?"

Torstyn takes his time answering. He's a direct thinker, not one for subtleties, and though Rúnr is impatient for Torstyn to understand, he waits. This is the whole of it and, like a ship able to navigate the endlessly roiling maelstrom of Hvergelmir from which all other waters have risen, if Torstyn can see how Rúnr thinks, there is hope.

"Because to kill you himself would not sway Skyjavík to his support," Torstyn says. "He may be our hero, but you're our champion, the first Berserkr in generations, and Odin does not give such a gift lightly."

It's a good point, but not the one Rúnr is thinking. "He could lie and say I attacked him. Say I insulted him. Some people will side with him so long as he gives a reason, any reason. No, he wanted me to disappear."

"The day after confronting us in the mead hall? People will see his motive."

Rúnr shakes his head. "The day after we dropped insults on him and his friends in front of a crowd. That's what people will remember, not how it started. They'll remember he asked me to sail with him, and I didn't say yes. He knew I wouldn't."

"You didn't say no."

"But I didn't say yes," Rúnr repeats. "And if I failed to appear at the Assembly . . ."

"He would call you a coward in front of the jarl. And by that, he would call the jarl a coward."

The drinking skin is empty. The brothers sit in silence, the sounds and smells of spring rising around them. Rúnr doesn't miss how often Torstyn's eye returns to the grave.

"But you did appear," Torstyn says.

"And tomorrow, when I lose the Challenge, I will be a criminal."

"Don't fight, then."

"Which is worse for Helvig, a son who is a criminal or one who is a coward?"

Torstyn picks up a stone and throws it. He's almost there. The closer he gets, however, the more Rúnr doubts his own plan.

"Velaug spoke a prophecy," he says.

"Tell me."

Rúnr hears the words in his mind. *Three times the god trance will take you. Three times on your journey as you seek the killer in the red house, the Temple of the Hanged God. There, Yrsa will have her vengeance.*

"I'll find the Painted Fenn, and my vengeance, within a red temple to Odin," he says, knowing well, as all do, the story of Odin giving his eye to Mimir's well, and then hanging himself upon

Yggdrasill for nine nights so that he could learn the runes of knowledge and know the truths of all the realms.

"We have no temples in Skyjavík," Torstyn says. A point Ubbein and Helvig have clashed over these past few summers, with the hero wanting to spend the spoils of their summer raids to build one, and the jarl wanting to spend those spoils on farming and smithing and keeping the mead and ale flowing in the hall.

"We do not."

"Uppsala," Torstyn says.

Rúnr doesn't allow his smile to show. The High Assembly of all the North, held every third year at the Great Temple of Uppsala to the east, where Odin stands tall with Thor and Freyr by his side. Rúnr and Torstyn went when they were younger with their fathers, and he has never forgotten how the temple's roof blazed red like fire under the setting sun. It was the most beautiful sight Rúnr has ever seen on dry land.

Save for the smiling face of his Little Bear.

"I cannot flee," he says. "I cannot retract my accusation, for that will still leave Ubbein's charge against me. And I cannot win."

"You can," Torstyn protests. "Fuck Odin and his trance. You rely on it too much."

Rúnr feels calmer than he has in a long time. "Has anyone ever beaten Ubbein? Has he ever been carried away in retreat? Has anyone ever even drawn blood from his flesh once, let alone three strikes? Listen, I cannot run, and I cannot win. And I do not need to do either."

"Then you'll lose. You'll be a murderer. Ubbein gains strength, and you'll be punished."

"I'll be exiled."

"Ubbein will demand execution."

"Helvig won't grant it."

"What if he does?"

"You must convince him not to. I'm the Berserkr. None will weep for my departure, but many will fear an attempt to execute me. What if Odin tries to stop it? What if the god trance takes me as the axe descends upon my neck? I'm a danger. The people will want me exiled, of this you must convince him."

"How is this a good plan?" Torstyn asks. He shakes the empty skin. "And why is the mead gone?"

This time Rúnr does laugh. He loves his brother. He'll miss him. "The gods want this. They've told me. I will be exiled, which means—"

"Which means you will not be forced to sail the summer raids," Torstyn says, understanding finally taking him.

"I will be free to go to Uppsala and avenge my daughter."

Torstyn stands. He's agitated. Ready for a fight. It wouldn't be the first time they threw punches at each other. It's what brothers do. But he paces instead.

"There has to be another way. You'll be an outlaw. No status. No protection. You'll lose everything."

"I already have. Let them take this land and this house. I'll never sleep here again. So long as they leave Yrsa to rest, I have nothing to lose."

"What if Odin revokes his gift?"

What if he does? Rúnr thinks, a cold fear in his gut—this he hasn't considered.

"Have you ever heard of such a thing, a Berserkr losing the god trance?"

"No," Torstyn says. "But what I know of Odin's mind could fill a droplet of rain with room to spare."

They share a mirthless laugh. Rúnr stands.

"I'll come with you," Torstyn says.

"That will harm Helvig more than anything I do," he says. "You are his blood. You must remain apart from me. The Challenge will be met tomorrow. I'll lose. I'll become an outlaw. Your father will need you against an emboldened Ubbein even more."

"You're a fool."

"I will return."

"When?"

Rúnr thinks of the other message Velaug gave. One word, as if outpouring many in that breath. *Survive.*

All the rest is just clouds and waves. Survive. For vengeance. For Yrsa. For Valhalla. Nothing else matters.

"When my exile ends. Protect her," Rúnr says, indicating Yrsa's grave. "All will be as the gods will it."

CHAPTER 14

The excitement on the beach is heavy. Rúnr feels it before his boots have touched the sand. Like for battle. Like the gods recalled by Heimdall sounding Gjallarhorn to call Ragnarök. Skyjavík has never held this many people, it seems.

The Berserkr and the hero. Who wouldn't want to discover which the gods favor most?

Torstyn waits at the edge of the crowd. His reaction to Rúnr's arrival is subdued, coming to meet him the way a gate watcher might greet a stranger.

"You can beat him," Torstyn says, his tone already defeated.

"I've decided," Rúnr says.

Torstyn embraces Rúnr. "What you've decided is a leaf on a storm's wind compared to what the gods have decided."

Rúnr doesn't argue. He kisses his brother's cheek. "The gods want me to find my fate."

"He's come!" a voice calls. There are cheers. And then jeers.

Torstyn releases Rúnr and they push their way to the beach where two boats wait and Jarl Helvig sits in his chair, brought out to the docks for the occasion. Thyri, Rúnr notes, is absent. As is Ubbein. A flare of hope is quickly doused. Ubbein is no coward. He'll come. And even if he doesn't, Rúnr will be bound to follow Helvig's raids wherever they go. There will be no sneaking off at night on stolen horses again only to return a hero. If he flees the raids, his exile will be permanent.

Torstyn tries to begin a chant of Rúnr's name. There is little support, the chant quickly turning to Ubbein's name. The air seems to shimmer with his reputation. Though the gods keep their counsel close, the people of the Opplands share their favor freely.

Rúnr accepts his lack of popularity the way a man accepts being told it is raining while standing hoodless in the deluge.

Torstyn holds Rúnr's shoulders. There are no words that matter now. The brothers part, and Torstyn joins his father on the docks, standing beside the chair, his face set grim. Leif joins him to stand behind Helvig's other shoulder. Two strong men to protect the jarl. It will have to be enough.

Rúnr looks out to the harbor. The waters are calm, the tide low, Thor's Island riding high. It's a small island, large enough for the two dozen men upon it to stand shoulder to shoulder in a ring, shields set at their feet, swords and axes held casually. Rúnr suspects they are chatting, calling favorites, making wagers. The men of the Circle are supposed to be half for each combatant, but finding a dozen to support Rúnr over Ubbein is a difficult task.

With the same inevitability he's undertaken all his tasks this day—the prayers over Yrsa's grave, the ritual washing of his hands after, the dedication of his body to Odin, and more—Rúnr accepts what is. His fight cannot be with those things he cannot change. His fight is with Ubbein. His fight is to lose.

Will the gods allow me to lose?

This is the question Torstyn hadn't thought to ask. It's the question Rúnr doesn't know the answer for. A Challenge is sacred, prescribed by the gods as a way to show favor and judgment. Rúnr knows he is innocent, that the men he killed were paid to take his life, but he needs to lose. He needs to be adjudged a criminal.

He considered visiting Velaug again, but he's certain she wouldn't be home. His fate is to seek the Fenn within the red temple to Odin. This he can only do if he's exiled, freed from his responsibility to follow Helvig's warriors on their raids. The decision is made. Still, he searches for Velaug, hoping for a smile or a nod, anything to confirm he's making the correct choice. He thinks he sees her, but the crowd is thick and pressing. The familiar color of her hair is lost. The crowd murmurs. The murmur becomes a roar. The roar, a thunder. Ubbein has arrived.

The people part, making way for their hero and many followers, more than were with him at Ivar's funeral. More strangers among them as well. And the lawspeaker. He should be with Helvig on the docks, not throwing his support upon one of the combatants. Luck is against Rúnr.

Which is exactly what he needs.

Ubbein joins him on the beach, his followers staying back with the crowd. The hero examines both boats while Rúnr waits, content with whichever one Ubbein rejects. The wagering begins now with the boats. The people know which is which, one lucky, the other not, some will say. Rúnr doesn't care.

"A good vessel," Ubbein says, choosing one.

Cheers rise from the crowd. The sound of coin changing hands is obvious. Rúnr steps to his boat. The lawspeaker appears and climbs the docks to stand a distance from the jarl, a supposed neutral party. Rúnr doubts it.

"A Challenge has been made," Helvig says, his voice booming. He stands, as is the way. "Have both challenger and challenged come to settle the dispute?"

"I have come," Ubbein says. Cheers follow.

"I have come," Rúnr says. Muttering follows.

The lawspeaker says, "Speak the Challenge."

The accuser speaks first, but in this instance, both have made accusations. Rúnr is unsure what to do. Ubbein is not. He raises his hands high.

"Rúnr Helvigson is a murderer and a coward, I speak," the hero says.

Those gathered chitter and chomp for more, but none speak out yet. They know their place. They know the rules. Rúnr must answer. But Rúnr's mind is running wild once more. *Rúnr Helvigson*, Ubbein said, making certain to place guilt on both jarl and son.

The lawspeaker has made his way to the docks and stands apart from Leif. Has he counseled Ubbein? Is he a party to what is coming?

"Speak, Rúnr, son of Njal," Helvig commands, prompting Rúnr from his thoughts while chiding him like a father telling him to get on with it already.

As with Ubbein's words, Rúnr notes the naming. Helvig is disowning him.

I do not blame you, he thinks, even as he fights back the disappointment and anger of hearing it aloud.

"Ubbein, son of Sigurd, is a liar and a bringer of assassins to Skyjavík. This is my defense and my accusation, I speak."

The people jeer and shout. A head of cabbage flies, barely making it to the sand. Another lands near Rúnr's boat. Some carrots wobble through the air. Leif climbs down from the docks, and the vegetable attack quickly ceases.

"Such are the accusations," Helvig says, silencing the people. "The gods demand all such Challenges be settled where three roads meet: that of right, that of wrong, and that of judgment. In the harbor of Skyjavík, three fish roads, fjords blue as Odin's eye, meet in such a manner, and therein floats Thor's Island. Do any deny the gods' favor upon this famed island where Gullveig returned to life for the third time with the power of foresight, the first seeress to walk among men? The place where Thor himself first rode the Bifröst to Midgard, the earth there scarred by his arrival?"

"None deny it, jarl," is the thunderous reply from all those gathered, a single voice of power and awe.

The ritual now complete, Helvig must call for the two combatants to enter the boats and row to the island. He does not speak right away, however, leaving Rúnr to eye the restless crowd. Most are watching Ubbein or Helvig. Eilif has come to the fore, his boots on the sands, with Gellir beside him. The pair whisper in turns to a group of strangers. There is nodding. Eyes turn occasionally to Rúnr.

"A word," Leif says, emerging from the crowd to join the combatants on the beach.

Though it is unusual for any to speak now, Helvig does not stop his Hersir. Leif comes to Ubbein and Rúnr holding three horns sloshing with ale. Rúnr wants to get on with it, to enter the boat and row to the island and fight, but he's also thankful for the delay. And the ale. He takes the first horn when it's offered. Ubbein takes his.

"Two men who have fought for Skyjavík stand before us," Leif says. "Two men who have stood as heroes among us. One is right, and one is wrong. The gods know how to decide, and as men, we know the old ways are best."

He pauses. The people voice their agreement to his words. It's the most words Rúnr has ever heard Leif speak at one time.

"I have fought beside both Ubbein and Rúnr," the Hersir continues. "I count this a dark day that one must be lost, a criminal deserving judgment. I count this a dark day that you cheer such an outcome."

He points to the people as if selecting each one. There is silence. He raises his horn and drinks. As does Ubbein. As does Rúnr, his confidence somehow shaken rather than bolstered by Leif's words.

"Enter the boats," Helvig says. "Row hard. Fight well. And may Skyjavík find Odin's favor afterward."

One more cheer from the crowd. Above them, two crows fly low and then soar high toward the southern mountain—Odin watching with interest, for certain.

Ubbein steps first into his boat. Rúnr follows suit. The people of Skyjavík surge forward to shove the boats into the water, and then it is a race to the island. Ubbein wins by a length. Rúnr has no care for such trivialities, but Ubbein stands proud of himself on the island's shore. Rúnr joins him and the two dozen warriors make room for them to pass. When the pair stand in the center, the warriors close the Circle and raise their shields. It is Rúnr's first time on the island. Challenging a Berserkr, even if the god trance cannot take him here, is not a popular move. Sand and gravel cover the land, with three jagged black lines, each the width of a healthy sow, cut deep into the earth from the east, the west, and the north, meeting in the island's center. The result of the Bifröst. A faint smell, like soot, hangs in the air.

Where the black lines meet lie two sets of arms: a sword and shield each. Ubbein circles them, finally choosing a pair. Rúnr waits patiently, growing calmer by the moment. The outcome is decided. What fear could he have? He takes up his gear. The shield is solid. The sword is young and made well enough, some wealthy man's weapon, as all swords begin. Though he prefers an axe, he's well trained on many weapons.

Ubbein slaps his sword against his shield. The warriors of the Circle do the same, making thunder.

"To blood," Ubbein says.

The rules are known. The first to draw blood three times is the victor. But not small blood. To score a point, deep blood is needed. Spraying blood. Dangerous blood. Rúnr tries to recall how many Challenges Ubbein has fought. There are songs for each, of course. Eight? Eleven? It doesn't matter.

"To blood," he says.

"To blood!" the warriors of the Circle shout in unison, loud enough for those on the beach to hear.

Surely there is a reply from Skyjavík, but Rúnr doesn't hear it. He's drinking in the moment, this time between sounds, fingers wrapped around his bear's tooth pendant. Ubbein, however, is impatient. He bangs his sword on his shield again and again. Rúnr exhales and slams his own sword upon his shield.

Survive.

The word strikes him as if whispered in his ear so that he almost turns to look for Velaug beside him. Is this what she meant? Could Ubbein seek his death here?

Men have died during Challenges, but never has a warrior murdered another on this island. Doing so would be an outlandish crime. A cursed act. Even Ubbein couldn't be so arrogant as to think he could get away with it, could he?

There's no time to think on an answer. Ubbein is fast with his first strike, and faster still with his second. The Challenge is underway and already Rúnr is on his back foot, battling for his life.

CHAPTER 15

Rúnr should have expected this—Ubbein eschewing the ceremonial first strikes by each combatant. This fight will be to spill as much blood as Ubbein can before the warriors of the Circle, with their shields thundering, can stop him.

If they even want to stop him.

Ubbein's sword flies as if flexible as rope, able to slash where it shouldn't be possible. Within seconds, Rúnr has suffered numerous minor cuts and scrapes, each receiving the same call from the warriors of the Circle: "Carry on!"

In the god trance, Rúnr would have torn Ubbein to pieces already, tiny shreds of flesh and muscle fit for salting and drying. The people of Skyjavík would be chanting Rúnr's name. Champion and Berserkr and Hero all in one.

And my fate lost, Yrsa's vengeance gone, as I go raiding, as much a prisoner as any thrall.

No, he must lose. But he cannot lose quickly or carelessly. Ubbein must feel Rúnr's strength and skill. The warriors of the Circle must witness a skilled duel. Only in this way can the exile be earned.

Ubbein slices wildly. Rúnr spins easily aside. Except it's not so wild a swing after all. Ubbein's ability to change momentum is uncanny, and Rúnr is caught off-balance, parrying and evading as he's never done before. Stumbling backward into a warrior's shield, the man shoving him roughly back into the Circle. Fate keeps him breathing as his boot catches a rut in the Bifröst lines. He falls, the slip keeping his head from being cleaved in half by the width of a finger. His beard isn't so lucky, a tuft of it shorn off and blowing away in the breeze.

Ubbein lets him regain his feet, a half grin on his lips that speaks of confidence like iron. Rúnr stands tall. Chest out. Shoulders wide. The Circle beats thunder, swords and axes on shields.

"I know it was you," Rúnr says.

Ubbein comes swiftly, his sword a blur, his shield a hammer crashing into Rúnr's own, throwing him back against the Circle wall once more. Again, Rúnr loses his footing and lands on a knee, exposed. Shoulder, back, arm, head—Ubbein has his choice. He cuts a gash in Rúnr's arm, bicep to elbow.

"First blood!" a voice from the Circle cries.

Tradition says a combatant must be allowed to regain his footing after a strike, but Ubbein offers no favor, charging the moment Rúnr is nearly upright. But Rúnr is no fool. He's set his weight and is able to twist aside and go low. He knocks Ubbein's shield high and kicks the hero below the knee. Ubbein stumbles. Rúnr finally has the advantage. Instinct presses him forward, hacking once, twice, then a hard jab. He misses Ubbein's heart by the grace of a quick dive away. Ubbein stands to face Rúnr. The two warriors eye each other. Rúnr didn't have to miss, and Ubbein knows it.

Because I must lose!

Someone from the Circle cries, "Carry on!"

Ubbein comes faster and even faster still. His sword work is dizzying, exhausting Rúnr, leaving him with more wounds on his arms and legs. Small blood, but enough of them will kill even the heartiest warrior.

"Come on," Rúnr says through clenched jaw, daring Ubbein to end this.

The hero obliges, his sword moving so fast Rúnr can barely see it. He misses a parry, and Ubbein stabs him in the thigh.

"Second blood!"

They face each other. Again, Ubbein comes fast, forcing Rúnr to focus too much on the sword. Ubbein's fist slams into his face. His nose crunches. His eyes water.

"Carry on!"

Ubbein comes again, but Rúnr's vision tightens to a point. Not the god trance. Just rage. He swings his sword like a man chopping down a tree, no finesse, no aim, just brute strength. It works. He lands a deep strike on Ubbein's hip. The hero backs away.

"First Blood!"

As Ubbein gave no time, so too does Rúnr attack again, quickly. This time it's Ubbein's feet that tangle. Rúnr slashes across his elbow, spraying blood.

"Carry on!" is the call.

"The fuck you call that?" Rúnr shouts about the obvious deep blood he's drawn, but there's no reply from the Circle.

Ubbein, his breathing more labored now, comes steadily. Rúnr parries. Feints. Nearly slices a hit, but Ubbein's shield does its job. Rúnr slashes down again and again until the shield's strappings snap. Ubbein is in danger.

I'm in danger!

The thought is so abrupt, Rúnr's sword goes astray. What's he doing? Ubbein must win. It's the only way Rúnr can be allowed to hunt the Painted Fenn.

It takes almost as much skill for Rúnr to miss his next slash as it would to strike home, making it seem a desperate escape by Ubbein leading to the hero's advantage as Rúnr's own shield is clubbed from his grasp. The follow-up knocks Rúnr's sword from his hand and him onto his ass, forcing him to crawl backward from Ubbein's sword thrusts.

"Had enough?" Ubbein asks once Rúnr is backed up near the Circle wall. If he's aware of what Rúnr has allowed him, he does not show it.

"Your beard," Rúnr says, making certain his breathing is labored, "looks like your sister's vagina hair."

Ubbein sets his feet and laughs deeply. Rúnr tenses. The coming pain will be terrible. But necessary. The Circle thunder grows louder.

"Say hello to your daughter in Valhalla," Ubbein says.

He means to kill me.

Fear fills Rúnr. If he dies, Yrsa will never see Valhalla. He digs his feet and hands into the sand, ready to spring. The hero comes. Rúnr launches. It's a good move. But all Rúnr has is his fists. He throws a glancing blow to Ubbein's skull. Ubbein never stops moving. He uses that same momentum to grab Rúnr's arm and throw him at the Circle wall. He tumbles through, warriors falling this way and that, Rúnr landing half in the water, choking on the salty drink.

Desperate, he searches for a weapon and finds steel.

There's no thinking now. No strategy. Only life and death. Rúnr closes his fist around the blade he's found. An axe. He shifts his grip and rises from the water, barely avoiding being gutted by a wicked cleaving sword. A killing blow. Rúnr means to return the favor and slams his weapon down on Ubbein's backswing. The two hold strong, nose to nose, until Ubbein shoves, breaking the stalemate. The Circle has reformed. Ubbein jabs, a feint. Rúnr blocks the follow-up. Ubbein spins. When he comes back for the counter, he's aging, his face rotting and shrinking against his skull, his hair falling out like soot, his eyes empty holes from which beetles crawl, like the wolf-thing.

Rúnr recoils, his advantage lost. The draugr-like Ubbein-thing seems to hold two swords for the speed it swings them. Three even.

How is that possible? Its breath is putrid, gagging Rúnr. It blinks empty eyes. One of its lids droops, then drops away. Rúnr fights the Ubbein-thing. He fights his own terror. He's losing to both. If any in the Circle see what Rúnr sees, they don't speak of it. The Circle holds. The Ubbein-thing runs a sword through Rúnr's belly.

I'm going to die.

Velaug's voice says, *Survive.*

It's enough. Rúnr grips his found axe, only now recognizing it. His own axe, *again*, though he reburied it with Yrsa last night.

Impossible?

The Ubbein-thing slashes at his throat. The axe parries, saving Rúnr's life, but it's a waning life. He clutches at the wound in his belly.

Survive.

It is all Rúnr can do to shout, "Mercy."

He falls, defeated, alone beneath the sky and Odin's circling ravens.

CHAPTER 16

Rúnr lies unconscious in Torstyn's bed, every healer the jarl could call upon bustling in and out. Torstyn knows he's useless here, begging pardon for how often he's in the way, but none of them make him as uncomfortable as the seeress.

He's not sure if it's because of who she is now or because of who she was long ago. He kissed her once, Velaug daughter of Olga. The girl Rúnr loved from the time he could walk, and she was too tiny to even sit upright without help. Rúnr would watch her, that pudgy bald babe, as she slept or ate or sucked her own little toes as if bewitched. Torstyn remembers Njal saying Rúnr would make a good protector for the future seeress. He remembers Olga saying such a role would never be enough to fulfill him.

It is her turn now to sit and watch Rúnr sleep. She has rubbed herbs and poultices on his wounds. She has asked the serving girls to prepare the leek and onion stew. Torstyn can smell it coming long before a girl—he can't remember her name, though he does recall with fondness her enthusiasm in bed—brings the steaming soup. When the girl tries to feed it to Rúnr, Velaug takes the bowl and shoos everyone out.

"I'm not going," Torstyn says.

Velaug does not reply. She doesn't even look at him. She touches Rúnr's lips to open them and pours the steaming broth into his mouth, most of it pouring down his beard and over his belly and into the bed. The impulse to protest seizes Torstyn, but he resists. Velaug is intent on her chore.

Someone new enters behind Torstyn. He knows the perfume.

"Mother," he says. It's the first time she's visited since Rúnr was brought here from the Challenge.

She touches his arm briefly but does not speak. Velaug places the bowl aside and raises her eyes to the rafters. Time passes. Torstyn finds his thoughts on the coming exile. Like facing an enemy shield wall, he seeks a weakness, a way around or through. But he knows his father, prompted by the onlooking bushy eyebrows of the law-speaker, will do as Rúnr predicted.

Velaug speaks dark words. Ancient words. His mother stiffens but remains by his side. The seeress places her lips above Rúnr's lips, almost close enough to kiss. She moves down, lips to chin, nose to his mouth. Nose to beard. To bare chest. To the belly wound covered in a jaundiced poultice. The room stinks of so much sweat and blood and stew and worry, Torstyn has no idea how Velaug can discern the reek of what's spilled over Rúnr from what might be seeping from his sliced intestines.

She raises her head from the wound and breathes deep. Back to the wound and then another deep breath, like a dolphin breaching. A third time.

"The wound is clean," she finally says, standing, her nose stained with blood and poultice.

"Bring Hrodny," his mother calls. "She's my best seamstress."

"Thank you," Torstyn says to both women.

His mother leaves. For a moment, it's only Velaug and Torstyn with Rúnr. He thinks of the summer before Rúnr's adoption, walking on the path with Velaug from the mead hall to her house. He reached for her. She didn't deny him, so he put his lips to hers. It lasted a breath, and in that moment, he knew it was only Rúnr's kiss she wanted. They've never spoken of it. As far as Torstyn knows, she's never mentioned it to anyone.

"Velaug," Torstyn says, though what he means to say next he's not sure.

"He will survive," she says. That's all. She leaves.

Hrodny arrives moments later, along with several other servants. Torstyn means to stay, but another thrall comes, one of Father's.

"The jarl requests you," the thrall says, then leaves promptly.

Torstyn remains where he is, watching the stitching and the reapplication of Rúnr's poultice, thinking all the while. He knows Rúnr is smarter than he is, but to accept losing seems like stupidity. Not that there's anything he can do now. Rúnr called mercy before he passed out, a coward's defeat. Ubbein would have won anyway, of course, by Rúnr's own design. So why? What part of Rúnr's plan did he not share?

Or am I too thick-skulled to understand?

"Torstyn!"

No thrall calling this time, it is the jarl's own voice. Torstyn's only option now is to make certain his father levies exile rather than the execution he's certain Ubbein will push for. And to beg the shortest exile possible.

"The wound is sewn?" Torstyn asks Hrodny.

She nods without looking at him, tending to Rúnr's other wounds. Two more serving girls enter the room. It's getting crowded. Hot. The jarl calls again. Reluctantly, Torstyn leaves his brother. Helvig is waiting in the mead hall, sitting upon the arm of the jarl's chair. The hall is empty save for Leif at one of the tables across the fire.

"The wound is clean," his father says. "Your mother told me."

Torstyn says, "The seeress says he'll live."

"The gods have work for him."

"But you do not."

"The law is clear," says his father.

"You know Ubbein hired those assassins."

"The law is the law."

Such a cowardly answer, the kind a man gives when he's been too long in a chair and not on the battlefield. It's shameful for Torstyn to think this, of course, but the thought is had. No point in apologizing for it now.

"You're not a lawspeaker," he says.

"You need to be all things and more as jarl," his father says. "We've had this discussion before."

"Then let's not have it again."

Has he ever let me direct a conversation, even once, in my life?

"Skyjavík is our responsibility," his father says. "What happens if you don't become jarl?"

"The same thing that happens if I do. Ubbein comes for the chair."

"He won't dare, not if we remain strong."

"Like he wouldn't dare hire assassins?" Torstyn says.

"You'll sit upon this chair while I still live." His father pounds it with both fists.

"That'll scare him off, an old man and a fool."

"You're no fool."

"Have you lied to me all these years, Father?" Torstyn asks, knowing both can count well the arguments they've had that have featured the jarl screaming: *My son, the fool!*

His father opens his mouth to speak but makes no words.

Torstyn says, "Whether it's you or I, soon he's going to make a new Challenge, and there's not a man in the Opplands who can defeat him on Thor's Island."

"Rúnr almost did."

"And now you'll exile him."

"Ubbein has asked for execution."

Torstyn can't believe his father is even considering it. That he would even give voice to it.

"You will exile him, Father." He's never taken this tone with the jarl before. "You will make him an outlaw. Strip him of all protections from bandits and assassins. You will expose him to the wilderness and the moods of the gods. You will do this for as short a time as you can justify."

Leif shifts at his table but doesn't speak. He's a serious presence, always nearby to protect the jarl and his family. Torstyn wonders if that even means protecting the jarl from his family.

"You speak Rúnr's words," the jarl says.

Torstyn fumes at the suggestion he could not invent, could not understand, such a plan. The fact that they are Rúnr's words only makes him angrier.

"The law says—"

"Fuck the law. How long will you exile my brother, your son?"

The jarl winces as if Torstyn has struck him. "Three winters for the unlawful murder of a man."

"So six winters for killing two assassins."

His father sighs. "Aye."

"There is one other matter," Leif says.

"What matter?" Torstyn asks.

When the jarl doesn't answer, Leif does. "The black chair."

Torstyn hadn't thought of this. He feels the fool once more, though Rúnr didn't mention the possibility either. "You can't," he protests.

"Tonight. We'll wake him if necessary."

"The *nithstóll* is for criminals!" Torstyn says of the carved chair upon which criminals must sit while awaiting punishment.

"What do you think your brother is now?" the jarl roars. "If he cannot sit tonight, he will tomorrow. The law—"

"Tell me of the law once more, Father, and you'll have no sons to follow you as jarl."

The jarl bows his head. His shoulders, Torstyn notices, are thin. Far thinner than he's ever realized. For the first time, he considers his father as old. As finite rather than monolithic. For the first time he wonders how many winters the jarl has left. Seven? Five?

Will he even live to see Rúnr return from exile?

With a cracked voice, his father says, "I loved her too."

It's Yrsa he speaks of, though it takes Torstyn a moment to understand.

"She was sunshine itself," Helvig says, and Torstyn knows it's true. His father never shied from showering his love on Rúnr's daughter, unlike the way he raised the boys.

What if I have a daughter one day? Torstyn wonders, the thought new to him. *Will he love my daughter as he says he did Yrsa?*

Shame fills him once more. And once more, he turns that shame to anger.

"We will both of us lie dead beneath Ubbein's sword before the next winter thaws if you're not careful."

"That may be," the jarl begins.

Torstyn doesn't wait for him to finish. He exits the mead hall seeking something . . . anything. A fight. A fuck. A fire to cleanse everything that has happened since he and Rúnr returned from the Fennvold. What he finds is ale in the marketplace and then a quiet spot to drink it beside his buried niece.

CHAPTER 17

"I see you," Rúnr says to the black-and-red kite.

It is small but bold and seems less a creature of the wild than it does the memory of a shadow. Until the quarter moon reflects in its eyes. Then Rúnr knows it's real.

"Have you come to watch for the gods?" he says. "Or to tell me a secret?"

The bird hops toward the beach as if daring Rúnr to join him.

"Very funny, little fellow," he says, lifting his hands at the wrists as far as the ropes binding him to the chair allow. "But as you can see, I'm quite tied up at the moment."

He laughs at his own joke, the inability to move along with the burning wound in his belly sending a thick pain surging up his chest and down his almost numb legs. The kite makes a sound much like a laugh.

"Ah, a wise bird after all." Rúnr chuckles again, then chokes on his own breath.

The kite jumps into the air and becomes part of the night. Rúnr doesn't know how long he has been here, or even how long he's been awake, but sunrise is still some hours away, so he watches the sky for the bird's return. He's bound to the *nithstóll* where it's been brought to display criminals, at the opposite end of the beach from where Ivar's funeral was held. There's little else he can do, except think.

His mind wanders a hundred snowy paths, and a hundred more sea roads, until he has no idea where one thought begins and another ends. He questions which is worse: pain or loneliness? He argues with himself that exile from the Opplands is the better choice to being lost in a black mist, allowed into neither Hel nor Valhalla. He remembers hunting with Torstyn and Helvig and Njal, and how poor his aim was with a bow. And how it's not much better now. He imagines gripping the Painted Fenn's throat, squeezing until the man's eyes pop from his skull. He recalls the Ubbein-thing and vomits down his own beard.

Torstyn would laugh. So much laughter for such a dark night. Rúnr's, the bird's, his imaginary brother's. Has there ever been a story of Loki Shapeshifter as entertaining as all this?

"You're awake," comes a familiar voice, as if Rúnr's own thoughts conjured the speaker.

He can't see his brother approaching, tied as he is to the punishment chair, which always faces the East Mountain, leaving the punished unable to see the harbor or the town.

"How long, then?" Rúnr asks when Torstyn comes into his view, a cup in hand.

"Six years."

"Six," Rúnr repeats.

"I tried to lessen it."

"No, six is good."

"How can you say such things?"

"It's as I expected," Rúnr says, suddenly very thirsty. "Is that for me?"

"Water. Our father forbids anything else."

Rúnr tries to nod. His head, bound to the chair, will not move. Torstyn pours the water into his mouth. Most drains away. As it does, Torstyn's face also begins to drain. To melt. Decay. Like Ubbein's. Rúnr squeezes his eyes shut, choking on the water.

"Too fast," Torstyn says. "Sorry."

When Rúnr opens his eyes, his brother is unblemished, though the pain on his face makes it seem he's the one being punished.

I need to tell him, Rúnr thinks. About the black mist and Ivar in the hot spring and the wolf and the Ubbein-thing. He's shared everything else with his brother, why not these horrors?

Because who could believe I'm anything other than cursed to hear of them?

"I could cut you loose," Torstyn says. "You could go now before the people arrive to throw mud and shit on you."

"If I flee, I can never return."

Torstyn offers more water. Rúnr accepts it, finishing what is in the cup.

"Will she come, do you think?"

Torstyn says, "The seeress?"

Rúnr blinks twice, the closest he can come to a silent affirmation.

"She sat with you while you were in my bed," Torstyn says, "tending you."

"Then this hole in my belly won't kill me?"

"She says you'll survive."

Survive!

That one word again. It's more heartening than the water Torstyn provided. It means his fate remains. He will find the Painted Fenn in the red temple.

"Hold," Torstyn says.

Rúnr can't see what his brother is looking at down the beach, but his stance doesn't tighten. He doesn't reach for his sword.

"Ho there, Leif," Torstyn says. "What brings you?"

Leif doesn't cross in front of the chair, leaving Rúnr to hear the conversation without being able to see the Hersir.

"Your father asked my service."

"To watch him?" Torstyn says.

"So you can get some sleep."

"Why should I care for sleep when my brother is treated this way?"

"It's the jarl's command."

"Go, Torstyn," Rúnr says.

"I will stand by your side until I no longer can."

"Then after sleep makes you fall, you can be woken by that same mud and shit thrown at me. Besides, I can't turn my head to see you at my side anyway."

Torstyn laughs. "You have sworn his safety?" he asks Leif.

Leif says, "I have sworn."

"I'll return before dawn," Torstyn says.

Before the shit-throwers arrive and the lawspeaker comes to speak my exile, Rúnr thinks, understanding his brother's meaning.

When Torstyn goes, the night grows quiet. Leif is silent as the breeze. In time, Rúnr sleeps. Or must have, because he wakes with a start, pain lancing up his arms and down his neck when he jerks to awareness. It's not yet dawn, but the tip of the East Mountain is touching a purple sky now.

"Did my brother leave any more water?" Rúnr asks.

There is no response.

"Leif?"

The Hersir is either asleep or gone. Either option is worrisome. A fluttering comes from the right. At the farthest edge of Rúnr's vision, he catches motion. The kite, returned?

Then more sounds. Boots this time, on sand.

"Leif?" When there's no reply, he says, "Velaug?"

"Sweet that you think the seeress would come to suck on your shamed cock, murderer."

Rúnr knows Eilif's deep voice immediately.

"Jealous I didn't offer it to you first?" Rúnr says. He should be scared, but he tells himself he's safe in his fate.

Until the sound of a sword being drawn argues that sometimes fates change.

"You're a funny man," a second voice says. Gellir.

The sound of another sword. "I'm going to cut off your prick and make you eat it before I kill you."

Rúnr struggles against the ropes fastening him to the chair. "You're quite occupied by my penis tonight, tree fucker," he says.

"That's it!" Eilif comes into Rúnr's view, sword raised.

Gellir puts himself between the tall man and Rúnr. "Wait. We can't, not here."

"He'll be easier to move in pieces," Eilif growls.

"The blood. You're going to wash it?"

Eilif trembles with rage. "I don't fucking care."

"You should." A new voice.

"Leif?" Rúnr asks.

Eilif kicks Rúnr hard in the chest, driving the breath from his body and blanching his vision. He sucks air, which makes him cough, almost choking. Which makes him vomit again, though there's little but the water to come up. He blinks away tears to the sounds of steel on steel. There is no one in his vision, but the fight is here. To his left. Behind. Left again. Quickly, Leif drives Eilif and Gellir before Rúnr, then to the right, out of sight again.

It makes no sense. Ubbein is getting what he wants in Rúnr's exile, so why send these thugs to execute him? Until morning he's still the jarl's son. Murdering him here, now, is a shameful act, one that will bring its own punishment on Ubbein. The hero is smart enough to know that he could simply wait and send Eilif and Gellir after him once he crosses the East Mountain into the wilderness. He'll have no protection then. His murder will require no blood price or trial.

There's a shout. Geillir's deep voice calling a curse, interrupted by a cry of pain. The sound of a sword through leather and flesh, then of a body falling. The feeling of something wet and warm against the back of Rúnr's head. He knows the feel of blood.

"You'll regret this," Eilif says. "And you, Rúnr Njalson, I will kill you."

Then Leif, sword darkened, stands before Rúnr. "I don't think we can stay here anymore," the Hersir says, cutting Rúnr's bonds.

Rúnr tries to stand, but his legs have no strength. Leif keeps him from collapsing. Behind the chair, Gellir lies, eyes open, as is his chest. Blood soaks the sand. Distant, Eilif is fleeing. Rúnr tries to go after him and again almost falls.

Leif hauls him upright. "No time for that."

"Torstyn," Rúnr begins.

"They can't let you go now. They'll return with more men, more than even I can fight. If you want to protect the jarl, come with me now."

Rúnr understands, though slowly, his brain as deprived of quick thinking as his legs are of strength. He nods and leans on Leif, and the pair make their way south across the beach.

CHAPTER 18

They are climbing the South Mountain before Rúnr gives words to what's troubling him.

"Why would Ubbein try to have me killed like that?" he asks.

Leif, forcing their pace, says, "That was the act of a small mind."

Rúnr, exhausted and still in pain, slips, nearly tumbling from the path. The ways of the South Mountain are treacherous in daylight, one of the reasons few people travel this way. Now, even with the sun rising, their progress is too slow. What's happened will soon be known, and they're not even to the ravine yet.

Which only prompts more questions from Rúnr's ever unfocused mind.

"Why south?" he asks. "Exile is over the East Mountain."

And why am I only thinking to ask this now? We should be entering the mead hall, calling Helvig and laying new accusations against Ubbein.

He looks at the sun cresting the mountains. "I'm not exiled yet."

"You are," Leif says. "In the minds of the people, you are. What could you say that would make this right? What could you accuse Eilif and Gellir of that Ubbein won't turn against you and Jarl Helvig? They caught me freeing you, he'll say. We murdered Gellir, he'll say. At the jarl's bidding, he'll say. So much will get worse. Come, we have to keep moving."

Rúnr leans on a thin tree. "What can we do, then?"

"Get you somewhere safe," Leif says. "With you by my side, my words are tainted with your guilt, but if I return alone and stand before the jarl and swear the truth, I can convince him."

"Ubbein won't let you."

Leif is quiet a moment, searching the path below, the way they've come. "As I said, that was the act of a small mind."

This time, Rúnr considers his words. Ubbein is smart. Wily. He's not petty. And that attack felt personal, like Eilif couldn't help himself.

"Ubbein didn't order Eilif to kill me," Rúnr says.

"I think Ubbein will find out about Gellir's death the same time everyone else does."

"Because Eilif won't run to him to tell of it," Rúnr finishes. "Which means there's still time to speak with Helvig first."

"Ubbein may not have ordered it, but he won't let it stand either. You're not safe in Skyjavík. Up there, I know a place, a cave. Everyone will think you fled east into the wilderness. No one will search here. Come."

The Hersir begins up the path again. Rúnr is tired. Confused. It all makes sense and yet doesn't. His belly hurts. As does his knee. He knows he must go east eventually to the red temple in Uppsala, but Leif is wise, and his reasoning seems sound. He finds a stout branch of solid birch the right length to make a good walking stick and with its help, he follows Leif.

"You have only the one sword," Rúnr says as they make their way.

"I do."

"I can't defend myself for long with a stick."

Leif looks back on Rúnr as if only now noticing the walking stick. "I've used this cave before," he says. "There's a cache of supplies inside. Some weapons. You'll be okay."

His mind skipping like a stone on the water, Rúnr thinks of Velaug, of Yrsa, of Torstyn.

"You have to tell my brother where I am."

"No one can know until Jarl Helvig decides how to proceed."

"Torstyn has to know. He could come. He will come."

"There's no time. I gave my word to your father, to both your fathers."

Rúnr's breath is labored from the climb. "Both my fathers?" he asks, having never heard of an oath between Leif and Njal before.

"We three—Njal, Helvig, and I—spoke the words for our sons when we were younger than you are now."

"Your son?"

Leif stops and allows Rúnr to catch up. "I had a boy but no marriage. We three spoke our oaths after you and Torstyn were born but before my son was. He came some weeks later but never took a breath."

"I didn't know," Rúnr says, his thoughts again on his own daughter.

Leif coughs and says, "We're almost there."

Again, he sets off quicker than Rúnr can manage, but keeping always within sight. For a moment, as the path turns, Rúnr thinks he sees movement below. A deer or a small bear? Or men sent by Ubbein? He quickens his steps as best he can. Fate will take him east when it's time, he must trust in that. When he catches up with Leif, they're near the deep ravine, more than halfway to the mountain's summit.

"Where's this cave?" he asks. Wherever it's hidden, he can wait out the search for him while healing, then trek up and over the mountain. From there, the valleys will lead him south but then east again. The wilderness is vast, with few roads and no need to travel in straight lines.

"Close," Leif says.

He crosses to the ravine's edge and waits. Rúnr joins him. Leif points uphill.

"There."

Rúnr squints. "I don't see it."

Leif's sword is in his hand seemingly without motion. Rúnr has time for a single thought—*By the gods he's fast!*—and then the blade is coming for his head. It's all Rúnr can do to keep his skull attached to his neck with an unsteady leap backward, but his legs are still weak. His body still unhealed. The walking stick tangles with his feet. He falls at the ravine's edge and Leif is on him.

CHAPTER 19

The walking stick is all Rúnr has. Good for support on a hike, or as a boy's training sword, but not much more. Too short to use as a spear. Not hearty enough to hold up against steel. But, Rúnr remembers Njal telling him once, when facing death, anything, everything, is a weapon.

I once saw a man take up a splinter from the hull of his ship, Njal said that day they were fishing out on the fjord, *and yank a tooth from his own jaw so that each of his hands held a weapon against ten bandits. It was a quick and brutal death, but one the gods surely appreciated. The Valkyries came for him that day, I can tell you, boy.*

With his father's voice in his head, Rúnr raises the branch defensively, defiantly. Leif's sword slices the stick in half like a knife through a sail. A mighty swing meant to end the battle quickly, but the branch deflects the blade just enough for Rúnr to keep from being split in half.

Rúnr scrambles to the side, twice more dodging Leif's blade as he gets to his feet barely an arrow's length from the ravine behind him. He's vulnerable. Nearly beaten. Leif, however, does not finish him. Sword lowered, the Hersir takes a step back.

A sign of respect? Or a ploy?

"You're supposed to serve the jarl," Rúnr says. Each hand holds half the walking stick, the piece in his left splintered at the tip and the one in his right cut clean at a good angle. He grips the pieces like they are seaxes, long knives meant for close kills.

"I've done nothing but serve Jarl Helvig since the day he first sat in that chair." Leif's muscles flex. He's confident. Determined.

As is my fate, Rúnr tells himself. *Which is not to die here.* But the gods are fickle. They can change their minds like the winds in a maelstrom. The luck they intend to give can be withdrawn, or even regifted to another, time and again in a breath. If he's to survive this, he can't rely on fate alone.

"The fuck you have," Rúnr says.

"Ubbein needs to be sent a message," Leif says. "He needs to be told his schemes are seen, and that his dogs should be kept on a tighter watch."

"What message does murdering me send?" The ground along the ravine is loose. Each movement sends sticks and pebbles dropping over the sheer edge, no sound indicating if they ever hit bottom. Space is what Rúnr needs. If he meets death today, it will come on the Hersir's sword, not in the blackness of the ravine where the Valkyries will not find him.

Like they cannot find Yrsa.

Leif's answer is a swift jab. Rúnr backs and turns, but the jab is a distraction. A knife has come from nowhere into Leif's off hand and slices deep into Rúnr's shoulder. Only the grace of some god keeps him from recoiling over the ravine's edge.

He swings as fast as he can with the splintered half of the walking stick, then jabs once, twice with the sharpened end. Leif doesn't even bother parrying, though he can turn the sticks to tinder if he chooses. He moves swiftly instead so that each of Rúnr's strikes hits nothing but air. Spent, Rúnr waits to be run through. Again, however, Leif doesn't take advantage.

He doesn't want my blood on his sword, Rúnr realizes. It's all about the ravine. Whether by discomfort or cowardice, Leif means his death in one way only. It's not much leverage, but Rúnr knows to take what he can.

"No one will know if you let me go," Rúnr says, seeking the right words to exploit Leif's hesitation.

"No one will know anything of your fate but what I say."

"Out there, exiled in the wilderness, an outlaw, is as good as death. Why this?"

"There're lands beyond the wilderness," Leif says. "Across the seas to the east and south where the mountains are twice as tall as ours, where the wheat blows in the wind like waves, where flesh-eaters roam, and where horse riders use bows taller than a man, loosing arrows with ease at full gallop."

Rúnr is not sure if Leif is speaking fantasies to distract him, or if he's having a change of heart and is telling him of mystical and dangerous lands to which he can flee, but even words can be a weapon when facing death.

"Impossible," he says, trying to keep Leif talking. "No one can draw a bow that tall from horseback."

"They don't like men of the North out there."

"I'm no longer a man of the North," Rúnr says. "I'm an exile."

Leif grunts, possibly in approval. Rúnr risks a look behind him. The ravine is like a giant's hungry mouth. He's overcome with a wild desire to leap into it. This thought is followed by another, that he should beg for his life.

And the shame of that idea banishes his fear, and he swings the sharpened stick.

Leif parries twice with the flat of his sword, then reduces the splintered stick to a useless twig. Rúnr makes as if to toss it aside but throws it instead. Leif ducks the stick, but Rúnr manages to knock the knife from his hand. Their weapons are, in number at least, even once more.

"What will you tell Njal in Valhalla after I kill you?" Rúnr says. "When he asks how you died, will you say to him, 'I tried to kill your son'?"

Leif swings his sword like a boy practicing his motions. "I'll tell him that I kept my oath—our oath, Njal and I—to our friend Helvig."

"It's good you have no sons," Rúnr says, the insult sharp enough to enrage most men.

Leif nods as if acknowledging, or possibly even agreeing with, this fact. "It's a shame Njal and Helvig do," he says.

"How much did Ubbein pay you?"

Leif, in an almost comical display, looks offended. "You think I'm an assassin?"

"What else am I to think?" Rúnr edges along the ravine, seeking the best place to make his stand. It is no straight line, this gorge, like an axe blow through the mountain. It's uneven like an old woman's teeth, and Rúnr chooses the place that gives him the most foot space.

"I'm sworn to protect Helvig," Leif says, his usual dour focus seeming to break a little. "Helvig! Not Skyjavík's jarl. I don't care one of Loki's lies for who sits in the chair. Helvig, Njal, and I swore it together, the three of us for each other, no matter what. We swore it by Odin's eye. No other bond may outrank that. Ubbein will be jarl one day sooner than another. He's too strong to stop. I'm not serving him. I'm saving Helvig's life."

Rúnr wonders if the Hersir has gone mad. "You should have let Eilif kill me, then," he says. "Since you're too afraid to wet your own blade with my blood."

Leif moves as if to strike a killing blow but holds. Maybe reconsiders. "Eilif is a braggart, and Gellir was a goat's hoof. Their blades in your chest would serve no one but Ubbein."

Rúnr closes the distance between himself and Leif. "And your blade in my chest?"

"Ubbein will owe me. And through that, he can have the chair so long as Helvig lives."

That's it, then. The trade almost makes sense to Rúnr. An oath on Odin's eye demands sacrifice. Wouldn't he cut down anyone who gets in the way of his vengeance for Yrsa?

Not anyone, he thinks. *Not Torstyn.*

"You understand now, don't you?" Leif says.

"You're a traitor."

Leif raises his sword in a show of respect. It seems he's done playing at allowing the ravine to claim this kill. His next strike will come from high. What Rúnr doesn't know is if it'll come in earnest or as a feint to set up the killing blow.

Rúnr raises his stick in return. The air is still and smells of melting snow. Somewhere, a bird calls. The scampering of woodland creatures is all around. Leif is fast and precise. No feint. His first blow takes a chunk from Rúnr's stick. His next two open wounds in each of Rúnr's arms. A jab forces Rúnr back to the edge of the ravine once more. Another reopens the wound in his belly given by Ubbein. Finally, Leif knocks the stick from Rúnr's hand. There's only one play left. Rúnr begs his hands and arms to be as strong as they've ever been. If he's going over the edge, he will take Leif with him.

Where's the god trance now? he thinks.

The Hersir flexes for the killing blow.

"Leif!"

Both Rúnr and Leif turn to find Torstyn charging up the path. Rúnr throws himself at the Hersir. It's enough to get inside his sword arc and throw off his balance. Enough to give Torstyn time to join the fray, his own sword driving Leif back, giving Rúnr space to get away from the ravine. Hersir and jarl's son exchange blows until the two face each other in a moment of calm like the center of a storm.

"You shouldn't have come," Leif says.

Torstyn angles to protect Rúnr, but in doing so allows Leif to set them both against the ravine.

"You shouldn't have abandoned your duty," Torstyn says.

"This is my duty."

Torstyn goes high. Rúnr goes low, trying to take out Leif's legs. He receives a knee to the side of his head instead. The crash of steel calls out two, three, four strikes between Leif and Torstyn as Rúnr tumbles aside to the ravine. Inside his skull is thunder. He tries to stand, the wound in his belly on fire, only to see Torstyn thrown down beside him, his sword far from where he lands. Leif turns to Rúnr, the killing blow aimed.

I'll see you soon, Little Bear.

Leif's sword comes down, but not into Rúnr's skull. Torstyn throws himself in the way, taking the blow where the neck meets the shoulder, but he's strong and grabs onto Leif, pulling him away from Rúnr.

"Dog's taint," Torstyn says, laughing, blood spurting from his wound and his mouth.

Leif gets his sword arm free. Instinct drives Rúnr to attack though he can barely stand. He manages a step as Leif sinks his weapon into Torstyn's stomach.

"No!" Rúnr shouts.

"Find him," Torstyn says, his eyes on Rúnr and not the man who has killed him.

Leif pulls his sword free and kicks Torstyn. Rúnr can only scream wild anguish as his brother tumbles over the ravine's edge into darkness.

Find him, comes Torstyn's voice.

Survive, comes Velaug's voice.

And Rúnr knows he will receive no more assistance today. No more allies. No god trance. He can stay and die, or he can flee and find his fate. It's no choice at all, really. He does what he must and changes direction. Down the path he goes, away from Skyjavík. Down the mountain, limping, scrambling, tumbling, his legs unable to bear his weight. Head over heels, plummeting like a tossed stone, fleeing like the coward both Ubbein and Berthe have accused him of being.

CHAPTER 20

The days are a haze of pain and fear. Nights are spent in caves, or burrows dug into melting snow drifts that Rúnr cannot remember digging, or beneath branches and shrubs and leaves pulled hastily onto himself not too near a game trail. He has no thoughts but for his next breath and the pain of his wounds, erupting with every step in his knee, in his belly, in his shoulders and arms and muscles. He hears no sounds but of the wilderness. Sees no signs of pursuers. Eats only what he can scavenge, berries and mushrooms. Drinks only what snow he can find to melt in his mouth, or what morning dew he can collect and pour from a budding flower. Though he doesn't risk a fire, he's at times as hot as the springs of the South Mountain themselves. Other times, he's as cold as a naked fool in midwinter.

"I have a fever," he tells himself. He has only recently emerged from the shadow of a tree where he slept in fits and starts, soaked in sweat. He thinks he's heading east, but every time he looks for the sun, he grows dizzy. On this day, it doesn't matter.

"Follow the sky," his mother, Alina, says.

"I can't see the sky," he tells her, for it's gray with clouds and smells of storm, only vaguely aware that his mother has been dead longer than his father.

The rain begins. It cools. Cleanses his mind. He remembers that he needs to drink. He tears his already tattered clothing and fashions a bladder to collect the rain. He drinks, standing out in the open as if on his own land. He shouldn't, he knows, it's dangerous for him out here, but he doesn't care.

He drinks as much as he can collect, then collects more and drinks that as well. Then he vomits most of it back up.

"Some ale next?" he asks the clouds.

The rain lessens, but no ale falls from the sky. He tries to walk, but his knee barely holds him. He finds a branch. Like the one he fought Leif with. Thinking of the Hersir brings anger. Anger brings strength. Strength gets him moving, but soon his thoughts of Leif turn to thoughts of Torstyn. Was he already dead when Rúnr fled or was he still falling down, screaming for a bottom that would never come?

He will never receive proper funeral rites.

Rúnr screams. No words. No intention. Just expulsion of everything inside him until he's on his knees and weeping. In time, the twittering of a bird calls. He opens his eyes, unsure if he has slept. The gray sky is darkening. The day is lost. His fever is raging. What isn't burning aches.

Survive.

He struggles to his feet. He knows he can't travel tonight. He must pass the fever. If he doesn't, he'll die. If he dies, neither Yrsa nor Torstyn finds vengeance.

"Are you in Valhalla, brother?" he asks, as he seeks wood for a fire. "Is there a seat for me beside you?"

And suddenly there's a fire. It's night. He's in a small copse. He doesn't remember coming here or starting the fire. The fever is taking his mind.

"Well done, boy," his father, Njal, says.

"I did it as you taught me." Rúnr doesn't look about for his father as he did for his mother.

"Fire is to be respected. Remember that. Like an oath, it is serious and sacred and must not be forsaken." Njal's hand appears—no more than that, not even an arm—and takes an ember from the fire and touches it to the seeping wound in Rúnr's belly.

The pain is excruciating, but Rúnr refuses to cry out.

"You will live," Njal says, a command rather than a prophecy.

"Yes, father."

Njal is gone. The pain in Rúnr's belly is gone. But not the fever.

"Am I to die here?" he asks the fire, looking deep into its core, into its whitest flames.

The flames answer: *Vengeance.*

Rúnr thinks he understands. "Thank you, Allfather."

Something crashes through the woods nearby. Despite the pain and the fever, Rúnr is to his feet.

Torstyn bursts through the trees. Half his flesh is blackened like Hel herself, half a corpse and half alive. His head lolls, barely attached. His ribs are crushed so that his chest is like a sunken apple.

Rúnr hears his own voice scream at the draugr's appearance, only for the thing to be gone in a breath as if it had never existed. Rúnr's vision twists and bounces like a foundering ship, until he wakes unaware that he'd slept. The sun is rising. Beside him lies a boar, a branch thrust like a spear through its mouth. Its flesh is cold, its heart silent, its breath still. Could he have killed it? Could it be a gift from the gods?

Either way, Rúnr knows he must eat. And drink. He crawls from the dead animal, searching the area until he finds a glassy black stone. It chips easily, creating an edge as sharp as any butcher's knife. He returns to the boar, each motion an agony, and shoves with all his strength until it rolls over enough to expose its belly. The black stone slices easily, making a perfect cut from hind to head. The next slice goes deeper, as it must, but the stench it releases throws Rúnr back as a wave of fluid and maggots erupt over him. He vomits into the mix, which only makes him feel sicker, his eyes watering. Grubs squirm over his arms and legs. He flings them away, squashing those that hang on. The boar's corpse belches a great sound and out pours the rest of its insides, rotting and putrid, a disgusting soup of half-decayed organs and miasma.

Impossible, of course, for such rot and decomposition in a creature that was only just killed this day.

"By Odin's breath!"

He's on his feet despite the pain. Running despite the delirium of the fever. Lost. Thrashing through branches getting even more lost. Until a bird chirps, insistent. Again, it sounds. There. A red-bodied kite, heavy on a branch. It calls once more, then takes to the sky.

Follow the sky, his mother said.

Rúnr follows the bird for minutes. Maybe hours. When he lags, it lands on a branch and calls until he finds his way. It's relentless, soaring with purpose to the edge of a steep-walled valley. Below sits a meadow, like a grassy fjord, still cold with the memory of winter, snow in drifts and bushes bare of leaf or flower. In the center stands a single grass-roofed house beside a small barn.

The kite circles above Rúnr, then swoops low to the house, landing on its roof.

"There?" Rúnr asks, his voice cracking. He places a hand to his forehead. He might as well be touching a hearthstone.

The kite jumps to flight and is soon gone, but Rúnr knows a sign when he sees one. Or thinks he does. If the kite is real. Or if it's a vision sent from the gods. Either way, he'll heed its advice.

He trudges into the valley, through snow drifts to his hips, finally coming to the house. A boy no more than six winters old stands in an open doorway. He regards Rúnr gravely, moving his mouth as if calling for someone, but Rúnr hears no voice. A girl appears from within. A girl with a face Rúnr knows.

"Yrsa," he tries to say. His throat tightens. His vision fails. He falls. And keeps falling.

CHAPTER 21

Thought comes before memory.

I am a man even as I am an animal. I live even as I am dead. I seek vengeance even as I hide from my deeds.

Memory comes before wakefulness.

Yrsa. Berthe. Torstyn. Ubbein. Wolf. Boar. Kite. House. Boy. Girl. Yrsa.

"Papa," a small voice says. Her head lolls back too far to be natural. Her throat is open like a sheep's when hung upside down for bleeding.

"Little Bear."

"You must kill the brute," she says, her throat opening and closing like a mouth.

"I will cut him down."

"When the brute is gone, they'll find me."

"The Valkyries."

"When the brute is gone, I'll feast in the great hall."

"Valhalla."

"When the brute is gone," she says.

She's gone. In her place, a column of empty smoke. Somewhere there's a distant roar, a feral creature. An angry destructor.

The voice of Ragnarök?

From the smoke that was Yrsa, two faces appear. A boy. A girl. One rots while the other is flush with life. They exchange—the rotting one regenerating, and the other dying, desiccating, disintegrating.

The smoke swallows the children once more.

"Sleep," a voice says. A kind voice. A child's voice.

It all unwinds, from wakefulness back to memory back to thought. Sleep comes and so comes the fear once more.

CHAPTER 22

Rúnr wakes. He's on his back. On a dirt floor. Inside a house. Flickering candles offer inconsistent light. He's warm, slick with sweat. There was a fever and many wounds, some severe, he recalls, though details remain blurry. There's the sound of scuttling feet about.

"He's awake," a small voice says.

The boy! Rúnr remembers. There's a girl as well. He cannot see them. He can barely move.

"How long have I slept?" he asks, his voice little more than a whisper.

The boy's face hovers over him. Rúnr expects to recognize it, but he does not. Nor the girl when she smiles above him. Her hair is lighter than Yrsa's. Her face chubbier. The similarity between these two, however, is apparent. They could be siblings, even twins.

"Drink," the girl says. She offers a cup.

Rúnr finds the strength to take it. Her fingers touch his. They are cold. His fever must remain. He manages to raise his head enough to drink. The cup offers water neither cool nor refreshing. It does give his voice strength, however.

"How long have I slept?" he asks again.

The children look at each other without answering. Rúnr returns the empty cup. The girl brings a rolled cape and helps Rúnr lift his head again so she can place it as a pillow. The house, Rúnr can now see, is choked with dust and disuse. Some of the roof beams are cracked, as are some of the walls. The door hangs crooked, showing that night is near. Rúnr's own house, unlived in since Berthe left, is in better condition.

The boy says, "The fever is almost gone."

Rúnr's hand goes to his abdomen. New stitches cover the old, the wound beneath healing well. He touches his knee next, still tender but no longer swollen. All over, his body aches but he can detect no serious lingering injury.

"You'll be all right," says the boy.

"Good as new," says the girl.

They smile to each other and then leave the house without a sound. Alone, Rúnr becomes aware of the sounds and smells of the house and the valley: a wolf's howling, birds singing, the clamor of insects, the melting of wax from the candles, the aroma of flowers, of spring in bloom.

Were there flowers in the valley when he found the house? He remembers snow.

"How long have I slept?" he calls out. There is no answer.

It takes all his strength to sit up. Pain comes with each motion, but it's the pain of stiffness and inaction, not damage. He'll feel better once he's moving, he decides. Another night, if the children's parents will have him, and then he can be off to the east. Maybe he can barter for their aid or some supplies with his own service—repair the door, fix the roof, whatever else he can do before tomorrow's midday.

I'm an outlaw.

It's a startling thought as much as it's a pointless one. So what? These people have helped him without asking his name. What purpose would there be in identifying himself or telling them of his exile?

I'm an outlaw, he thinks again, this time considering what that means. He's owed nothing, not even hospitality. Responsible for nothing, not even a return kindness. But he can be better than what is owed or what he's responsible for. He stands. Stretches. Everything hurts. His clothes are tattered, little more than rags. He has no boots. No armor. No cloak. But he's alive.

He makes his way to the door and examines the damage. It won't take long to repair. Such work surely must be worth a few days' rations. He considers where he thinks this valley lies, a fortnight's crossing of the wilderness on foot to Uppsala, probably, though with his injuries it could be more. Ample food and water are out there to be found, but setting out with supplies would be best.

"Boy?" he calls out, trying to open the door carefully. The wood cracks. The door falls outward revealing the evening. He becomes aware that he's shivering.

Rather than go outside, Rúnr moves slowly about the house, seeking clothes. Dust lies thick on every surface. His stomach rumbles, but he finds no food or drink. Three empty cups and a chipped bowl sit on a table with a wobbly leg. There's a chest in one corner, empty but for dust and spiders. Against one wall, he finds a pile of rags that stink of age and mold. He wraps them around his feet, wondering after the children and their parents. Perhaps they've all gone to hunt or gather food or collect water. He recalls a barn and returns to the door. The snow he remembers is gone. Flowers grow in clusters, and in full bloom nearby. Could he have slept a week? Longer?

What must Helvig be doing now?

He imagines the jarl declaring execution for Leif, but it's a fool's thought. There were only two witnesses to Leif's betrayal. Torstyn and himself. His imagination now finds Leif drinking heartily beside Helvig, consoling his friend for the loss of his sons. Who will Leif blame? Ubbein? Not without someone else to speak support.

Me, then.

Yes, that's how it'll go. The adopted Berserkr slipped his bonds and killed Gellir and fled. Leif and Torstyn followed. The jarl's true son was killed, his body thrown into the ravine. Leif cut down the criminal and heaved his body into the ravine after Torstyn's. Nothing left to do but curse Rúnr's name and move on.

Dizziness strikes Rúnr like a blow from an axe. He tries to lean on the wall, misses, and tumbles outside onto the fallen door. Getting to his feet is more difficult this time, but he manages eventually. The sound of running water, a light trickling, comes from nearby, the opposite way from the barn. It takes many careful steps, limping and resting, to reach a narrow creek. The water is fresh and cool. He cups his hands and drinks his fill and then sits to rest a time.

Night is upon him when he stands once more. The moon is recently full—could it be two weeks since Rúnr fled from Leif down the mountain?—and casts a clean light to guide him around the house to where the barn slumps, its door shut. It's in worse condition than he thought, its roof ready to collapse with the next storm. The air here is strangely still, and he's filled with the idea that he shouldn't stay. That he shouldn't be here at all.

"Boy?" he tries to call, but his voice breaks.

For the first time he wonders if the children have parents. It's this thought that pushes him forward. They helped him, maybe saved his life. If they're on their own, he'll help them. The door, the roof, even the barn—he can fix it all. It'll take time, but his trek to the creek and back has proved he needs more than a night or two for his strength to return before he can cross the wilderness.

"Are you in there?" he says, his voice somewhat stronger.

He pulls at the barn door. It resists, then opens stiffly, a long time since it's been used. Inside is a hay-strewn floor marked by timbers fallen from the roof. Broken sheep stalls. Some piles of rotted lumber. And, sitting up against a bale of hay, two small bodies.

Though they're sunken and blackened, as bodies become when they're mummified by the cold of winter, there's no mistaking them. The boy and girl, the brother holding his sister, long dead. Throats cut.

Rúnr's breath floats white as a cloud. His hands and legs tremble.

"Who healed me, then?" he whispers.

There are no answers from the barn. He turns to go and finds another body propped up against a deteriorating, wheelless wagon as if watching over the children. This one, too, is old and black from the cold. A man. The father, his throat cut like the children, a rusted carving knife gripped in his hand.

Suicide. After finding his children murdered?

Or after killing them himself?

Rúnr thinks of Yrsa, not just for the manner of death around him. He thinks of her having survived the raid. Of her being taken rather than killed. Of her being sold as a thrall among the Fenns. Of her dying slowly of starvation or a wasting illness. He thinks of all this and knows what happened here.

This father, seeing death was coming, whether violent by bandits or slow by plague or starvation, gathered his children to him. He told them to close their eyes as he readied the knife he once used to prepare their meals. He drew it lovingly through their flesh and throats and their lives.

Rúnr looks between the father and the children. This is their place. He does not belong here. He tries to go, to leave, but his eyes remain on the father. On his hand, no longer holding a rusty knife. Clutched there now is Rúnr's own axe.

Impossible!

Yes, impossible. Like finding the axe at the hot springs and again during the Challenge. Impossible like the way Rúnr sees the living wither and die before his eyes, like the wolf-thing and the boar that was rotted inside as if it had been dead for months. Dead like this family. Like Yrsa.

"Is this your doing, Odin?" Rúnr says, hand going to the bear's tooth around his neck. "Is it yours, Hel? Or Loki Mischief Bringer?"

Gods don't answer mortals with their voices, but the axe is answer enough for Rúnr. He kneels to take it, but the father's dead hand won't let go. He pulls, ready to jump back, half expecting the father to rise like a draugr protecting its barrow hoard. There's no struggle from the corpse, however. A last pull frees the axe. The body falls aside revealing a pit dug into the dirt floor beneath the wagon. In the pit, a cache of barrels.

Again Rúnr waits for the undead to protect its trove. Torstyn would laugh. As would Ubbein and Helvig and Eilif and Njal. Such is the way of the Opplands. Laugh and enjoy and revel in the life the gods have given them. It's a way Rúnr has never felt comfortable in, like wearing another man's clothes.

"Apologies, friend," he says, shoving the father's corpse farther aside so he can take the barrels, three in all. It is not a fine thing to take from the dead, of course, but Rúnr thinks—he knows somehow—that these barrels are a gift, as was the care the dead children provided.

The first barrel holds scraps of cloth that may have once been a fine shirt, a few coins, and a gold torc, ornamented with knobs and the heads of deer, goats, and wolves. A wealthy piece, perhaps treasured since the man took it as a trophy on a summer raid, but not enough to buy life from death, it seems.

The second contains a warrior's stash. Mismatched but well-conditioned armor, including a mail shirt, boots, thick leather plates for one leg, two forearms, and a shoulder, and an iron helmet. He lifts the helm. It's solid and well made, and too small for his head. He lays it aside. There is also a steel and tinder, a shoulder sack, a spear, a knife, a bow, and nine arrows. A good omen for the number of realms and the number of nights Odin hung on

Yggdrasill. This dead father, Rúnr thinks, must have once been a fine warrior indeed in his youth.

The final barrel offers a stock of dried fruits, meats, and fish, along with a small cask of sweet mead, three or four days' worth altogether. Enough supplies to get him healthy. Enough time to regain his strength. Enough bounty to convince him that Odin has not abandoned him.

"Until the food and mead are gone, then," he says, as much to the children as to the gods who might be listening. For now, he'll bring these barrels into the house, and then he'll rest.

CHAPTER 23

The morning after the food runs out, Rúnr wakes in the children's house feeling good. It's the first semi-restful night he's spent in weeks, though it was still haunted by dreams of Yrsa wrapped in shadow, and in that shadow, he thought, though surely, he misremembered, there were others skulking about in the darkest distances. Other dead, lost perhaps, like Yrsa.

The brute lives, she said in that dream. *Why have you not killed the brute?*

I'm trying, he wanted to tell her, but he woke suddenly, beset by doubt and fear.

This is how he's spent his days, as trapped in his doubts as Yrsa is in the black mist, his mind wrestling with fate and choice and responsibility while his body mends.

Yrsa or Torstyn?

His oath to avenge his daughter versus his duty to avenge his brother.

How does a man choose between his responsibility as a father and his obligation as a brother and warrior? He hefts his axe, imagining it biting into Leif's ribs. It's not a large axe, not heavy compared to others, but it must have seemed so to Yrsa that night.

"I should have taught you better," he says, but she was only four winters old. The need to show her such things hadn't been there.

If she was a boy . . .

He forces himself away from the thought. Berthe knew no haste to train Yrsa like a warrior. Wondering *if this* or *if that* is just his unfocused mind seeking distraction. He grips the axe and wills it to tell him his path. To his surprise, the axe seems to answer. The way is simple, it seems to say. Fate first. And then, when Yrsa dines in Valhalla, he'll return to take the blood price from Leif. That settled, he dresses in the armor he found in the barn and hangs his axe from his belt. It's time to leave, after one more task for the children and their father, who have lain cold for so long. He will do for them what he did not do for Yrsa—he will send them into death with the warmth of fire.

It's midmorning by the time Rúnr has dressed in the armor and collected the supplies. He's tired, sweating, breathing hard. Certainly all signs he should wait longer to depart, at least another day, but he can no longer stay here.

He brings the chipped bowl outside and lays it beside the door and takes the bow and the arrows and heads into the trees hoping for a pig or a deer. He finds a hare instead. Tracks it awhile, finally creeping up to it near a small stream. The bow is not of quality, but it doesn't matter. Such weapons have never been his strength. It takes three arrows to bring the animal down, one of which he's able to recover from a tree, leaving him with seven. A lucky number.

Back at the house, he makes a small fire where he can see both the house and the barn and sets the hare and the bowl beside it.

"I would offer a horse, a dragon, if I could," he says to the sky. "But a sacrifice of need in the absence of abundance, we are taught by Odin, is a fine gift. This is what I offer, and what I ask. Blood and strength."

With the knife, he opens the hare groin to neck and holds it above the bowl so that its blood is collected. When there are only drips left, he sets down the hare and takes a stick from the fire and blows out the flame dancing on its tip. He dips the stick into the bowl and swirls it so the blood twists like a storm.

"For Odin," he says, taking the stick to stand before the house.

"For Thor and Tyr," he says, flinging the blood over the door and walls, returning to the bowl when necessary to rewet it. He's never done this before, only seen it done by the old seeress. Which makes him think of Velaug, the new seeress. He wonders if he's doing this ritual for the first time before even she has. He thinks of her fingers, thin and strong and sure, unlike his thick and clumsy hands. He knocks the side of the bowl, nearly tipping it over as he tries to gather more blood on the stick.

"Fuck," he mutters, then curses his broken mind, its thoughts never where they should be.

Why is it never Berthe's hands I think of? he wonders.

He can't allow shame to distract him. This ritual is important. He must find focus.

"For Frejya and for Hel." He continues flinging blood over the house until it seems right. He then takes the bowl and the stick to the barn and splashes blood here as well. When finished, he returns to the fire where he drops the stick into the flames. It flares and pops.

He places the bowl on the ground and kneels before it and places his hand in the remaining blood—thick and not cool—until it coats his fingers. He brushes them through his hair and beard. He paints his face, eyes to jaw. He streaks his arms, elbows to wrists.

"For vengeance and Valhalla," he says.

He raises the bowl and drinks what remains. The blood is salty and tastes of victory and fate.

"For Yrsa."

He guts the hare and puts the meat on a stick to cook. The innards he brings to a tree near the house and ties them together and kisses them and hangs them from the highest bow he can reach, to bring the gods' eyes to this place where terrible deaths have occurred.

"Like this?" he hears Yrsa say as he does so.

He closes his eyes and sees her trying to tie a loop on the end of a rope, learning at his side how to be a sailor.

"Almost," he says in the memory.

He shows her once more. This time she gets it.

"You'll be sailing before winter," he tells her.

She beams with pride.

He opens his eyes. She's not here, of course. His mind cannot even stay focused on an offering to the gods. If he continues this way, he'll offend one of them eventually. Maybe all of them.

He returns to the fire and takes a burning log and holds it high. No words now. Either the gods are watching, or they're not. He throws the torch onto the thatched roof, which catches quickly.

While it burns, loudly and without apology, he takes another log from the fire and goes to the barn. He knows he should go inside, but he doesn't. He can't. Instead, he waits outside, half certain the children will appear. When they don't, he speaks to them anyway.

"I can offer only my thanks. And the peace of fire."

The groaning of the burning house is the only reply.

To the father he says, "I don't know you, but I trust you did right by your family, friend. May you feast well in Valhalla with your children beside you."

He throws the log onto the barn's roof. It catches immediately, like the house.

"Find peace and glory."

Rúnr watches the house and barn burn for some time, the smoke funneling into the sky. Will it twist west toward vengeance for Torstyn? Or east toward vengeance for Yrsa? Will he bend his will to an omen of smoke, return to Skyjavík if that's what is shown, find Leif, find Ubbein, take the price for Torstyn's blood, then go east, maybe with Helvig's blessing, with a horse and supplies and maybe warriors to accompany him through the wilderness?

But the smoke only coils up and up, no direction at all but to the sky. No hint. No omen. Until a bird circles the smoke funnel. A red-bodied kite. The bird seems to hover in place, floating rather than flying. Then it soars with purpose. East.

"Very well," Rúnr says. He'll travel east, as fast as he can, toward Uppsala and the red temple. Toward fate and vengeance for Yrsa.

PART TWO

"It's better to be betrayed than to trust no one."
—*The Saga of Fljótsdæla*

CHAPTER 24

It's the funerals.

Three years Erasmus has spent in the North, and in many ways, he feels like a Northman. He dresses like them. He's learned their language, though it still feels complex and overly breathy sometimes. Their pagan rituals are not so different from what he grew up with, if he allows himself to see them objectively, like the scholar he once was. Their morning routines still give him pause, but it's simple enough to avoid the shared cleansing bowl with its water full of grime and snot and blood. He is an *erlendr*, after all, an outlander, a foreigner like the other merchants and mercenaries and slavemongers who populate the market seeking to sell their wares or themselves. Or other people.

The temple, with its height and stern lines, is also not so different from home. Smaller of course. And there's only the one. But prayer has not been at the forefront of his daily routine for many more years than he's spent here in Uppsala. He misses neither congregations nor sermons, was not welcome to them anyway at the end. Before he left.

Can God still see him, this far from the Reigning City?

He and I have come to an understanding, Erasmus thinks, as he straightens his wares.

A fair covenant, all things considered: Erasmus does not ask His presence here in the North, and He does not ask Erasmus to attend His laws.

Haggling at a nearby tent gets loud. A new merchant, barely three days set up in the market, is pointing and shouting at two Northmen. The merchant—Erasmus can't remember his name—is powerfully built, attractive, and with skin like the deepest tanned leather. And he's offended by an offer, it seems. Though this is the largest market in many days' travel, the people of these lands are not good negotiators. Not like at home. There, it's an art. Erasmus learned it at his father's hip, though he took a different road when he became grown. The irony of his lot now, here, is not lost on him.

One of the Northmen levels an insult at the merchant. The other Northman tries to settle with peace. The merchant is selling spices, not the most popular of choices for the North. They like their food boiled and bland here. They like their negotiations short and contentious, though they're honest in bargaining. Rarely does a Northerner try to swindle a seller or present forged coin. What's happening now, however, is getting tense. Erasmus isn't one to put his nose in another's business, especially when that business involves armed Northmen, but he finds his feet taking him from his own tent to his neighbor's.

Bad idea, he thinks when one of the Northmen touches a knife at his belt.

The Northman's friend puts himself in the middle.

"This one will not be here long," the peacemaker says. "Not with the way he bargains."

The angry one puts his knife away. "Not with the reputation he's building."

"Come," the friend says. "The funeral will begin soon."

The pair go north, out of the market, as do most of the others who are shopping. Funerals are not good for business, though that's not why Erasmus dislikes them.

The merchant looks at Erasmus as if offended at his approach.

"You'll learn their ways," Erasmus says.

"They'll learn mine," the merchant replies.

Erasmus shrugs. Domenico, one of the slavemongers, has also come near. He's friendly enough, but Erasmus has never liked his company. Slavery here, with those enslaved called thralls, is more common than in the Empire, but it seems to Erasmus that many slave keepers treat their thralls as members of their household more than as property. The slavemongers, however, are often harsh, and Domenico is one of the harshest.

"He won't last long," Domenico says to Erasmus, his voice low enough to keep the spice seller from hearing. He's a Christian from the Empire, though none of the merchants here make a habit of displaying their religions, or of using their native tongues. They all speak Northern here.

Bacceva, a Radhanite seller far from the regular routes those Jewish merchants usually travel, says, "Hope he lasts long enough to show me some of his private wares."

Domenico laughs.

"What do you think, Erasmus?" Bacceva says. "Is he my type?"

"Who isn't?" Erasmus says.

Bacceva winks, then she and Domenico begin talking about the weather and how quickly it has turned warm, as if this can be considered warmth, Erasmus thinks as he returns to his tent with a shiver. If funerals are the one thing that make him most uncomfortable in his life here in the North, the winters were the most difficult for him to come to terms with on his arrival, the springs here colder than the winters back home.

And yet, Erasmus has come to enjoy these winters. Not for the cold. For the way the people here embrace the challenge each winter brings. And Yule, it turns out, is not so different from the celebrations of the Empire, the way its people come together with a single mind for joy and hope around Christ's Mass.

The bells in the temple ring. The ceremony is about to begin. What few people were still browsing leave. Only the merchants are left, and some of those whisper hasty deals with their neighbors to watch their tents so they can witness the event.

"Are you going?" Bacceva asks Domenico.

"No, but I can watch your tent if you want to."

She forces a laugh that's both mocking and insecure. "No one watches my pieces but me."

Erasmus would prefer she does go, both of them for that matter, but he doesn't say anything. He's uncomfortable, his stomach in knots as if awaiting bad news. The way he used to make himself sick with worry when he lived on the road in the early days of his exile.

These damned funerals!

And these Northmen die at such alarming rates. They rush cheerfully into battle, refuse common medicines in the face of fever, kill each other for the sake of an insult that should be little more than a snowflake melting on one's shoulder. There's not been a week without a violent death in his entire time in the North.

Today, however, is different. More important. Not a simple funeral for a warrior. This is a lord's burial. Everyone in the city is expected to attend. Except outlanders, of course. They may come or go, stay or leave, so long as they don't interrupt.

A breeze comes, blowing maps from his table, forcing Erasmus to scramble to keep from losing some of his most valuable product. He's a seller of knowledge, of maps and poems and ancient tomes, unlike most of the others here. There's the Frank selling weapons, the Bulgarian selling spices and grains, the Saxon selling carved totems and hand tools. There's Domenico selling his slaves and Bacceva selling an impressive array of jewels and relics, their provenance changing with her customers' needs. A Christian will find the finger of Jesus Christ on one of her tables, or a nail from the True Cross. A Northman moments later will learn the nail is from the bindings of Fenrir, Father of Wolves. A Saracen will discover the finger belongs to the Prophet of his religion. And so on it goes in the market. Spices. Fruits. Boots. Drinks of all kinds.

And from the north, as if to remind Erasmus he shouldn't forget the funeral, there's a rumble of approval.

The first time a lower noble died, Erasmus went to his funeral. He still has nightmares about the Angel of Death. The barbaric parts of the funeral—the blood, the slaughter, the fire, the invocation of gods—he accepted; he still accepts. He's in the North, after all. What they see as proper, Erasmus understands as simply primitive ritual. He's an educated man, taught in the greatest and wisest city in the world. The rituals and traditions of that city, he knows, were not always the same. But knowing this, even accepting this, cannot bring him to accept—or not fear—the Angel of Death.

With a face as white as bone and eyes blackened with pitch, she'll come forward through the crowd to the great ship that has been built for this occasion. She'll come to the young woman who is now standing before the ship, a thrall owned by the deceased, offering her body to her dead lord. This young thrall has spent the hours prior to the funeral intoxicated and having sex with the dead man's friends and family, saying to each, *It is for him whom I serve that I do this.*

The Angel of Death—they call her *kjósa*, the chooser of the dead man's path—will take the thrall about the throat and squeeze with a strength equal to a man's until the thrall's eyes go red and her body stiffens. When the thrall falls, the Angel of Death will lift her like lifting a babe and carry her to her deceased lord and place her at the man's feet.

Erasmus shivers at the knowledge of what is happening so close by then sets about fussing with his stock. He turns a book of poetry so that it's in the tent's shadow rather than the sun. It's old, after all, and requires care.

"Which god are those stories of, friend?" a Northern voice asks in the language of the Empire.

Startled, Erasmus nearly knocks the book from its stand. It's some months since he's heard another speak his native tongue. He sizes up the speaker, an absolutely massive warrior with bright blond hair and beard.

"Whichever fits your need," Erasmus says, the language of his childhood uncomfortable on his lips.

The man chuckles. "A good answer. My need for gods is not so great at the moment, however. What about yours?"

"Less than some, I wager." A politic answer, the kind Erasmus has learned to offer.

"The jarl's esteemed brother-in-law, you mean?" The man has switched to the Northern language to ask after the lord whose funeral captures the city this day.

"It's a joyous occasion," Erasmus says, relating the common words of respect for the dead, oddly relieved to speak the man's language.

The big man grunts and busies himself among the maps and scrolls and books under the tent, touching many of them as if measuring their worth by his fingertips. He shows more reverence for these works than many Northerners, and he moves with more grace than his size implies.

"Can I help you find something?" Erasmus asks.

The wind turns. The smell of smoke fills the market. Erasmus looks north to find smoke rising.

"She finishes," the man says of the funeral and the Angel of Death.

Yes, she will speak more words now that the ship is set to burning. It's been ignited by a naked man walking backward, a torch in hand. Within the ship, the jarl's brother-in-law lies in his best clothes, or perhaps even better clothes than any he wore in life. He's surrounded by gifts of fruit, meat, ale, and more. The heads of sacrificed animals lie around him, as do many weapons, for these Northern pagans believe he will travel to an afterlife of hunting and of battle. A sword or axe is clutched in his hands upon his chest.

Only now, with the flames reaching high, will the Angel of Death quit the scene and enter the Great Temple of Thor, Freyr, and Odin, and she will not be seen again until the next funeral. Not by any eyes, Northern or foreign.

Has she gone yet? Erasmus needs to know before he can breathe easy.

"She has gone," the man says.

Erasmus flinches as if the man has made to strike him. "How can you know?"

"Have you not seen a funeral? It's a glorious thing. Even from here, I can feel it. I can feel *her*."

"I cannot," Erasmus says.

"Because she has gone."

The man's certainty sets Erasmus at ease. Which only begs more questions, but for now he has a customer.

"What is it you said you're after?"

"A map," the man says.

"A map? Yes, of course! I have maps." Erasmus is into his persona now, one of the most successful sellers in the market. "The best maps in all the North, for I'm the most traveled man you'll meet."

"I've heard this. It's why I've sought you out."

"And who speaks so kindly of me, if I may ask?" For surely, it's either patron or rival. Keeping track of each is important to a merchant's success.

"A bird."

Erasmus can't tell if the man is being serious or not. Northerners believe in many supernatural beings and events, even animals that speak, though Erasmus finds it uncomfortable to be in a conversation about one. "Have you traveled far on that bird's recommendation, friend?"

The big man smiles like a wolf whose found a trapped rabbit. "Call me Garmr. And you are Erasmus, the merchant from Miklagard—the great city that calls itself Constantinople—yes?"

Erasmus's stomach turns once more at the naming of his home. He's never told anyone his story.

"I am Erasmus the Gatherer, of Macedonia," he says, offering the place of origin that he has told to all who ask. Regathering his wits, he says. "And you, friend Garmr, you're from the East, I think, by your voice? You are Rus?"

"From the East, yes, arrived by ship yesterday among the Rus."

"By ship so early in the season. It must have been a difficult voyage."

"A god was surely with us."

The conversation has wound itself back to the beginning. "Well, then, good Garmr, what kind of map may I supply for you? Would you like to find the land of the Danes or the rich Saxon Isles?" These are the common requests. Erasmus suspects Garmr desires something more exotic, but he knows better than to offer his best pieces right off.

"Not these." He says no more.

It's to be a game, then. Erasmus likes the challenge. Once, he wrote poems and told stories to the wealthiest men and women of the world, each word an art cut from his mind the way a master sculptor finds the shapes in his marble. Selling is its own art as well, though not so rewarding to the soul, perhaps. Even still, this Garmr presents a challenge, and Erasmus means to savor it.

"I can show you the ways through Iberia," he says with a dismissive hand as if it's nothing. "Or do you seek the road to the legends of Rome itself?"

A smile forms within Garmr's beard.

I have him!

"Rome, you say? That is tempting. But, master gatherer, it is, in fact, to your homeland I wish to go. To Miklagard. It's your best maps I seek, the ones you do not put on display."

A serpent coils around Erasmus's intestines. The Angel of Death herself could not have disarmed him as readily as this request. Maps to the Reigning City are not difficult to come by, but Erasmus has in his possession some that offer detail beyond any others that have ever been drawn. Taken from the emperor's own library.

How could anyone know of such treasures?

A thought next—Garmr came with the Rus. How many ships arrived yesterday? A single one can carry thirty or more men. Thirty or more warriors.

And their fleets can be dozens of ships.

What could a fleet of Rus, among the most violent men in all the world, want in Constantinople?

Who cares? I owe nothing to my homeland.

"Do you intend to travel so far?" Erasmus asks.

Garmr waves a large hand. "We each go where the gods determine. My fate lies south and to the east."

Fate. Gods. There is no questioning either for these Northmen or their cousins the Rus. For Erasmus, coin rules the day. If this man will pay what his best maps are worth, it could finance half a decade's living. But to be the one to send an army of murderous Rus into the heart of the Empire?

Then again, it's not like Constantinople is a hidden city. It's the light of the world, so it calls itself. It's not difficult to find.

"Well, you're in luck," Erasmus says.

"Not just of the way to Miklagard," Garmr says. "I seek maps of the city itself."

I owe nothing. I am owed!

"Such maps are quite valuable."

Garmr nods. "Then I assume you keep them in a safe place."

The maps are, in fact, in a chest below the very table Erasmus is standing behind, but he will not admit as much. "As you say."

"And you'll need time to gather them?"

"Of course. Shall we talk price?"

Garmr opens a pouch and shows three large gems inside, one green and two blue. Erasmus feels his teeth tingle.

"This is a first payment," Garmr says. "Twice the coin it would take to purchase every piece displayed in your tent will also be yours when I have the maps I need."

It takes all Erasmus has to keep his voice even. "That sounds like a fair deal."

"A man will arrive in the coming days. An Opplander, though dark of beard and wearing mismatched armor, like those handed down from a confused father."

"A friend of yours?"

Garmr smiles as if the answer is obvious. "When this man comes, I'll return. Upon Hel's shroud and flesh, I tell you this. Have the map for me, then."

Erasmus has not heard an oath upon Hel in his time in the North. Most swear upon Odin and his remaining eye, but this Garmr is an odd Northman, it seems. To that thought, isn't Garmr the name of Hel's hound?

Garmr coughs, noting that Erasmus is taking too long to reply.

"Yes, when the Opplander comes. As you wish."

Garmr tosses the pouch onto the table and leaves, his going seeming to drain Erasmus's strength. It's all he can do to gather the pouch to his breast and peer cautiously inside. The gems are all there. Elation fills him, making him want to sing, followed by fear. He glances at the other merchants. Have they seen what's in the pouch? Are they conspiring already?

Though he's never done so before, he finds himself wanting to close up his tent early, but that would bring suspicion. No, he must remain here as always. Every minute of every day until the stranger in mismatched armor arrives. Until Garmr returns. His life, he suddenly fears—suddenly *knows*—depends on it.

CHAPTER 25

It was the largest city Rúnr had ever seen when he was ten winters old. Like the deepest lakes in all the North, Uppsala insisted upon its place in the world. In the years since, it seems to have only grown larger, sprawling wide, unlike the Saxon cities he's raided, which try to stand as tall as towers can be built. As he looks down from the western hills, it looks to Rúnr like a painted battle map, except instead of upended ale horns and shaped rocks representing enemy warriors and small fortifications of timber, the city is of stone and wood and color and size. Every building is painted. Every roof is bright. The Great Temple, its own red roof rising tall, cannot be missed, pointing to the sky, to Asgard itself, maybe, which could be the only place Rúnr might imagine more color in all the realms.

Unlike Asgard, however, Uppsala has no wall, no fortifications. It sprawls, trusting like a sleeping bear that no one will be foolish enough to attack it.

But Rúnr hasn't come to admire the city's size or color or architecture. It took more than two weeks to cross the wilderness. He slept in fits. He walked whenever the sun shone. In rain. In wind. Through pain. He hunted. He fought off a wolverine, who decided after a few tries with its sharp claws that the interloper wasn't worth the trouble. He endured. And now he needs rest, so close to his goal.

"Am I so close?" he asks. Who? Himself? Odin?

Three times the god trance should take him before he finds the Painted Fenn in the red temple, and yet he hasn't become Berserkr since the Fennvold.

Doubt slows his pace as much as exhaustion and discomfort. Has he made an error? The god trance has never come more than once in a week. How can he be a fortnight or more from his goal when it stands right there?

Maybe I shouldn't waste time with thinking and questioning.

He pushes on, passing the first few buildings—farms and barns spread out across the plain—that mark his entry into Uppsala. Beyond them, before entering the city proper, he must cross through a row of trees that reminds him again of his visit here with Torstyn so long ago.

"Bet I can climb that one faster," his brother said of a hanging willow.

"What about that one?" Rúnr said, pointing Torstyn's attention off toward an oak only to skip into a run before his brother knew what was happening, clambering up the willow. Shouting insults at each other. Laughing all the way to the top.

The memory, and its pain, come as unexpected as a snake bite.

"I will return for you," he says, a promise not to forget his purpose.

On the outskirts, the temple was there before him like a standing stone marker, but once he has entered the city, among so many people bustling this way and that, the horizon becoming lost behind its many roofs, Rúnr finds his sense of direction clouded. Was he heading straight for the temple, or does he need to find a street turning . . . north? West? Being in a forest of the tallest oaks is not so disconcerting as this feeling of being lost so close to his goal.

He finds a cross street and stops and closes his eyes. So many voices. A warm sun. The smell of the sea. The sounds of a market. He opens his eyes and turns southeast. The docks are that way, his nose tells him. East to the market, his ears tell him. And northeast to the temple, his memory tells him as he plots out the city based on what he saw from the hills, so northeast he goes, deeper into the city where more and more buildings are constructed of stone rather than wood. Somewhere a man curses. A fight follows, spilling onto the street Rúnr walks. He maneuvers around the two brawling men, keeping the temple in his mind, until someone else tries to get involved in the fight and shoves Rúnr to do so. Rúnr shoves back. The man he faces is bright eyes and scarred, only half his face able to grow a beard.

"I've a mind to beat your ass to tears too," the man says.

Rúnr tenses, anger rising within him. Not the god trance, but maybe he could force it, make the first of the three times foretold come now so that he is that much closer to meeting the Fenn who killed his Little Bear. But there are women nearby. Men who are not warriors. Thralls. An old man, blind by the look of him, sitting on a stool with his unseeing face turned up to the sun. And children.

If the god trance comes now, they will all die.

"You don't want to do that," Rúnr says, trying to keep his calm. He has no allies here. The god trance is followed, always, by the slow awakening and the sickness. Whoever the Berserkr doesn't kill will bleed him out while he rises from the depths.

He turns his back to the man. Who shoves him again. Rúnr throws an elbow. Instinct. Reflex. He catches the man beside his ear. The man drops like a stone thrown overboard. A cheer goes up. Rúnr stands as still as possible. He waits, but no feeling of the god trance comes. He exhales as those around him go about their business, the two fighting men taking their altercation further up the road. Tense and clenching, Rúnr starts for the temple once more.

He finds the mead hall first. It's taller than Helvig's, and twice as long, atop a hill within the city, carved stairs leading to tall, painted doors. He follows the road around the hill, pressing into throngs of people moving in the opposite direction. Clogging the way Rúnr means to go. Soon, he's pushing and shoving just to keep from being dragged away like a leaf on a stream. The smells of bodies and sweat, of smoke and spices, cling to those around him. The languages of foreigners fill his ears.

"Watch it," a man says, elbowing his way by.

Rúnr looks after the man, who pauses to look back. Something is wrong about the way he glares. Then he sees it, just a flash—a hand reaching for his belt. He slaps the hand away. A boy yelps and dashes off into the crowd. Rúnr tries to sight him, like aiming a bow for a bounding squirrel. The man who bumped him, he notes, is gone. A simple con, and he fell for it, which is only half his anger at the moment when he realizes his belt is light. His hand finds only an empty space where his axe had hung.

Rúnr spares no more time, running, shoving violently through the crowd before he's even identified his target. He knocks a woman aside. Pushes a man shouting at a thrall. There—the boy! People are making way now, allowing Rúnr to catch the thief by the arm. The axe comes up, a threat more than an attack. With his free hand, Rúnr wrenches the weapon from the boy.

"If you're going to use it, kill quickly," he growls.

"If you're going to carry it, tie it better to your belt," the boy says, squirming. He can't be more than eight or nine winters old. His face is gaunt. He's thin as a sail. His hands are dirty, and his fingernails are nearly chewed away. His teeth are the color of autumn leaves.

Rúnr holds him tight, probably bruising his arm. He could bring the thief to the mead hall and watch him be flogged, or maybe even executed, for his crime. The boy surely knows this as well but shows no fear.

"Do you know the temple, boy?" he asks.

"Do you know the sky, foreigner?"

It's the kind of comeback Torstyn would have spat, which makes Rúnr smile.

"Be careful who you and your father steal from."

"Lagho's not my father."

Rúnr sees no need to reply.

"I could work for you instead," the boy says.

"Why would I want that?"

"I can get anything. You could protect me from Lagho."

"Why would I care one bull's testicle for you or this Lagho?"

"I'll pay you half."

"Tell me the way to the temple and you can go," Rúnr says. He's not come all this way to be distracted by local problems.

The boy tries once more to pull his arm free, but slumps when he sees he's not strong enough.

"It's there, around that corner. Probably so full you'll lose more than your axe inside."

"Why's that?"

"The funeral," the boy says. "Did you just walk into town?"

"I did," Rúnr says. He lets go.

The boy crouches like a scared cat, ready to pounce or flee. "What about Lagho?"

"Your problem, not mine," Rúnr says, setting off in the direction the boy indicated.

The crowd does indeed get fuller as he enters an open square from which rises the Great Temple, like a mead hall that has grown up and up. Like a hero rising above all other warriors on the field of battle. Sitting upon a stone block foundation, it's twice the height of the tallest firs of the Opplands. Two towers soar above its east and west corners, and across these, from one to the other and then around smaller peaks at the north and south corners of the roof, a great rope the thickness of a strong man, of Thor's own arms, drapes taught, effectively encircling the temple. Along this rope sit many birds, adding their caws to the endless voices of the city. And the roof in the midday sun, as Rúnr remembers, is red as an apple's flesh.

Here now, before the temple like a boy before his father, Rúnr takes pause. Should he even be here yet, having not found the god trance, let alone three times? Should he seek a fight? Should he seek wisdom? Sleep? He needs to find answers.

His eyes wander the square. To this right, upon a slight ridge, grows a tree of modest height but massive girth, as if trying to match the temple's height with its own width. Beside the tree, a spring flows running noisily into a well. Rúnr considers what to do, deciding in the end to tie his axe tight to his belt before proceeding among so many people.

"I'll tell you its secret," the boy says, beside Rúnr once more.

"The temple has a secret, thief?" Rúnr keeps his eye on the boy while checking his possessions.

"How can a temple have a secret?" The boy looks at him askew, as if he's the greatest fool walking the land. "I mean the tree."

Rúnr knows this is part of another deception, but his mind is splitting, finding too many roads to travel.

"It's the World Tree, don't you know?" the boy says.

"Yggdrasill? This?" Rúnr says, for surely, it's a joke. The World Tree holds all the Nine Realms and more, its trunk passing through Midgard, its branches growing into the infinity of the gods. This is a large tree, for certain, but so large as Yggdrasill, he thinks not.

"All foreigners say stupid things like this," the boy says.

"What can it matter if I believe you or not?"

"If you don't believe me, you don't believe Odin, who hanged himself, wounded, upon this tree for nine windswept nights."

The boy sounds so much like a priest, Rúnr considers taking him by the shoulder and bringing him into the temple so that he may leave thievery and find a better purpose. He's here to find his own fate, however, not change another's.

"A coin, then, for letting you have your axe back?" the boy asks.

"I'll let you keep both your hands."

The boy pouts, at least half for show. Rúnr likes him more than he should, and for that he digs out a single coin from his purse and hands it to the boy.

"Thank you, sir. Truly," the boy says.

"Disappear," Rúnr tells him.

The boy does as he's told, slipping into the crowd like a snake into the water. Rúnr watches as long as he can, then turns his attention to the tree. It has godlike girth, this is true. But it's short. Like he imagines a dwarf. Yggdrasill? If so, he nods reverently to it. If not, he does not linger, crossing the square to the temple.

Its doors stand open for all to enter and, as the boy indicated, there are more people than should be within. Rúnr needs both patience and strength to work his way inside, where candles and torches light the way, the air humid and hazy with smoke. The main corridor is long. Many of the men and women here stand bowed or kneel in supplication along the walls. Their whispers to the gods are like the buzzing of bees. Rúnr proceeds, threading himself carefully to keep from disturbing anyone's prayers, seeking any painted faces.

"It's not time," he mutters. Each unfamiliar face quickens his pulse until he reaches the terminus. Here, the temple is wider than it appears from the outside. Here, before a broad and noisy crowd, rise three great carvings half the height of the temple itself. Thor, standing before the others, the hammer Mjölnir in his hand. Seated then is Odin, his ravens of thought and of remembrance, Huginn and Muninn, upon his shoulders. And third, also seated, is Freyr, his phallus standing so erect it nearly touches his chin, his arms wide, inviting those who seek his blessing of fertility.

In the presence of these gods, and of those clamoring for their favor, a confidence rises in Rúnr. It will be here, before Odin himself, that the Painted Fenn is found. He shoulders into the crowd, his care and doubt abandoned, reaching the center of the room. Turning in circles to see each face, knowing he is about to bring blood in this house of the gods. But again, he sees no Fenn. Again, his confidence wavers.

I'm here on the gods' words, he reminds himself, but he feels small. Weak. Lost. Desperate, sweaty, empty.

He searches the faces of the carvings, of the gods themselves, for hope. The slightest twist of a grin upon Thor's lips? A glimmer of knowing in the emptiness of Odin's sacrificed eye? The tremor of a nod from Freyr?

But the Fenn is not here. Vengeance is not here. Fate is not here.

Despair clutches Rúnr as he finds himself leaning against Odin, the wood smooth and cool, yet with the warmth of life inside. The thrum of a heartbeat. Odin is listening.

"I have come, Allfather, as you commanded," he says. "Where is my enemy? Where is my vengeance?"

"Your vengeance?" a familiar voice says. "Or your daughter's vengeance?"

Rúnr refuses to turn. He refuses to accept. He waits for the Allfather to speak, but it's as if the temple has gone silent.

Was it all a lie?

Has he come here, has he been brought here, for some purpose other than revenge?

"Come, Rúnr," Velaug says. "We must speak."

He turns but refuses to meet her eyes. This is his rebellion. He examines her sandaled feet, her braceleted wrists, her braided hair peering from within a hood. The gods betray, he knows. They do as their personalities and whims demand because that is what they are. But Velaug—he cannot accept she has played with him the way gods do. He has to trust, even as he finds himself hating who she is, which only brings him to hate who she was.

She waits patiently. Silently. Until he accepts, he must give in. He bows his head.

"Then let us speak," he says.

CHAPTER 26

She leads him to a quiet part of the temple where few candles burn and no one else crowds them. Here, they're free of the sharp odors of so many bodies pressed together. What had been a thunder-din of voices is now a low murmur, as if the walls and floor and ceiling are thrumming with life. This is a holy room though no gods stand within. At least, none Rúnr can see.

She faces him and waits.

"How are you here?" he asks.

"The same as most," Velaug says. "It's not so far or so difficult to come east. Even you seem to have managed it."

It's all he can do to keep from shouting, or from grabbing her by the throat. "I have no patience for games. Why are you here?"

"I go where the gods demand."

"Riddles," Rúnr says. She's never left Skyjavík before, never traveled to where other seeresses speak the gods' mysteries, so far as he knows. He spits at her feet, regretting the act before the glob hits the floor. The gods do not take such offense lightly.

"I say what the gods demand," she insists.

"Fuck you," he says. He means it cruel, but it sounds more like he's begging her to do just that.

Velaug takes down her hood. It is her—his friend, his former lover, the seeress who spoke his prophecy only weeks ago. And yet, he doesn't think it is her anymore. The fear this brings is the coldest ice.

"What did you expect to find here?" she asks in the way a seeress should.

"You know."

"A Fenn, his face painted with the serpentine twists of Jörmungandr. You expected to see this face turn to fear at the sight of you."

Rúnr does not like being known so well. "As you told me."

"I told you no such thing."

Her words come like a father striking down a child's fantasy of adventure and glory. Njal took this tone with him sometimes, occasionally with a grip on his shoulder—often with the sting of a quick backhand.

"The temple—" Rúnr begins.

"You expected to face this Fenn and shout your daughter's name and to slaughter him before Odin and Thor and Freyr."

The temple seems to pitch and tilt like a tiny boat at the sea's mercy. He reaches for a wall, for stability, and finds only Velaug. She grips his forearms, her hands frigid.

"You expected to suffer a great wound and die in glory here in the gods' sights," she says, "and thus be taken to Valhalla."

"No," Rúnr says, finding his footing. "Not this last part. I won't die here."

"This is true."

"Torstyn," he says.

"Will be avenged."

"You know?"

She nods. The flesh of her palms grows warm upon his arms.

"Does Helvig?"

"He knows he's lost two sons."

I could be there for him, Rúnr thinks. He could comfort his brother's father. He could bring justice to Skyjavík. But at what cost? At what delay for Yrsa?

"You're not done here, Rúnr."

"The Painted Fenn will come?" he asks hungrily.

"Not to this place," Velaug says, letting go of his arms.

Frustration now, Rúnr's emotions coming and going the way his thoughts usually do.

"I don't understand," he says.

"Then you're not the man I hoped, the one I thought the smart boy I remember would grow into."

"By Thor's beard, can you speak to me like a human, like the woman I thought the girl who loved me would grow into?"

She bows her head, for the first time an honest display. Has he shamed her or angered her? When she meets his eyes again, there's no hint either way.

"I'm meant to speak the words the gods give me," she says. "Just as you are meant for your fate."

"We stand within the red temple. Where is the Painted Fenn?"

"We stand within a red temple."

She ticks her head to the side like a bird. Waiting.

For me to understand something.

Fear comes again, a new wave making thunder when it crashes. He's feared failing Yrsa for weakness or a lack of skill. He feared failing her when he entered the Circle against Ubbein and when Leif slew Torstyn and when the fever almost ended him. These are the ways men fail, and if the gods deem it so, there's nothing he can do about it.

But to fail simply because he's not smart enough?

A bird trills high above in the rafters, causing Rúnr to look up. To find understanding rain down upon him.

"I have come to the wrong temple," he says.

Velaug's smile is genuine. Familiar. The smile she used to give when they stole a kiss behind a barn, or after they fucked near the hot springs on the South Mountain. The smile that said she would prefer a lifetime in his arms than five lifetimes as the voice of the gods.

"Speak your fate back to me," she says.

He says, "Three times the god trance will take me before I face Yrsa's killer in the red Temple of the Hanged God. There, Yrsa will have her vengeance."

There's consideration in her eyes at first, then pride. And love, he thinks. He doesn't know what she sees in his eyes, but if she would allow an embrace, she would feel his desire. And would that be so wrong?

"You will travel far," she says.

"Do you know where the temple is that I must seek?"

She looks away. "No more than you know what vengeance means."

He wants to strike her mouth. He wants to kiss her lips. It's all he can do to keep from stabbing her in the heart after.

"Rúnr, your fate is like the Nine Realms, varied and chaotic." She makes a circle with her hands so that he sees her face through her fingers. "If I show you Midgard like this, am I saying it is small?" She turns her hands parallel to the floor. "If I show you Midgard like this, am I saying it's a hollow disk?"

"The seeress speaks in riddles again."

"The boy refuses to grow up again."

They hold each other locked, eye to eye.

"Your fate is unchanged," she says. "There is a man here who seeks you."

"Not the Painted Fenn?"

"No, not him. Go to the market, to the map seller."

"He has a map to the temple I seek?"

Velaug's answer is to leave this quiet part of the temple. Rúnr follows her to the main corridor where they're surrounded by so many people. Here, Rúnr feels more alone than he did in the wilderness. Velaug stands in the center, forcing Rúnr to press against her. She must feel his need for her, but he doesn't flee from it. He presses closer. She brings her lips to his ear.

"Three times the god trance will take you," she says. "But not like before. And each will exact a toll."

He thinks of the Raumsdair Berserkr again, how he lived in the wilderness after being driven from his home. How he attacked travelers like a pack of wolves all held within his solitary skin. How, when his own father came bearing love and hope, he murdered and ate the old man. How, in the end, it took more than twenty warriors to bring him down. So the story goes.

"Do you know how this ends?" Rúnr asks.

"No. The gods are not omniscient. Only the destiny of Ragnarök is certain," she says. After a pause, she adds, "Be careful, Rúnr."

"Is this you speaking or the gods?" he asks.

If she's angry at his question, she refuses to show it. If she feels the same desire as he, she refuses to return it. The crowd filling the temple is relentless. Growing violent. Someone bumps Rúnr's hip. A boot stomps on his foot. A heavy shoulder knocks him aside, forcing him to spin full around to face Velaug again, but she's gone. He's alone among so many, defeated for not finding what he sought here. Renewed for knowing his fate still waits out there.

And that's enough as he works his way through the crowd to find who seeks him.

CHAPTER 27

"You're him," a merchant calls from a wide tent casting a heavy shadow. He's nearly as old as Helvig and has the thin hair and soft gut of a lawspeaker.

The market is triple the length of Skyjavík's, and twice its width, not to mention at least double its noise and smells. The merchant's tent is across the market's flow, which moves like the currents of the sea, the shoppers keeping to these currents as if by instinct. Rather than cross it, Rúnr joins it, circling until he comes to the merchant who has shouted for him.

"You're the map seller?" he asks.

"Erasmus. And you're the Opplander in the mismatched armor."

"Did Velaug tell you I'd come?"

"I don't know a Velaug."

"The seeress of Skyjavík, did you speak with her?"

The merchant pales as if in sudden terror. In a low voice he says, "This seeress, she—she is the Angel of Death who performs funerals in this city?"

"No, each city or jarldom has its own seeress, its own *kjósa*. An angel, you call her? I've heard this word. It's Christian, no?"

Erasmus looks about again. "Maybe we shouldn't speak of such things here."

A man's god is his business, both of Rúnr's fathers taught him. In all the seas he's sailed, and the lands he's raided, he's encountered more gods than he can count or name. If they were strong gods, he would have died many years sooner, as Njal did. That witch's god was not one to trifle with, even if Rúnr did prevail. The Saracen god, the one they call Allah, has also proven strong to Rúnr in his travels. The Christian god, on the other hand, he's never found strong enough to defeat a Northern foe, but if a man wants to pledge himself to such a god, who is Rúnr to sway that person from their own folly?

"Very well," he says. "How do you know me, then?"

"The large Rus, Garmr. He said you—you would seek me out looking like a man in confused armor. I must say, friend, that description fits you well."

Rúnr studies the merchant, trying to decide if the man is playing with him, for what person would choose the name of Hel's hound for their own? Such a name would risk disfavor from the gods.

"I don't know a large Rus called this name," he says.

"Well," the merchant says, "he seems to know you, or at least that you would arrive in the appearance you currently display."

Perhaps the question isn't whether this Rus knew my father, but if he knows Velaug.

"And this Rus man spoke with you today of my arrival?"

"No, my friend. He was here days ago during the funeral."

Rúnr finds this discomforting. Days ago, he was in the wilderness, crossing mountains. None knew if he would survive to see Uppsala.

None save, perhaps, the gods?

He thinks again of the man's name, Garmr, and finds it chilling to think perhaps Hel has taken enough interest in him to send her guard dog to aid him.

"So where is this Garmr?" Rúnr asks.

"He said he'll return to gather the maps he's purchased when you arrive."

"A map? To a red temple?" Rúnr does his best to contain his excitement.

"He didn't say anything about a temple."

Before Rúnr can ask more, he's bumped hard by a blond man shouldering his way by the tent.

"There's plenty of room," Rúnr says after the man.

The man looks over his shoulder as if sizing up an adversary. Rúnr's instincts awaken as someone else bumps him. He turns, his feet becoming tangled with another's so that he almost falls, catching himself on one of the merchant's tables, sending scrolls and maps flying. When he finds his balance, a woman faces him, well-muscled with wheat-blond hair wrapped tight above her ears. She flexes her arms. The first man comes to stand beside her. Different heights but same wide mouths and gray eyes. Siblings for sure. Twins, even. The man's stance leaves no doubt he wants a fight.

Striking first is always best. Except when it isn't. And Rúnr is not here to brawl.

"My mistake,"' he says.

"Sweating cock," the man says.

Rúnr is thirsty, he suddenly realizes. And hungry. Which makes his willingness to take an insult weaken. "Do you lick your mother's vagina with that mouth?" he says to the man.

The woman slides to the side. The man makes as if to spit in Rúnr's face. The natural reaction is to take a step back. Too late, he recognizes what's happening. The woman's leg catches the back of his knees, and he tumbles ass over head out into the flow of the market. He bounces off someone, then takes a knee to the side of the head before landing on his back, the air slammed from his lungs. Gasping, he gets to a knee, the market's currents ceasing and a gap forming around him and the twins.

"Too easy," the man says.

The woman produces two short-bladed swords. "He's not done yet."

The man draws his own sword, though neither advances, allowing Rúnr to regain his feet and take a few sharp breaths. A mistake to give him this much time. He reaches for his axe, only to find it stuck to his belt. Tied tight.

The fucking thief!

There's time for nothing else. They come in concert, a pattern Rúnr recognizes and is able to evade while untying his axe. The lace gets tangled. The man's sword creates sparks against his shoulder armor. The woman lands a kick to his thigh. The limp he nursed through the wilderness returns eagerly. The axe comes free. Rúnr leaps back unsteadily to reset.

"Nice axe," the woman says.

The pair spread to flank him. The crowd shouts with anticipation and joy. No one is going to intervene. As Rúnr would have it.

The man says, "Not much of a weapon for a man."

"Cut her tits off easy enough," Rúnr says, trying to anger him, get him to act rashly in defense of his sister.

The man doesn't take the bait, moving to keep Rúnr out in the open. The woman licks her lips and finds an advantageous angle. Around them, voices call out wagers. Rúnr is not favored to win.

The man comes with a feint. Rúnr parries with his axe but is left vulnerable. The woman is slow to take advantage, giving him a mere scratch on the hip. Another mistake, he thinks, until the man comes again, forcing him to turn his back to the woman to defend himself. They're good, each move positioning him closer to defeat. The woman dashes in, quicker than a rabbit, and opens a wound in his thigh. She could have run him through but either missed the opportunity or chose not to. There's little time for Rúnr to decide which as the fight becomes a hailstorm of strikes and parries and last-second dodges. The crowd shouts for blood. Rúnr obliges, bleeding from many small nicks and cuts.

"Is this the best you have?" he says, breathing heavy as he draws a knife.

"Is it yours?" the man says.

It is not!

Rúnr attacks in a fury, forcing the man to block the axe and open himself to a bite from the knife. Rúnr doesn't strike, however. He spins and manages to knock one of the woman's blades out of her hand, the blow leaving her off-balance. Rúnr springs, ready to end their advantage and make it a one-on-one fight.

A massive warsword swings down, separating Rúnr from his attackers.

"Enough!"

All three turn to the voice. The man wielding the warsword is the largest he's ever seen. Not so tall as Eilif, but with height and width enough to give him godlike proportions. Shining blond hair, with a beard to be proud of, and hands like a smith's hammer, he eyes Rúnr with . . . joy?

"Not bad," the woman says.

Her partner says, "He'll do, I think."

"Yes, he'll do nicely," the large man says.

"He'll need to be quicker," the woman says.

"I think we'll find he's everything we need, Ingirid. You and your brother may spend your time as you please. We'll meet at the docks in the morning."

The siblings depart without a word, though the woman looks back at Rúnr, her glance catching him watch her go. She offers a crooked grin and disappears with her brother into the crowd as the flow of the market returns.

"You're Garmr, then?" Rúnr says, thinking this man is not nearly old enough to have adventured with his fathers.

"And you are Rúnr, son of Njal." The big man turns to Erasmus with a hint of mischief that reminds Rúnr of Torstyn and says, "Time to close up the shop today."

The merchant stiffens. "It's only midday, I can't close."

"You can't stay open and still prepare for our journey."

"Journey? I—I have the maps. Our deal?"

Rúnr rubs his many relatively small wounds, blood dotting his arms and legs, some of it beginning to clot.

"Show me," Garmr says.

Hands shaking, Erasmus produces a number of maps. Garmr looks at each in turn, dropping them onto a nearby table until he's gone through them all. Then he sifts through the pile and picks one back up. Looks at both sides.

"This one."

"Only—only one?" Erasmus asks.

"I will pay the same."

"That's agreeable."

"With one additional requirement."

Though Garmr speaks as if discussing the details of a great feast, the threat in his words is palpable. Rúnr finds himself enthralled by the exchange before him.

"I—one?" Erasmus says.

"Find me at my ship at dawn," Garmr says.

"That's all? I—yes, I can do that, friend Garmr."

"And keep this map safe for me, will you?"

Erasmus stammers his agreement, fumbling about to lock away the rest of the maps in a chest he drags from beneath a table. While this happens, Garmr places a massive hand on Rúnr's shoulder.

"Do your wounds need tending?"

Rúnr rolls his shoulders. "No."

"Good. Do you have a place to spend the night?"

"I'll make do."

Erasmus makes quite the racket locking objects away in various chests, talking to himself about who he might trust to care for his wares.

"We leave in the morning," Garmr says.

"Do we?" Rúnr asks, understanding what's about to be proposed. Velaug told him to come here. Garmr knew he would arrive. The two must have spoken, which means his fate must lie somewhere along the map Garmr is purchasing. He won't ask after it, however. Not yet. Better to hear more of what Garmr is proposing.

"Our fates are entwined, my friend," Garmr says. "For at least a time."

"Says who?"

"The gods. Who else can make prophecy?"

Despite himself, Rúnr finds Garmr likable. Not trustworthy, exactly, but worth trusting for a time. He wonders if the big man knows the bargain he's striking, and with whom. Few would knowingly seek out a Berserkr as a traveling companion. They are for battle and for forgetting.

"Have the gods told you I can be hired so easily?" Rúnr asks.

"I'm not hiring you. I'm offering you a way to what you seek."

Rúnr doesn't like the answer, but he decides to bide his time until morning.

"Erasmus," Garmr says. "Our friend needs a bed for the night."

Erasmus, barely loud enough to be heard, says, "My home is—is tiny."

"I'll find my own bed," Rúnr says. "But tell me, why would you trust a man you just met on this journey of yours?"

"Why would you?" Garmr grins big as the sun. "At dawn, friend," he says, and then departs.

Erasmus has gone off to speak with another of the merchants nearby, leaving Rúnr to consider the journey, the maps, and where to find a bed for what will probably be a sleepless night. Which brings to mind the woman he's just fought, called Ingirid, and her crooked grin.

CHAPTER 28

The docks are not what Rúnr expects. In Skyjavík, they're built from the beach along the harbor. But Uppsala has no harbor. It lies locked between the hills to the west and the marshy plains to the south and east. It is south where the ships dock, a far walk from the mead hall where Rúnr spent the night.

The sun is almost risen above those marshes when he sees the river and the first ships moored along its length. And what a sun! He's never seen the like in all his travels. In the Opplands it appears suddenly, growing with haste, atop the mountains where seconds earlier there had been only a hint of the coming day. Here, the morning calls forth its coming with a slowly brightening sky and then, red as the fires of Muspelheim, the sun rises like Odin's one eye seeking the truth of dawn, perhaps the most honest hour men know . . . save for that immediately following sex, he thinks, his mind slipping away from the now to the then. To Berthe. To Velaug. To the woman from yesterday—Ingirid, like the best and worst parts of both Berthe and Velaug: strong, mysterious, dangerous, angry, and something enticing.

The now. The now!

Yes, the sun, the docks, the ships, so many of them. Merchant ships and fishing ships and longships for speed, for war, and for crossing the widest seas. It's upon one of these Rúnr expects to find

Garmr, but whether or not he'll sail with the man is yet to be seen. The red temple may not be here, but he doesn't know if it's where Garmr is offering to take him either.

He has the gold torc from the dead family in the wilderness. He could buy his own ship with it and sail all the rivers and seas until he finds the red temple—but it wouldn't be enough to buy a crew, let alone one he can trust.

"Hello, friend," the map merchant calls. He's well awake for the early morning, though worry lines his face. "I thought you might not come."

Rúnr doesn't know why this merchant would care either way. "I've not yet committed to going farther than this."

"Because you seek some other direction?"

"What can it matter to you?"

Erasmus flinches. "I remember you saying something about a red temple."

Rúnr's instinct is to speak no more of it, but fate doesn't work alone. It takes courage and boldness and strength to reach what it dangles before a man. It takes wisdom to know when to ignore instinct.

"I thought it was this red temple." Rúnr points north toward the town center.

"For what purpose?"

"My own purpose," Rúnr snaps. Again, Erasmus recoils. He's like a child who's been beaten too often, which inexplicably makes Rúnr want to comfort him. "My fate, given by the seeress," he says more gently.

"The seeress you—you called Velaug?"

"Yes."

Erasmus looks into the sun as if considering. "The map Garmr has purchased, it's of the way to the Reigning City, and of Constantinople itself."

"Miklagard," Rúnr says, using the Northern name. "It's the greatest Christian city in the world, I've heard. What of it?"

"Constantinople is not just a Christian city, though it sometimes forgets this."

"The great Christian emperor allows other gods in his city?" Rúnr is surprised by this revelation. The Christians he's heard of, and the few he's ever spoken to—most of the ones he's met have been on the battlefield, where conversation does not flourish—have always been adamant in the righteous domination of their one weak god over all others.

"Allows, not allows. What's legal is not always what is."

"Now you sound like a seeress," Rúnr says.

Erasmus seems both pleased and confused by this statement. "What I mean is, there are many who live in the city who are not Christian."

"People of the North?"

"Not when—when I left, some now maybe."

Rúnr finds this hopeful. "Fenns? And temples to Odin?"

"The former is possible. The latter, certainly not."

"Why are we talking so much of it, then?" Rúnr asks.

Erasmus says, "I think you might have it wrong, about the temple."

Reflex tells Rúnr to slap this fool so that he stops wasting words and time, but something else—that part of him that wanted to comfort the merchant, perhaps—tells him to wait. To ask.

"What do I have wrong?"

"The Cathedral of Holy Wisdom," Erasmus says. "It's the largest temple in all the world."

Considering the temple in this very city, Rúnr has doubts, but he motions for Erasmus to continue.

"Do you know the story of Jesus?"

"The Christ God who wins wars in robes and without a sword?" Rúnr says. "I don't fear him."

"But do you know the story?"

"If you wish to tell it, do so already."

Erasmus starts and stops with barely a sound escaping his mouth. "First, may—may I ask w-why you seek this red temple?"

Rúnr searches for Garmr and the twins but sees no familiar faces. "Vengeance," he says.

"Upon a building?"

Rúnr almost laughs. "For a murder."

"How do you know the murderer will be in such a temple?"

"I told you. Fate. Prophecy."

Erasmus nods. "Will you share the words of this prophecy?"

"You sound like my father testing my knowledge of knots," Rúnr says, giving voice to a thought he hadn't intended to speak aloud.

"I think I can help you."

"Why?"

"Because I—because Garmr sc-scares me, and you do not."

"Then you're a fool."

"I'm an old fool, which means I've learned when to trust and when not to," Erasmus says. "So far."

Rúnr considers this. He finds neither the merchant nor Garmr all that trustworthy yet, but if this map man does know something of temples . . .

"Very well. She spoke to me of the red Temple of the Hanged God. Do you know the place?"

Erasmus thinks a moment. "Jesus was crucified," he says.

"Good for him."

"He was nailed to a beam crossed over a pole." Erasmus spreads his arms wide. "Hanged, as you say."

Rúnr is alive with confidence and questions. "The Hanged God. And the temple, this place of wisdom you spoke of?"

"In the heart of Constantinople where Garmr seeks to go, built of red brick and red clay and red tile, gilded in bands so that it shines red as the sun itself when there are no clouds in the sky."

Rúnr's chest is full, the way it becomes before battle. The way it is when he's near Velaug. "Truly you speak?"

"I've seen it myself countless times."

Rúnr rises as tall as he can seeking Garmr, the man who will be his way into Christian lands. A long journey it'll be, long enough for the god trance to find him three times. This will be his way, if he can find the cursed Rus and his lackey twins.

"Opplander!" Ingirid approaches as if knowing he'd be on this very spot.

"You sail to Miklagard, then?" Rúnr asks.

"Garmr will tell you of it."

"Why don't you?"

She tilts her head at him. "Follow me."

"Where?"

"The ships here belong to locals," Erasmus says. "Travelers and foreigners must dock further south."

Rúnr understands. It's about safety, especially for a city with no walls. Smart.

"You too, merchant," Ingirid says.

"Me—me too what?"

"Follow."

Erasmus looks to Rúnr, who has no interest in being part of the man's decision. He's after what Garmr offers. So he follows, wondering at Ingirid's role. She, like her brother, is Rus. She is well armed. A good fighter, as he knows from yesterday. Do the Rus have business in Miklagard? If so, it must be new business. Otherwise, why would they need a map?

"There," she says, pointing, after a long walk.

Garmr and Ingirid's brother are where she indicates, readying a ship, though there's no other crew at work upon it. As they get closer, Rúnr sees it's a *knarr*, a merchant ship, though shorter and narrower than any he's seen before. Strikingly, it's not nearly as deep as a standard *knarr*, which is often built for sea travels. Rather, its draft is like that of a longship, suited for speed on river raids. Most striking, he counts only four benches and four oars.

"This?" Rúnr says.

"The best ships are made by the best crews," Garmr says, with the familiar jocularity that reminds Rúnr once more of Torstyn.

"And where is this excellent crew?"

Ingirid's brother makes it clear with a shot of snot from his nose that he thinks little of Rúnr and less of the merchant.

"Don't mind Ingimar," Garmr says. "He's just protective of his sister."

"I don't need protection," Ingirid says. She gets to work loading supplies onto the ship with a glare.

Rúnr notes bags of barleymeal and butter. Standard ship's provisions, though closer to a full longship's fare, it seems, than what should be needed for a four-oared vessel. They're either planning to join with more ships or preparing for a long voyage indeed.

"Quite right. Are you hungry, then, Rúnr? We have fruit already on board."

Hungry for information, not fruit, Rúnr says, "Tell me of your plans."

Ingimar makes another sound. He looks even more like his sister today, though where she hangs short swords on her belt with the ease of practiced hands, his weapons—a sword and a bow—are leaning beside the ship.

"When we're on our way," Garmr says.

"I think you'll be on your way without me if we don't talk first."

"And you?" Garmr asks of Erasmus.

The merchant looks startled, as if shaken awake from a nap. "Me—me what?"

"Do you need to hear it before we set sail?"

"I—I'm not going."

Garmr's grin grows so wide it seems it might split his beard and skull besides. "We are all five of us going," he says with such sternness there can be no doubt.

Rúnr says, "Why do you want me?"

"Relax," Garmr says. "You and I are not enemies."

The words seem to force their intention upon Rúnr. He does relax, despite his desire not to.

"I've sailed more seas than most men," Garmr says. "This ship, and our hands, will serve us well. And since we travel to the same place, it only makes sense that you join us."

Rúnr holds his own idea of what makes sense silent and close. "How is it you know where I intend to travel?"

Garmr merely grins some more.

"Tell him already," Ingimar says.

"If it'll get him on board before the sun rises any higher," Ingirid adds.

"The Oppland Berserkr himself," Garmr says, arms wide, his voice too loud.

Rúnr's hand finds his axe as he searches those along the docks for any who might have heard of him, any who might know to send whispers back to Ubbein or Leif. Ingimar stops his toil and comes closer. Ingirid puts a hand to her belt. Erasmus nearly trips over himself to back away until he bumps into a barrel meant for another ship.

"Hold there, friend," Garmr says. "As I said, we're not enemies."

"Maybe it's not you I'm concerned with," says Rúnr.

"Please," Garmr says. "It's only the five of us and the gods who know where you stand beneath today's sun. No man here will betray you for your past deeds."

"Or woman," Ingirid says.

"Upon Hel's shroud and flesh, I tell you," pledges Garmr.

Rúnr doesn't like the invocation of Hel herself, especially from a man called Garmr. More than that, it brings Yrsa to mind, and the sudden fear that the black she walks within might be the misty shores of the land named for its queen: Hel, that ninth of the realms where the misfortunate and the dishonored dead go.

Papa.

He looks up, expecting to see her, but it's only the twins.

"Listen," Garmr says. "It has been foretold that we can only succeed with one of Odin's champions at our side. For a time, this gave me pause as no Berserkr has walked the lands of the North in many generations. But now, here you stand."

"Not much of a fighter for a Berserkr," Ingimar says, hopping down from the ship, his confidence at odds with his narrow shoulders.

"Would you see the god trance up close?" Rúnr demands.

Ingimar smirks and stands there as if lord of all the world.

"Grow up," his sister says.

"We were promised a great warrior, and all we get is a fat merchant and this guy."

"Exactly as I planned," Garmr says.

Ingimar is about to say more, likely to try to force Rúnr into another fight—for which Rúnr is flexing and ready, even desirous—when Ingirid puts a hand on her brother's shoulder and whispers into his ear.

"Fine," Ingimar says. "But what good is a merchant who can't even fight?"

"On this, I agree with my brother," Ingirid says. "One kick and this one would crumble like a leaf in the autumn. At least we know Rúnr can take a punch well enough."

"His job is to kill, not get punched."

Rúnr grows frustrated with all of them. The bickering is like him and Torstyn when they were young. Too much bravado, not enough wisdom. And even less knowledge of details. What lies ahead? He must know. He must be certain the red temple awaits.

"Tell me your plans now," he says.

"Or what?" says Ingimar.

"Shut up already," his sister says. "Tell them, Garmr, and let's be on our way."

"Great sir," Erasmus says, taking a bag from his belt. "I have brought the—the map you asked for. Please take—take it and go on your way. No—no further payment needed."

"In a moment," Garmr says.

"But I—"

"In a moment!" Garmr shouts.

Crews nearby stop their work and stare. Even Ingirid and Ingimar tense.

Garmr seems to go from larger than he should be to smaller as if by will alone. "Apologies, friends. Erasmus, have patience. The gods need us to work out some details."

"Your gods," Erasmus says weakly.

"What did you say?" Ingimar says.

"We will not fight among ourselves," Garmr says. "None of us are so foolish as to think our gods are the only ones of the whole world, are we? Now, gather round. Here is why we sail."

Rúnr finds himself pressing in like a child at a campfire ready for a story. The twins and Erasmus do the same, the merchant situating himself as close to Rúnr as possible, like an orphaned cat choosing its new owner.

"We seek vengeance and treasure in whichever order they present themselves," the large man begins.

"You've heard of vengeance and treasure, haven't you, Berserkr?" Ingimar says.

Rúnr is unsure how this baiting can serve the man. "All men know of vengeance and treasure," he says.

"Are women not part of your world?" Ingirid asks.

The question catches Rúnr off guard, the way Velaug often does. "I—"

She laughs, as does Garmr. Her brother glares. Erasmus says nothing in Rúnr's shadow.

"The Romans have built a fortress on the Don, the great river of the Empire's east," Garmr says. "The White Fortress, it lords over the waters, controlling who sails the way, massive chains crossing the river to keep out those who do not pay or are not welcome. The wealthiest empire in the world, and they want more and then always more again, is this not so, Erasmus?"

"Is he the expert, or the map seller?" Ingimar asks.

"He's both."

With all eyes on him, Erasmus clears his throat. "Among us, yes, I—I can claim the most familiarity."

"And your assessment?"

"You sp-speak true."

Ingirid waves a dismissive hand. "The White Fortress was a gatepost our people, the Rus, once navigated freely," she says. "In these last years, however, the Romans have restricted trade to those called Khazars and cut off trade with us altogether."

"This is your vengeance, then," Rúnr says.

Ingimar says, "And our treasure. What they will not trade, we will take."

It seems a fair goal to Rúnr, though a horrendously poor plan. "And you do this by sailing other rivers from here to attack the heart of the Empire with three men, a woman, and a merchant?"

"One woman worth two of you men," Ingirid says.

Her brother tries to speak, but she silences him with a look.

Garmr, seemingly amused, says, "But we are not the axe coming for the Empire's head. We are the tip of the sword whose point will open its throat. The Rus gather in Kyiv as we speak and will sail in one month. We will arrive in Miklagard first to welcome them."

"Rurik has come to Kyiv?" Ingirid asks.

"The Rus chieftain will remain in his hillfort on Lake Ilmen until he is needed."

"I still don't see what good the four of us can do," Rúnr says. Then again, he doesn't care one duck's clenched ass what this group wants him to do once they arrive. The moment he sees the red temple Erasmus spoke of, he'll quit these fools to find his fate. Until then, he can play a part.

"Five," Garmr says.

Erasmus stutters again, "B—but—"

Garmr ignores him entirely. "We sail this morning. Our way is through the heart of the Christian lands."

"Where we'll kill every one of them we see," Ingimar says.

"Maybe not so many," Garmr admits. "But we'll raid and kill and burn. We'll carve fear into their hearts as we go, making the chaos of a hundred ships so that the Empire must turn its attention north and west."

"And while the Empire fears one direction . . ." Rúnr says, understanding.

"The Rus fleet will burn the White Fortress and then fall upon Miklagard like a swarm of wasps," Ingirid finishes.

"Like Thor's own thunderbolt," Ingimar adds.

Garmr grins like a bear with a mouthful of honey. It's a good plan, Rúnr thinks, if they were fifty instead of five, with many ships rather than one.

"You think we're not enough," Garmr says. "Do not look surprised. The doubt is obvious on your face. You see, there's no winter in Miklagard."

"I don't—this is not true," Erasmus says. "There is winter."

Garmr continues without allowing an answer or even looking at the merchant. "It's a land of ever-summer, and while we were bundled in the snows of winter, one of the Empire's larger southern strongholds surrendered to a Saracen army. All their might, especially their fleets, are focused on the Saracens, but I have word this has left the emperor nervous about his enemies in the west."

"So we'll give them an enemy from the west," Ingimar says.

"It doesn't matter how few we are," Ingirid says. "It only matters how loudly we can make the Christians cry in fear."

Garmr stares into Rúnr with such intensity, it seems he's stoking a fire in Rúnr's chest.

"I p-prefer not to sail," the merchant says.

"You prefer?" Ingimar kicks a stone at the merchant. "You prefer to let us go slaughter your people without a word to calm our blades?"

"I—you—I . . ." Erasmus appears close to tears, seeking help from anyone who will oblige.

Rúnr has no interest. He's thinking his way to the red Christian temple.

Garmr positions himself in the middle of the other four, effectively protecting Erasmus. "You will sail with us," he says. "Or you'll lie forever at the bottom of these waters."

"The map," Erasmus offers weakly.

"Show me," says Garmr.

Erasmus hands over the map, which Garmr examines. Each time the big man flips it one side to the other, Erasmus squeaks like a mouse.

"Yes, this is the one," Garmr says. "Keep it safe for me, with great thanks."

"I—but I can't," Erasmus says.

"But you can. I know all the things you can do and have done. No, don't fret. I'm not your enemy, nor do I care to bring you to Miklagard in chains. I'll not shed your blood, I tell you. I'll bring you to the crossroads of your redemption. What path you choose when we get there is up to you."

Erasmus stammers but can hardly make the sounds of a word.

"It's settled, then," Garmr says. He puts the map in the merchant's hands and presses those hands to his chest. "Now, keep it well and safe. Swear it upon the gods and Hel herself."

Terrified, eyes wide and darting, Erasmus nods agreement while mumbling something. Rúnr hears the word *god* in the mess.

"Excellent," Garmr says. "Now, Rúnr, you have something to ask in return for your . . . services?"

He does, though he doesn't like that Garmr knows it so readily, any more than he likes continued oaths to Hel.

"I do."

"Not coin."

"No, not coin. A promise. Tell me we'll walk the streets of Miklagard."

"Do you doubt us?" Ingimar asks, again like a man seeking a fight.

Rúnr ignores him. "We sail as a crew, yes? And Garmr is our captain, yes?"

Garmr looks at the twins. They nod in unison.

"Then I ask the captain's word that I'll walk the streets of Miklagard."

"Upon Hel's shroud and flesh, I swear it," Garmr says.

A second oath to Hel. A dangerous game, but what other kind can Rúnr play?

"Are we all happy now?" Ingimar says, throwing his hands wildly. "Can we sail so we can kill some Christians already?"

Garmr frowns at the man. Rúnr does the same. Even Ingirid seems fed up with his cantankerous theatrics. This is not the way Rúnr envisioned finding his fate, but the destination is all that matters. He waits for Erasmus to be prodded on board and then follows, the last of the five. One step closer to the end.

CHAPTER 29

Ingimar enjoys the first day. The sun shines. The wind is fair at their backs. The sea is welcoming and there's no need to place oars in the water. Each does their job well and silent.

Except the map man.

Ingimar doesn't know what kind of man can be lost on a ship, but surely, it's a man not worth having at sea. The map man whimpers deep in the hull like a babe who has lost his mother's tit. He vomits over and over. He's even pissed himself. Better to throw him over the side now. That would make Ingimar happy when so much else leaves him feeling like there's a bull inside his chest goring at his ribs to thrash free. But Garmr, their captain, won't have it. The map man is important to him. And Garmr, who holds the steering oar at the stern, is important to Ingimar and Ingirid. For now.

Even if Ingimar has to put up with Garmr calling out the waves he finds beautiful and the clouds he sees as shapes like sheep in a meadow or dolphins fucking. When another ship is sighted on the horizon, he shouts its name as if there isn't a ship in the world he's not sailed upon.

Ingimar is certain he's a liar, but so what? Liars win wars. Meanwhile, Ingimar does his part. Ingirid does hers. And the Berserkr does his. That one has no grace and no humor, but he knows how to sail and how to walk a ship at sea without flailing. Ingimar downs his third mug of beer, thinking how it might feel to break the Berserkr's nose and watch his eyes make tears.

"Are you not watching?" Ingirid says.

Ingimar looks round to find her scowling. The Berserkr watches him as well. Black-bearded bastard.

"I see it," Ingimar growls. The sail is slack. The morning is long gone. It's time to eat, but that won't happen anytime soon. He pulls at the rigging, making this rope taut and that one loose. The sail remains limp as an old man's cock.

"Oars," he says.

Garmr stands tall, a hand to his brow seeking the horizon. "Aye," he says. "To oars."

Three move as one to lower the sail, working as if they've been a crew for years. Ingimar didn't know what to expect from the Berserkr, but in this the man does not disappoint. The way he looks at Ingirid, however; the way most men look at her: considering, imagining, lusting—well, there are many problems that will have to wait.

"Are you planning to help, Map Man?" Ingimar says.

"I don't—I've never sailed." If chattering teeth could make wind, there would be no need to lower the sail.

"Sit there," Ingimar orders, pointing to the bench behind the Berserkr.

Ingimar and his sister take the starboard oars, Ingirid in the front.

The map man sits, looking at the oar like it's a snake. "What—what do I do?"

The Berserkr gets up, wordless, and places the map man's oar in the water. "Watch me," he says. He pulls three powerful strokes, listing the ship starboard. "Now you," he says.

"Like this?" the map man asks as his oar barely kisses the sea.

It's too much to allow. Ingimar brings his oar in and stands. He'll make sure to find the map first, then the dead weight goes overboard.

"Leave him be," Ingirid says. Always taking another's side.

"Empty hands lead to sunken ships."

"He'll learn," Garmr says.

"Is this what you want to wait for, Berserkr—a hairless vagina of a Christian to learn to sail?"

The Berserkr keeps his eyes ahead and rows hard. Coward, maybe, or fool. There will be time to find out. Ingimar has sailed this way before, though not as far as they'll go this spring and summer. He knows what waits ahead.

"Don't call me that," the map man says.

"He has a spine, then?"

The map man looks down and tries to row.

"Sit, Ingimar," Ingirid says.

"Maybe when I see everyone pulling their weight."

"Sit, Ingimar," Garmr says.

This is predictable. Has there ever been a disagreement with Ingirid where other men have not chosen her side?

"Row, for the sake of the Valkyries," Ingirid says.

She's focused, the muscles in her arms and back and neck taut. Rowing hard. If Ingimar doesn't join her, she'll brag all night at the lengths she pulled the ship compared to lengths he didn't.

"If all the people of Miklagard are like this one," he says, taking his bench at his oar, "we'll not need to wait for the fleet. You and I will be enough to burn it to the ground, sister."

"Aye," she says.

"Aye," Garmr says with a laugh.

"What say you, Berserkr?" Ingimar asks, finding rhythm with his sister.

"I say row," the dour bastard says.

The map man loses his grip on the oar. The sound of it skipping on the water is unmistakable, as is the crack of the inboard portion of the shaft when it jumps from his hands and slams him in the chest. He cries out but manages to grab the oar before it slips into the water. Ingimar laughs until he falls out of rhythm.

"Do something with him," Ingirid tells Rúnr.

"Can you cook him?" Ingimar asks, laughing violently now.

"Show him how, Rúnr," Garmr says. "The rest of the days here at sea, we'll rotate our places on the benches at half the regular time."

The Berserkr begins speaking directions to the map man, forcing Ingimar and Ingirid to stop rowing so that the lesson can proceed without starboard pull. A waste, of course. No soft-middled fool like this will ever learn to row properly. Better just to rotate now and put the map man on the steering oar so Garmr can take a bench.

"He'll steer us to Jörmungandr's scales," Ingirid says, as if knowing his thoughts. A thing she does more often than he for her thoughts.

"Or right back to Uppsala if he stays at an oar."

Soon enough, and faster than Ingimar expects, the Berserkr declares the map man ready to row. The four take their benches and follow Ingirid's lead. It's not steady, but they cut the sea road well enough for Garmr to begin humming. And the Berserkr to stamp his boot. And Ingirid to pick up a chant. And Ingimar to take the chant to a song. And soon they're like a true crew, swimming the sea south, five fates come to one.

CHAPTER 30

The second day begins with wind but no sun. Then sun but no wind. Then, like night at midday, comes the storm. Ingirid is at the steering oar, but it's Garmr who calls it from the first port bench.

"Tie it all down," he bellows.

Ingirid stands before remembering her place. At the steering oar, she must hold their course. It's up to the other four to make the ship ready. Three, really, as Erasmus can barely row yet, let alone do anything else.

"Get deep into the hull," she shouts at him when he stands there like a confused goat on a cliff, unsure how to go up or down.

He takes the order well and hides near the beer. That one aside, the rest of the crew take to one another quickly, without orders or bickering. Lines are grabbed. The sail is tended.

"The merchant's oar isn't tied," Ingirid shouts when she sees it jitter against the hull.

Rúnr hands off a line to Garmr, who takes it as he should, and attends to the oar. Though Ingimar is at the bow and she can't hear his voice, she can see his mouth working. Never did learn when to shut up, always a word to start a fight, or escalate one, or create one where there had been no rancor moments earlier. It'll only be a matter of time until he and Rúnr make fists for each other, and she doesn't think Garmr will stop them so long as they're not endangering the ship or the journey.

A coin on Rúnr, then, she thinks, indulging a moment to watch him tighten the sail with his strong hands and powerful arms so that it's not damaged. The coming storm will not be gentle. Neither is the Opplander.

The sea becomes angry. The wind shrieks so that even Thor's goats could not be heard over it.

"I'll take it," Garmr says of the steering oar.

Ingirid does not loosen her grip. "It's my turn."

"Good luck with that argument," Ingimar says to Garmr, working a line nearby. "I'd rather fight the storm in a fishing boat."

Garmr laughs. "Pray we don't lose you, then, good Ingirid."

Across the sea, maybe, she thinks, *but not upon it.* That seeress all those years ago was clear on this point. Across the sea Ingirid's fate waits. She'll not drown this day. Of the others, however, she cannot be so certain.

CHAPTER 31

The third day is like the first. Calm seas. Good wind when it chooses, and good rowing when it's needed. Like now. Garmr is at the steering oar. Erasmus is in front of Ingimar. Rúnr is behind Ingirid. What a view the Berserkr has. Garmr laughs to himself, then sets his eyes on the sea once more.

They'll see land before the sun sets and reach it in the morning, a day earlier than he anticipated. The storm could have thrown them east or west. Instead, it carried them south. Luck is at their back.

"You row like a lame cat trying to jump," Ingimar says to Erasmus.

"You talk too much," Ingirid says.

"Tip of the sword," Ingimar says. "More like splinters from a stick."

Rúnr tries a song. No one picks it up. He stops. Then Ingirid continues it. Soon, they're all singing, even Erasmus, who has learned some of the words. *On no other ship could four such as these find a rhythm*, Garmr thinks. Luck, and the favor of his Lady, is at his back, as it ever is.

A shame one of this crew will not see the grandeur of Miklagard.

A great shame indeed.

CHAPTER 32

The land rises from the sea the way it always does: in a haze, in uncertainty, and then, finally, in a teasing mockery. *Yes, you found me,* it says to Rúnr as they sail into a wide bay. *Against all odds even with the winds and the gods at your back. But finding me is only the first part, the easy part, you optimistic fools.*

Rúnr doesn't speak the lands he sees, nor do Garmr or the twins. Likely they know, as he does, that it's not fine to celebrate a simple act of survival when the surviving is not yet complete and their boots have not yet touched dry land.

"Is that land?" Erasmus says.

"Idiot," Ingimar mutters.

Garmr stands tall at the bow and points, and the ship follows, slipping into the river and the surrounding forest like a worm into the mouth of a hungry bird.

"Village," their captain says, indicating the jagged lines of rooftops along the coast, a wide flung but not so large fishing hamlet.

"About time," Ingimar says. "To blood."

"Split," Ingirid says, pointing ahead to the east away from the village to a gap in the trees, like a missing tooth.

Garmr looks east and west and east again. It's the first time Rúnr has noted indecision in the man. He finds it disconcerting.

"To oars," their captain says. "This one's not for us."

"Fuck all!" says Ingimar, though he follows orders and takes to his bench, lifting his oar. "Look at that place. No wall. No tower. We could take all they have, gold and women, and be done before supper."

"East," Garmr repeats.

"We came to bring blood and war," Ingimar insists.

"We came to be smart."

"War is not with men, it's with fear," Erasmus says so boldly everyone stops to listen. "Those who are conquered by fear will suffer until death and only death frees them."

Ingimar looks as if he's going to say something, but he closes his mouth just as quickly. Rúnr isn't sure how to reply. It's not the words, though they reach something in him he doesn't quite recognize yet. It's the way the merchant says them. He's not yet asserted himself since the moment Rúnr met him. But here, now, he does.

Why?

"These are not your words," Ingirid says.

"No, they're old words, more than a thousand years from the past."

"From a wise man."

"Yes."

Rúnr is impressed with Ingirid's knowledge.

"A conqueror," she says.

Erasmus says, "He was."

Ingimar mutters something cruel. Rúnr imagines he was a boy often picked on, one who hated when the odds turned against him. He imagines the relief Ingimar must have felt when his sister stood by his side. And the humiliation at having only a girl to aid him. Yes, that's the grimace on his face now.

"Would you all like to suck each other's cocks while you read poetry?" the angry twin says.

"Feel free to suck mine," his sister says.

Garmr laughs.

"I was a poet once," Erasmus says, mostly under his breath, but Rúnr hears.

"Our map man is correct," Garmr says. "We come to make fear more than blood. For now. Let the village lie unmolested so that we can bring havoc to the next one we find. Let these Christians wonder from which direction we come, and in what direction we go. This is our purpose, yes?"

"Yes," Ingirid says.

Ingimar, his eyes still on the village, says, "It is."

Erasmus remains silent, as does Rúnr. Havoc sounds like delay to him. He aches to sail fast and straight down the Christian rivers to Miklagard, but this is not his crew. And even if it is a temporary arrangement, even if he's no more than a mercenary among them, he will not speak out against his captain. Such is how crews fail and ships flounder and only whispers of the dead return.

"We sail on, then," Garmr says.

And so they pull their oars, with their captain at the steering, and row into a dense forest with a canopy so thick it's like dusk within.

"Beautiful, isn't it?" Garmr says when they've left the sea behind.

He points at a tree and names it. Then a bush. Some other plant Rúnr doesn't recognize. A forest is a forest, whether in the North or on the Saxon Isles. But a forest is unique as well, and he cannot help but see the beauty around them in a similar fashion to the excitement Garmr shows as he names what surrounds them. Sometimes in a language familiar and sometimes not.

"You've sailed these lands before," Erasmus says.

"I've sailed every waterway the world knows," is Garmr's reply.

Ingimar spits into the river. "The east bank is higher than the west."

"So it is."

Rúnr sees this as well, now that it's pointed out. Not a strange geography in itself, but the height of the east bank is notable. He wonders if it's an omen, and in that wondering finds his thoughts back home. With Yrsa at the hot spring on the South Mountain. A dozen memories tied into one like a great rope. She, complaining of the hike. She, washing her hair with Berthe beside her. She, holding his hand as they collect flowers. Like Berthe, she liked purple ones.

"What if a bear comes?" she asks in a memory that both happened and didn't. The question came from her lips, but not at the springs, Rúnr thinks. It matters little. Inside his mind she asks it, and he answers.

"A bear won't come."

"How do you know?"

Here, Berthe gives him a look. *Tell her what you are,* his wife's eyes say. But that might frighten her. Or bring more questions he cannot, or will not, answer.

Those who are conquered by fear will suffer until death and only death frees them.

An ancient man's words spoken by Erasmus, they have no place in this memory, and yet here they are.

"Because you're my Little Bear," Rúnr tells her. "And one bear here is enough for any day."

Berthe scowls. Yrsa smiles. She hugs her father. He pulls her close, like pulling an oar.

"You row like the map man," Ingimar says, bringing Rúnr to the now.

He's lost their rhythm and stutters his work to regain it. He seeks the sun through the trees, finding only broken shafts of light at a steep angle. Evening it is, then. He's been lost in his mind a long time, meandering like the river.

"Idiots everywhere," Ingimar says.

"Shut up already," his sister, at the oar behind Rúnr, says.

"Not my fault he can't keep time."

"Hush," Garmr says like a father to his children.

"You brought him," Ingimar complains. "Said we need him. The gods want us to need him, or whatever cockshit words you used."

"Silence," Garmr says.

This time, his word is followed. He points. To the west, above the trees, rises a point. No one needs name it. Like a good crew, they put aside all animosity. They are focus and purpose, for there rises the steeple of a temple. Rúnr almost loses his rhythm again, pulling too hard, leaning forward, rising off his bench to see. Is it red? Is it the one?

No, the roof is thatched and of dark wood.

"Now we have fun," Ingimar says.

"*Now* you may have your blood," Garmr says.

CHAPTER 33

"Poppies," Garmr says.

Ingimar wants to grab a handful and shove them into the man's mouth to shut him up. Never before has he known a man—*a man!*—to be so obsessed with a land's flora.

"For healing," Ingirid says.

"If they're not for rowing, they can fuck off," Ingimar tells her.

"Past the field," Garmr says, indicating a gravel beach on the west bank where they can moor the ship.

Push. Pull. Push. Ingimar puts his might into his oars. He has no other worry now. His sword is sharp. His bow is taut. He needs only feel his boots on the beach and he will introduce so many Christians to their weak god.

Even better, he'll see the Berserkr in action. None in his lifetime have witnessed such a thing and survived to tell of it, not in his lands anyway—lands that lie farther northeast across forests almost too gloomy and heavy to travel by land. All this way he and Ingirid have come, from Lake Ilmen west through Eistland, across a dangerous gulf to the place of the Sámi. Across a sea to the land of the Swedes. And then over that sea once more to here. All to be many weeks still from Miklagard.

All to fight beside a Berserkr. That is Garmr's insistence.

"It's time," he says to his sister.

She nods, her eyes on the Berserkr as they hit the beach with barely a sound, knowing his meaning, as she always does. But frustratingly, he doesn't know her thoughts on the Berserkr. Does she doubt as he does, or is she simply curious? Excited?

He stows his oar, as do the others, and looks back at Garmr, remembering their conversation after testing the Opplander in the marketplace.

"The gods say we need him," Garmr had insisted.

"Him? The gods told you his name?" Ingimar had asked.

"How many Berserkrs do you think there are?" Such a goat's answer, a woman's answer, coming from that broad-shouldered man.

But here they are. "Come, Berserkr," Ingimar says. "Fight by my side."

"I don't think that would be wise," is the Berserkr's answer.

"Afraid I'll see you stumble like you did at my hand?"

The Berserkr climbs from the ship without answer.

"You know it's not wise to stand near a Berserkr," Ingirid says.

The map man, working on leaving the ship, stops with a leg dangling over the edge. "Why not?"

"The god trance makes a man kill," Ingirid says, "like a ferocious bear, the stories say."

"Is it true?" Ingimar asks. He has no need for other's fear but finds himself curious. "Ever eaten a friend?"

The Berserkr straps a shield to his arm but otherwise doesn't seek armor. "Not yet."

The threat is clear, but Ingimar laughs as he collects his weapons and gear. He's seen bravado before.

"This way," Garmr says, his great warsword over his back.

Ingimar sets off but is stopped by the mewling of the map man.

"I'm no fighter," the sorry merchant says.

"The amount of dead weight we carry," Ingimar laments.

"And yet," the Berserkr says, "we keep *you* with us."

Ingirid laughs so hard she snorts and slaps her belly.

"You fight with him, then," Ingimar says. "And you, Map Man, stay here so I don't accidentally cut off your head."

He doesn't wait for a reply. It's time to fight. He sets off the way Garmr pointed, stepping on as many poppies as he can.

CHAPTER 34

The closer they get, the taller the temple reveals itself. Might as well be a giant cock, Ingirid thinks, like on the statues in the Great Temple of Uppsala—it's all men know: cocks. Those tiny, crooked wart-covered ones above their balls. The iron and steel ones they use to split flesh. And the massive wood and stone ones they build to convince themselves they have something to offer women and gods.

She slinks through the woods behind Garmr and Rúnr, her brother already headed off in a different direction. Probably seeking a hill under tree cover so he can use his bow, firing long, thin cocks like the manliest of men.

She can't help a smile at that one.

"Here," Garmr says, waving them to some bushes. He's mostly shadow as night rises, but a large shadow she finds easily.

Rúnr kneels beside him, spying the village that pools around the temple. To Ingirid, it's the luck of the gods this night. The village is well lit by fire and torch, and lively, which is what strikes her. The whole population must be here, gathering in the open space before the temple as if for some event. A feast? A sacrifice? It doesn't matter. There are a hundred of them, maybe more, but half are children and women who appear no more familiar with a sword than a Danish bride is with cock on her wedding night.

By Freyja, I've got cock on my mind.

She refuses to look at Rúnr, focusing instead on the Christians. Of the men, none look to be armed. A good fight for two score warriors, but here they crouch numbered five in total—no, four; the map man either waits at the ship or has fled. And surely these Christians have weapons somewhere. Four against half a hundred.

I'm forgetting the women, just like Ingimar does.

Four against a hundred, then. Impossible.

"Speed and surprise," Garmr says, as if knowing her mind the way Ingimar sometimes does. "This is how four beats a hundred."

Ingirid is not so certain, but she wants to find out. Almost as much as she wants not to die here in this nameless land. Not for fear, of course. She and Ingimar have a goal. Rurik's goal. Burn Miklagard to ash so that the world will sing of the Rus for a thousand years.

"Do you see Ingimar?" Rúnr says.

Garmr seems to concentrate more than look. "There." He points. "On the rooftop."

Ingirid can't see him, but the place Garmr points is ideal to aim upon the Christians and rain slaughter. Four against eighty, maybe, once Ingimar is out of arrows.

"The gods will see us tonight," she says.

"We will make such fear, the Empire will turn its eye before two more sunrises."

"Only if we let some live," Rúnr says.

"Live? Death makes fear."

"The dead don't—" He bites off his own words.

"Don't what?" Ingirid asks.

"They don't speak of our victories."

Garmr laughs, a hand over his mouth to keep quiet. "Our Berserkr is wise. Very well, let one or two live and flee and scream of our deeds."

Ingirid isn't sure she agrees, but she's not so opposed as to make an argument of it. The idea of mercy turns her eye behind them, to the ship. The map man. He hasn't betrayed them yet. Hasn't come screaming to his fellow Christians of danger in the night. She wonders if it's because he's fled somewhere else entirely.

"He won't betray us," Rúnr says when she looks back toward the river.

She asks, "You know this how?"

He shrugs. Ingirid wants to grab him by those shoulders and slam him to the ground.

"What if he flees, then?" she says to Garmr. "He has your map."

"He does," admits their captain.

"You trust him?"

"I trust him as I trust each of you. And I know we need him. That's enough."

"Then why isn't he here to fight with us?" This is the question she's meant to ask. It's been in her mind like a thorn since they set sail.

"Each of us will bleed and shed blood on this journey."

"That's not an answer."

"It's the only answer there is."

"He's not fighting now."

"We fight now," Rúnr says. "He'll fight later."

"Spoken like a Berserkr," says Garmr.

"Have you met many?"

Garmr opens his mouth, then closes it without speaking, as if afraid of revealing something dangerous, or forbidden. Ingirid has never seen him scared. This isn't fear, but it might be close, and it unsettles her.

Ingirid tries to hold Rúnr's eye, to see if he noticed Garmr's reaction, but the Berserkr is focused on the enemy, cold and dispassionate like a mountain in a storm. Then something changes. His eyes widen. His mouth drops open a little. Like he's seeing something horrific she can't see.

"What is it?" she asks.

He blinks, licks his lips. "Nothing."

She's certain it's not nothing. "You saw something."

"I didn't."

Maybe this is just how Berserkrs are. She cracks her knuckles. "Let's do this already."

"When it ends," Garmr says, "take only what treasure you can carry."

"Understood." They have far to travel and their ship is only so large. And there will be treasure beyond imagining in Miklagard.

"Be sure your brother remembers."

"He'll remember," she says. *He just might not care.*

Garmr whistles like a wren. A big one. At the edge of the village crowd, a woman falls. A boy. A dog with a whimper. Two men. Confusion sets in slowly. Another man drops clutching his chest. Another woman.

Forget the women, for fuck's sake, Ingirid thinks, hating the dismissal but knowing full well Christian women are not the threat Rus women are.

Rúnr begins rocking back and forth, rising to full height, like a bull readying to charge.

"Wait," Garmr says.

Two more men fall. Someone screams. The confusion rolls like a wave through the whole of the village. This is the moment. No one running yet, but chaos waiting in their veins. No leader. No focus. Like chickens waking when the wolf comes.

"Now," Rúnr says.

He goes. Garmr goes behind him, leaving Ingirid to move north, cutting off any escape around the temple.

Ah, the spear-din!

It's the thrill of a hunt, of an open ocean swim, of the sight of the world from the top of the tallest mountain. It's the thrum of heat, of a teasing touch, of a cock penetrating deep. It's the best of life, making death is.

Her swords are part of her, as much as her fingers and her wrists. What she lacks in strength to slice bone in a single strike, she makes up for with speed and the sharpest of blades. A man clutching his gut. Another his throat. A spurting thigh that will drain a life's blood. A hand, that she can sever. A foot. Half a face. She is painted in her enemies' lives, licking it from her lips, refusing to wipe her eyes. Let her vision be red this night. Let the men fall before her while the women scream and flee. Let the others kill them. Let her brother. For her, the glory is in the number of men she kills.

Nearby, Rúnr slams into a man armed with only a shield, and the pair go tumbling into a house. A dog comes snarling for Ingirid. She sends it limping away, then follows Rúnr into the house. He's standing over the man, now dead, his skull split in two. Before him, a young girl, maybe seven winters old, is quivering on the floor.

"I could let you go," Rúnr says, though he must know the girl doesn't understand. "If you promise not to fight, I could leave you here to hide. Can you do that?"

The girl seems to understand and bobs her head eagerly.

"Go!"

The girl scrambles across the floor to the back of the house and slips underneath a bed. Rúnr turns, clearly surprised to find Ingirid standing there.

"Mercy in war is weak," she says.

"She's a child," Rúnr says. "She's not at war."

He goes around her and leaves the house. Ingirid wants to shout after him that *all* mercy is weak, but she knows better. Which makes her angry. She kicks the dead man. It doesn't improve her mood. The little girl, peering out from under the bed, is weeping. A memory starts to rise. A baby girl struggling to breathe. She would be about this age now.

"No," Ingirid says, stamping down the memory. She leaves the house without looking back.

Outside, she finds Garmr making a road of bloody heads lost from their bodies. And Rúnr down the way killing with brutality despite what she's just witnessed. And there, finally, she spies Ingimar. He's left his bow somewhere and is fighting with their father's sword. The Christians have not yet formed a defense. They scream and run. No armor. Little more than spades and hatchets and clubs in some of their hands. A bald man in a dress stands before the temple spouting words like they can be weapons. She roars. He trembles but holds forth a gold cross-sticks hanging on a rope around his neck.

Left sword frees the gold. Right sword frees the hand from the wrist. Left sword opens the man's dress where a mother sometimes gets opened to let out a baby. Right sword fills his mouth when he screams in pain. He'll never scream again.

She kills as she runs, nearly tripping over a girl, barely old enough to be married, her torn clothes falling from her shoulders, huddled on the ground. A baby in her arms, wailing thing.

The memory tries to surface once more.

Ingimar appears, blood rolling down his face like rain. "Look at this one," he says.

She knows her brother's mind. This young mother with large suckling breasts. Ingirid stabs the girl through the side of the neck, then the baby after. Two swift strokes, a painless end for each. A mercy, she tells herself as her brother complains, calls her a bitch, and hurries off after a trio of fleeing men.

The memory fades.

Is this regret she feels, or pride?

Garmr and Rúnr come from opposite directions to join Ingirid before the temple. The three of them have been painted in victory. All around, bodies lie like stones on a beach. The grass and dirt of the village is slick with blood. Garmr holds his warsword as if it weighs as little as one of her own. Rúnr's breathing comes in heaves, but he is still Rúnr. Not the Berserkr. She's relieved. And disappointed. By the look on his face, she thinks he feels the same.

Ingimar returns. "There may be a few hiding in houses, but the rest are in there." He points at the temple.

Garmr says, "Let the hiding few live. They will tell our story."

Ingirid asks, "How many inside?"

Ingimar goes to examine the temple, doors first. Then walls. All the way around. It takes time. Shouting and crying comes from within, but no one tries to escape. Around them, the village is still.

"Locked up tighter than a duck's ass," Ingimar says on his return. "Maybe half the village inside."

"Half a hundred dead, then, at the hands of four," Garmr says.

"They'll sing songs of what we did here tonight," Ingirid says.

Garmr, voice heavy and certain, says, "Tonight is only a part of what will be sung."

At this, Ingimar beams. "Find their gold?" he asks.

"Inside," says Rúnr, pointing. "Their temples are their vaults."

"We have no need for this village's gold," Garmr says.

"You may not," Ingimar says, starting for the temple.

Garmr stops him with a hand. Not violent, but not gentle. "There will be more gold than any one ship can carry."

Ingimar bites his front teeth. Ingirid knows that face. He doesn't want to back down.

"How do you know?" her brother asks.

"Everyone knows of the treasures of Miklagard."

"Of course I do!"

Ingirid hides a grin. Her brother is brave and sometimes even close to wise. But he can be fooled, too, and Garmr knows how.

"When we've completed our journey, you'll never have need to raid or plunder again," Garmr says. "Upon Hel's shroud and flesh, I tell you this."

Ingimar breaks a wide smile. "All right, then. What about this place?"

"Burn it," says Garmr of the temple.

Rúnr rocks foot to foot.

"Something to say?" Ingimar asks.

Rúnr says, "The children inside."

"What about them?"

"We agreed to let some live."

He's relentless, their Berserkr. Ingirid can't help but admire him for it, even as she's still angry at him. Or at herself because of him.

"We've let enough live," Garmr says.

Rúnr's jaw clenches. As does his fist. He puts his axe on his belt and stalks back toward the river.

"A Berserkr with no stomach for killing," Ingimar says. "Exactly what we need."

"Shut up," Ingirid tells her brother.

"Burn it," Garmr says again.

Ingimar sets about the task. "Is a man's job suddenly too much for you, then?" he teases his sister.

Without a word, she joins him. They are crew after all, given an order by their captain. Soon the temple is alight. A pyre. A statement. Ingirid hopes the Christian god is watching. She hopes he is afraid. She knows no matter how much fear he feels, it won't be enough.

CHAPTER 35

Night.

Erasmus isn't sure when it came. He's huddled in the ship, in the hull, he thinks. Maritime details have never been forefront in his life. He's spent more time on a ship over these last few days than he had in all his previous years.

Why?

He could have fled, couldn't he, instead of following these murderous barbarians?

Maybe not overboard, he's not much of a swimmer, but at night while they camp. Or now.

He almost laughs. Now. All that matters now is the blood, the ever-expanding pool that's been steadily edging toward him since . . .

The sky was still dusky when the three villagers came running from the death wielded by Garmr, Ingirid, Ingimar, and Rúnr.

My companions, Erasmus thinks, pulling his legs up tighter as the blood creeps closer. This is why he hasn't fled. He knows it, even as he fears what it makes him. They tease. They dismiss and degrade him. But they also accept him. It's been so long since anyone has. Since he's let anyone try.

Suddenly, he has to pee.

The blood comes to within a hair of his boot. He feels it as if his foot is naked, and the fluid is boiling hot. He slams the back of his head against the ship, tightening himself into an even smaller ball, which only makes him need to pee more. So much blood from just two people.

The third fled, screaming into the forest before the crew returned from doing their slaughter.

I've done mine.

The three came without a care at concealing themselves. Two men and a woman. They saw the ship and must have taken it for a place to hide or thought they could sail it themselves to get away. They hadn't expected to find Erasmus cowering below. One of the men shouted at him, threatening. Erasmus knows the languages of this land, but he couldn't hear the man's words. All he could hear was his heart hammering inside his chest.

The crew returned shortly after to find Erasmus standing over the bodies, sword in hand.

Oh, how they congratulated him, even Ingimar. Slaps on the back. Kind words. Praise even. How he enjoyed it even as his stomach twists to think of it, the celebration of deaths he caused. He weeps. He can do so now because the others are off gathering supplies and treasures from the dead. He should have wept then, when the bodies were still warm, but he'd been unable to do anything but stare at what he'd done.

Things have not gotten much better since. The blood is closer, and he can't curl up any tighter, and the night stretches on and on.

In God's name, who am I?

He thinks back to who he used to be. A man of words, poems, and histories and all the beauties the Empire has magnanimously recorded over the centuries. A man who loved rather than killed.

Could he be any farther from the one who looked upon him with such passion, that face that once gave him such peace and filled him with such joy and love?

He makes no attempt to stop his weeping as the blood oozes ever closer. It will reach him soon.

CHAPTER 36

Are you not ashamed?

Rúnr starts, an obvious flinch at the sound of Yrsa's voice, one that Ingimar picks up on.

"Hear an owl? Or a big scary vole?"

They're camped on a pebbled beach beneath a moonless sky. Erasmus is off gathering another haul of firewood, Garmr arranging what's already been brought. Ingimar skins two rabbits and a squirrel. And Ingirid cleans and sharpens her blades, for they recently come from the slaughter of a farmstead up the way.

And I must have fallen into a nap, Rúnr thinks. How else could he have heard Yrsa's accusation?

The dream has come each night over these weeks, as always, but Yrsa's denunciation of her father growing stronger the closer the crew gets to their goal.

It's not been an unpleasant journey, though—the dreams, and the moments of seeing faces decay before his eyes, notwithstanding. They sail the river when they can. They portage the ship when they can't. They travel by day and set camp along the riverbank at night. Hunting and gathering at dusk and dawn. Raiding and killing when Garmr deems the time opportune. Sometimes they pass within pissing distance of a monastery or a procession of Christians, horse and carriage and at the march, along a riverside road without an arrow loosed at the enemy. Other times, Garmr calls to fight, often to seek out a village or homestead the rest of them cannot see or hear from the ship.

They've found their rhythm as a crew, keeping to Garmr's orders. Sailing steadily south and east through tall, thick, green forests or near open plains of dancing grass or within sight of cragged mountains that seem always in ill humor. Ingimar complains and picks on Erasmus, who does what he's told with a sullen acceptance, his role mostly that of gatherer in the beginning. But Rúnr and Garmr take turns teaching him how to sail, how to fight, how to repair the ship and cook the meals, how to be part of a crew so that now he's no worse than a boy on his first raid. An impressive improvement, to Rúnr's mind.

Meanwhile, Ingirid impresses at every task while often speaking a shrewd counterpoint to Garmr, a fact some captains can't handle from any man, let alone a woman. Garmr, however, seems content to call a vote more often than not when there's disagreement.

And Rúnr, he mans the rigging, he rows in time, he hunts, he fights, he kills. There's no reason to do otherwise as no other action will bring him to Miklagard sooner—a fact he both hates and has made peace with. Their ship will travel at the speed of the river, the wind, and the crew's oars. No faster. And the truth is, he's enjoying himself. He's never been part of a true crew before. He's a Berserkr, after all.

Then there's Ingirid. He hasn't missed her eye on him. He hasn't tried to hide his own looks at her. She's not attractive the way Velaug is. She's more like Berthe. Strong. And in that strength, sensual, though she doesn't indulge it.

"You fight well for a coward," says Ingimar to Rúnr, at least half in jest. He's grown far less antagonistic the longer the crew sails together.

Rúnr says, "You fight well for a dead man."

Garmr snorts. Ingirid coughs to cover a laugh.

"We're all dead," Ingimar says, still caked in blood from the recent raid, making no rush of going to the river to wash. "But I'll spend eternity in Valhalla. Will you, Berserkr?"

"Shall we find out?" Rúnr says carelessly.

Ingimar laughs. It's the response of a friend. A brother. At the start of their voyage, such insults were meant to cut. Among strangers, such words could lead to violence. Here, they could lead to the dissolution of the crew. To the loss of the way to Miklagard.

Now, however, for this crew, they've become routine, their venom neutered.

Rúnr forces a smile but his mind drifts back to Yrsa, then to the two girls he found hiding in the barn at the farmstead. Too young yet to be married off. He wanted to tell them to flee, but the twins came. Ingimar shrugged. Ingirid shook her head. Ingimar grunted. Ingirid nodded once, solemnly. An agreement. This is the way between them, speaking without words. Ingimar grabbed one of the girls by the arm. Ingirid shoved the other outside and followed, her mood dark. When she was gone, her brother skewered the remaining girl with his sword.

Routine.

Let one live.

Never two.

After, while Ingimar and Garmr made slaughter of the injured across the farmstead, Ingirid caught Rúnr's eye from the corner of the barn. A nod of her head brought him to her. He couldn't help recalling similar rendezvous with Velaug, but it was words Ingirid wanted.

"You never kill them," she said.

"Who?"

"Girls."

"I don't spare women."

Ingirid stood close to him, her sweat and the smell of battle making a heady scent. "Children, then," she said. "You never kill *them*."

"Is it a problem?"

"What do you think of when I do?" It was an oddly vulnerable question from her.

"I don't judge your choices," he said.

She nodded. "I won't judge yours, then," she said. They stayed together like that for a longer moment than necessary.

"Is that thing ready to roast?" Garmr asks.

Back to the now for Rúnr. Ingimar tosses a rabbit, too high, forcing Garmr to leap to catch it.

"Hope your aim with a bow is better," Rúnr says.

"I hope your aim with my sister is farther from the mark," Ingimar says.

Ingirid looks daggers at her brother. "Hope you find a seal to fuck."

"Don't you worry about me. I get whatever I need."

Erasmus chooses this moment to emerge from the trees, arms laden with branches.

"Just to your tastes, eh?" Ingirid says, barely able to get the words out for her laughter.

Erasmus freezes as if under the aim of an archer, eyes wide. Such fear he demonstrated often in their first days together, but not so much recently.

"Get the fire started already, Map Man," Ingimar says. "We're hungry."

And that's the end of it for now. Tomorrow night will bring other strife, some for fun and some for insult. Like a good crew.

Thinking this, Rúnr settles near the fire and waits for supper. The night is warm. If they continue south long enough, he thinks, they may find a land that truly does not know winter. He almost laughs at the idea.

The food comes soon enough, with Garmr on Rúnr's left and Erasmus on his right, the twins across the fire. They eat with vigor and grunts and belches, drinking the beer they've taken from the dead, their own casks having gone dry some days ago.

"The stars here are the same," Garmr says. "And yet they're different."

Rúnr looks up. "I see the same stars. It's the lights of the Bifröst I don't see."

"We're beyond the reach of the gods here, then," Ingirid says.

"Not so," says Garmr. "There are many ways to travel. Look at us, see."

"The lights of the North," Erasmus says, "are the breath of Aurora, goddess of the dawn, according to the old ways of the Empire."

Ingimar says, "False goddess," and spits.

Erasmus wipes his chin. "It's their truth."

"I thought their truth is the Christ god."

"It wasn't always."

The conversation goes on a time recounting Roman gods and Northern gods and the stars. Rúnr listens without listening, his mind winding through its own caverns, their trail of ideas as disconnected as his own, until it comes back to the stars.

"You've traveled far, yes?" Rúnr asks Erasmus. "Seen many stars?"

Erasmus nods.

"Do you know this river?"

Garmr leans in to listen. It occurs to Rúnr that none of them have asked the river's name before now. There's power in a name, he knows. Everyone knows. How have they not thought to ask?

"The Danube, I think," says Erasmus.

"A great river?"

"Very long, yes."

"And it goes all the way—"

"It does not," Garmr interrupts. "We'll sail another fortnight or so, and then we'll trade the river for the land."

"And what," Ingimar says, gnawing on a bone, "put wheels on our ship?"

"I have made arrangements."

"What does that mean?" asks Ingirid.

"It means we'll arrive in time."

There's silence among them awhile. Bones are chewed and tossed into the fire. Beer is passed around. Ingirid's eyes find Rúnr more than once. A distraction. One he decides he can't afford. She's bored, after all, on a ship with four men. One her brother. One old enough to be her father. One her captain. Rúnr is all that's left. A passing fancy.

And yet, there was that conversation behind the barn. There is the way she seems to watch him at times, approving of the way he fights or sails or builds a fire.

"Is it truly worth all this?" Erasmus says.

Rúnr thinks he's missed part of the conversation. "Is what worth all this?"

"War. Vengeance. It's one or the other with your people, always. But the five of us going so far to kill so many. Is it worth it?"

Garmr and Ingimar exchange looks, one of intrigue and the other of disgust. Ingirid seems thoughtful. To Rúnr, the question is more than foolish. It angers him.

"It is worth it," he says. "It's required for what has been taken."

"It's our way," Ingirid adds.

Erasmus, his face full of compassion, asks, "What has been taken?"

"Trade routes," says Ingimar.

"That's not why you've come," the merchant says to Rúnr.

Rúnr seeks a place in his own mind that is neither rage nor sadness. A place where Yrsa doesn't watch him. He cannot find it.

"My daughter," he says.

Erasmus takes the beer Ingirid offers and passes it to Rúnr without drinking. Rúnr passes it to Garmr.

"I'm sorry for the loss of your daughter," Erasmus says.

"You don't understand."

"No, I don't. So much focus on retaliation instead of healing, on more death instead of living."

"You're going to find yourself indulging the former rather than the latter," Ingimar says.

Rúnr says, "You live among us. You see our ways. You build wealth from our purses, but you judge our ways of justice?"

Eyes full of conviction, Erasmus doesn't back down. "I do judge when your ways make no sense. Vengeance only begets vengeance."

Rúnr is both surprised and impressed with this. There is steel in this old man, he thinks, though it seems it's wielded only when necessary.

"A typical Christian idea," says Ingirid.

Erasmus shakes his head. "How would you know? I've lived among your people. Have you lived among others? And hear this, each of you. Wanting peace instead of endless violence isn't foolish and it's not a uniquely Christian desire."

"Sounds Christian."

"I do not speak for them."

"You speak for cowards, then," Ingimar says.

Rúnr notes that Garmr is silent and watchful.

"It's not cowardly to want to live."

"I say it is."

"When does the cycle of violence end?" Erasmus asks.

"When there are none left to kill," Rúnr says.

"And what do you know of bravery anyway?" Ingimar says. "I haven't seen you lift a weapon in actual battle yet."

"I've killed."

"You've defended, like a cornered mouse who got lucky with a swipe of its tiny claw."

Erasmus pales a little. "I have no quarrel with the people you kill."

"As I said. Coward."

"Because I've not bled with you?" Erasmus says. "But I have bled, this I promise. I've suffered as much as any of you, but I've not sought vengeance for my wounds."

"But you can," Garmr says, finally joining the conversation. "Soon enough, we'll be to your homeland, and then you can seek that vengeance."

"That—it's not my way."

Rúnr finds the merchant both distasteful and endearing. Like a child to be protected. To be taught.

"Forget about vengeance, then," he says. "What about fate?"

Erasmus takes a moment to answer. "What about it?"

"Do you seek yours or let it find you?"

"That is God's decision."

"Maybe, but I know mine."

"And I, mine," says Ingirid.

"And you?" Erasmus asks Garmr.

Their captain nods.

"And your fate," Erasmus says to Rúnr, "is the red temple that you told me of, yes?"

"I've not heard of this," Ingirid says.

Rúnr sees no reason to withhold the details. Erasmus knows. Garmr seems to know. Why not the twins?

"The Oppland Seeress spoke my fate not long ago," he says, feeling Ingirid's attention. "Vengeance against my daughter's killer waits in a red temple. I thought she meant the temple in Uppsala, but now I believe it's the red temple of Miklagard. Three times from that day we spoke, she said, the god trance will find me before I will have vengeance."

"God trance," Ingimar says. "You fight well enough for an Opplander, but I've seen no bit of Berserkr in you."

Nor has Rúnr felt it in himself. In its place, a growing impatience. And fear, though he'll show neither to this crew. "See it too close," he says, "and it may be the final thing you see."

"We brought you for a reason."

"I came for a reason."

Ingirid says, "Has the god trance come for you since you received the prophecy?"

At her voice, Rúnr finds he's angrier at her brother than he should be. "No," he admits.

Ingimar tosses a bone as if to say, *See what I mean?*

"Your fate, then?" Rúnr asks.

The twin looks to his sister, who only shrugs. "I've not asked to know mine," is all he says.

"Fate is only one destination in a life," Garmr says. "Not asking won't change it."

Ingimar says, "Maybe, but it's my fate. My choice."

Garmr picks at his tooth. "What of you, Ingirid?"

"I will seek vengeance in a land far away," she says. "Across a sea, with the blood of vengeance on my hands, is where I will die."

"Vengeance for what?" asks Erasmus.

Ingirid fixes him with a squinting stare. Then Rúnr, then Garmr, then her own brother. "That was not spoken at the time."

The beer returns to Rúnr. This time he drinks, then passes to Garmr, who drains it.

"What of you, Garmr?" Ingimar asks.

Their captain clears his throat. "In Ragnarök, many gods, many animals, and many people will die. I'm no exception."

"Then Ragnarök comes soon?" Ingimar asks with the tone of one humoring a child.

Garmr shrugs.

"You'll not speak of it?" Ingimar presses.

Their captain says, "A man's fate is his own."

Ingirid coughs and kicks a pebble his direction.

"A warrior's fate is their own," Garmr corrects.

"Unless it affects kin or crew," Ingimar says, speaking of custom that is nearly old enough to be law. "Then the truth of it should be spoken."

Garmr picks up the pebble and tosses it in his palm. "As you say."

Erasmus says, "Ragnarök is the end, yes? I've heard many speak of this legend, but none have explained it to me."

"It's no legend," says Garmr, his voice heavy like thunder.

"If you don't understand it, you shouldn't ask about it," Ingimar says.

Erasmus says, "How can I learn if I don't ask?"

Rúnr is struck by the man's curiosity at such a dangerous subject. Also, he notes that Erasmus is no longer stuttering like he did at the outset of the journey.

"Don't learn," Ingimar snarls.

"Do you want to know the truth of it, Christian?" asks Ingirid.

Erasmus puts his palms up. "Please don't call me that."

"I'm going to sleep." Ingimar marches off to the ship and climbs inside.

"Listen close," Ingirid says, "and know what all know, from the Allfather to the osprey. Ragnarök is the war between the gods of Asgard and the ranks of Hel."

"A final battle between good and evil." Erasmus rubs his chin.

"No," Garmr says forcefully. "The Aesir are not good. Hel is not evil. These are foolish, children's ideas. War is between men."

"Men, eh?" Ingirid says.

Garmr throws his hands in the air and grunts in exasperation. "Between people. Towns. Nations. Call it whatever the fuck you want. There is no evil in Ragnarök."

"I think I understand," says Erasmus.

"I doubt it," says Garmr.

"My point," says Ingirid, "is that Ragnarök is an ending, but not the end. It's one time around the circle, but what circle do you know of that has an edge? This age of the Aesir, the gods, most of them, will cease for sure, but the circle itself remains for the next trip around. After flames lick the stars and blacken the sun, the gods who are prophesied to return will travel from Hel and collect in Idthavöllr in a great hall to drink and hunt together. And Líf and Lífthrasir will come forth from Yggdrasill, where they hid during Fimbulvetr, into a green field, and these two will repopulate the earth from their seed, and Midgard will be a place of eternal springtime, with no horrors or monsters left to torment humanity."

Garmr drops his pebble and nods his approval of the explanation. Rúnr also finds it elegant. Unlike the words of a seeress, it's direct and without dissembling.

"Two people, a man and a woman, in a green garden," Erasmus says.

"It is so."

"Have you heard of the Garden of Eden?"

"A Christian legend," Garmr says. "I've had enough of this talk."

He leaves the fire and enters the darkness, and they do not hear him anymore.

"Which legend is the Garden of Eden?" Rúnr asks. He knows of the Christ god and of the way Christians hide their holy men in monasteries, but of the rest of their beliefs he has cared little to learn.

So why care now?

He looks across the fire at Ingirid, leaning forward to engage the conversation.

His voice low, Erasmus says, "It's where God makes the first man and the first woman. It's not only Christian, though. The Saracens speak of this garden as paradise as well."

"Paradise, like Valhalla?"

"Not exactly, no. God created the garden for the living, not the dead."

"Which god?" asks Ingirid.

"There is only—my people believe there is only one god. I don't wish to offend you by saying this."

"You don't offend me, Christian. But you might consider if my gods are listening."

"Don't call me that. I don't call you pagan. My name is Erasmus. And the garden is where all of humanity begins." He breathes deep as if thinking.

"What is pagan?" Rúnr says.

"It—well, it's you. It's anyone who follows many gods."

"It's an insult, then?"

"It wasn't always. My point is the Garden of Eden. It's interesting that the end of your religion meets the beginning of mine."

"Ragnarök is not the end," Rúnr says. "Have you not listened to Ingirid? You Christians see only your way. This is why you die so easily."

Erasmus stands. "Do not call me that," he reasserts. It's the most violent action Rúnr has seen him take. The realization that he's placed himself in danger is plain on his face, but he doesn't sit, and he doesn't apologize. He stares at Rúnr, waiting.

For this, Rúnr gives respect. "I will no longer call you this."

"Nor will I," says Ingirid. "But I can't make promises for my brother."

Erasmus laughs, quietly and uneasily. "I'm going to sleep in the ship," he says.

Soon, it's only Ingirid and Rúnr at the fire.

"Tell me about your daughter," she says.

He reacts the way he might if he accidentally touched the fire, pulling back, protecting his wound. But just as quickly, the pain leaves. He finds he wants to talk about her. Not too much. Just enough to remind himself.

"She was ferocious," he says.

Ingirid laughs. "I bet."

"She wanted to learn everything, from tying knots to building ships. She always had a smile."

"Dark eyes like you?"

"No, blue like her mother."

"Where is her mother?"

"Dead." It's difficult not to let his voice carry his guilt. "She found the courage I could not at the time. She divorced me and went north for vengeance just as the blizzards came. She was never seen again."

"I'm sorry."

They are silent awhile.

"Have you ever traveled this far south?" Ingirid asks.

"No, but my father told of lands that appear on no map my people have seen. My mother . . ." He finds he doesn't want to talk of her now.

"She was not a Northerner."

He combs his fingers through his black beard. "You can tell?"

Ingirid gives that crooked smile.

"You should sleep," he tells her.

"You'll hold watch?"

"I will."

She comes to his side of the fire. "I'll watch with you."

He nods his acceptance and turns so that his back is to the fire. So that his eyes can adjust to the night. She sits beside him, her thigh against his.

"You're slow," she says.

Rúnr says, "I've killed as many as you."

"Slow of mind, fool," she says, taking his beard in her fist and turning his face. "Slow of eye and of mind."

She pulls him close. Their mouths meet. Their tongues battle. Their hands grope and grapple. She is strong like Berthe and bold like Velaug, with not a hint of modesty or submission. In moments, they're naked by each other's hands. It's deep into the night before they find sleep.

CHAPTER 37

A portage is no more difficult than rowing or fighting or fucking. It's rhythm and teamwork. Their ship, upside down and over their heads like a giant hat—their gear either secured inside, thanks to an intelligent system of hooks and latches, or being dragged on a sled behind—is much lighter than a raiding longship. Which doesn't make it light work at all. Rúnr's shoulders ache and his back is tight as a fist at the bottom of his spine. It's the sixth portage so far. Maybe the twentieth he's ever done, and he hates it more than the gods hate Loki Mischief Bringer's chaos.

"Are you sure this is the right way?" Ingimar complains.

They're half a day in, the longest portage of the journey, forced by a trio of storm-downed trees damming a bend in the river. The four men haul the ship with Rúnr first, Garmr in the back, and Ingimar and Erasmus in the middle, the merchant often tripping over roots or stumbling across loose stones. If their hands weren't holding the ship, Rúnr is certain Ingimar would have strangled their map seller by now.

Rúnr raises the bow above his eyes. No sight of Ingirid, who's gone ahead to scout the way back to the river. Though she's almost as tall as her brother and Erasmus, the difference is enough to tip the ship at an unwieldy angle.

"She went this way," Rúnr says, noting the cut bushes and branches widening the path, if it can be called that. "Wait, I see her."

She comes at a jog, one sword in hand. "Not far," she reports. "There's a place we'll need to lay down the ship and cut through some trees. After that, the river is in sight."

"I guess that's good news," Ingimar says.

"Give strength to your arms and legs," orders Garmr, "not your mouths."

The march continues, with Ingirid leading the way. Sweat beads on Rúnr's hairline and runs down his face, tickling his eyelashes and nose. The air in this forest is as wet as the hot springs themselves. Heavy as Odin's breath, smelling of mud and rain, yet no rain has fallen in over a week. He distrusts this place because of it. When the sky promises a storm, that storm should come.

As if hearing him, the sky chooses to let fall its rain.

"This is going to help," says Ingimar.

"At least you're under there, dry," Ingirid says.

The rain sounds like tiny war drums against the ship's hull. The ground immediately turns to mud, forcing Rúnr to think his steps to keep steady. As the bow, if he falters, the ship falls. If the ship is damaged, it'll be many days repairing it, meaning longer to reach Miklagard. Longer for Yrsa to walk in the darkness.

Worse, they're running low on supplies, their last raid coming five days ago, a farm that yielded little reward. More days spent in this forest and not on the river means greater chance of those supplies running out. And what a failure it would be if his Little Bear never sees Valhalla because he lies starved to a husk in this forest.

These thoughts turn to others. The desire to punch Ingimar when he complains so much. Asking Erasmus more about the red temple of Miklagard. The bounce of Ingirid's breasts when she is astraddle him. Those breasts becoming Berthe's, naked and wanting their first night together. Becoming Velaug's, young as he once knew her. What if Velaug nursed Yrsa instead? What if Yrsa's father had been Torstyn? What if Torstyn had loved Rúnr like a woman rather than a brother?

What if Rúnr went into the winter for their daughter, for revenge, instead of Berthe?

What if I went alongside her?

On it goes like this. Were he under torture, he suspects, he still wouldn't find the singular focus his crewmates know. His mind, his life, both lacking the simplest way of doing anything. Making great quandaries of all things: Could they arrive a day sooner if they raided one fewer village? Would that cause him to miss the Painted Fenn at fate's appointed time? What would he sacrifice to be there now? His life? His crew's? Erasmus? Ingimar and Ingirid? Garmr? His friends?

Yes, he thinks, they are his friends.

Am I the kind of man to kill a friend in pursuit of fate?

He knows the answer as he knows his own heartbeat: He'll happily kill them all if fate demands it. To avenge Yrsa, he'll take off Garmr's head, open the merchant's chest, cut Ingimar in half.

But not Ingirid.

Yes, he tells himself. *Even Ingirid.*

A liar speaks only lies. This, in Velaug's voice inside his head.

A liar thinks only lies. This, in Ingirid's own voice.

He shakes his head carefully so as not to lose step, but the sweat on his face, this itch in his nose, is going to set his mind to madness. He scrunches his face. Feels the tickle deep inside his nostrils. Braces himself. Sneezes. And nearly loses his balance.

"Watch it, raccoon tits!" Ingimar shouts.

"Pay attention," Ingirid tells her brother.

He says to her, "Want to take a turn carrying this?"

"What do you think?"

Rúnr thinks he would like to watch her pull off her wet shirt. Three nights of the past week, she's come to him after his watch.

They don't speak of it during the day, just trade covert smiles and occasional lingering touches, but there is a *something* between them now, like an invisible rope. Like the air right before Thor throws his lightning to Earth.

He enjoys it even as he doubts it. He craves it even as he avoids it. Of women, he's aware he knows little, but he does know that Ingirid welcomes him to her bedroll. And he knows that when he lies with her, he thinks less of Berthe and Velaug and Yrsa. Until sleep comes and the dream and the black mist. The closer they get to Miklagard the more certain he is there are other things in that black mist, shapes, shades, even beasts lurking, watching, waiting.

"Three times, you were told, then?" Erasmus says.

"Three times?" Rúnr asks, thinking he's lost himself in his many thoughts and missed the beginning of a conversation.

"That night we spoke of fate, you said you were told the god trance will take you three times before you come to the red temple."

If it were Ingirid asking him about this under the moon, when they lie entwined after sex, he would likely be happy enough to answer. Here, in portage, with all the crew listening, however, he's less keen on the conversation. But neither can he avoid it.

"Yes, three times," he says. "But the seeress made no mention of the number of days or months that would correspond to the three times."

"Eh, I've known more than one seeress," Ingimar says. "They're all the same, twisting details until they're like a knot tied by a child who doesn't know what she's doing."

Yrsa knew what she was doing from the youngest age, Rúnr thinks. Knots and threadwork were as natural as feeding at Berthe's breast for her. Never once did she tie a mess that had to be cut apart. He smiles at the memory of her holding up a sail's knot, beaming her smile.

"Just like yours, Papa," she said, the two of them out in the harbor at dawn for some lazy fishing.

He's glad the ship hides his face.

Ingirid asks, "What is it like?"

Other than Torstyn, no one has ever asked Rúnr this question. He wants to tell her it's pain and fury and exaltation. It's being cut and fucking and seeing the face of Odin all at once. But these are thoughts flying into and out of his mind like ravens racing to and from a battlefield.

"It builds and it's sudden," he says. "It's like any battle-rage, but then more. It's—" He almost tells her it's not worth it, but that would be an offense to Odin. "This is what you should know of it: When you see the god trance upon me, and you will know it when you do, or when I tell you not to be by my side, be far away."

None of the crew reply. Soon, Garmr begins to hum a rowing tune. Ingimar picks it up. Even Erasmus knows it by now and joins in. Rúnr does not. Each step brings them closer to their goal, to his fate. And for the first time, he fears reaching it.

I'm tired, he thinks. *And hungry.*

Yes, that's it. That's all. He joins the song, his own voice deep and from low in his belly. Some minutes later, Ingirid calls a halt.

"The trees that need cutting are ahead," she says.

Rúnr slows, then stops, keeping feel for the march behind him. As one, they raise the ship and take turns slipping out from under it, to grasp it by the gunwale, so that when they all have it, the ship can be turned and lain down. Rúnr first, then in order, with Ingirid taking her place behind Erasmus at the stern. The process is smooth and without incident, leaving the ship sitting on the ground beneath the thick canopy of trees, the rain still falling.

"The river is there," Ingirid says, pointing.

Sure enough, through the trees, Rúnr sees the river flowing strong from the rain.

"Let's have a moment and drink," Garmr says.

"I'll get the skins," says Ingimar without a hint of complaint.

Soon, they're passing waterskins—their ale having run out days ago—with the rain slowed to a falling mist.

"It's late in the day," Erasmus says. It's plain what he means. Rest is needed.

"We'll make way for the ship," Garmr says, "and then make camp on the beach."

"A wise captain," agrees Ingimar.

Rúnr notes Ingirid's eye on him and thinks she'll come to him tonight. Or maybe, if one of the others takes the earlier watch, he'll go to her.

"What's that?" Garmr says, standing and looking at the tree line to the west.

"Tracks," says Ingimar.

Garmr turns to Ingirid. "Did you not scout the area?"

"They weren't there," says Ingirid.

"You're certain?" asks Ingimar.

"I know how to find tracks."

Ingimar points. "And yet, there they are."

"Are you saying I failed?"

Rúnr gets on a knee beside the tracks. "Men. Recent in the mud."

"Here," says Garmr, kneeling closer to the trees.

More tracks, clearly boots, crater the mud to the east and west, along the tree line. Heavy. Not hunters. Armed and armored enemies.

"Listen," says Ingirid.

Rúnr is already gripping his axe and retrieving his shield from the ship. The others arm themselves similarly as the enemy comes from the trees. Four from each side. Eleven more from the same path over which they've just brought the ship. There will be no escape without blood.

"A trap," growls Ingimar.

And such an obvious trap it is now that it's sprung. All the raiding Rúnr and crew have done, all the killing and burning to spread fear—it's worked. The Christians of this vast forested land heard and cowered and called for soldiers, and those soldiers marched the river, watching the ship day after day, finally slipping ahead to where they knew of a narrow bend. They found the downed trees, or cut them themselves to give appearances, and dragged them across the river to force the portage, to herd the crew to this spot where they could not escape with their ship. To outnumber and ambush them.

"Let's not make it so easy on them," says Garmr.

"Agreed," says Ingirid.

The crew adjusts positions to best account their strengths as learned from these weeks of raiding and fighting. Ingimar on one end with his bow. Gamr on the other to have room for his war-sword. Rúnr and Ingirid in the middle to rush the line.

"I'm ready," Erasmus says, behind them. He's armed himself with a sword and shield, though his grip is weak and will cost him his protection after a solid blow. Still, there's no hiding from this fight, and the merchant knows it. Rúnr respects that.

"Stay back and away from our swings," he tells the merchant as he eyes the enemy. Each wears mail. Some hold shields. Some swords, and some spears. Among the nineteen, one comes forward wearing more mail and steel plates than Rúnr has ever seen shared among three men. Striking him will be like striking stone.

"Shield wall?" Ingimar asks.

"You each have a unique talent for killing," their captain says. "Use them. And protect the ship."

They each know the importance of this command, but Rúnr's mind doesn't find the ship. It finds Ingirid's blue eyes. He wonders if the Christians would give her a proper funeral.

"Protect Erasmus too. All depends on him."

"On him?" Ingimar says.

"Do you want to have a conversation, or do you want to make blood?"

"Blood," says Ingimar with a grin.

"Blood," his sister agrees.

Blood, Rúnr thinks, weighing the difficult odds standing between him and his vengeance—between Yrsa and Valhalla.

The rain increases and runs in rivers off their helms and armor. One of the Christians speaks hurriedly to the heavily armored man. Another shakes his head and says more. One wants to charge, it seems. Another speaks patience. They're not of one goal as a crew must be. This is good. It's hope.

The heavily armored one, the leader surely, shouts a battle cry. The rest raise their swords and spears and echo the call. They come.

Rúnr's belly becomes a rock. His tongue becomes fire. His skull grows thick. He touches his bear's tooth as his vision tunnels to a point.

"Away!" he shouts to his crew, his friends, as the battle-din rises and Rúnr's mind falls. Like sinking.

I'm drowning.

Yes, that's what it is. He's drowning, but not beneath the sea. He's drowning into someone else, something else, that is not himself. Men scream. Blood flies. A hand falls. A leg at the knee. Half a skull. He's no longer drowning but rising, two men as one. A killer and a father. Engaged and uncaring. Enraged and calm.

He is himself and a god.

No, don't think this—the gods will not like it.

He bites his shield and tastes lightning.

Fuck the gods. I am Berserkr!

CHAPTER 38

Something is different. Wrong.

Bodies and limbs pile high somewhere, but he is not there. Blood falls like rain, but he is not wet. He is himself within someone else. Like a man on a ship without sail or oar, at the sea's mercy.

Because I am Berserkr.

The thought is jarring. He's never known himself when within the god trance. It comes. It takes him. He wakes later. But this . . .

Three times the god trance will take you. But not like before. And each will exact a toll.

"Papa?"

He's in a black forest of trees with no shape. Somewhere distant, he knows a black beast lurks, but beside him is a girl he knows. His chest swells with love and fear.

"Stay inside," he tells her. "Be brave."

Only they're not inside. Nor are they in the black forest anymore. They're simply in black. Like night without stars. A place of shades and shadows lost from all light.

"Papa," the girl says. "Follow me."

He follows as if it's the only thing he could ever want. She runs. He tries to chase, but running in the black is like running through the fjord's shallows. He knows only one thought: He must keep the girl safe.

"We're close," she says, shoving through the black the way she used to shove through goats loitering on the road.

"To what?" he asks. His voice sounds foreign.

She stops and points. "Lo, there, Papa. The world."

And it is truly all of Midgard before them, with greens and browns as far as any eye can see. There's no blue, however. Not of the sea nor of the sky. What there is, rising before them, is the tallest mountain ever seen. Tall enough that its summit is lost to view. Tall enough that it must surely be piercing the dome of the sky.

"Himinbjörg," he says, for the home of Heimdall the Watcher it must be.

"No," Yrsa says. She continues to point.

When he looks from her to Himinbjörg once more, it is no longer a mountain but a Jötunn, a godlike giant. A corpse of stone. Hrungnir, of course, slain by Thor. Except it's not Hrungnir either. The face is that of the Painted Fenn, the one who murdered the girl.

Purpose is blinding, deafening, encompassing all but the tiniest fractal of thought: *Vengeance now. Not in the name of a god, for no god saved my Little Bear. Vengeance for me.*

For Yrsa.

"Stand, Fenn," he cries. "Face me and know death has come for you, murderer of children!"

He strikes with his axe at the giant's face, but it's a face of stone, and the blow creates only sparks not wounds. The giant does not stir.

"Papa, the eye."

The giant's closed eyelids wait high above. He climbs, the girl beside him, until he reaches the first eye and strikes with all the might of his body. The lid opens. There is no eyeball, only the black.

"Inside, quickly," the girl says.

She goes first, and he follows. They make no sound as they travel from the black into a light so bright he can see nothing at all. Snowblind. Until vision comes and they stand before a man of stone, his flesh impervious. Within the black, the cloud-murk, the stone man comes.

"Your axe will not help, Papa," the girl says.

He wields it anyway, and it bounces off the stone man like trying to chop a boulder. The stone man swings fists of bedrock, slashes with talons like mountain crags. It's all he can do to keep from getting hit, for surely his bones will shatter under such a blow.

"The joints, Papa."

He understands and ducks below a vicious swipe. Instead of backing away for distance, he dives close, grappling with the stone man, wrapping his handgrip around the bicep. Leveraging with a boot in the stone man's gut. And now he pulls with all his might until a tremendous seam appears at the shoulder. Bone bursts and within the stone, sinews and tendons and arteries split and tear until the arm rips free and the stone man cries out in agony and falls to a pool of pebbled blood, the wrenched wound gaping.

Like a spear, like a trophy, he holds the stone arm high and then uses it to crush his enemy's skull with a single killing stroke.

"It is done," he says. Around him is only the black and no reply. "Yrsa?"

The black moves about him like serpents. Someone screams. He knows pain. He tastes blood. He feels . . .

I feel!

Wet.

Warm.

Falling.

Landing.

Familiar hands on his face.

"He fights well after all."

And then nothing.

CHAPTER 39

The whole of the armored man's shoulder and arm, in bare flesh, hangs below the serpent's head at the ship's prow. It's the day after the ambush, with a soft rain, no wind, and Rúnr at an oar, his head thick as wool and full of distant thunder. Worse than any rising after a god trance he's previously experienced. But this was no normal god trance, he understands. Nor will the following two be.

Is this the toll? An aching head and a Thor-sized hangover? He can handle this, he thinks. But what if the toll grows with each god trance? What if as the Berserkr he becomes weaker or can suffer injuries?

Why shouldn't I be wounded? he thinks, looking over the crew. Ingirid lost a chunk of her ear during the ambush. Her brother suffered a deep wound above his knee causing a limp. Erasmus, they say, acquitted himself well and was rewarded with a hole in his shoulder and two lost teeth. Garmr says he was struck mightily, but Rúnr sees no injury upon their captain. Rúnr himself has countless cuts and bruises from these weeks of raiding. He wonders if his crewmates are bitter that he's not suffered more.

Ingimar takes up the rower's song from his sister. They push and pull in rhythm, Garmr's deep voice adding to the thunder in Rúnr's head.

He'd been offered the steering oar when he woke, the memory of fighting the stone man fresh in his mind. The crew had already cut a path through the trees and readied the ship to sail, so he declined to take what was Ingirid's turn at the steering. The rotation matters in a crew. Why should his suffering be counted more than another's?

Why should I care for anyone else's suffering?

But he does care. Neither Ingimar nor Garmr is like a brother. Erasmus is no father. And Ingirid may be his lover, but there's no commitment between them—and since the ambush, she's been more distant toward him than before it. Despite it all, they're a crew. In Skyjavík he had friends and kin but never felt more than a tolerated outsider. Here, among strangers known to him barely a month, he's one of many bound to each other as strongly as the words of fate can say. And he likes it.

And of the toll?

Never before has he known himself within the god trance. Never before has he recalled the actions of his Berserkr self.

But were those his actions? And what of the black? Has he fought within it before? Is it the place of the god trance?

The greater question: Has he always had an ally within the black? If so, surely that ally could only have been Yrsa since her death. What of before?

He counts the times he was Berserkr before the night Yrsa died. Twenty-two, that was. Of course it was. Nine for Odin's nights upon Yggdrasill, and thirteen for Baldr's death at the trickery of Loki, the uninvited thirteenth guest to the handsome god's feast. He remembers nothing of those twenty-two times.

Despite himself, Rúnr seeks Huginn and Muninn, Odin's ravens, in the cloud-spotted sky.

"All right, I'll admit it," Ingimar says, continuing a conversation from earlier that morning, which itself had begun sometime the evening before. "The Berserkr is worth it."

Ingirid, more grim than her usual bright natured self after a battle, says, "No one asked you."

"Which is why I'm admitting, of my own. A good face for me, don't you think?"

"A good face for you is one I don't have to see when I wake."

"You prefer his face, black beard like a Saracen thrall?"

Rúnr turns, a retort sharp on his tongue, ready to slice in defense of his mother, but he holds the words. Ingimar talks to talk, not to intend. An insult from his lips is forgotten by him long before it's forgotten by the insulted. It's a wonder the man has not met Challenge after Challenge to his own death.

Rúnr sets his attention instead upon the armored man's arm, torn off from the body by his own bare hands—by the Berserkr's hands, he thinks, for surely there is some division between himself rowing and thinking in this moment and the version of himself that fights in the god trance—so his crew has told him.

"Thinking of all the ways that big strong hand can stroke you?" Ingimar says.

Erasmus coughs and loses rhythm before quickly recovering.

"Thinking of all the ways I can slap you with it," Rúnr says.

Ingirid laughs a little.

"Think of all the ways that man's steel armor could benefit a warrior," Garmr says at the oar behind Rúnr.

"So long as those wearing it don't face a Berserkr, eh?" says Ingimar.

"This Berserkr, Rúnr, I mean, is the only one, though," says Erasmus. "Isn't that so?"

Ingimar says happily, "Only one I've ever met."

"Only one I've ever heard of taking breath in our lifetime," Ingirid says.

"It's a long time since there's been one," Garmr agrees.

Still considering the armored man, who Erasmus earlier called a *bogatyr*, using the local language word for a hero, Rúnr says, "I can hear you."

"Of course you can," Ingimar says. "Berserkrs are known for their listening as much as their killing." He gives himself fully to laughter while somehow keeping time with his oar.

"May I ask?" Erasmus begins. "The god trance, how does it work? How does it start? I don't understand."

"Of course you don't, Christian," Ingimar says, the words potentially malicious but the tone playful.

"A jarl may ask Odin Allfather, for a warrior, a champion, to fight unwinnable battles," Garmr says. "If Odin favors the jarl, he may grant such a champion, a Berserkr who becomes an unkillable warrior when the odds are poor and defeat is imminent. A slaughter-beast who, while in the trance, is all fury and blood and death."

"It sounds . . . impossible." Erasmus scratches his beard. "It sounds like a difficult life."

"It's a great honor," says Ingirid.

Rúnr feels her eyes on him but says nothing.

"A rare honor," Garmr adds. "Rúnr is the first Berserkr in generations. He may be the first of many in this age. Or he may be the last Odin ever grants."

"I think I understand," Erasmus says. "I would like to write this down, maybe someday when we're dry."

Ingimar and Garmr laugh. Ingirid does not.

"I have a question," Rúnr says before thinking all the way through what he wants to ask. Or how to do so.

"Well," Ingimar says after some time. "Are you going to ask it, or do you want us to guess?"

The memory of disliking Ingimar is not so distant for Rúnr, and it returns often the way Thor's lightning splits and lights the sky.

"During the fight, was there—did any of you see a black mist?"

"There was rain," offers Ingirid.

"Cloudy," says Erasmus. "Little sun."

"I saw dead men," Ingimar says, still laughing.

"A black mist is no common thing in Midgard," says Garmr.

Rúnr turns as much as he can, but Garmr is intent on his rowing and betrays no insight. Still, it's a curious response. All these weeks, and Ingimar is no longer the one Rúnr fears trusting. It's their captain, Garmr, who withholds, like a seeress speaking in riddles at times. Like the god Mimir knowing so much more than can be shared with mortals or even Odin himself.

"Do you see a black mist when you enter the god trance?" Erasmus asks.

Rúnr doesn't know how to answer. Every time? This one time? Now and ever more after?

"I remember nothing of what I am or what I do when I'm Berserkr."

"Not even tearing off a man's arm?" asks Ingimar.

Not the armored man's, Rúnr thinks. The stone man's, however, he does. And the black and Yrsa. He remembers so much, yet none of it as the others remember. Maybe this is the toll Velaug spoke of. Such disunion between action and memory, enough to bring most people to madness. But he's known a fractured mind so long, it's not a toll he must fear, he tells himself.

Not a toll I must fear, he repeats.

"Nothing of it," he says.

"What of other things, then?" Ingirid asks.

"Other things?"

"Does a Berserkr only fight?"

"What else could one do?"

"Hunt," says Garmr.

"Build a ship," says Ingimar.

"Cut a mine into a mountain," suggests Erasmus.

Ingimar says, "My sister wants to know if a Berserkr can fuck."

Garmr laughs like the booms of an earthquake, drowning out any rebuttal Ingirid may have.

"The god trance is not for fucking," Rúnr says of the foolish question—the dangerous question—while keeping his oar in rhythm.

"Break a woman in half, would you?" Ingimar says, still laughing.

"You're not the first man to boast like this," Ingirid says mirthlessly. "None ever live up to it."

The laughter is so loud it would announce them to any Christians near the river. Even Erasmus joins in.

"I would not be a man," Rúnr says, like Ingirid finding little humor in this topic.

A man's arm torn from his body is not the worst thing he's done within the god trance. Though he doesn't remember doing them, he's seen the results. They haunt his dreams. Eyes wide in horror upon heads flung far from their shoulders. Bodies torn in half at the waist. Enemies hacked so small the remains could feed newly hatched fish. And the bite marks. He can't know they're from his own teeth, but he knows they're not from any other man's. Gouges torn from flesh in ways only a wolf might, but with no wolf tracks nearby.

"Seems like it might be worth the risk," Ingirid says, the first hint of playfulness in her today.

"At least wait until we make camp," Ingimar says. "Tough to row with you riding his cock and him killing us all."

"A Berserkr does not fuck," Rúnr says, seeking an end to the conversation.

"A gelded champion!" Ingimar says.

"Definitely not that," Ingirid says. "I've seen it."

Ingimar shouts as if calling to another ship, "Maybe Berserkrs like cock more than tits, then."

Erasmus coughs and loses rhythm.

"Do they not have cock lovers in Miklagard, Map Man?" Ingimar asks.

Erasmus says, "You're quite interested in cocks today."

Garmr laughs even louder than before. "The Christian wins this round!"

"Don't call me that," Erasmus mutters.

Rúnr hears him, but it doesn't seem the others do. Ingirid is shouting jibes at her brother, who is threatening her with a hunting accident. Garmr seems content to laugh and row and point out exotic trees and their exotic names, while Erasmus seems most willing to row and speak only when needed in defense.

On like this they go, with Rúnr trying to focus on the only thing that matters: The god trance has taken him once. There are two left to come, and Miklagard and his fate are that much closer somewhere beyond the southern horizon.

CHAPTER 40

He's waiting for Ingirid, away from the fire. She knew he would be, but still it took some courage on her part to come into the darkness with him. After what she's seen. After what she's decided she might tell him.

"Your brother has the watch?" he asks. He's sitting against a tree, his black hair and beard masking his face in the night.

"He has the watch." She doesn't mean to sound so . . . formal.

She sits cross-legged, close enough he could touch her. Neither moves for a time. Her bandaged ear, what's left of it after the battle two days ago, throbs. She presses two fingers to it, which relieves some of the pain.

"Can you still hear?" he asks.

"I can."

More time passes. Night birds *chwak*. Small animals scurry.

"It's not the same now, is it?" he says.

"Rúnr—"

"It's okay. It must be terrifying to see."

The god trance, he means. He doesn't have to say it. She doesn't have to guess. "You—it was, yes, terrifying. But exhilarating as well. A real Berserkr."

"I knew you wouldn't come last night. I thought maybe not tonight either."

The truth Ingirid won't admit aloud is, she's not sure she was going to come ever again. But not because of what she saw. What she witnessed him do—that's why she did come. No, what she's wrestled with since she saw him in the god trance is this sudden, awful urge to share her story with him.

"I'm here," she says.

"What did I do?"

"I didn't see it all."

He turns his head. The fire, though not close, flashes in his eyes. She slides closer to him.

"I saw arrows and spears break upon your armor and your flesh," she says. "I saw your eyes grow even darker, deeper. I saw you—it was just my roused battle-sweat, surely—but I saw you grow larger."

Rúnr grunts gently.

"The enemy came in threes and fours, and I had to battle well. When I saw you again, you were on your back, the man's knee on your chest, but you had his arm twisted. You reached inside his breastplate and gave a roar like a bear swallowing a wolf. Then I lost sight of you once more, but I heard the ripping and the rending of his muscle and bone as you tore his arm from his body."

"What did I do then?"

"The next time I saw you was when our enemies were all slain, at least seven of them by your hand. Why do you think the god trance came that time and not another?"

"I asked a seeress once. She spoke only riddles, and not good ones, if I'm to judge."

"Because we were so outnumbered, maybe."

"I've always assumed it comes at those times when, if it didn't come, I would not survive. Did you see me . . . return to myself?"

"You were lying on the ground among the dead. I thought—" *I thought the impossible, and it nearly broke me.* "I thought maybe the stories of a Berserkr being unbeatable were wrong."

He laughs, the kind that hides pain. "Was I snoring?"

Now she laughs and past memories of joy and anguish flood her mind. Now the words come. She can't stop them. "I had a daughter once," she says.

There's no rush in his response. This pleases her, as if this night might last as long as they need it to.

"I am sorry for you," he says. Then, after more time, "Tell me about your daughter."

It's as if a blacksmith's anvil is lifted from her chest. No one asks this. Even Ingimar has not spoken of it since the night she died.

"Saanna." Saying her name is like breathing free after being held underwater. "Her name was Saanna. I was old enough to marry, but I wasn't married. She was born with no eyes and too weak a heart. She lived just over a week."

Her voice breaks as she remembers. Her mother, Predslava, was gone by then, lost to a fever. Her father, Osmond, was gone too, lost during a summer raid. All she had was Saanna and Ingimar, and all her brother did was chide her.

"We don't name them before the first gift to the gods on the ninth night of breath," he told her when she whispered the girl's name shortly after she was born. "Just take her to the sea and leave her. There's no other future for her, sister."

But he was wrong. There were eight days for Saanna. Eight nights of her snuggled to Ingirid's breast. Eight nights of flesh against flesh, mewling and blindly grasping for her mother. Eight nights before her breath finally left her.

Rúnr doesn't chide her. He takes her hand tentatively, as if expecting her to pull away. She does not, instead entwining her fingers with his. The night passes like this without the need for more, for either of them.

CHAPTER 41

The parapets of the fortress, clad in brick and lording over the river with a sternness befitting the gods, are as red as the setting sun. Rúnr sees it first at the steering oar while the others row hard, heads down, all of them sweating like Rúnr can't ever recall in the North—and Erasmus insisting all the while, with summer still a few weeks away, the heat will only increase.

"Is this it?" Rúnr asks, for the city surrounding the fortress sprawls double the span of Uppsala. "Is this the temple of Miklagard?"

The others look up but no one stops rowing.

"It's not," Erasmus says, wearily.

He doesn't consult a map. No one asks him to. He has proven himself accurate time and again so that Rúnr has wondered more than once if a map is even necessary with him along. He knows the names of the rivers they travel and the towns they pass. He's even told them just yesterday, Rúnr now remembers, that they are in the land of the Bulgars. Clearly this is not Miklagard yet.

He sighs. Ingimar grumbles. They row on.

The way has been difficult since the god trance. Five days on the river, most of it at the oars or portaging the ship, and what towns and monasteries they've spied have been fortified and too large for an assault from the five of them. Supplies are running low again. Tempers are running high. Ingimar is a storm of bluster and threats. Erasmus, growing thin now and muscled so that he could almost resemble an old warrior, is more skittish than he's been, but he stands and speaks more like one of them than not. Even Garmr's good humor is lessened of late. As for Ingirid, she comes to him most nights now, though they spend as many of those nights simply talking quietly and sleeping comfortably as they do enjoying each other. For Rúnr, it's a pleasant change even if the heat continues so that he can't help but think that fire is cooler than this Christian air.

There's beauty too. More green than he's ever seen, and not even a hint of snow atop the highest peaks they pass. He finds himself too enthralled to even listen to Garmr as he names trees and massive insects that each buzz like a bee swarm.

In all this, he finds comfort repeating Velaug's words over and over within his head. In remembering Yrsa helping cook soup or chase down a stray sheep. In the way Ingirid eats, rows, hunts, and what more? She's quick with her blades, wise in battle strategy, and fearless in the fight. She shouts freely and kills with joy and lies content beside him at night in a way that Berthe never did.

"It's Ruse, I think," Erasmus says a time later.

"So it is," says Garmr.

Ingimar is the first to lift his oar from the water. "A place you know?"

"A place I know."

"High walls," Ingirid says.

"We're not here to raid," Garmr says.

"We have little to trade."

"We have him," Ingimar says, nodding at Erasmus.

Ahead, the river bends. Fortifications are built on either side. This ship will not pass through safely.

"We beach there, at the turn," Garmr says. "Tell us of this city, Erasmus."

"What's the point if we're not raiding it?" asks Ingimar.

"I asked, is the point." Garmr's tone leaves no doubt who remains captain.

"They call Ruse the Red City for the bricks that come from the river's clay," Erasmus states.

"The Red City," Rúnr muses. Maybe it's not Miklagard he seeks. A city of this size must have a temple. A red temple in a red city. He rises to his feet, steady though the ship lists some. "Is there a temple?"

"There was the last time I was here."

"How long ago was that?"

"Twenty years, about."

"And this temple, for what god?"

"It's a Christian temple."

Rúnr feels it coming now. Fate.

"Dedicated to Mary," says Erasmus.

Rúnr feels it fleeing now, like the last drops of beer from a horn. "Mary?"

"The mother of Jesus."

"Not hanged?"

Erasmus shakes his head. "We're not in the place you seek."

"Let's burn it all," Ingimar says. "We can watch from here and see what's left after everyone inside has cooked."

He means it to start an argument, Rúnr thinks, but no one speaks against the idea. They're hungry, their meat gone three days ago. Thirsty, their water gone two days, leaving them only the flowing river water to drink.

We don't belong this far south, Rúnr thinks.

Opplanders have traveled far, of course, but this far? And still they remain weeks from Miklagard. It's almost too much to comprehend—the gods sending him so far to avenge one buried beside his own house.

"There," says Garmr, pointing to tree cover. "And fear not, friends. Meat and ale and more will soon be with us."

"So far from the city?" Ingirid asks.

"This is where we must be."

Ingimar doesn't offer the complaint Rúnr expects as they row to the sandy beach and climb from the ship and stretch in the last rays of the sun. There will be no relief from the heat, however, Rúnr has learned. Even night in these lands is like a sweaty armpit after battle.

"Stopping here is foolish," Ingimar says. "We should kill and run."

"If you think the night is enough cover," Ingirid says.

"Or even simpler, sneak in like thieves and take what we need and be gone."

"It is a walled city," Erasmus says.

"And you're an old man," Ingimar says. "What other facts should we trade?"

"I'm telling you of the place you want to raid."

"How about we trade him for a basket of mutton?"

"Let him speak," Rúnr says. Most of Ingimar's antics are like the summer mosquitos of the Opplands. A small nuisance not worth his attention when there's hunting or fighting to be done. But sometimes, he wants to punch the fool just to see his mouth bleed.

"Thank you," Erasmus says.

Ingimar glares. Ingirid gives a sideways look at Rúnr, but he's not certain what it means.

"The walls here cannot be climbed," Erasmus says. "Thieving is impossible without someone letting us in. And it's a large city, even if it's barely the breadth of a single parish in Constantinople. The five of us can't possibly affect an attack here."

Rúnr does not miss the way Erasmus includes himself in the count.

"We're not sneaking inside," Garmr says. "Nor are we raiding or laying siege."

"What are we doing, then?" Ingirid asks.

"Waiting. See the trees there? Bring the ship so that it's not so easily seen from the river."

They do as ordered, dragging the ship with Ingimar grumbling the entire time, what's left of the armored man's arm dangling and bouncing as they go. They're nearly to the trees before Rúnr hears the dogs, and then the horses after that. He springs away from the ship and reaches for his axe.

"Ambush!"

Ingimar is at his side, with Ingirid flanking wide.

"Hold!" Garmr calls.

"Do you not hear?"

"I hear. Hold and meet friends. Fight and lose much more."

"Don't like it," Ingimar says. His bow is in hand, an arrow nocked, when three men and two dogs come through the trees. A fourth man can be seen in the shadows of the woods with two, maybe three, horses. "I can halve their number before they get closer."

"Stay arms," Garmr orders.

He approaches the men. Words are exchanged, Rúnr noting there doesn't appear to be anyone translating. Within a few moments, their captain returns.

"Our reputation has grown," says Garmr.

"This is why we've come, to hear what others say of us?" says Ingimar.

"I expected to have to send a messenger in the morning," Garmr continues without pause for Ingimar's gripes. "But knowing we were nearing, my friend has kept men along the river the last few days. They heard us as they were preparing to quit for the night."

"Your friend?" Ingirid asks.

"He'll come in the morning. For now, we make camp, but no fire."

"Who needs one?" says Ingimar. "My ass is a swamp."

Garmr grins the way he used to before the voyage became so difficult. Seeing this gives Rúnr confidence. It'll be a good night, he thinks. Erasmus gathers their remaining vegetables, carrots and leeks mostly, and hands some to each.

"A good night, it'll be," Garmr muses, looking up at the sky. "And my friend Vasil will come at dawn with all I've arranged."

Erasmus coughs up a carrot and spits it out. He looks about wildly a moment before drifting away from the ship into the shadows of the trees where he sits pensively. No one seems to notice but Rúnr.

"And what is it you've arranged?" Ingirid asks. "We have nothing but trinkets from our raids thus far. How can we barter for all we'll need to complete our journey?"

"There's always something to barter."

"Oh, just explain what we're trading or shut up already," says Ingimar.

Garmr pops a leek into his mouth and chews thoughtfully before speaking. "Our ship."

CHAPTER 42

"Welcome," Garmr says, arms wide.

Five of them have come through the trees this morning, equipped like warriors though Rúnr thinks they're more like inexperienced mercenaries relying on appearance as their best weapon. Their bright cloaks are too long, apt to be caught under foot, and of a thin material that can offer no protection or warmth. Their swords hang at their belts, undrawn. Two hold spears. Good solid-looking weapons. One even points his, sort of, at the crew. The other's spear points at the birds and the clouds and the gods above.

Rúnr moves cautiously to Garmr's right while Ingimar and Ingirid take position to protect the ship. None of them know if Garmr was serious last night about trading it as he refused to answer questions before finding a loud, snoring sleep. Between Rúnr and Ingirid, there was some speculation but no conclusion. All Rúnr is certain of now is that these five do not appear to be interested in the ship, nor do they seem skillful enough to sail it.

"Did we volunteer to train children?" Ingimar says.

One of the men with a spear calls out into the woods. His voice is answered by another from the trees.

Erasmus hisses an unfamiliar word. Rúnr looks back to find the merchant's eyes locked on the five.

"Do you know what they're saying?" Rúnr asks. When Erasmus doesn't answer, he shouts the merchant's name.

"What—yes," the merchant says. "He's telling someone that it's safe."

"Dumb as well as dressed like fools," Ingirid says.

"Keep calm," Garmr says. "We don't want to scare these wee lads, do we?"

Ingimar laughs and spits in the direction of the five. The one with his spear high takes a step forward but is stopped by the other spearman. They argue. Ingimar spits again. The coming of boots through the woods ends the conflict before it begins. Four more come through the trees, all mounted upon healthy mares, three of them equipped like the five, and one dressed like a lord, though Rúnr has never seen a lord so colorful in all his life. The man's cloak alone looks like a rainbow vomited upon a swallow.

"Is that you, Vasil?" Garmr calls. "There's gray in your beard now."

The lord, Vasil, comes forward, motioning for the eight warriors to hold back. Ingirid and Ingimar move to flank Garmr. Rúnr lets his hand find his axe but doesn't raise it, trusting their captain's lead.

In the language of the North, Vasil says, "And yours is as yellow as ever, my friend. Is such a thing possible for the years it's been since we shared a drink?"

"What is, is possible. Isn't that so?"

"Wise words. Whose?"

Garmr finally lowers his arms. "Yours!" He laughs uproariously.

Vasil joins him with his own guffaws while motioning for the warriors to relax. Not one of them seems to, but Vasil pays them little mind. He dismounts with skill, and once he's down, Rúnr can see he's a large man with a round belly, approaching Erasmus's age.

Against the obvious concerns of his warriors, Vasil crossed the distance between the two lines and he and Garmr embrace.

"Shall we share a drink today?" Garmr says when they separate.

"I've awaited such with great anticipation," replies Vasil.

"I hope you've brought good spirits, my friends. I'm sorry to say ours have run dry."

Vasil doesn't appear surprised by this. "Of course, my friend." He motions at his attendants. Two of them dismount, each bringing a three-legged stool that had been tied to their horses. The stools placed, they return to their mounts again, one now bringing goblets and the other two ceramic carafes. Their job done, the attendants stand silent by their horses.

"Guess we're not invited," says Ingimar when Vasil motions for Garmr to sit opposite him on one of the stools.

While the lord pours from one carafe for himself and Garmr, Ingirid separates herself from her brother to approach Rúnr.

"I don't like him," she whispers. "Or them." She nods at Vasil's entourage.

"We trust Garmr," Rúnr says, though his words sound more like a question to his own ear.

"Do you really think this guy wants our ship?"

"Doesn't seem a sailor."

"Maybe we can sell him something else."

"What do we have?"

Ingimar comes to where they stand. "I still say we trade him." He nods at Erasmus, who doesn't seem to be listening.

"Enough for an ale, maybe?" Ingirid says.

"Doubt it."

Rúnr leaves the twins to speak with Erasmus, eyes never leaving Vasil's men. He doesn't like them. Not for being formidable, for they clearly are not. For their apparent inexperience. There is little more dangerous to a shaky truce than an idiot who acts rashly.

"How do you know them?" he asks.

Erasmus says, "I don't—I've never met them."

"But Garmr does, so what can you tell?"

"They're Radhanites."

"Should this mean something to me?"

"Jews. Merchants, of a network that touches the farthest lands the Greeks ever dreamed of, in all directions."

"The North?"

"Part of my trading routes, yes."

"And this man, Vasil?"

"I know nothing of him."

"But you know their words."

"Yes. The men at the trees speak with bravado. They whisper of the ways they can kill us. And what they could do to . . ." He looks to Ingirid.

Rúnr almost laughs out loud at the thought that these men, even seven against one, could bring Ingirid to submission.

"Well," says Garmr standing, the personal portion of his meeting with Vasil complete. He points to their ship. "Here it is."

Vasil rises from his stool and walks the ship's starboard length, then again the port length, until he comes to stand beside Garmr.

"It's a beauty," Vasil says. "As promised."

Ingimar places himself between Vasil and the ship. "It's not for your eyes or hands."

Rúnr sees Ingirid's frustration with her brother in the way her shoulders sag for the briefest moment before she jogs the field to stand beside him, swords drawn. Which brings weapons to bear from Vasil's men.

Which brings Rúnr at a run to Ingirid's side, axe in hand.

"Friends, friends," Garmr says.

Vasil speaks a heavy command in his own tongue. His men waver, uncertain. Rúnr suffers no such indecision. He's locked on to the one still mounted as the first to die.

"Put your weapons away," Garmr says. When none do, he speaks again. "Ingimar, you pile of splintered hooves, put your sword down now."

"There's no barter you can make that's worth our ship," Ingimar says.

"You'll sail over the mountains, then? Or portage this fucking thing to within sight of Odin's breath so high over the pass we must take?"

Mountains! Rúnr longs to see them, suddenly, deeply—to know how they compare to the mountains of the Opplands. A strange feeling, like an unexpected hunger at the mention of a roasted boar.

"Is this the way?" Ingirid says.

"It is."

"Let our map man tell it."

Garmr sighs. "Erasmus."

The merchant doesn't move at first. Garmr calls him. This time he comes, though Rúnr can see much of the old fear—that which enveloped him when he first joined the crew—in the way he walks. But after all they've seen and done together, what can be feared here?

"How is the way to Miklagard?" Garmr asks.

"East, to the sea," Erasmus says, head bowed low. "Four or five days, maybe. Longer if we spend time foraging or raiding. Another four or five across that sea to reach Miklagard."

"Where they'll see us coming a day away, vulnerable on the water. What about by land?"

"If there's a pass over the mountains, with good horses we could make it in eight or nine days, perhaps."

"A knowledgeable friend you have," Vasil says to Garmr. To Erasmus: "Do I know you, friend?"

Erasmus says, "Certainly not."

"I feel I might."

"This is our merchant and map seller," Garmr says. "From the city itself we seek."

"I, too, am from Constantinople," Vasil exclaims. "Your face seems so familiar. Perhaps you knew my father, Solomon?"

The way Erasmus hunches, Rúnr thinks he's about to be sick. But he straightens right away and turns to look Vasil in the eye.

"I left the city many years ago," Erasmus says. "I was no more than a boy. You could not have even been born then, I would think."

A lie, Rúnr is certain, but a lie to a potential enemy is no worry to fret over when there are weapons drawn. He holds his position.

"Kin of a sort, then," says Vasil, "even if we don't know it. Will you all come feast with me in the city?"

"I think that would not bring the proper attention on you from the lords of the city," Garmr says.

"Quite right. Quite right." Vasil laughs.

"Tell me, our bargain is in good standing?"

"Yes, yes. Of course. I forget myself. The trees here are thick, however. You understand. Your exchange for the ship waits on the road."

"As agreed?"

"As agreed."

Rúnr notes the way Erasmus slinks back to the river.

"You won't be insulted if we examine it," Garmr says, no question found in his tone.

"Of course. Of course." Vasil sweeps his arms wide as if the entire river and forest are his gift.

"Ingimar, Rúnr," Garmr says. "Go."

Ingimar, like a tree, doesn't move.

"The deal is struck. I ask once more, do you want to carry the ship over the mountains? Or risk arriving too late to our destination?"

"Go," Ingirid tells her brother.

"How will we know if the deal is honored?" Rúnr asks.

Garmr says, "You'll know."

With a shrug, Ingimar sheaths his sword. Ingirid and Rúnr put away their weapons as well. Vasil instructs his men to do the same.

When it's done, Ingimar and Rúnr pass through the woods. At the road, two more men wait with a pair of strong horses and a wide wagon. The men back away, but not too far.

"This is worth our ship?" Ingimar says.

Rúnr doesn't think so, but he understands their position of need. "It's what's necessary," he says.

"Make sure these twats don't stab me from behind." Ingimar approaches the cart and looks inside. "Is this all?"

Rúnr comes to see and finds supplies enough for a few days. Salted meats, fish, barrels of beer, breads, and vegetables. And enough empty space for much more to be added. It seems a good haul, but worth a ship? Surely not.

This he means to say to Ingimar, and that perhaps they should consult with Garmr, but when he looks upon his crewmate, he finds instead a hollow cheeked ghoul, flesh peeling back from his rotting skull.

"Do you hear me?" the draugr-like Ingimar says. Continuing before Rúnr can shake off the vision, he says through decaying lips, "I've had enough of these games."

The Ingimar-thing draws his sword and runs through one of the men. The other, eyes wide, opens his mouth to scream.

Rúnr takes his axe from his belt and throws it in a single motion, the blade splitting the man's face. He falls with a thud. A horse snorts in discomfort. Birds fly from the trees. All else is still. When he turns to Ingimar, his crewmate is whole and youthful once more.

"Why?" Rúnr asks, taking a moment to close his eyes before retrieving his axe. He's known since they met that one day, Ingimar's rashness would put them in danger. That it comes so close to Miklagard, with the way laid out before him, makes it difficult not to split the fool's chest. But he is crew. They are five and will not function efficiently as four. And for that, four would be three because, despite their closeness, he is sure Ingirid will take her brother's side. He places the axe on his belt.

"Needed something to balance the trade," Ingimar answers. He heads back into the trees, laughing merrily.

By the time Rúnr catches up, Ingimar is standing beside Garmr grinning like a fool.

"Alescki will be your man," Vasil says to Garmr. "It's arranged."

"You've done as promised," Garmr says. The two men clasp hands. Then Garmr's eyes find the blood on Ingimar's forearm. "What is this?" their captain asks.

"All is well," Ingimar says innocently.

Rúnr feels the change in Ingirid. It's her brother's tone. She knows what he's done. Her hands go to her swords again.

"What have you done?" Garmr seems to grow larger and darker in stature as he says this.

There's a shout from the woods. Rúnr turns. Two of the men are missing, having gone to check on the wagon, perhaps. Another shouts. The bodies are found. Potential friends are now enemies. Rúnr wields his axe.

"Fool!" Garmr says, even as he grabs Vasil by the throat.

"No, wait," Erasmus shouts.

Ingirid spins into action as Vasil falls dead, neck broken, on top of the two carafes, crushing both. She slices into Vasil's men like a feral cat among a litter of mice. Rúnr does the same, felling one of the mounted warriors with a well-placed throw. Ingimar, laughing as if all is well in the world, draws his bow and downs the other two horsemen. Rúnr retrieves his axe and continues to kill. Swinging, chasing, hacking. In minutes, the fight is over. The crew stands, unharmed. The Radhanites lie in pools of blood.

"I should cut you to pieces," Garmr says, coming for Ingimar.

Ingirid stands in his way. "Don't," she tells him.

Rúnr thinks he'll plow over her like a bull over a chicken, but he stops.

"There were armed men at the wagon," Ingimar says. "They weren't going to let us leave."

Garmr seems to consider this, his tongue lashing out as if tasting the truth of the words. He goes to Vasil's body and kicks the pieces of the carafes, their wine spreading like blood.

"Be away from my sight," he says. "Both of you."

Ingirid leads her brother into the woods, in the direction of the wagon.

"You had a hand in this?" Garmr asks.

Rúnr says, "There were armed men."

Garmr, growling deep in his throat, turns to Erasmus. "Do you still fight with us?"

"I—we should not have done this," says Erasmus.

Garmr paces like a wolf. "Do you still fight with us?"

"We are," Erasmus says carefully, "crew."

"Strip it," Garmr says of the ship. "Everything we can use or carry, rigging to sails to nails. Get those cursed twins on it too."

"And you?" Rúnr asks.

Garmr stalks off into the trees to the south without an answer.

"You did know him, didn't you?" Rúnr says to Erasmus.

The merchant says, "I knew—I knew of him."

Another lie? Rúnr can't be certain. He heads into the trees to find the twins. They're arguing beside the wagon when he arrives.

"It's not the time to question our captain," Ingirid says.

"Rurik was wrong about him," Ingimar claims before seeing Rúnr. "What of you, come to argue as well?"

Rúnr says, "We have to leave this place."

"Strip what we can from the ship?" Ingirid says.

"Aye."

"I'll get the sail," Ingimar says. "Wonder what he has in mind for the return home."

At this, as the twins head back into the trees, Rúnr's care for the current moment is lost. Yes, they need to be gone before they're discovered. Yes, there are secrets piling up among the crew. Lies as well, which pains him even as he knows it shouldn't. He's not here for them, he insists within his mind. He's here for himself. For Yrsa. For the gods who want him to mete out this vengeance.

Except, he seeks more than one vengeance. From Miklagard, he means to return to the North, to face Leif and Ubbein for the death of Torstyn. What happens now is not—cannot be—isolated from what happens next. Without a ship, how is he to return home?

CHAPTER 43

"A good ship it was," Garmr mutters.

Ahead, not so far now compared to when they set out this morning, drab bister mountains rise like a wall. Like the body of Jörmungandr, the terminus of Midgard itself.

"He says that once more, I'm going to run him through," Ingimar says.

No one answers. All eyes are ahead. Or to the trees on either side of the road. Though the people of this place are poor—their two raids since they left Vasil and his men dead at the riverside yesterday have returned no gold and little of use, save for some dried fruits, nuts, and a meal's worth of tart wine—it remains a dangerous land they ride through upon Vasil's horses. Garmr, Ingimar, and Ingirid lead the way, with Erasmus and Rúnr's mounts pulling the wagon. As on the ship, this is a rotation they share.

And through each rotation, and the two raids, their captain has said little but to lament the ship he'd planned to trade away in any case.

"We'll meet the pass with sunlight remaining," Ingirid says.

"A good ship."

Ingimar pulls up his horse. "Now's the time," he says to his sister.

"It isn't," she tells him.

"Time for what?" Rúnr asks, recognizing the same conspiratorial look between the siblings he noted yesterday.

"Reminding Garmr what we've come for."

Ingimar grunts his agreement.

"Do all Northmen care so for their ships?" asks Erasmus.

"*Stígandr*, I called it," Garmr says. "Did I tell you this? *Swift Traveler*."

The merchant gives voice to Rúnr's thoughts: "I've never sailed a ship with a name."

Ingirid says, "We sailed into the land of the Slavs on a ship called *Eljun*. *Endurance*."

"Who cares for a ship's name?" says Ingimar. "I care for meat and mead and fucking."

"There's meat in the wagon," Rúnr says.

"Don't look at me for fucking," Ingirid says to her brother.

"Nor I," adds Erasmus, his voice barely above a whisper.

Garmr laughs.

"He remembers humor," says Ingirid.

"I remember," their captain says. "Sometimes deep thought is more important, though."

"Did your deep thoughts conjure anything useful?" Ingimar asks. "A plan, perhaps?"

"A plan?" Garmr says. "Are we in need of a new one? We have our goal. We have our map and our map man. We follow the road over the mountain. Then to Miklagard." He kicks his horse to a trot.

The twins, after a shared look, follow, forcing Erasmus and Rúnr to count their start with the horses so that one doesn't pull the wagon unbalanced over the other. It's a pleasing moment for Rúnr, feeling like a crew again. He knows he shouldn't invest in it. Whatever their goals after Miklagard, he doesn't share them. But to feel a part rather than apart—he relishes it. As he relishes the view of the mountains. After all their time aboard the ship, to be on horseback now, and to ascend nearer the gods, offers a contentment he's not felt in a long time. It reminds him of the South Mountain. The hot springs. Of peace.

"We seek a man called Alescki," Garmr says when they've matched speeds, the wagon trundling along briskly.

"So there is more of a plan," Ingimar says.

"You might have heard it from Vasil himself if you hadn't forced his death."

"He would have forced ours."

"Not my friend."

"You have such confidence in a Christian?" Ingirid says.

"He was a Jew," Erasmus says.

"As if the difference matters," says Ingimar. "The warriors at the wagon meant to slaughter us when our backs were turned."

Ingirid says, "It doesn't matter now."

"The wagon has supplies for the three days over the mountain," Garmr says. "Plus room for much more. The more will come from Alescki, in a town called Syanka on the other side of the pass, already paid for by Vasil in our name. This is what my ship was worth."

"Syanka?" Erasmus says.

"You know of it?"

"I know the name. The word. It means a shadow."

"Why should I give a fuck what words mean in their language?" Ingimar grumbles. "Their word for a sweaty asshole can be ball-sack for all I care."

Rúnr's frustration with Ingimar has grown since yesterday. He bites back a retort that will have them all at each other's throats. "Tell us," he says to Erasmus.

"I only speak of it because I've heard of places with similar names," Erasmus says. "Places best to avoid. Places where old spirits torment the living."

"You're trying to scare us, like a child's story," Ingirid says.

"Go on," says Garmr, whose beard is dark and bright in the sun all at once.

"The word means not just the shadow of an object. It can mean the shadow of a man. It's sometimes given to a place to make it seem less welcoming to . . . well, to travelers like us."

"A shadow, like on the ground, you mean?" Ingirid asks.

"No, no. Not shadow exactly . . . I'm not sure of the word in your language. A shade. A soul. The shadow of his life."

Ingimar's mount slows. Ingirid looks back, her brow creased. Rúnr thinks he knows what Erasmus speaks of, remembering well the stories boys would tell at night around a fire, or that men would tell in foreign lands under moonless skies.

"There's an Oppland story," Rúnr says. "A greedy man promises to look after a neighbor's sheep one Yule. The neighbor's wife is ill, and he's lame having lost a leg in battle the previous summer. The greedy man tends the sheep in the deep snow the first night and then the second, but when it becomes clear none are watching, he begins to bring the sheep from his neighbor's land to his, two per night until he's left his neighbor with half a flock while doubling the size of his own."

"We have stories like this as well," Ingirid says. "The greedy man was not sated, however. He wanted all the sheep and so during a great snowfall, he went out to bring the rest to his land, but one—the last one—ran off. Unwilling to let it go, he kept after the animal until the snows were too deep, and he froze to death."

Rúnr finds himself impatient to pick up the story once more. As much as he's always enjoyed hearing great tales, he's never been a teller of them. Here now, riding toward these dire-looking mountains, the telling is all he wants. More than a drink. More than Ingirid beside him in the night. He wonders if this is what the great skalds feel when they sing their poems. What Velaug feels when the gods speak through her.

"The next night, with none in the village yet aware of what's transpired, the dead man rises, rotted and black," Rúnr says, remembering Ingimar's decayed face near Ruse. "The man was held by the curse of his own greed to the place where he died, forever haunting that land. Attacking any who dare approach. A scourge that no hero yet has been able to vanquish in a dozen generations."

"Draugr," Ingimar says. He spits, as one must when speaking of the cursed.

"A cairn-wight," Ingirid adds. "A dead man who wasn't cremated, who returns to life to plague the place where he died or where he's buried."

Rúnr's mind turns to Ingimar once more, and the Ubbein-thing. His stomach rolls uncomfortably. Then he thinks of Yrsa, unburned in the ground of his home. If he fails to find the Painted Fenn, will she face a similar fate?

"In any case, Syanka is the place we go," Garmr says. "And we must go quickly. Look, the spring storms are late this year, Vasil told me. He'd hoped we'd miss them, but it seems they will not miss us."

Rúnr's attention moves back to the mountains, to the sky above that's grown black like the darkest of storms. Like the skies of Fimbulvetr are told to be.

"That's a big storm," Ingimar says.

As they ride, the black grows like a river overflowing its banks until it seems it might swallow the world.

"Like angels at war, Vasil said these storms could be," Garmr says. "Dangerous and worth our care."

"Angels are idiot Christian ideas," says Ingimar. "I've sailed worse storms than any that's found me on land. We need not fear what terrorizes Christians."

"We terrorize Christians," Ingirid says.

The twins share a laugh.

"Vasil was a Jew," Erasmus reminds them.

He is ignored as they ride on.

Eventually, Ingirid asks the merchant, "Have you seen storms like this?"

"Only from afar, but there are stories of God's wrath flooding the world."

"What wrath could match Thor's thunder?" Ingimar boasts.

The answer, Rúnr fears, might be the very storm into which they're riding.

CHAPTER 44

The mountains are taller than those of the Opplands. If Rúnr thought them a wall from a distance, as the road rises to the pass, he now thinks they're every wall ever built. Perhaps they're the world itself, and he's only lived his lifetime in shallow foothills, never knowing what truly lies out there.

It's not the height that gives him pause, however. Or even the black clouds swirling above like the ocean's maelstrom in the sky. It's the shape of the peaks. He thinks again of the world itself and knows he doesn't stand upon the slopes of Jörmungandr's flesh. He stands upon the bones of Ymir himself. This road, his spine rising to his shoulders. A place people were not meant to stand, let alone climb.

Yet climb they do.

"This pass will take us direct, over the mountains to Syanka," says Garmr. "From there, the road flies straight to Miklagard."

"Says your dead Christian friend," Ingirid says.

Erasmus shakes his head. The gods add their thoughts by cracking the sky with lightning. The following thunder rolls like waves. Rúnr keeps his horse steady, but Erasmus is not an experienced rider. His mount rears, dumping the merchant, and circles wildly before bolting back the way they came. Rain falls hard and with purpose.

"Hold," Garmr orders, his voice competing admirably with the thunder, when Ingirid kicks her mare to give chase. "We're not going backward."

"We'll be walking if it happens to four more horses," Ingirid says.

"Then we'll walk. Forward."

Rúnr, of a similar mind to Garmr—forward to Miklagard no matter what—hands his reins to Ingimar and dismounts to help Erasmus, who is dazed and muddy.

"Are you broken?"

"I don't think so," says Erasmus.

Ingirid rides near, speaking, but Rúnr can't hear her. She dismounts.

"We should walk," she says.

She signals the same to Garmr, who nods and passes the message to Ingimar. Down a horse, they decide to hitch a third to the wagon to help with the growing mud on the road. Garmr keeps his mount's reins firm in hand. The storm, as if offended at their passing grows fiercer and the sky darker until Rúnr cannot tell if it's day or night.

"We have to reach the top," Garmr says, the five of them huddled as close as they can be so voices can be heard.

"Agreed," says Ingirid. "Too dangerous to camp on this incline."

"Then what?" her brother says. "Sleep in the wagon and hope we don't drown?"

Rúnr doesn't find the rain so uncomfortable, but the air has gone from too hot to too cold in a snap. He's shivering, though he does his best not to show it. A Northman cold in the south—how Torstyn would laugh!

"We could carry on through the night," he says.

"We could stop whining like babies and remember we have the ship's sail to make camp," says Ingirid.

"Always have to be so smart," her brother says.

She sticks out her tongue in the most childish way. The most attractive way, to Rúnr. Ingimar flicks water from his fingers at her. She laughs. They press on, the remainder of the day fading fast as the pass brings them up near its height.

"Finally," Ingimar says with the summit in view.

The ground rumbles in response.

"Together," Garmr shouts.

The road roils beneath their feet, then half the road simply disappears. Gone in a mudslide, no more than a horse-length to Rúnr's right. Erasmus clings to his arm like a child. Staring into the darkness where the road had been seconds ago, Rúnr doesn't shake him off.

"Carefully," Garmr says.

"Yes, we see that," Ingimar says.

The ascent soon levels. Rúnr guesses it must be well into the night now. The mountains rise high to the east, the road dotted with bushes and small trees. The crew is soaked and beaten down, yet they continue, slowly. Too slowly.

"We can't go all night in this," Erasmus says.

Rúnr watches the words on his lips more than he hears them. There's no shame in calling a camp, he knows. It's late. The pass has them far above the world below. A misstep would send them over the edge, but they're closer by the day to Miklagard. To vengeance.

"There!" Only Garmr's voice carries. He's pointing to a ridge of boulder and stone, a row of short trees growing off it at an angle. "We'll make shelter with the sail."

I will not be halted by a storm!

Lightning strikes close enough to turn the sky white and fill the air with the scent of burning earth. Thor does not like being challenged.

Rúnr knows when to listen, even if he does so begrudgingly. The process of making camp is slow. They're soaked as the drowned when it's complete. No fire will burn. None complain, save for the horses who don't fit beneath the sail. These they tie to the wagon, and then to a tree. Cups and skins are set in the wagon to collect the rain, and food and drink are brought under the sail so the crew can huddle together and try to find warmth, the sky splits with blinding light every so often, thunder rumbling their bones.

"Tastes like piss," Ingimar says of the wine.

"You'd know," his sister says. "And the taste of boiled boots too, eh?"

"You promised we'd never speak of that."

Garmr laughs. A promising sound, Rúnr thinks, as he joins his captain.

"Shut up, cow fucker," Ingimar says.

"You sound jealous," Rúnr says. "Miss your favorite cow?"

"Miss your mother's cunt."

Words that would bring violence any other time, with any other crew, Rúnr knows to accept from Ingimar. To play on and add to. "Mine's dead. Trade for yours?"

"Stop," Ingirid says.

"Taking his side, sister?"

"Would you have me take yours?"

"You'll have to fuck her to get it, it seems," Garmr says, still laughing.

Ingimar pouts. "Not my type."

Rúnr can barely keep from laughing long enough to say, "She doesn't moo?"

Ingimar is on his feet, as tall as he can under the sail, going for Rúnr. A punch lands. A counter strikes off mark. Mud is thrown. Then a stone from the side, hitting Ingimar. He stops and looks at his sister. She, crouched, not hiding her grin, points at Erasmus.

"You fucking map fucker," Ingimar says. When he goes for Erasmus, however, he slips in the mud and lands face-first.

Rúnr thinks he might piss himself from laughing so hard. Ingirid seems in a similar state, as do Garmr and Erasmus. Soon enough, Ingimar is sitting on his ass, face caked in mud, snickering. With the next crash of thunder, so strong the ground seems to billow beneath them, the mood evens. They sit in a circle, Ingirid and Garmr at Rúnr's sides, eating and passing the wine.

"How far to Miklagard after we meet this man Alescki?" Rúnr asks.

"Less than a week, I would think," says Erasmus.

"You think?" Ingimar says, with more humor than malice. "Tell me again why you're here. I've not seen the map you carry, nor have I seen anyone else look at it. Seems to me we need one or the other—the map or you. Why both?"

"I could say the same for you and your sister, no?" Garmr says. "One or the other is good, why have both?"

"You'd go into battle with even fewer numbers?"

"Same answer to you."

"What of the walls?" Rúnr drains a wine skin and sets the empty to collect rain.

"The walls of Miklagard make the walls of Ruse look like twigs," Erasmus says.

Garmr wipes his beard. "Shall we look at the map?"

"Don't trouble yourself on my behalf," says Ingimar.

Erasmus passes his eyes from one to the other, seeking direction. When neither speaks, he removes the folded map from inside his shirt. It's wet but not damaged. He unfolds it and hands it to Garmr, who glances but does not study. With the map in his hands, Rúnr can see there's a second map on the back, this one of a city with streets and buildings labeled in a wavy script. There's also a series of lighter lines, sometimes made of little more than dots, running across and through streets and buildings. What they signify, Rúnr doesn't know.

"The walls won't be a problem." Garmr folds up the map and hands it back. "Who has a story to tell?"

Ingimar tosses an apple core into the center of the circle where a fire would be. "That's it? No more talk of Miklagard and walls?"

"We'll talk more when we're close enough to see the walls," Garmr says. "Now, we're cold and wet, set at a dank camp upon a distant mountain. It's a night for stories."

"I can tell the story of Ragnar Lothbrók," Ingirid says. "He sailed more than a hundred ships to the Frankish capitol of Paris and set to plundering its riches."

Rúnr knows this history well, the invasion of Paris occurring when he was a boy. There were no stories he preferred more than those of Ragnar.

"Not that story," Garmr says. "I want to hear your stories."

"You know ours," Ingimar says.

"Erasmus," Rúnr says. "What brought you to the North?"

The merchant looks at his hands. "I'd rather not talk of it."

Same, but it's you or I . . .

As if to make the point, the sky lights and thunder smacks. Outside, a horse's complaint is barely heard. The ground rumbles once more.

Garmr smiles. "The gods want to hear your tale."

"I—it was long ago," Erasmus says. "I was a poet. I told you this before. A poet and a scholar."

"Yes, you have," says Ingimar. "Is there an exciting part?"

"I spent much time at the court of the emperor, my charge to record and to research what he wanted to know, day or night. Also, I tutored his family. Siblings, children, any close or distant kin who sought knowledge, I was at their disposal. He—there was a night. I fell in love."

"With the emperor?" Ingimar asks, elbowing Garmr and laughing.

"No, no. I met—it was a not a love that could be allowed, so we kept it secret. I was not royal, you see. I—there were promises made. Betrothals that couldn't be broken. We kept on like conspirators. Like thieves. Until we were caught."

"A fight, then? If you're not going to tell us of her breasts or the smell of her cunt, then some action, yes?"

"You're a pig's testicle" Ingirid says to her brother.

The twins argue a moment, while Rúnr watches Erasmus. His eyes are damp. His hands wring together. This is a difficult telling. "You were punished," he says. "We understand. You had to leave."

"I was imprisoned," Erasmus says. "When—after I got out, I was shunned. There was nowhere to go, so I went west. Then north. Along the way, I met some distant kin who taught me their ways as traders. This is how I came to Uppsala."

"A good story," Garmr says, gathering another wineskin.

Ingirid places her hand on Rúnr's forearm. "Your turn," she says.

"I've told my story," Rúnr says.

"Not all of it," Ingirid says, looking into his eyes.

Rúnr finds he can't deny her. Not upon this mountain beneath this storm, so close to the gods—it's a night for sharing as a crew. Garmr offers the wine. Rúnr takes it. Drinks deep.

"I've spoken of my daughter, Yrsa, my vengeance and the red temple. There's more. Before I came to Uppsala and met you, I was an outlaw exiled from my home. Before that I watched my jarl's Hersir, my protector since I was a boy, murder the jarl's son, my brother. Before that I lost a Challenge, defending myself in the Circle against the accusation of murder because I killed assassins sent for my head. Before that, my brother and I slaughtered an entire village in the Fennvold seeking the painted man who killed my daughter. Before that my wife divorced me for not going sooner in search of vengeance, then she went during the coldest of winter and perished in the snow. And before that, I lived in a small house and was content."

Thunder makes the mountain shake. The wine comes around again. He holds a mouthful as if holding his breath before diving below the water. Then he tells of that night, being woken by the sounds of the invaders. The words come from deep inside. He has no need to think of which to speak next. Berthe ready to fight. Yrsa holding his axe. The Painted Fenn coming into his house. The battle. The god trance.

"I came back to myself quickly from the god trance that night, sitting on the floor, a weight upon me I did not at first understand, and the Painted Fenn bleeding, limping, fleeing into the night with blood on his blade. I tried to go after him. By Odin's beard and eye I tried, but the weight . . ."

Now his eyes grow wet and his vision blurs. His words catch in his throat.

"It was Yrsa in my arms, body limp, eyes open, throat as well all the way to the bone, her grip on my axe still strong." He laughs a little. "So strong."

Ingirid places a hand on his shoulder. No one makes a joke about their intimacy.

"Berthe came in and saw. She took Yrsa but not before I promised my Little Bear that the Valkyries would come for her. I swore it, but they have not come. They will not come until I kill the one who cut her down."

CHAPTER 45

Rúnr seems on the edge of tears, holding desperately to a semblance of stoicism, as if emotion is weakness. Ingimar makes a face. Ingirid knows better, however. There's no weakness in mourning a lost child. No weakness in showing pain to those close to you. Erasmus seems to know this as well, his head tilted in empathy. Garmr also, nods approvingly.

And Ingirid remembers. Her mother. Her father. Her baby girl, Saanna. Her guilt, her culpability, is as alive now as it was then while she watches Rúnr seek his next words like a coalfish gasping for water upon the beach. His guilt is real and true. She doesn't begrudge him this, as she feels her own like a knife alive inside her, slicing away more and more every night. Yet for that, the pain has been lessened of late, she realizes. As if it's now a shared burden between her and Rúnr, each of them carrying a little of the other's through understanding. She squeezes his shoulder.

"May you find your vengeance," says Ingimar earnestly.

At this, Ingirid is pleased, for her brother hasn't taken to friendship in a long time.

"May you find it," Garmr says.

"Yes," says Erasmus. "May you find it."

Rúnr sits silent, the crew sits silent, leaving Ingirid to consider her role, and his, ahead. The advantage of having a Berserkr when they reach Miklagard is obvious, but it's what comes after that she now weighs. There will come a time when she and her brother must face Garmr—named for an agent of Ragnarök—as foe not captain. In such an endeavor, Rúnr's strength added to their own will be essential.

Is this why she's so drawn to him?

It is not.

She's used men before to achieve goals. That is not what she's doing now.

Thunder rumbles. The rain shifts direction, slanting the sail they sit beneath so that it drains behind Garmr.

"May I ask more?" Erasmus says.

Ingimar settles down so that he's almost lying flat. "Ask what you want. I'm going to find sleep." He closes his eyes.

"I want to ask about vengeance."

"You don't understand what it is?" Garmr asks.

"I understand why you seek it, for the pain of wrongs done to you or your loved ones, but won't it then continue, never ending?"

"Continue?" Ingirid says, uncertain of the man's intention. "Vengeance ends the killer's life, and if he's an unjust person, he'll not find himself in Valhalla."

Erasmus thinks on this a moment, his face going through contortions as if the process of thinking is a physical one.

"And the worthy dead go to Valhalla?" he asks.

"They do," says Garmr. "If they die honorably in battle."

"And this is what you each seek for yourselves?"

"We do," Ingirid says, having to turn her head occasionally for the diminished hearing in her damaged ear.

"Then why the need for vengeance? Your loved ones who have died are there, correct, in the place you want them to be—the place they want to be?"

The question is as startling as the next crash of thunder, this one louder. Closer. The ground shakes.

It's a test, Ingirid thinks. The storm. The questioning. This entire campaign. She'll do what the gods demand and prove herself.

"Valhalla—" she begins, ready to declare the difference between the joy of the afterlife and the responsibility of this life.

"You don't know a fucking thing," Rúnr says, eyes dark as the storm. "My Yrsa does not feast in Valhalla. She won't until her murderer is met and killed."

He seems ready, even hungry, for Erasmus to disagree. Eager to raise arms. Ingirid notes Garmr smirking within his beard, seemingly calm, but his hand creeping toward his sword. Erasmus appears shaken and shaking.

"And you will kill this Fenn," she says quickly. "The laws of love and life and the gods demand what they demand, a person's destination in Valhalla regardless."

"I didn't—I mean no offense," Erasmus says. "I'm seeking to learn."

Rúnr grunts. Maybe a word. Maybe just the noise. Ingirid takes it as permission for Erasmus not to fear violence tonight. The merchant, after a look to Garmr—whose hands are now folded across his belly—seems to take it the same.

"Of vengeance, then," Erasmus says. "You'll seek yours, but what of theirs?"

"Whose?" Rúnr asks.

"The people you kill. This Painted Fenn has kin, yes? His family will then seek vengeance against you, will they not?"

Ingirid understands the words but not the meaning of the question. "All who are wronged may seek a price."

"He has no kin," Rúnr says. "I've already killed them all."

His tone, his strength, draws first approval from Ingirid. Then desire.

"His jarl, then? Or a brother who's been away for a time and discovers what you've done. If he comes and kills you, won't your family then seek vengeance on them?"

"I have no family," says Rúnr, as if he's admitting an ill deed. "When I'm killed, there will be none to find vengeance for me."

When, not *if*. As it should be, Ingirid thinks, for a warrior should die in battle.

"No," she says. "I'll seek vengeance for you."

"Thank you," Rúnr says.

"And then someone comes for you," Erasmus says to her. "And then your brother for them. And so on."

"And on," Ingirid says, thinking he understands but doesn't comprehend.

Erasmus licks his lips thoughtfully. "It's a circle that never ends."

"It's the way we live."

"And the way we die," Rúnr says.

"As the gods demand," Garmr says. "But it's not never-ending, as you say. All vengeance prices end after Fimbulvetr with the coming of Ragnarök."

"But you've told me Ragnarök is not an ending."

"Correct." Garmr points as if Erasmus has been caught stealing. "After Ragnarök, the blood prices of before, even those unpaid, become null. But new wrongs traveling along the circle will call for vengeance."

"It all comes back to this, then," Erasmus says.

You get it now, Ingirid thinks. The circle. The rotation of life and death without end. Seeking pleasure in the big and the small. Again, her attention shifts to Rúnr. He's thoughtful, bordering on morose. She understands why and thinks that when she lies in his arms later, their sleep will be cathartic.

Thunder rocks the mountain, shaking it unlike before. Ingimar sits up.

"Under attack?" he asks, his words thick with sleep.

Another jolt shudders the mountain. Erasmus cries out and grabs at nothing, for there's nothing stable. Until the quaking stops.

Ingirid climbs out from under the sail, swords in hand, expecting dragons and angry gods. What she finds instead is much worse.

"The horses," she says, looking at the void where they were tied to the wagon.

The others join her at the edge of a new cliff where the road has given way, sending their wagon, mounts, and all their supplies into a great chasm.

CHAPTER 46

"We need to find food," Erasmus says.

"Amazing you haven't been made King of All Christians, with such insight," Ingimar snaps.

They trudge on, each carrying a heavy length of the ship's rigging ropes and a narrow strip of its sail, sweating so that there isn't much difference in how drenched they are now versus during the storm. A day has come and gone since the storm wore itself out. Since the loss of their horses and wagon. Little sleep since then. Less water. No food. And now, on foot, evening approaching and still two or three days before they come to Syanka where they can resupply.

"Yes, getting killed hurts," Ingimar continues. "Women have tits, birds fly, and hungry men need food. Isn't that wise and grand?"

"And most idiots have cocks," his sister mutters. She's a little ahead of Rúnr, eyes always forward.

They all know they must go south. They must find food. They must succeed.

I will, Rúnr thinks, taking comfort in his fate. Only to quickly lose that confidence for the uncertainty Velaug's prophecy casts on his companions. He doesn't want to see them harmed, but what a warrior wants is less important than what needs to happen on a battlefield. Everyone knows this. He keeps on, thoughts shifting to the rest of the sail they no longer have, rolled tight and lying beside the road like a corpse. A burden they can no longer bear without a wagon.

They're like that, his crew. Essential, until they're not.

He eyes each one. Ingimar's bow will be necessary if they can find game to hunt. Garmr's sword would be missed in any fight. Ingirid's steel, her strength and determination, make them all the better for this quest. Erasmus, even he's become a warrior, to the addition of his knowledge and his map.

But only Rúnr can kill the Painted Fenn.

Somewhere above, birds cackle.

"There," Ingirid says, pointing.

Ingimar already has an arrow nocked. "Where?"

"I heard them."

"I can't shoot sound," Ingimar hisses.

Rúnr, a shielding hand to his brow, sees movement against the cliff far up. "Higher, below the crag, the one that looks like Garmr's beard."

"My beard does not—"

"Shut up," Ingirid says.

Garmr doesn't object. Erasmus moves from one side of Ingimar to the other.

"I see it," the merchant says.

Ingimar passes his aim erratically. "I don't."

"Shoot it," Ingirid says.

"What are you seeing?"

Ingirid gets behind him, up on her toes, places her hand on his shoulder and points. "Shoot there."

Ingimar looses the arrow. It plunks the mountain with a hollow sound and falls away, lost. No one speaks. Rúnr squints but can no longer see anything.

"What was it?" Ingimar asks.

"Eagle, maybe," says his sister.

"Vulture," Garmr says.

"Did you see it?"

"It was a vulture. We need to keep moving."

Rúnr wants to agree. He wants to grab their captain and shake him and shout that they need food or nothing else will matter. He wants to pull a handful of leaves from a tree and chew them until he can swallow. Come tomorrow, he might try this. The day after, it'll be strips of his shirt. Or from his boots. Has he ever been this hungry?

"Maybe we should try a little flesh," Ingimar says. "Back of the arm. Thigh. No real pain. Good meat."

Rúnr can't tell if he's joking, but no one tells him to stop speaking.

"I mean, some of us are softer than others," Ingimar continues. "More tender."

Erasmus, knowing full well what everyone else knows—that Ingimar is speaking of him—doesn't wait for more. "Are you volunteering your tender unused ball sack?"

Ingimar pulls a sword. "You fucking Christian. Forget your flesh, I'm going to drink your blood."

Erasmus, no longer the weak, rounded man Rúnr first met, pulls his own sword, though it's plain he doesn't want to swing it in anger. He's a man who finds his strength in fear. An ally good in battle but maybe not so much in a fight for temper or sport.

"How about we drink both, yours and his," Ingirid says, "and see which tastes sweeter."

Rúnr licks his cracked lips. They're in danger of turning on each other. He's heard of crews falling apart like this on the open sea, cast about with a torn sail or lost oars, unable to find shore. There have been stories of the unthinkable, what Ingimar now jokes of. It's talk the gods would not appreciate.

"We'll not need to eat each other, I think," Garmr says. "We've all been days without food before. Keep your wits."

"Not sure the fat one has," Ingimar says.

Though it's been weeks since Erasmus could be called fat, no one objects. All the better, to Rúnr. Let Ingimar burn his frustrations out the way Torstyn used to. When he was most frustrated with his father or his lessons, he would climb. Or run. Or fuck. Sometimes he and Rúnr would go off to hunt just to be away from Skyjavík. The South Mountain, near the ravine where his body now lies, they tracked every kind of animal and bird imaginable. Down the mountain and up. So high it was cold even in the summer.

"I have an idea," Rúnr blurts, suddenly full of energy. Such a simple plan, he should be angry he hasn't thought of it until now. Though weakened from lack of food, he jogs farther down to a sheer drop on the east side of the road.

"We used to gather eggs," he says as the others follow. "On mountains or the cliffs over the fjord, or sometimes out by the sea, where men can't climb unless they have rope. See, there!"

They each lean over the edge to see what he sees: a nest snug against the cliff, half obscured by a jutting rock, some ten man-lengths down.

"I don't see a bird," says Erasmus.

"If the gods are with us," Rúnr says, "there'll be eggs."

"A long way down," says Ingimar.

Ingirid says, "I should go."

"She's our best climber," Garmr says, a fact no one disputes.

"It's not just the climbing," Rúnr says. "It's the rigging. The balance. I almost fell more than once."

Ingirid says, "And I've never fallen."

"You've never climbed this way."

She grins. "And you've not done it in how long?"

"Since I was a boy. Torstyn and I would take turns, with—" He catches his tongue before speaking Leif's name. "We took turns, one climbing and one the anchor, then switching. It was a contest. Whoever could gather the most eggs won their choice of the lot."

"You're much bigger now than when you were a boy."

"Stronger too. It's a fair trade."

Ingimar says, "He can handle it. Better his ass falling down the mountain than yours."

Ingirid gives up the argument with a shrug. "Show me."

The rigging is not complex. A rope to tie around his waist, some stakes at the top to anchor it, and a pouch made of the ship's sail. Rúnr gives it all the same eye he would a ship before sailing or an axe before battle.

"Be careful," Ingirid says.

Her brother rolls his eyes. "Thank the gods mother is here."

She ignores him and kisses Rúnr on the mouth, a rare display in front of the whole crew. No one says a word about it.

The first bit is a climb like any other. Soon, however, a soft rain begins to fall, and the way grows treacherous. A fine moss grows in every crevice, slippery to both hand and boot. When Rúnr reaches the rock above the nest, he flattens himself against the cliff and collects his nerves. His stomach growls.

He braces his feet and shoves off the cliff and lets the rope slide through his palm, dropping below the jutting rock and swinging back toward the nest. He grabs at the ledge and almost loses grip, arching his back, grabbing frantically, getting his fingers into the grit and stone. He gives himself a breath, then pulls up onto the ledge, the nest wide and welcoming with four big eggs inside and no bird in sight. Four in one nest! Surely the gods are with him.

He collects the eggs carefully, one eye on the skies above and below. When he has them all, he begins the climb back up. More difficult. Longer. Exhausting. As he nears the top, he shouts to the crew, "You can pull now."

No reply. Perhaps the blowing winds are too much for them to hear, so he continues to climb, finally pulling himself back up to the pass where the crew are all facing away from him.

"Thanks for the help," he says.

Garmr turns first, smiling wide. "Look what Ingimar did," he says.

Their captain steps aside as Ingirid comes to Rúnr and looks him over, seemingly satisfied with what she sees.

Behind her, Ingimar is pulling one of his arrows from the breast of a golden feathered eagle. "One shot," he says proudly.

"What about you?" Ingirid asks.

"Four eggs," Rúnr says, though he's less satisfied now than he was.

"What's wrong?"

"Nothing."

"Come on, then," she says.

She sets to making a fire while Rúnr watches Ingimar begin plucking the eagle. They already had the eggs, he thinks, killing the mother eagle as well just feels . . . excessive.

Garmr claps a big hand on Rúnr's shoulder. "We will eat well tonight," he says. "And then, to Miklagard."

"To Miklagard," Ingimar says.

Ingirid says it. Garmr shouts it. Rúnr can't help but repeat it.

Even Erasmus joins as the crew chant it over and over, making their destination known to the mountains, the wind, the sky, and the gods.

CHAPTER 47

A half day's march from the mountains, three days after Rúnr collected the eggs, the crew finds Syanka, a fenced village nestled in the mountain's crook. The bustling of farmers—though what they might be farming in such rocky and barren terrain, Rúnr doesn't know—and herders of hogs and goats is plain even from this distance. A good omen. Below is no draugr-blighted ground as Erasmus seemed to fear.

"Not so dangerous looking," Ingimar says as they make their descent.

Garmr grunts an agreement.

Rúnr sets his sight farther afield, spying flatlands the color of wheat to the south. North and west, the mountains. East, teeming lands and the shimmer of dank waters such as can be found in meres and marshes. His stomach grumbles, but it's simple hunger now rather than the threat of starvation. The gods deserve thanks—or will if this Alescki comes through as promised.

What Rúnr took for a rudimentary herder's fence around the village is revealed to be more substantial, at least at intervals, the closer they get. An odd construction, actually, with lengths of formidable barrier interspersed with post and beam sections low enough even a lazy cat could jump over them.

"Rebuilt," Garmr says.

Rúnr agrees. And recently too, the cut ends of the logs say.

"A battle," Ingimar says.

"A raid," his sister replies.

When they descend fully from the mountain, setting them on level ground with the village, the people of Syanka begin to come, lining the fence at its low sections.

"Not so welcoming," Ingirid says.

Ingimar says, "Maybe they didn't get Vasil's message."

"Maybe they don't plan to honor the deal," says Erasmus.

At this Garmr stops and glares at the former merchant. "Maybe we'll discover their intention better if we approach rather than guessing from a distance."

"Do you speak their language?" Rúnr asks Erasmus.

"I've not heard their language."

"You knew the name of their village," says Ingimar, "and what it means."

"I know the word. It could have been given to the village a century ago. Three centuries. Who's to say the people here speak that language?"

"You're to say," Garmr says. "Go."

They continue together until they can make out the individuals of Syanka clearly, armed it turns out. Hearty and bearded men. A few women with the look of farmers and workers. Axes, shields, spears, and spades threaten from their hands, though Rúnr thinks it's mostly a show. Still, five against a village is not so easy without holding the initiative of surprise. Even less easy without a Berserkr under the god trance, and he doesn't feel it coming for him. Yet.

"Possible," Ingimar says softly, surely weighing the odds of success, same as Rúnr.

"Doable," says Ingirid.

"Unnecessary," says Garmr. "Go, find Alescki," he adds to Erasmus.

The merchant sighs but doesn't argue. Shoulders back, posture strong, he approaches the fence while the rest of the crew wait. A lifetime from the merchant who first boarded Garmr's ship, Rúnr thinks, as he watches the villagers' faces and stances for any hint of danger. Halfway between the crew and the fence, the distance of the longest of longships, Erasmus sets his feet.

"Hello," he begins, then repeats the greeting in five other languages Rúnr doesn't know.

A black-haired man comes to the fence. He argues with two others, then climbs the fence to stand, sword in hand, alone before Erasmus, an easy spear's throw between them. The man speaks a single word. Erasmus repeats it. A conversation grows, halting but respectful, it seems. While this continues, Rúnr considers the village. Nearly three score watch from the fence, mostly men, but the village is large enough for twice that. So where are the rest?

Rúnr hears the name Alescki from Erasmus. It's repeated by the villager, who shouts it back over his shoulder. The name is repeated three times more by others.

"He's coming," Erasmus says to the crew.

It doesn't take long. Alescki is nearly as old as Erasmus, taller, and with keen eyes. He comes to the fence but does not climb it. The black-haired man Erasmus has been conversing with moves to speak with him.

"You're the ones come with Vasil's recommendation?" Alescki calls in the language of the North, his voice deep and strong.

Erasmus looks to Garmr for instruction. A nod from their captain says the crew should join their merchant.

"The one I spoke with is the village chief," Erasmus says. "He's aware of our deal with Alescki but spoke of a new development."

"What development?" Garmr asks.

"He wanted Alescki to speak it because it's his deal."

Garmr tugs at his beard and looks at Rúnr, who shrugs. They'll either fulfill the deal or there will be blood. The shadow of a bird, huge wingspan, crosses them.

"We are the ones come from Vasil, on his word," Garmr says to the older man. "I'm Garmr, Vasil's good friend."

"I am Alescki, also Vasil's good friend."

"Shame our mutual friend isn't here to suck someone off," Ingimar mutters.

"Then we're agreed on fulfilling our friend's deal?" Garmr says.

Alescki says, "Prove you are his friend."

A grumble escapes Garmr's chest as he produces pieces of a ceramic jar from a pouch at his belt. "There was trouble on the pass," the captain says. "A landslide took nearly all of our supplies. This is what Vasil intended us to bring, this very fine wine. I apologize on my friend's behalf and understand that we may need to renegotiate portions of our deal."

"Renegotiate my ass," says Ingimar.

"Shut your mouth," Ingirid says to her brother through gritted teeth.

Rúnr watches Garmr spread out the pieces of the jar in his hands, surprised as much for the appearance of Vasil's wine carafe, which he never saw Garmr collect, as he is for how politic their oft-bloodthirsty captain is being.

"A shame," Alescki says.

"Truly," Garmr agrees. He places the pieces of the carafe on the ground, then faces Alescki once more. "I must admit, coming on Vasil's word, we expected somewhat more of a welcome."

"On another day, you might have had it."

Alescki doesn't rush the pause, letting it linger until Rúnr thinks he might have to go pull the man's tongue from his mouth to make it speak again.

"We've suffered a tragedy," Alescki finally says.

Garmr breathes deep and nods to Erasmus. Diplomacy is best left to those who know its ways.

"My—our hearts feel for your tragedy," Erasmus says. "We too have suffered loss. May I ask of yours?"

Ingimar paces to Rúnr's right. "Waste of time."

"I've been asked not to speak of it," Alescki says. "Unless . . ."

"We come at Vasil's word," says Erasmus. "Such word must be worth a trust."

Though the chief has not spoken a word of their language, it seems he understands enough and motions for Alescki to lean over the fence. While they speak quietly, Ingirid comes to Rúnr.

"Do you feel anything?" she asks.

He knows she means the god trance. "No."

"A difficult fight without help."

"It won't be a fight," Garmr says. "Not yet."

Rúnr wants to agree, but doubt nags.

Alescki coughs, ready for the crew's attention once more. "I'm to speak for our chief as he does not know the words in your language."

"We listen," Garmr says.

"I'm to say you may not come into Syanka."

Ingimar takes his bow from his shoulder, slowly. The villagers along the fence begin shifting nervously. Ingirid flexes her knees and arms. Rúnr seeks archers within the village but finds none. Garmr wipes the back of his hand across his mouth. What he says next will determine the day's blood. Or not.

"And of our deal with Vasil?" their captain says.

"That deal, I'm sorry to say, died when Vasil's wine was lost."

"What's so special about the fucking wine?" Ingimar says.

"A new deal, then, friend?" Garmr says, his smile wide like a lynx about to pounce.

"Are you strong enough warriors to kill a man?" Alescki asks.

"One man?"

Alescki looks at his chief, who nods. "Are you strong enough warriors to kill all of us?"

Garmr stares down the chief, who looks away. "We are."

"We should just do it," Ingimar says.

Ingirid's swords are out now. If Alescki means violence, he's giving the crew too much time to prepare. Rúnr chooses his route to the fence, a crossing way to keep arrows from finding his flesh. A man with dark bushy eyebrows will be the first to fall to his axe. Even Erasmus seems ready, tight but not tense, anxious but not afraid.

"Will you hear a tale?" Alescki asks.

The question is unexpected, even leaving Garmr silent a moment. He nods at Erasmus.

"We will," Erasmus says.

"In the days of my mother's mother," Alescki begins, "riders came from the dirty waters to the east. A strange place for riders, of course. Most ride the plains. But these were dark times and a dark people, if they even were people. They rode on bloody mounts, forsaking armor and even clothing. They . . ." He says an unfamiliar word.

"He says *androphagi*," Erasmus says, repeating the word. He turns to Garmr, then to Rúnr. "Flesh-eaters, of a legend older than Rome itself. Cannibals."

Ingimar spits. "We thought draugrs were bad."

"They came and took and promised to take more unless we gave willingly," Alescki says. "So we gave. Yearly, when the spring storms darkened the mountains, they would ride from the dirty waters and surround us and wait until we handed over what they desired. But not since my mother's youth have they come. In the years between we built this fence so that if they came again, we could keep them out." He pats one of the newer beams. "The fence did not work."

As Alescki speaks Rúnr becomes aware of something missing more than numbers. A feeling that something is not right in the village, though what it is he cannot say. Only that there's a feeling of absence. A thing that should be but isn't.

"They've come again, these riders?" Erasmus asks.

"With the spring storms like in the old days. They tore through our fence like it was built of twigs and took . . . what they wanted. And after, they promised a return at summer's height."

"What did they take?"

What is gone has left a hole in the village, a feeling of absence. And it's a familiar feeling, though Rúnr cannot yet name it. Though it makes him suddenly uneasy. Sweaty. Ready to run—though if toward danger or from it, he doesn't yet know.

"They took three, like in the old days." Alescki says. "But they demand thirteen when they return."

Thirteen again, returning Baldr's death to Rúnr's mind, the death of beauty among the gods.

"Thirteen what?"

"Children."

Rúnr recognizes it now. Only men and women at the fence. No children. No sounds of their play from further in the village. Are they hiding? Are they hidden away, the last great treasure the village has? He looks over the few women at the fence again. They're grim. Their eyes hard, unforgiving. In them, he sees Berthe. He sees himself. His pain.

"We were promised supplies for two weeks," Garmr says. "Coin and repairs for our gear."

Alescki bows his head. "It was a difficult winter. If we give them what they ask, there will be fewer than ten remaining. If they come a third time this year, there'll be none left."

"We were promised, Alescki."

The chief eyes each of them. He's a man ready for death, whether it comes this day or the next. A man in control of nothing, willing to choose the day of it if nothing else. But Rúnr no longer wants to fight these people. These fathers and mothers in mourning.

"What do you ask of us?" Rúnr says. He feels Garmr's attention on him for speaking out of turn, perhaps. Or maybe for salvaging the moment.

"Our deal is not broken," says Alescki. "Hear me, please. We will give double the food and water promised. Horses for the way that you may keep after. Carts. Five times the coin. We will give all you need and desire if you will do for us one thing."

One thing. No need to say it. The request is as obvious as the mountains. Garmr motions the crew closer. When the crew is together, he lays out his hands, palms up. A request for votes.

"I'm not chasing flesh-eaters," Ingimar says. "Better to kill these fuckers than go chasing such things."

"Is there truth to it?" Garmr asks.

"There are stories," says Erasmus.

"Stories are for children," Ingimar says.

"Are you scared of children's stories, then?" his sister says.

"Fuck you."

"Many stories begin with truth," Erasmus says.

"Like Berserkrs," Rúnr says, more to himself than the others.

"You're not just a story," Ingirid says.

"That's the point," says Erasmus.

"He doesn't eat people."

But I've seen bite marks.

It's not a comfortable thought. Thankfully, remaining locked onto a single thought is not a curse Rúnr bears. He thinks of the women at the fence. Of their children taken. Of the riders who've taken them. And eaten them.

"We don't need this," Ingimar says. "We can take what we want from here. Look at them. They can't stop us."

"Ingirid?" Garmr prompts.

"We don't need it," she says.

"What'll we eat the rest of the way?" Ingimar argues. "Our boots next? And flesh-eaters? You want to go after them?"

"I don't. We don't need any of this. The village. The flesh-eaters. We should move on. We'll find food. We have the whole way."

"These people are not our enemies," says Erasmus.

Ingimar snaps, "They're not our friends."

"Your vote, Rúnr?" Garmr asks.

Rúnr's attention remains on the women, their cheeks withering before his eyes. Flesh blackening. Rotting so that they're no longer women but like the wolf at the hot springs. Like the Ubbein-thing. A jowly woman's jaw falls off. A snake slithers from another's ear. One other opens her dress so that black insects burst from her nipples in streams, taking to the air on wings red as blood.

"Rúnr?"

He turns. Ingirid is watching him with concern. To her side, Erasmus seems afraid. Could he have seen what Rúnr saw? He looks to the fence again, but there's no rot among the women now. No insects or gaping eyes. All is still, save for a commotion to the side. A small head pops up over a low portion of fence, causing a woman to clutch at a little girl holding tight to the rail. A few seconds. She meets Rúnr's eye. She says a word—a name, perhaps a sibling taken—then she's pulled away and woman and child disappear into the village.

"We can find these riders," he says, wiping his sweaty palms on his thighs.

"It's to you, captain," Ingirid says.

To Rúnr's ear, there's contempt in her saying *captain*.

"I vote we track the riders."

"Fucking stupid," Ingimar says.

"Do you wish to be captain?" asks Garmr.

Ingimar scratches his beard and mutters.

"Then the vote is made," Garmr says. Hands open to his sides, he approaches Alescki and the chief. "How far?"

"Two days," Alescki answers.

"Then we need horses and food and water for four days, enough to take us and bring us back for the promise of what is owed."

"You shall have it, if you'll give your word."

"Upon Hel's shroud and flesh, I tell you," Garmr says, "we will avenge your children."

Alescki hesitates. He converses with the chief. There's head shaking. Rúnr thinks he can hear the name Hel.

"It's not vengeance we seek for them," Alescki says. "It's their return we want."

The twins exchange looks. Rúnr doesn't have to guess their thoughts: If the riders are cannibals, there may not be children to return.

"We'll return to you all we can."

"It's agreed." Alescki bows. "We'll have your provisions brought to you."

"Waste of time," Ingimar says.

Rúnr doesn't disagree. He hates adding four days to the journey, but the little girl at the fence, what she might suffer from these flesh-eaters. "Can we afford four days?"

Garmr looks up at the sun, then south. "We can."

Ingirid nudges Rúnr, directing his attention to where the chief is climbing back over the fence, the beams rocking beneath his weight. A weak point, for sure. Just in case.

CHAPTER 48

Not even midday and Ingimar is already certain this detour is a mistake. Not just because he thought so from the start. Because it's dividing the crew. Ingirid is dissatisfied with the vote, which puts her at odds with Rúnr. Which puts him at odds with Ingimar. Which drives a greater distance between his sister and the Berserkr. Which leaves the crew held together by Garmr's will and their shared desire—the gods-be-cursed need, at this point—to set sights on Miklagard and see it burned to the ground.

Like that fucking village could be burning now, Ingimar thinks.

And there goes the map man at Rúnr's side like a dog, contented as one too. Yes, he's more a part of the crew now than when they set out, but he's still not one of them. And always siding with Rúnr, lending his votes double the weight. Driving a wedge into the crew, separating them at the ribs like a ship being pried apart. He's the real problem. He always will be an outsider.

Ingimar's under no illusions, of course. He knows he's not the most pleasant man to sail with. He knows if not for his sister, he'd have been left behind on this raid or that one years ago. But here, for the first time, he's felt a part of something. A member and not just a tagalong.

And just as good, or maybe even better, is the friendship growing with Rúnr. Few spend long enough with Ingimar to understand his humor or desire his company, but the Opplander fits like a familiar shield. And long it's been since Ingimar had a man reliable at his side.

"What do you know of these riders?" Garmr asks Erasmus as they top a rise, each member of the crew upon a horse provided by the people of Syanka.

Ahead, the land flattens and darkens. The mere itself seems farther off than two days.

"Of these, nothing more than I've already told," the map man says.

"Then what good are you?" Ingimar asks.

"What good is asking this question?" Rúnr says, his mood foul since they left the village.

But even in such a mood, Ingimar understands the question is a reflex and not an insult or a grudge. It's a disagreement between friends, part of a crew's *comradeness.* Or whatever it's called—Ingirid would know the right word for it. Words were never Ingimar's strength, save for when finding ones to insult someone else's prick or mother or tiny hands. He laughs at the thought.

"A joke?" his sister asks, riding near.

Ingimar spreads his arms wide. "We're the joke, I think."

"For seeking these children?" Rúnr says.

"For wasting time." He points to the sun. "Every villager could be dead by now. All their food and water and supplies and gold could be ours instead of spending four days to collect a small piece of it."

"We voted."

Since when did the rules of a vote matter to you? he thinks but does not say. *We're only here because we ignored a vote.*

Garmr came to Ingirid first—of course, for it's always been her name spoken with awe—then to him with Ingirid at his side, proposing this journey, this crew of five, rather than the traditional band, and approved by vote.

"It feels bad," Ingimar says.

"I've seen no omens," his sister says.

Rúnr rides ahead of them, speaking with the map man. Garmr is behind and to their right, as if at the steering oar. Or as if watching the twins. Another joke because Ingimar doesn't, and never has, trusted their captain. Not his endless beard nor his choice of name, for surely Garmr is no man's true name. To spend your days branded the same as Hel's pet hound is not the decision of a mind to be trusted.

"We're a good crew, even with this captain," Ingirid says softly, knowing his thoughts, as always.

"We're going to have to do it during the invasion." No need to say what. They both swore. Once Miklagard burns, Garmr's usefulness to the Rus ends and his threat to Rurik's power begins, even if their chieftain doesn't see it. Garmr must die before they begin the journey home. "Won't be easy, though."

He doesn't just mean the fight itself, for Garmr is formidable. He means that the man has made himself popular with all the Rus in Rurik's camp. He'll need to be dispatched quickly and in secret. But also, their captain seems to know well more than any man should, which means he'll be difficult to take by surprise.

"We'll manage."

"Your Berserkr can help, if you tell him to."

"Don't speak of him like that," Ingirid says. "He's not a pet."

Maybe not, but the point is the same, so Ingimar simply stays quiet.

"He'll help," Ingirid says after a moment. A quick decision. Or one already made. Maybe she's not so in love with the Berserkr as she seems. "Will you still be Hersir as Rurik promised?" she asks.

Ingimar has considered this often recently. "I will, but maybe not right away."

"Oh?" Her raised eyebrow says she knows what he's thinking.

He says it anyway. "If I'm going to be Hersir, I should prove I can lead first."

"To lead you need a crew."

"We have a crew."

"We'll be less when our captain is gone."

"We'll have a new captain."

This time Ingirid is quiet for a time. "You'd continue to travel, sail and raid, rather than return home?"

Another question Ingimar has thought on much. "What's home? Look at how often Rurik complains about being stuck, ruled by that chair as much as he rules. There's nothing else for me there. I go where you go. Like always."

"Like always," she says.

Ahead, Rúnr and Erasmus split, Garmr going to speak with the map man, and Rúnr riding alone at the fore.

"Unless you want to return home," Ingimar says.

"There's nothing for me there either."

"Not even marrying Rurik?"

Ingirid sneers. "He wasn't serious."

"He was. Very."

"I'm not going to marry Rurik."

"What about Rúnr?" Ingimar asks. He's pushing now. He's going to make her angry, but he can't stop himself. He never could. Another reason to hold on to this crew, as much of it as possible, for as long as possible—they put up with him.

"He's not interested in marrying."

"You seem to know a lot about men and their marriage desires."

"You don't need to worry about what I know. I'm not marrying. I'm not going to be a chieftain's wife or a warrior's wife or a farmer's wife. Especially not a farmer's wife, you understand. I'm not going to till and harvest and birth a litter like some dog."

"Maybe tell him that." Ingimar points at Rúnr.

"Is it a fight you need, brother? Or are you still sore you were outvoted?"

"It was a poor vote. Four days might matter."

"Garmr thinks it won't," says Ingirid.

"Maybe."

"Think it like this, then. How many stories are told among our people of you and I for killing? For burning? For taking gold that was once someone else's?"

"Many of you," he says, unable to keep the sting from his voice.

"My stories are your stories."

He knows she means it, sharing all she is able with him, but knowing it doesn't change the truth. He's sat among warriors singing songs, and for every time he's heard his name spoken, it's Ingirid, daughter of Osmond, who is named five more times.

"Now think it like this," she continues. "Ingimar, rescuer of children from the flesh-eaters."

He wants to like it. He wants to embrace it. But he says, "Think of it like this: Ingimar, rescuer of children only to set them to spear and torch afterward for some coin and a beer."

"Then don't," says Rúnr, having drifted back near them.

"Don't what?" Ingimar spits, angry at himself for being overheard, for letting Rúnr get near without realizing.

"Don't think of it. Don't do it."

Ingimar begins a retort, then changes his mind. He kicks his mount to a trot, overtakes Garmr and Erasmus to ride alone in front and be angry.

Twilight falls. In the distance, the shimmer of water, impossibly far. A trick of the eyes and the light, perhaps, for he knows they should reach it tomorrow, as he knows he should trust his captain and crew.

"Well, the crew at least, I will," he says to his horse.

The horse ignores him. Well enough. His crew are the riders not the mounts. And though they're spread over the landscape, they're his and he is theirs. A good crew. Almost a family, even. Another one of those thoughts he won't say out loud. Even his sister might not fully understand that one.

Then again, maybe things will go well, and she will. Maybe she's even thinking the same right now.

CHAPTER 49

"What did you see at the fence?" Ingirid asks.

Erasmus snores nearby, but not so close as to interrupt her and Rúnr. Garmr and Ingimar are on the other side of the fire. It's late. The night is lit by a half-moon. Rúnr rolls onto his elbow and looks at her. She enjoys the way his eyes touch hers first, then down to her bare body, then back to her eyes as if trying to pretend he didn't look.

He says nothing.

Most men are easy. They get that one look at her breasts, get one fuck, and all they can think of is another. For a glimpse, they'll tell others' secrets. For a touch they'll tell their own. For a fuck, they'll swear anything, give anything.

Well, some secrets have been shared, which both scares and comforts her.

He's not a man to take me as his wife, she thinks. Of course, that's good. But here, as part of this crew, they work well together, and she'd be lying if she said she felt nothing for him. Erasmus could lose his head, and she would carry on without much worry. Garmr could be cut down, *will be* cut down, and she'll not lose a second of sleep for it. But if Rúnr or her brother fell, that knife of guilt inside would grow impossibly large, impossibly vicious.

"I saw the way your eyes went distant. Tell me the truth," she prompts, even though theirs is not a relationship of truth, exactly.

It's one of trust. One of aligned goals. One of . . . feelings. Real ones, complicated ones.

"I see . . . things sometimes," he says. "Things that aren't there."

More secrets, then, she thinks.

"That child, the little girl?" She felt that tug at the sight of the kid—that pestering pull on her heart and bowels that sometimes accompanies seeing other mothers' daughters. She wonders if it's the same for him. If he faces those same questions:

Why does this child live, and not mine?

Why a Christian and not my daughter, pledged right and proper to Odin and Asgard?

If he feels that same jealous rage, how can he fight it, not act upon it, not slay those children who live blissfully unaware while his daughter walks in darkness?

"Tell me," she says when he doesn't reply. Once she would have sought advantage over a man for his secrets. Now, she finds she wants to know just to know. Maybe even to comfort him a little, save him from what pursues him if she can.

He breathes heavy, the exhale catching in his throat making him shudder. He coughs. Lies back. Closes his eyes.

"I see horrors," he says. "I see death in animals that aren't there. I see rot on faces that live. I see the dead alive and feel their hands on me and speak with them."

A fist forms in Ingirid's throat. These are not idle things for discussion. What he speaks of is a mark from the gods. A curse.

I should tell Ingimar, she thinks. A cursed member of the crew could bring everything down.

But she doesn't rise. She remembers what her mother said the night she died, a thing Ingirid has long chosen to forget.

"You saw this at the fence?" she asks, needing to hear more.

"The women. Dead. Alive. Both at once."

"They were alive."

All the confidences she's traded over the years, used for her and her brother's own gain. The choice is simple. Do it again. Deliver what's been confided in her to her brother and her captain. Save the crew. Save the mission. But the way he's looking at her, as if he needs to tell her, as if he needs her . . .

Or am I the one who needs him?

"How often?" she asks.

"Not every day."

"Does it coincide with the god trance?"

He takes his time answering. "No."

She thinks it's not the truth, but maybe not a lie either. He doesn't know. But she does. Somehow, she knows as sure as she remembers the feel of Saanna against her flesh. Her mother had a touch of the sight, an ability to know things that will come to be. She was no seeress, just a woman given to fevers and ramblings that sometimes came true, but Ingirid remembers well now her words.

"The seeress didn't tell you full. She didn't speak it true," her mother said, her eyes closed, brow set with sweat from the fever that would take her life that night. "A man with sight and none will be your guide. A man who knows death and life at once will show . . . will be . . . who . . . oh the gods . . ."

"Show me what?" Ingirid demanded. "Guide me where?" She pounded on the body that was no longer her mother until Ingimar came to take her away, their mother's last words as cryptic as any prophecy.

And now here she is, crossed with Rúnr, a man who sees nothing but black in the god trance, and who sees rot and death where the living stand. And her fate? Vengeance in a land across the sea, that's all she knows. Vengeance for her father, she's always assumed, but what if it's something else? What if it's for an act not yet complete?

"You're scared," Rúnr says. His eyes are open now.

"I'm thinking," she replies.

He chews on his bottom lip, his beard so black in the night.

"Sleep," she tells him.

He looks as if he might argue, but she puts her hand on his chest. He puts his hands behind his head as she lies against him. Too comfortable to be safe, but she stays. They're heading for bad times, for blood and pain. She feels it like a storm beyond the horizon. But it's not here yet, so she closes her eyes and listens to Rúnr's breathing, to his heart beating, and eventually she sleeps.

CHAPTER 50

"Bad idea," Ingirid says as they trek into the mere-lands.

Rúnr does not disagree. He'd expected brackish waters and dank muck, like the meres of the North, not a waterfall pouring over a ridge into a shallow lake surrounded by drooping trees. Though the lake looks shallow enough to wade across with a dry beard, he's wary of what lives beneath the surface—this discomfort more than a little influenced by what he saw at Syanka's fence.

That girl from the fence came to his dreams last night while Ingirid slept, her arm draped across his chest. First Yrsa visited, as always, then the girl came, face melting like ice during the thaw. Belly distended, the flesh squirming as if snakes were trying to escape. And then her melted face slipped away like a dropped mask, a leaf on the wind, and the wolf-thing from the hot springs burst from her skull. And then he woke, sweating, Ingirid still on him.

"Sleep," she mumbled.

But he couldn't, choosing to just lie with her until dawn, clutching his bear's tooth pendant, seeing in each shadow the girl's face, the melting done, its flesh like hardened beeswax, lumpy and wrong of shape. Despite seeing this, he somehow felt safe because of Ingirid's touch.

A fool's feeling.

"Something's wrong here," Ingimar says, raising his voice to be heard over the waterfall.

"Which way?" Ingirid asks.

Erasmus answers when no one else will. "Still east?"

"Your confidence is wonderful," says Ingimar.

Rúnr dismounts and goes to the water and sets his boots in to the tops of his toes, willing whatever lives beneath the dark water to show itself.

"Doesn't seem the place for riders," Ingirid says.

"Doesn't smell right, either," Garmr adds.

He too dismounts. The others follow suit. Ingimar plucks a rock from the shore and skips it out into the mere. Does something rise in the final splash, something serpentlike and curious?

Rúnr closes his eyes, willing them to see only the truth.

Was the wolf-thing not true? The children who wrapped my wounds?

"I smell it too," Ingirid says.

Rúnr inhales deeply but smells nothing other than the mere. He opens his eyes.

Ingimar throws another stone. "I smell the map man's sweaty fat ass."

"There's more fat in yours than mine," Erasmus says.

It's a good retort, but no one laughs. They're too tight. Looking too hard for an enemy, which is when they usually appear from a different direction. Rúnr retreats from the water and kneels. The rocky banks make it impossible to find tracks. But farther from the mere, along the path around its way . . .

"There." Rúnr points.

Garmr goes first, toward the waterfall. "Horse tracks."

Ingimar joins him and scouts ahead a few more lengths. "Maybe."

Rúnr thinks there's no maybe to it. They've come this far after their quarry. Surely, they're close. But that nagging feeling won't leave him.

"Tie off the horses," he tells Erasmus.

Ingirid joins Rúnr as he goes to Garmr near the waterfall where the waters are brackish and churning.

"Look," their captain shouts to be heard over the waterfall. "They've tried to wipe their tracks clean."

"Why would they do that?" Ingirid asks.

"To hide their comings and goings," Ingimar says, joining them.

"Thank you for explaining the obvious. I meant, why only here. They can't have done so all the way out to the plains." She points the way the riders must have gone.

Which is the problem, Rúnr thinks. They must have gone that direction, away from the waterfall where the waters seem to bubble with writhing, ill-contented sea beasts.

Ingimar has no fear, however, and takes his bow and pushes it into the water. "Not so deep."

"Go all the way," Ingirid says dismissively, her attention the other direction, still on the horse tracks.

Rúnr, however, is intent on Ingimar wading deeper. Erasmus arrives as the water reaches Ingimar's belly. If there's a monster here, it'll come now. Rúnr takes his axe from his belt and goes ankle deep into the water. There's motion inside his skull, like waves breaking on rocks. Like the sound of the waterfall. The god trance considering this moment, perhaps. Or just the effects of too little sleep, too many dreams, and too much anticipation.

"Be careful," he says, his voice sounding like his own mother's from years ago when she would catch him doing foolish things boys do, like leaping from a barn's roof into a pile of hay at Torstyn's urging.

"This is as deep as it gets," Ingimar calls.

"Catch us some dinner and I'll care," his sister says.

"Do you hear that?" Garmr says.

Rúnr turns to his captain only to find his eyes drawn to the drooping trees instead. Muscles clench and ripple his legs, arms, hands. His vision begins to tighten. Something is coming. Within and without. Almost too late, he understands.

"The trees!" he says.

They rotate as one, a good crew—the last action of theirs Rúnr sees. His vision is a point, his thoughts on their mistake, the waterfall masking the sounds of the charging horses as they burst from the trees, light and fast, flesh painted black with pitch, the men bright toothed and the women bare breasted. Spears and tall bows in their hands—tall as a man, and the flesh-eaters as well, just as Leif warned before he murdered Torstyn.

Among the riders, one woman wears a bear's skull like a helm and its fur and flesh as armor. They connect eyes as the riders break like waves against the crew, so many so fast they can't be counted. Poor odds, perhaps the worst Rúnr has ever faced. Pressure builds within his head so that his skull must split. His brains must spill. He welcomes her charge, this bear-mother, this savage-queen, biting the rim of his shield as he waits, his being falling away like a torn shell until all that remains is what Odin Allfather demands.

CHAPTER 51

"Papa."

He's in the black. The beast of this place stalks somewhere beyond sight, but he feels it closer this time.

A girl takes his hand. He doesn't know who he is or why, but he knows the black and he knows her.

"Stay with me," he says.

"Lo there, Papa. The world."

And it's all of Midgard before him even as it's no more than a single mountain rising higher than eyes can see. And here, at its base, the flatness of the world. And here, in that flatness, a dark tarn churning with brine-beasts.

"Deep," she says.

And deep he goes. Into the water. Into the mire. For a full day he swims, finally emerging into a cavern that must be capped by the dome of the sky. The girl is here, holding his hand still, though she did not swim with him.

"The shadow-hag," she says.

"I'll kill it."

She squeezes his hand. "I know."

The hag comes, galloping upon a horror beast with seven taloned legs. The first pass, he cuts the beast from under her. She rolls and rises, elongated into a shape mocking all things that walk and crawl and fly. Grim and savage with death-blue eyes shining in her bear-skull face, her black mane a tangle of rusted chains, half-rotted skulls dangling from each link, she screams. Strings of flesh dripping from her fangs, wicked and savage, she charges. No creature has ever moved faster. It's all he can do to throw the girl aside and fling himself into the mud before the bearish fiend comes round again.

To his feet, he stands his ground, surrounded by blood-painted imps riding fleshless mounts galloping upon six arms, not legs, each. With bone blades the imps hack at his flanks, but they are nothing compared to his strength. He swipes them aside with hand and axe. The hag comes, slamming into him like thunder, his shield broken, his axe lost. Into the dregs they roll. Arms around arms. Legs around legs. Claws and fangs rip at his flesh-armor but do not pierce. Heavy fists slam his bones. This pain he feels high and low, shallow and deep. She is winning, endless grip driving him to his knees.

"Papa," the girl says. She points. A knife on the muddy ground.

For this, for her, he rises, bringing the shadow-hag with him. She tires. Seeks to end him with one last crush, but he's not yet spent. He grips the knife, its blade sharp and hot for blood. With a tremendous heave, he throws her down. Knife high, he strikes, the blade ringing as it cleaves her flesh-house, biting deep into her spine.

The shadow-hag is no more. Mist evaporating into the black.

More imps come. These he slashes to portions and chunks, seeking the girl, his Little Bear. But she's gone. All around is becoming the black. A final imp with a sun-bright mane. He plunges the knife into its throat, leaving the blade there as the black takes him.

"Little Bear," he says, but it's only him now. And distant screaming. A familiar woman's voice, full of such pain.

And then nothing.

CHAPTER 52

The Berserkr walks among them, cutting down enemies whether they fight from foot or from horseback. Every scream, every death, is an exaltation for Garmr. He separates himself quickly from the others so that he can whirl and slash and slay with his warsword while keeping watch on the Berserkr and his beautiful art.

The first time the god trance changed Rúnr from warrior to Berserkr, Garmr was surrounded, his view obstructed, and he saw little of the slaughter. But now he witnesses it all.

What a glorious day!

He wants the bear-queen for his own, but she sees what he knows: The Berserkr is the danger. She urges her horse on without a care for Garmr. So be it. He'll take in numbers what he can't in status for the glory of his Lady. The result will be the same. He hacks off limb of horse and man, guts woman and beast, thinks he sees tiny gnawed upon fingers spilled from the stomach of one. Some horrors even he cannot stomach, so he sets to killing more, and then even more, suffering none to flee. Determined to rid Midgard of . . .

It's as if a bell suddenly tolls within Garmr's being. A turning point that changes all to come after. A fate found.

He cuts down a man, seeking the moment through raining blood. There, at the edge of the water. The mystery falls away and he sees the choices he has made are ratified. The choices he will make are clear. Relief and a greater burden at once, as life has ever been, and he throws himself into the killing with more vigor even as he watches a friend fall.

CHAPTER 53

The odd thing is how Erasmus enjoys it.

As a young man, the thought of blood curdled his stomach. The sight of it made him feint. He'd pricked his finger on a flower's thorn once and stuck the bloody digit in his mouth and woke later on the ground, alone and scared, certain he was dying. From a thorn prick.

He ducks below a charging rider's spear and slashes at the horse's hind leg. It rears, throwing the rider, and Erasmus is on her. She's strong, grabbing at his sword and rolling him until she's on top, holding her spear, the killing blow, aloft. For a moment, he finds humor in the situation, his murderer atop him like this, naked from the waist up as these riders, these flesh-eaters, prefer.

Erasmus the Gatherer would never have imagined himself here. Erasmus the Exile, wanderer of the world, would never have lasted a breath in a battle such as this. And Erasmus the poet, the scholar, the lover? That fool who'd read and written of such battles with fervor and pride and faith in glory . . . Is there anything further from the truth of violence than the writing of it?

No, that Erasmus could never have conceived such a moment as this.

She screams and slams her spear down. Erasmus twists. The spear strikes empty ground. He knees her ribs, knocks her spear away. Gets to a knee, but she's fast and produces a wicked dagger, slashing at his eyes. Quickly, she's atop him once more, her bare breasts nearly in his face, so he does what he can, biting her nipple, tearing through flesh, tasting blood, drinking it as she howls in pain, her aim ruined. He punches her in the throat. Knocks away her blade. Spits her nipple into her face and runs her through.

And looks for more as he licks his lips, loving the taste, knowing finally he's one of them. A Northman.

Erasmus the Northman, Eater of Nipples.

He giggles as he drives his sword through a man's spine. Chortles as he hammers the crossguard into another's jaw before disemboweling him. Screams to the gods—every name he can think—for more enemies to kill, more beer to drink, and more blood to bathe in.

The gods.

For how can there be only one in a world of such violence and beauty? How can he deny the truth of Thor's thunder and the grandeur of Sól's setting sun and the wisdom of Odin's eye in the ravens that follow battle?

He thought he belonged once. He had family. Friends. Community. A place at the emperor's court. More recently his spot with the merchants of the North. But it's here he truly knows belonging. Among this crew. His crew, with whom he can share a secret, or not, and feel no shame of it either way.

No shame at all? Then why haven't I spoken my whole truth?

An axe dislodges an iron plate from his forearm, pain striking up to his elbow. He swings wildly, forcing his attacker back into the lake. Just a boy, naked from the waist up, same as the rest of them, eyes wide. He comes again, but his axe is as short as his arms. Erasmus has the advantage and counters. The boy flees across the waters, right into carnage.

The Berserkr.

Erasmus has taken care to keep his distance from the chaos that is Rúnr within the god trance. Enemies fall to his axe and knife like rain from the sky. Into this, the boy runs and is swiftly cut in half at the belly. Erasmus doesn't look away, so he doesn't miss what comes next. Ingimar, pressed back by two flesh-eaters, is unaware of his position. He dispatches one. The other goes low, forcing Ingimar to dance even farther back.

Erasmus tries to shout, but his tongue is thick with blood and fear and realization: The crew is about to be shattered.

Ingimar turns. The Berserkr drives his knife forward. Ingirid screams.

CHAPTER 54

Only when the screaming stops does Ingirid realize it was her.

Nothing moves. Not the waves of the lake nor the wind nor the crew nor the flesh-eaters. They're all still, carved totems. Except Ingimar. His head snaps back. His arms flail wide. His legs go limp.

Ingimar falls.

Everything else snaps back into motion.

Ingirid bounds into the fray, ducking below the Berserkr's blade, to her brother's side in the shallow water. She lifts his face and cradles his head. There's more blood, it seems, than water in the tarn.

Someone shouts her name. She looks up, expecting to see the Berserkr bearing down upon her, death wearing Rúnr's face, but it's Erasmus cutting down a flesh-eater and then standing over her and Ingimar like a guardian. Nearby, the Berserkr slays two more flesh-eaters. Garmr massacres another. There are none left to kill.

Erasmus kneels beside her. "Let me help," he says.

Ingirid looks at her brother. One eye open, one closed. Chest still. She won't be one of those women who cry and shout and beat their fists on a body. Ingimar is gone. Only vengeance remains.

"Take him," she says, pushing the body to him.

She rises and faces the Berserkr. He's standing by the water's edge looking right at her, eyes narrowed and empty. Those eyes then roll back in his head, and he falls backward beneath a drooping tree.

"As it must be," Ingirid says. She finds her swords in her hands, no memory of unsheathing them. Two strides take her almost to the drained Berserkr.

Garmr stands between them.

"Wait," he says.

She has no desire for words and goes around, but he slides with her. Blocking her.

"Move," she says.

"We need him."

"He killed my brother."

"I'm sorry."

She tries the other way around but again Garmr stands between her and her goal. "I'm owed this," she says.

"Take what you're owed when our job is finished."

She screams a battle cry and charges.

She's on the ground before she feels the blow that put her there. By the gods he's fast!

She gets to a knee. To her right, Erasmus has dragged Ingimar from the water. She uses her swords to help get to her feet. She feigns exhaustion and defeat.

"Don't," Garmr warns.

She does anyway. And again he puts her on the ground. And again she regains her feet. She can't beat him, her captain. Not alone. Not when he's expecting her. So she begins to pace a line. Before her, Garmr leans on his warsword, its point digging into the dirt.

"Give him to me," she says.

Garmr holds her eye. "I will not."

She paces back and forth until she's worn a rut. And remembers, of a sudden, her mother taking her hand long ago.

"Knit slowly, fair love," she'd said.

Where were they? In the small home that sheltered Mother, Father, and two children? Probably there, yes, but the memory is without context—just her mother's face and words.

"Yes," she said. "Knit slowly enough and he'll forget you. That's when your needle can find his throat."

How old could Ingirid have been then? Six winters? Eight? What man was her mother speaking of? What kind of lesson was that to teach such a young girl?

The perfect lesson, she thinks as she looks at her brother, dead on the ground beside the man who killed him. Her crewmate. Her friend. Her lover.

"He'll not escape me," she says.

Garmr says, "As it will be."

His nonchalance enrages her, forcing all her willpower not to attack a third time, for she's certain he won't let her escape unharmed again if she does.

"If you won't let me have him now," she says, "then leave him. Let him flounder alone in this foreign place."

"His fate is tied to ours."

"But not to my brother's, is that it?"

A crack in Garmr's facade. But is it a grimace or a grin?

"Tied to it quite well, I would say," he replies.

She stops pacing. Erasmus comes from the lake carrying water in a beer skin, having taken it on himself to clean Ingimar—to clean the body. For that's all it is now. A body. Like Baldr lying dead after Loki tricked Hodr into slaying his twin. But unlike Baldr, Ingimar will not return after Ragnarök. No, her brother is lost to her forever, having gone with the Valkyries to dine in Valhalla.

Unlike your daughter, Rúnr!

She almost shouts it but can't force the words. Because it's too cruel? Or because Rúnr isn't yet awake and will not hear?

Or because I don't know where my own daughter dines?

"We'll give him a proper funeral," Garmr says.

But Ingirid doesn't care for funerals. Her mother got one. Her father. Her baby. What did those funerals accomplish but keeping her tied to empty bodies longer than necessary?

"Do what you want," she says. "I'll not wait for it."

She abandons the line she's paced, going to their horses. Five in all, though four is their number now.

"We made an oath to seek the children," Erasmus says from his knees, wiping blood from the body's face.

Fucking oaths! "Then I'll go find the children," she says.

"Ingirid," her captain says. "Fate cannot be avoided."

"What do you know of fate?"

"It cannot be avoided. Trying only brings it anyway but with cruelty."

"Ingimar didn't try to avoid it. He didn't ask about it. He didn't want to know. What cruelty did that save him?"

"Asking, or not, doesn't absolve a man of what the gods next deem necessary."

"What do they deem necessary?" She raises her face and arms to the darkening sky. "What more do you want to take from me? How thirsty for my pain can you be?"

The echoes of her shouting fade slowly.

"What the gods see, they see," Garmr says. "What they do, they do. But they can't plot the future or control fate."

"What do you know of it? Because you're named for Hel's pet, you think you see their ways?"

She doesn't miss the way her words hit, as if he's been struck. Somewhere within his beard, his mouth works words that never sound. There's a weakness there, but what is it?

Does he think he truly is Hel's hound, Garmr, guardian of Her realm's gates?

"The gods are not infallible," Garmr says, voice rumbling, words slow. "They see and know, but that's not the same as plotting pieces on a war map."

"Then your bullshit about fate, about needing Rúnr alive and Ingimar dead, could be wrong."

"Ragnarök will come as foretold. So too will we come to Miklagard as I've been told, four in number with the Berserkr among us. Vengeance for your brother will have to wait."

Vengeance for your brother.

In a land faraway, across a sea, with the blood of vengeance on my hands, is where I will die.

All this time, could it have been Ingimar's death she's been meant to avenge?

"Four in number?" Erasmus says. His task with the body done, he stands.

"What are you going on about?" Ingirid asks.

"He said he was told we would come to Miklagard, four in number," Erasmus says.

Garmr growls low in his chest. The three of them stand at angles to each other. Ravens arrive for the bodies along the water's edge.

Ingirid says to their captain. "You were told four in number?"

"We all have a fate," Garmr says. "You heard Rúnr's. Three times he will become Berserkr. This was the second. The third won't come until we walk the streets of Miklagard. If you want vengeance, you'll have to wait until then to see Ingimar's killer."

But separating Rúnr and Berserkr is not so simple when they wear the same face. Nor is that the point of what Garmr is saying. Or what he's not saying.

"You knew one of us would die," she says.

"I knew the Berserkr would live to see Miklagard," Garmr offers, "no matter the blood on his hands."

"Whose blood were you told it would be?"

Garmr's eyes flash. Anger? Fear? Both, Ingirid thinks, because she knows the truth now: he's known all along who would survive this journey and who wouldn't. The Berserkr could not die. The map man could not die, for if he was expendable, he'd have been tossed overboard long ago. And surely Garmr himself was not to die. It was always going to be her or her brother, at Rúnr's hand, he knew.

He knew!

And now I know where the blame lies.

Upon Rúnr, the Berserkr, of course, but no more than a mother bear should be blamed for its instinct to maul a man who gets too close to her cubs. But the one who nudges the poor man to try to pet the cubs . . . The one who sees the mother bear and doesn't say so . . . That is the one who should pay the price.

The one who must pay the blood price.

Knit slowly, fair love.

Yes, slowly, for there are two who deserve her swords now. It doesn't matter that she could no more stop the killing than she could break the circle and end Ragnarök itself. Every death must be paid for—blood for blood. It's the law. The way of gods and mortals without exemption. But it's not her way to shout such intentions and step into the Circle for a Challenge. She will knit slowly.

She points at Rúnr. "Keep him away from me."

Garmr sheaths his warsword. Whatever she saw in his eyes—fear, anger, doubt—is gone. He's their captain again, confident, like a man who knows the truth. Or who lives comfortably within lies, like Loki Mischief Bringer. Good.

"When we're finished," Garmr says, "when the fleet has come to Miklagard and we sail home in victory, if you wish my hand in helping you take blood for your brother's death, I will offer it."

Yes, knit slowly enough and he'll forget you. That's when your needle can find his throat.

"Swear it," Ingirid says.

"Upon Hel's shroud and flesh."

"Let's go find the children," she says, mounting one of the horses, satisfied that Garmr won't see her needle coming.

"What of him?" Erasmus asks, still standing beside Rúnr.

Ingirid rides off the way the flesh-eaters came, protected by the knowledge that fate has taken the one it meant to take. She'll live to see Miklagard, as will the other three. And once the city burns, she'll kill her captain. And then her lover.

CHAPTER 55

Rúnr opens his eyes. He's been awake for some time. He's heard Ingirid and Garmr arguing. He's heard them ride off. He knows what he's done though he doesn't remember doing it.

"You're alive," Erasmus says.

"Better than some." Rúnr's voice is hoarse. His vision sways as he sits up as if his mind is sloshing inside his skull. He looks at the body.

Ingimar seems almost peaceful, like he's asleep.

If I close my eyes and lie down again, can I swap with him?

Wouldn't that solve everything?

No.

"I'm sorry," he says, though the one who deserves his apology is no longer here.

"What can I do to help?"

"Water," Rúnr says.

Erasmus offers a skin. Rúnr drinks heartily while Erasmus talks to him. Where the others have gone, perhaps. Or a story of some kind meant to soothe his guilt. Whatever it is, Rúnr's fractured mind cannot follow, his thoughts, like gulls scattered by storm, flying every direction.

What will he say to Ingirid?

Should he turn back now and return north?

Is his vengeance for Yrsa more important than for Torstyn? Is it more important than Ingirid's for her brother?

How far are they from Miklagard?

"Is it worth it?" Erasmus asks.

"The god trance?"

"This journey to Constantinople."

The answer, Rúnr thinks, is probably no in both cases. "I swore an oath."

"A hundred thousand people have broken oaths. The world moves on. Kings rise and fall. There's always death. Always those seeking vengeance."

It's too much for now, for coming fresh from the god trance.

"Why are you here?" Rúnr asks.

"Your people would say fate."

"And your people?"

"As you know not the way the spirit nor the bones are joined together in the womb of a woman with child," Erasmus says, "so you know not the works of God, creator of all things."

"What part of this is meant to make me feel better for what I've done?"

"None of it."

For a moment, Rúnr considers finding his axe and splitting the man's skull, but the urge passes quickly. Erasmus is crew. He is a friend. As is Garmr and Ingirid.

As was Ingimar.

This thought he shoos like it's a cat inching toward his dinner.

"Where have they gone?"

"To find the children, as we promised."

"A hundred thousand people have broken oaths," Rúnr says. He means to say it with humor, but it doesn't sound that way.

"If you want to go north," Erasmus says, "I'll go with you."

It's the most honest and loyal thing anyone other than Torstyn has said to Rúnr in a long time. Immediately he regrets his earlier thoughts, and all they've done to this poor merchant. For the first time in weeks, Rúnr truly looks over the man—barely recognizable as the map man from Uppsala. Here stands a warrior. A Northman.

"I'm sworn twice," Rúnr says. "For vengeance and for the Rus. I'll go on to Constantinople."

"Then we best meet the others and find the children."

He remembers the little girl at the fence at Syanka. In his memory, her face melts revealing another beneath: Yrsa's. And her face melts revealing one more: his own. His stomach roils. He vomits.

"Are you okay?" Erasmus asks.

Rúnr wipes his mouth and beard. "Happens sometimes after the god trance."

Erasmus retrieves his axe and offers it. Rúnr takes it. They nod to each other and gather the rest of their things and lead their horses after Garmr and Ingirid.

CHAPTER 56

The cannibal camp is out in the open, in the plains so vast they might as well be an ocean. Smoke rises from their fires. Their homes are little more than huts, quick to erect and quick to strike. Nomadic people, migrating the plains the way reindeer migrate the North, Rúnr thinks. He sees no fear of attack in the camp. No worry for defense. Perhaps because they're so mobile. Or because their warriors are fierce. Or because they rely on reputation and fear.

Whatever the reason, it's a mistake.

By the time Rúnr and Erasmus arrive, there's nothing left but burning huts and bodies. Garmr and Ingirid have made short work of what appears to be mostly old men and women. The warriors must have all come to the ambush.

"Will she kill me?" Rúnr asks as they ride into the middle of the carnage, seeking his crewmates.

"Probably," Erasmus says.

"Ho there!" Garmr calls from the far side, where the grass grows taller.

"I see no children," Erasmus says.

They dismount. Garmr approaches.

"Where is she?" Rúnr asks.

"Where are the children?" Erasmus asks.

Garmr says, "There's nothing living here but us."

Their captain leads them into the grass until they find a clearing full of sprawled bodies, dozens of them, some whole and lined side by side, many strewn piecemeal or in piles. And in the center of them, sits Ingirid, her back to the crew. The stench of charred flesh is so thick it's like drowning.

"Did you do this?" Erasmus asks, coughing.

Ingirid doesn't rise or turn. "Why would I do this?"

"I found her sitting here," Garmr says.

"Ingirid," Rúnr begins.

"Now is not the time," she snaps.

"They butchered them here," Garmr says. He adds no more.

Erasmus, gagging, leaves.

As Rúnr looks over the dead, he finds the face of a boy, eyes frantic, lips working but making no sound. All around, more eyes blink at Rúnr. More mouths gape. Dismembered hands crawl like crabs over piles of arms and legs that slither like lugubrious serpents. Rúnr stifles a retching shout and backs away.

"Throw up somewhere else," Ingirid says.

"No, I—" But when Rúnr looks again, the dead are just that: dead.

"There were no children in the camp," Garmr says. "None of their own."

"Their women can't have children," says Ingirid.

"How can you know this?"

"They took these from the village, hoping to consume them, to correct whatever is broken in their own women."

"She's right," Rúnr says, though how he knows it, he can't say. It sounds correct. That's enough for him.

"I don't need your words," she says.

Garmr shifts his weight. "We'll ride on, make camp elsewhere."

"No," says Ingirid. "We'll camp here." She stands. Turns. Looks at Rúnr as if seeking something.

He stands silent, telling himself he's ready to accept whatever she does next. She comes toward him. He tenses but refuses to reach for his axe. She passes him, back through the grass toward the camp.

"It'll be all right," Garmr says.

The same urge to strike Erasmus that Rúnr felt earlier takes him now, whispering that he should end Garmr's life. He doesn't.

Garmr smiles. "We'll stay here tonight," he says. He leaves Rúnr alone with the bodies.

The brush of movement sounds from a pile. Rúnr doesn't wait to see the cause, following Garmr. The crew undertake the labor of moving the dead off to the clearing where the children lie, to keep distance should any predators or scavengers come.

That done, Garmr builds up a large fire at the edge of the camp, as far from the bodies as possible.

"We should return to Syanka in the morning," Erasmus says.

"We should go on to Miklagard," Ingirid says.

"We promised."

"To bring their children back. Would you bring those butchered corpses?"

"We can tell them, at least," Erasmus asserts.

"Vote," Garmr says. He sounds sleepy.

With Erasmus and Ingirid's votes known, it's to Rúnr. There's no choice, really. They've delayed long enough. He's been delayed long enough. Somewhere in the distance, he's certain he can see Yrsa waiting impatiently. "We have the horses we need, and there's plenty of food and drink here for us to take."

"The gold we were promised?" Garmr asks like it's a formality.

"There'll be enough of it in Miklagard," says Ingirid.

"Move on," votes Rúnr.

"Agreed," says Garmr. To Erasmus he adds, "Do you still have the map?"

Erasmus starts to produce it. "Of course."

Garmr puts up a hand to stop him. "Stitch it into the inside of your tunic."

"Why?"

"The closer we get, the more we'll need it, wouldn't you say?"

Erasmus looks to Rúnr who can only shrug—why start questioning their captain now?

"Okay," is all Erasmus says as he gets to work.

Soon, night is fallen. Ingirid takes the watch. Garmr snores while Erasmus sleeps with his back to the fire. Rúnr chooses a spot farther from the fire beside a hut and closes his eyes, but movement opens them again. Ingirid comes, he knows by her sound before he sees her. He could reach for his axe, but if she wants his blood tonight, he finds he cannot begrudge her that. He waits.

And she lies beside him. After a moment, he sits up on an elbow and looks at her, expecting grief and the need for comfort. He finds instead eyes of steel reflecting the fire.

"Ingirid," he begins.

"No," she says. "No apology tonight." After a time, she asks, "Why will the Valkyries not bring your daughter to Valhalla?"

The question surprises Rúnr. Then it makes him think of Torstyn and their ride to the Fennvold when he asked the same question. Now, however, Rúnr is not so conflicted about answering. "I've thought on this for a long time, and I can't know for certain, but I am Berserkr. I should have been able to protect her."

"You should have, but you are Odin's champion. His chosen. Why punish you? Why punish your daughter for your failure?"

This is the part Rúnr still struggles with. Why punish Yrsa? And the answer, if perhaps it is *the* answer, comes to him in such a succinct way he's surprised it hasn't occurred to him before. "Because my failure is a dishonor, an affront, to Odin Allfather, and I must redeem myself in his eye."

Ingirid makes a noise that might be agreement. Then she says, "Do you believe in fate?"

"Believe in it?" Fate is. He doesn't understand how someone can believe in it any more than they can believe in the sun or the moon. Each is. As fate is.

She places a hand on his chest. "That it's told to us infallibly?"

"Do you suspect lies told about your fate?" he asks, his thoughts going to Velaug and Berthe and Yrsa and Torstyn and Leif. They go to Helvig and Thyri, to Njal and Alina. They go to vengeance and guilt and Skyjavík and Miklagard.

Ingirid comes close to his ear. "I will tell you of fate," she whispers. "Ours was known to Garmr from the start, and he never spoke the truth of it: my brother or I would not live to see Miklagard."

Rúnr doesn't reply. He wonders why Ingirid is telling him now. Wonders what he would do if he discovered Velaug knew Yrsa would die that night and had not told. Would he blame the Painted Fenn all the same, or would there be blame to share for Velaug?

Would I still love her if I knew such a thing?

Ingirid begins undressing him. He lets her. She climbs atop him.

"I'm sor—"

She slaps his face. Hard.

"I'll tell you when it's time to apologize," she says.

He nods, thinking again of Velaug.

The sex is angrier than usual, more so than any he's ever known. She slashes his chest and back with her nails. Grinds his ribs, legs, groin with her elbows and fists and knees. Pain and pleasure twine together like serpents until they're both spent and covered in sweat.

"He could have saved my brother," she says. "He could have given me a chance to save him."

"By killing me?" Rúnr asks.

"He chose not to. Because he wanted Ingimar to die. Do you understand?"

"Yes."

"Do you believe me?"

Though there's no knife to his throat, there might as well be. Even still, Rúnr finds he does believe her. Or wants to. Which is, maybe, enough.

"I do."

"We must finish our mission first. We must fulfill our oaths as crew. But you owe me."

He understands what she's asking before she speaks it.

"Your vengeance waits in Miklagard," she says. "You deserve it. You shall have it. This is what I swear and what I offer: I help you find your vengeance, and then you help me find mine."

"Against Garmr," he says.

"He'll no longer be our captain once Miklagard burns. You see that, yes? It won't be a betrayal then. You owe me."

She touches him, ready again. He's not, but he's getting there.

"Say it," she says. "Swear it."

"I swear it, on Odin's eye."

"Swear it on Hel's hound, of the same name as our captain. Swear it on Garmr's teeth and hide."

"Upon Garmr's teeth and hide, then."

"As do I, on Garmr's blood and Odin's eye," she says. "We are bound, Rúnr."

"We are bound," he says.

She pulls his mouth to hers and soon the night grows even fiercer between them.

CHAPTER 57

The next week goes much the same as the first weeks of their campaign, though on horseback rather than ship. Though without song and banter. Though with four not five. Though with the sultriness of summer nearly upon them. For that, Erasmus spoke the entire truth—summer in these lands will undoubtedly be sweltering and relentless.

Still, they ride. They kill and steal when they can or must. They face the sun at times and have it at their backs at others but always progressing south. They double back and skirt around some farmsteads while burning others without pattern. They're close to Miklagard and must make the eyes of the city turn their way so that what is coming from the east will not be seen.

"The fleet approaches the White Fortress," Garmr says.

It's midday. Behind them, the horizon is darkened by the smoke from a burning tower. Erasmus called the city Hadrianople. Too large and too populous for the crew to raid, but its towers, numerous and well-spaced from each other, made easy targets. They chose one and killed the soldiers inside and set it alight and then rode west to the river where they doubled back toward their goal of reaching Miklagard before two more dawns.

"How do you know?" Rúnr asks.

"Can't you smell it on the wind?"

"I smell death and ash," says Erasmus.

In these moments, Rúnr feels Ingimar's absence most. No quick jab or sharp barb. No complaint or threat to fight over the smallest perceived injury. He imagines Ingirid feels it as well. Theirs is a confounding relationship, though he can't say he resents it or blames her for it. Beneath the sun, she keeps her distance and does not speak much. She kills with perfunctory efficiency, her previous joy in battle no longer visible.

Beneath the moon, she comes to him most nights, creeping, as if plotting to cut his throat. He holds his breath and touches his knife, just in case. Sometimes, they fuck. Often, she simply lies beside him, as if listening to his heartbeat.

Now, she rides the same way. Back to him in silence.

"I smell nothing," Rúnr says.

Garmr points ahead. The worn ruts that they've been calling roads since they traded their ship to Vasil—and then killed him on Ingimar's actions—are paved with stone ahead, large blocks cobbled together.

"Roman roads," Erasmus says. "We're close."

Rúnr squints into the distance. "I see no great city."

"How far?" Ingirid asks. It's the first she's spoken today.

Erasmus retrieves his map and spreads it out best he can. "If we stop raiding, we'll see the city's outer walls tomorrow."

"Still trying to save fellow Christian lives," she says in a way that sounds a lot like her brother.

He rolls up the map. "Do I look like a Christian to you?"

"You don't look like one of us."

"He's sworn to our mission, same as you," Garmr says.

Ingirid spits, again like her brother so that Rúnr half expects that when she turns, it'll be his face he sees instead of hers. And why not? Has he not caused enough deaths to be pursued by one each day until Ragnarök comes?

"You could carry the fucking map," she says to Rúnr.

"We are each more than what we carry."

She opens her mouth, then snaps it shut and rides ahead, the first to mount the road, her horse's hooves making a sound like woodpeckers on stone. The urge to chase her down and apologize for what he's done, to offer his life if she wishes it, overcomes Rúnr so that he kicks his horse ahead. Only to pull up seconds later. She deserves more than a groveling apology. If she wants his death for what he's done, she'll ask it. Or take it.

"There are some things we can't make better," Erasmus says.

Rúnr hadn't noticed him riding close. "What can you know of it?"

"I know you're hurt by what that other man did."

"There is no other man." Or is there? It's never occurred to Rúnr to think of the Berserkr as separate from himself. How could he think it? Not remembering what he does is not the same as not doing it.

"He seems someone else to me, the twice I've seen him."

They ride onto the road. In the distance, Rúnr sees shimmering heat rising, and within that, perhaps, the shape of something more.

"All I mean is, she seems to have forgiven you enough to continue toward our goal," Erasmus says. "Maybe that means you can forgive yourself enough as well."

Rúnr turns. Garmr is hanging back, only now approaching the road, like a steersman at the ship's stern. Behind him, the smoke looks like a tree reaching the clouds. Like Yggdrasill.

"Have you forgiven yourself?" he asks Erasmus.

"For what?"

"For what you've done with us."

His face darkens some. "Yes. And no."

"Then why should you speak to me of forgiveness? What does it even mean to forgive myself? Who cares what I think of myself? The gods only care for what we do, or what we don't do when we're meant to. You can't understand."

"Because I'm not one of you."

"Yes." It's a hurtful thing to say, Rúnr knows. They are—they *were*—crew. What are they now?

"I only meant to help," Erasmus says.

"There's no help for what I am."

"What will you do, then?"

"What I've sworn."

"Vengeance."

"Yes."

"Burn Miklagard."

"Yes." Rúnr notes this is the first time he's heard Erasmus use the Northern name for his former home.

"And then?"

"Whatever the gods will." It's enough of an answer. No reason to explain his willingness to lay his fate at Ingirid's feet. To allow her to decide if he'll return home to avenge his brother or leave that to others and let her take her own vengeance from his blood.

"You're an enigma, Rúnr. But I'm glad I met you," Erasmus says. "All of you."

Rúnr doesn't want to keep talking—he's content to let his mind run its way, from Miklagard to Ingirid to fate and his own death and the gods and what minds designed this road—yet words come from his mouth in any case. "Even though you've become . . . this?"

"I'll need forgiveness as well, I guess."

"From which gods?"

"Maybe all of them."

"Even the Christ God?"

Erasmus laughs. "Jesus has never been my god."

"Eyes!" Garmr calls.

Rúnr turns. Their captain rides calm, but he's twisted on his horse, looking behind them. At first, Rúnr sees nothing but the

Yggdrasill-like smoke. Then, from its base, its roots, a hint of movement. More than a hint.

"What is that?" Erasmus asks.

Now Garmr kicks his mount to speed. "Riders," he says as he passes.

Many of them, Rúnr sees now, in pursuit of the crew. He too kicks his horse, as does Erasmus. Soon they're riding fast with Ingirid. Rúnr imagines the walls of Miklagard somewhere before them, trapping them between stone and a thousand Christian soldiers chasing them from Hadrianople. A glorious death for story and song, but a poor one for the four of them, short of their goals.

"There," Garmr says, pointing. A village to the southeast. A place to hide or, at worst, a defensible place to make a stand. "Kill everyone you see. Meet in the middle."

No questions. No votes. They are crew, and this is battle. They ride hard, charging into the village on a line, leaping a low chicken fence, darting for the center, expecting cries of fear and the smell of blood as they strike, but there's no resistance. No sound, other than of the chickens. The place is abandoned.

"This isn't right," Erasmus says when they come to the center.

Ingirid spins her horse round and round, seeking someone to kill. Garmr sits calm on his. Erasmus continues to tell them how bad a place this is. And Rúnr understands why, all the birds of his mind coming to a point: this place, within the circle of the village, this open space perfect for drawing enemies in and sighting them with archers from the surrounding rooftops—this is obviously where they would make their stand. Which is why . . .

"We shouldn't have come here," Rúnr says at the same time the archers appear.

And riders from the east and south.

"Back west," Ingirid shouts.

A line of arrows hits the ground in front of her horse, causing it to rear, throwing Ingirid down. Erasmus jumps from his mount to help her. Another line of arrows keeps him from reaching her. Garmr draws his warsword, but he doesn't swing it, holding it at his side, point down, instead.

"We're caught," he says.

All this, Rúnr watches, axe in hand, seeing no way out. The riders from the west arrive. They're surrounded now. He closes his eyes but feels nothing coming. Of course. They're not in Miklagard. They're nowhere near the red temple. The god trance will not come today.

A Christian shouts.

"He says to drop our weapons," Erasmus translates.

Ingirid gets to her feet, seemingly unhurt. "Why don't they just kill us?"

"They need to know what we know," Garmr says. "They need to know if we are alone or part of something more."

"So tell them. Then we can get to killing."

"The one who wants to know isn't here. They're going to take us. We're going to let them."

"How—what do you know, Garmr?" Ingirid demands.

Rúnr answers for their captain. "This was the plan all along, wasn't it? This is how we pass through the walls that no one can steal through."

Garmr drops his sword. It rings heavy and loud. "We can only put Miklagard to burn from the inside."

Erasmus drops his weapons, to a look of disgust from Ingirid. Rúnr grips his axe tighter, understanding but not liking, or trusting, Garmr's plan. Ingirid eyes Rúnr, seeking a promise, he thinks. That they'll not die unarmed. That their promise to each other will not end here.

He throws down his axe and climbs from his horse. The soldiers come, spears prodding, archers still holding bowstrings drawn. The first of them reverses grip and smashes his spear shaft into Ingirid's temple. She falls. Rúnr shouts but is prodded by five spear tips. Erasmus is kicked to the ground and silenced. Rúnr and Garmr remain standing. The soldiers close in. Rúnr can feel one behind him. He tenses. Feels the blow to the back of his head, then nothing more.

CHAPTER 58

These are my people.

These four words are all Erasmus knows. All he'll let himself know.

These are my people.

The soldiers who lured them into the trap. The ones who kicked him, punched him, left him hurt, bleeding inside, that blood running from his nose and mouth and ears every so often. The ones who covered his head in a bag and threw him over a horse and rode him somewhere dark. Somewhere underground by the smell of it. Somewhere people piss and shit themselves out of fear. Somewhere worse than that fear could ever imagine.

All the while, the bag on his head. All the while, no talking. No responses to his questions.

Until now. His eyes are still adjusting to the light after . . . hours? Days? His grumbling stomach and dry mouth say a day or so. The air here is cleaner but not quite fresh. Familiar. He's been here before.

Miklagard.

Constantinople.

The heart of the Empire.

His vision returns slowly at first, then all at once in a painful flash. He's lying on his back on the floor, old stone ceiling above.

Old stone walls around. Cool, smooth, well-kept floor beneath. Easier to clean up that way.

These are my people.

A face comes into view. Grimy cheeks. Bad teeth. Eager eyes.

Panic fills Erasmus so that he almost forgets his name. But it's not the same man. It's been too long. Or there are more of them employed in this occupation than he knows, and luck has placed him with a new one.

Luck, not God.

Whoever Erasmus once was, he's a Northman now.

"They tell me you speak our language," the rot-toothed man says.

These were my people.

"I do."

"That will make things easier. Tell me, how many more ships are coming?"

They'd never discussed this—what to say if captured, what to admit to when asked hard. If he says they're alone, a single crew, the emperor will waste no more time focusing on the west. If he says they're a fleet coming down the rivers of Christendom, there'll be more questions. Many more questions.

What will Garmr say? Nothing? Something?

The rot-toothed man grins and disappears from view. Erasmus feels his boots being removed. Then pain. It's cold at first, somewhere specific though he can't quite pinpoint where. Then it becomes hot. Someone is screaming—it sounds like his own voice. The torturer's face reappears. Erasmus clamps his eyes shut.

These were my people.

In the darkness, he sees Rúnr, Garmr, and Ingirid and prays to all the gods they're spared this hospitality.

CHAPTER 59

These people think their dirty little man with his knives knows how to torture.

They think they're safe within their walls, but there was a tear in the bag they put over her head, and Ingirid saw it all. The way they came, thrown over horses, bouncing down the paved road until the walls came into view. For a moment, at the sight of those walls, being bound and hauled like wares for sale no longer mattered. So white they could have been snow. So high they must have been built by the same hands that erected the walls surrounding Asgard. Then into the city of stone. Roads, houses, columns, all clean, all white. Still bouncing with the horse's gait, hearing the jeers of Christians as they were paraded down street after street until they were taken underground. Thrown into a wagon. Taken deeper below the earth. Dropped onto a hard floor. Dragged here, then left alone for hours, maybe a day, in torn clothes, hands and feet bound, head still in the bag. No food or water. Only the faces she saw through that slit to keep her company. And she remembers each one with their crooked noses, scars, and receding hairlines.

They think they're safe. Like this man thinks, having come to her with a sickly grin and bad teeth. He takes off the bag and leans over her. Breathes on her like the stench of a hog's ass. Says nothing as he disappears down the length of her body. Her boots are removed. Cold steel touches her bare foot.

"I have questions," the man huffs, speaking her language.

"Ask them already," she says.

Pain slices through her other foot. She refuses to wail or flinch. Another slice. She remains silent but can't help her toes curling.

"I have questions," he repeats.

"Tell your mother."

He laughs. His face reappears. He punches her in the chest, right between her breasts, driving the breath from her lungs. An ache, like drowning, grows in her core.

"How many more heathens are coming?" he asks.

"Need more feet?" she manages to say. It feels like a god is standing on her rib cage. Good, because nothing less than a god is going to stop her. She's going to burn this city to ash and take every piece of gold she can carry. She's going to piss on every garden she sees and cut open every bitch she finds so that nothing will ever grow here again.

And then Garmr.

And then Rúnr.

And then, if possible, she'll find this fucker and cut him open one slice at a time and wear his shit-colored teeth as a necklace.

He shows her a knife. She shows him her smile, all teeth.

It gets much worse from there.

CHAPTER 60

It takes six of them to hold Garmr. He's broken free of every knot they've tied around his arms. The six are not happy. They don't want to be holding him, to be this close while the thin one with the mossy teeth does his work.

Garmr doesn't mind. Pain is nothing.

"Lay him down," the one says.

"We can't," the one holding the rope around Garmr's neck says.

The one with the bad teeth looks at Garmr's boots and frowns. "How many more of your kind are coming?" he asks in the Christian language.

Garmr doesn't answer.

He asks again in the Northern tongue.

"One hundred ships," says Garmr.

"You answer more easily than the others."

"I fear nothing."

"You should fear what I can do."

"Do you fear what I can do?"

"No."

"You'll die a fool."

Nervous shuffling of six pairs of feet.

"One hundred ships of four each?"

"One hundred ships of forty each, down the Rhine, down the Vistula, down the Danube, down the Maritsa. We come flying flags of your doom from the North."

"Why?"

Garmr laughs. "Why not?"

The hand at his wrist slips, just a little. Garmr yanks his arm free and throws a wild swing. He feels flesh split and bone crunch. There's shouting. The sensation of impacts. But pain is nothing when it doesn't serve his purpose. He's proven his point. Now he needs to make certain they believe him about the ships coming down the rivers. He needs to make certain they can't see which of his words are truths and which are lies.

He kneels and lets them hammer away at his back and head. He lies down and lets them think they've won. He listens for their breathing, ragged and worn past endurance. He listens for the gods and hears the slightest whisper. It's time.

"I bring a message for your emperor," Garmr says.

"Don't do that again," the one with the bad teeth says. "Take off his boots."

"I bring an offer."

"Tell me," the one with the bad teeth says while the others struggle with Garmr's boots.

A tremor of fear runs through Garmr. Will they strip his breeches and find the knives strapped to his hip? He can't give them a hint. He can't fail his Lady. "I will speak it to the emperor himself and no other," he says.

"Then you'll die with your offer unspoken."

"I promise you I will not."

A flick of pain breaks through. Garmr's thigh has been sliced, shallow but painful. This man knows what he's doing.

"Is your message still so important?"

Garmr licks his lips. "It is."

The one with the bad teeth taps a fingernail against them. Garmr knows he has the fool.

"Each of us who was captured has a piece of the offer," Garmr says. "Together or one at a time, we will each speak with the emperor."

"The others have not said such a thing."

"It's not their duty to do so. It's mine."

"Who do you speak this offer for?"

No hesitation. Garmr knows there cannot be. "Gunvald Stone-Chest, Warchief of the Danes."

"Very well."

More slicing. More pain, like rain coming through a failing roof. All as Garmr knows it must be, for he serves only one master, and She will have her way. Upon Hel's shroud and flesh, he swears it.

CHAPTER 61

Strong arms drop Rúnr onto cold, hard ground. The coarse-woven bag is finally pulled from his head, scraping his lip as it comes off. There's little light, but it's too much and he squeezes his eyes shut. His bonds are cut, but he has no strength to stretch his arms or legs. His shoulders ache. His feet scream. A door rattles and locks again.

"Finally," someone says.

Torstyn, Rúnr thinks at first. Then, Ingimar. But no.

"Looks worse than you," says another.

This voice he thinks he knows. "Velaug?" he croaks.

"Must have hit his head too many times."

"Helvig?"

"Open your eyes."

It hurts to do so, like they're gummed together. He manages to bring his hands to his face and rub away what's there. The light doesn't hurt so much now, coming from a hole crossed with metal bars above. *Far* above. He grunts and seeks familiar faces. Finds ones he both expects and doesn't.

"Ingirid," he says.

"We're all here," Garmr says.

Ingirid makes a face and noise. In a corner, as much as there are corners in this round hole, Erasmus sits folded up to himself rocking. Opposite him, a pile of rags pulses every so often. Eventually, a rat pops its head up and then digs back into the rags. Now, too, Rúnr notes a door, so short even Ingirid would have to duck low to go through.

"Locked and more solid than ironwood," Garmr says.

Indicating Erasmus, Ingirid says, "He's useless, like when we met him."

Something takes over in Rúnr, a need to slow everything and take control. All his overthinking, all his scattered minds, come together. Erasmus is terrified, he sees, but not like when they met him. Not cowardly. Affected. Pummeled by something Rúnr can't see—something familiar to Rúnr, not in what it is, but in how it attacks. It's fear in Erasmus, yes, but not fear of what he doesn't know. Rather, it's fear of what he *does* know.

"Looks like they tortured each of us," Garmr says.

"Some more than others," says Ingirid.

Only now does Rúnr note their conditions. Like him, they're barefoot, clothes torn, faces bloodied but not broken. The wounds on their feet, he's certain, match the pain in his own.

"Why did they separate us, only to put us together again?" Ingirid asks.

Garmr stands, less steady than Rúnr has ever seen him. "I told them to."

Ingirid gets to her feet as if she's been challenged. When she sways, Rúnr stands to help but must put a hand on the wall, which is slick with moisture, to keep himself upright. His feet feel like they're on fire, but the pain is somehow less horrible than he expects.

"I'm fine," he says.

"Why would they do what you told them to?" Ingirid asks Garmr.

"The one with the bad teeth—we all met him?" Garmr says.

Rúnr nods. Ingirid does the same. Erasmus continues to rock back and forth, but he looks up and nods.

"He asked us all the same questions too?" Garmr says. "How many invaders? From what directions?"

"Among some other conversation," says Ingirid.

"What did you tell him?"

"To fuck himself."

Garmr smiles a little.

Rúnr says, "I didn't speak a word."

"Erasmus?" Garmr prompts.

"I . . . I told him we—I know nothing," Erasmus says.

"Say it again," Ingirid says.

"I told him nothing."

She menaces toward him. "I don't believe you."

"Calm, Ingirid," says Garmr.

She turns to Garmr, as much venom in her eyes for him as for Erasmus.

"We will all answer their questions soon enough if they keep cutting us," Garmr says.

"This is true," Erasmus says.

Rúnr is certain of it as well, as much as he's certain that fighting among themselves will not help their mission, the fleet, or his own need to find the red temple. Until this moment, that goal has been kept in the depths of his mind, buried beneath the fetid bag over his head, the torture, the fear of what will come next. But now, he looks up at the hole again, too high to reach even if they stand on each other's shoulders. He needs to get out of here. Needs to see this famed city. Needs to walk its streets until he comes to the red temple. And he'll build a ladder from this crew's bones to do so if necessary.

Will I?

Any doubt is shoved away.

"I like you better when you're silent like a scared boy," says Ingirid to Erasmus without looking at him. She casts a glare at Rúnr, then returns her attention to Garmr.

"I told him we each bear a piece of a single message from Gunvald, Warchief of the Danes," their captain says.

"How many lords do you serve, you traitorous fuck?" Ingirid shouts, menacing toward him despite her wounded feet.

"There is no Gunvald," Garmr says. "I pointed their eyes west, that's all."

Ingirid, fists clenched, says nothing.

"Whatever your plan is, tell it now," Rúnr says, much of Ingirid's ire in his own voice.

"He is my plan." Garmr points at Erasmus.

Their map man is no longer rocking. He seems oddly calm to Rúnr, as if he's made a decision that's been plaguing him. Garmr now paces their prison, tracing a hand along the wall as he does, pausing every so often to push gently. When he stands before Erasmus, he takes his hand from the wall and sits down beside the former merchant.

"It's daylight," Garmr says.

Rúnr can't help looking up. The little light coming from above looks to be torches and candles, not sun.

"We're deep underground," says Garmr.

"How do you know this?" Ingirid says. "How do you know where the fleet is and everything else you know? Why did you insist on his map and then never look at it?"

It seems she might go on, keep pushing, but she stops. Waits.

Garmr says, "We have time for a story."

Ingirid bends down, wipes blood from under her foot, and flings it in Garmr's direction. "I don't want to hear your stories."

"It's not my story."

Erasmus seems more himself now, watching, though he says nothing.

"Stories are a waste of time," Ingirid says. "I've not come this far and killed all those Christians just to die within the city we're supposed to be attacking."

"Are we certain we're even within Miklagard?" Rúnr asks.

"We are," Erasmus says. "Near the Hippodrome and the palace. And since we came over the mountain, nearly half the people we've killed have not been Christians."

"How can you know they were not?" Rúnr asks.

"Their clothing," Erasmus says, "and their words. And . . . I know there's many in and near the city who don't follow the Christian god."

"Followers of Odin, then, or Thor?"

"No."

"Saracens?" Ingirid asks.

"Some. Others follow gods even I've never heard the names of. And still more, like Vasil—he was a Radhanite."

"A Jew," Garmr says.

"Jews are liars, and their god is a demon," Ingirid says. "And this is a poor story for when we're trapped in a dungeon."

Erasmus lowers his head to his knees once more. At first, Rúnr thinks it's sadness or even shame. But for what? His head throbs and his jaw hurts and his feet . . . He leans back on the wall and slides down so that he's sitting like Garmr and Erasmus. His mind is seeking too many answers to too many questions. How to escape? Where to go once they do? Will the Painted Fenn be in the temple?

"How many Jews have you met?" Erasmus asks, sadly.

Ingirid says, "None."

"Two at least," Erasmus says. "Vasil . . ."

So obvious now, Rúnr sees. "You."

Erasmus nods.

"This is why you brought me, isn't it?" he says to Garmr. "It was never about the map."

"The map was useful," Garmr says. "It may be again. But no, we could have found our way without it. It's time to tell your story."

Erasmus shifts uncomfortably. Takes a deep breath. Looks at each of the others around the cellar, his eyes lingering on the door a moment, before bringing his glare to Garmr.

"How did you know?" he asks.

"It doesn't matter."

Ingirid says, "It does."

Garmr picks his teeth with his fingernail. "Do I ask why you choose Rúnr to fuck instead of me or Erasmus? No, it's what you know to be the right choice."

"Jealous I didn't choose you?"

Garmr grins. "Erasmus owes us a tale. You'll appreciate it, I promise."

Ingirid finally sits and waves her hand, either to go on or to dismiss the three men altogether.

"I am a Jew," Erasmus finally says. "I was born in Constantinople's Jewish Quarter, not far from where we sit. I was the son of a rabbi, what we call our priests. I wasn't meant to preach like him, however. I studied, yes, but I wanted to write my own stories, not just read them. I learned languages and became the best of the scroll keepers in all the city. My talents for translation and scribing made me in demand. And from that, my lyrics came to the attention of the emperor himself."

"You already told this bit," Ingirid says. "You fucked the empress, or her sister or someone."

Garmr laughs. Rúnr, however, sees pain in Erasmus and understands this is not far from the truth.

"One day, while I was reciting a translation of a Greek poem to the empress," Erasmus says, "her younger brother came to hear, and soon the empress was called away, and it was just he and I. He was so taken with my reading, he asked the next day to see me again, to hear one of my own poems. Our . . . relationship was bright and intense and secret by necessity."

"*Ergi*," Ingirid says, the insult for a man fucked by another man coming listless from her, as if she speaks it for her brother, who never shied from a chance to abuse Erasmus.

"Of all the things the gods care for," Garmr says, "I can tell you that who a man loves is not of their concern."

"Now you know the minds of the gods?"

"Do you know the story of Thor, the bride? Or of Odin, the medicine woman? Did not Loki make himself a mare to love a stallion?"

Rúnr knows the stories well, of course. Thor dressing as a giant's bride to retrieve his stolen hammer, Mjölnir. Odin dressing as a medicine woman to seduce a princess of famed beauty. And Loki, his act of love producing Sleipnir, the eight-legged horse who would be Odin's own steed.

Ingirid paces, clearly trying not to limp on her damaged foot. "Is this story going somewhere?" she asks.

"It will take us somewhere," Erasmus says. "We were happy for months, he and I, until we were caught one night. It wasn't bad enough I was seen as taking advantage of the empress's brother, but being a Jew—and legally only allowed to love another Jew—I was accused of bewitching him. The charge against me was treason."

"Did he not speak on your behalf?" asks Ingirid.

Erasmus takes a moment. Wipes his eye once. "He accused me himself in front of the emperor and the empress. I was put in prison to await execution. It was an old cell, little more than a drainpipe no longer used since newer sewers were built a hundred years ago. I escaped and fled home, but news of my crimes had reached my family. My parents wouldn't take me in. My friends refused me. My *rhabbí*, my teacher, Vasil's father, closed his door to me."

"Vasil did know you!" Rúnr says.

"It was his father who called the city watch after he turned me away. Vasil was just a boy then. I was left with no option but to flee the city, my home."

"How does any of this help us now?" Ingirid asks.

"Your escape," says Rúnr, thinking he understands.

Erasmus nods. "My escape."

Ingirid slaps the wall "You were in this hole?"

"Yes."

"This exact stinking hole!"

"This oubliette, yes."

"You knew." She points at Garmr.

Their captain grins while Rúnr feels suddenly warm with a sense of expectation. And purpose. Fate moves so many hands. Was this forbidden love all those years ago, so far from where the gods of the North roam, orchestrated just so he could one day find vengeance for his daughter? A silly notion, and yet here they are, with the ending of the story about to be told.

"We're below a tower," Erasmus says. "Beside a cistern. Surrounded by brick and mortar and what is called here cement. I was a scholar, remember. I knew the city's history. I knew its architecture. I knew that when this tower was built, the existing sewer was turned into dungeons that, because they were so close to the palace, were designated for special prisoners. Nobles, traitors, and the like."

"Which is why you insisted we speak to the emperor," says Rúnr to Garmr.

Their captain says, "It is."

"What's a sew-war?" Ingirid asks.

"Underground trenches for the disposal of waste."

"Rubbish? Why not burn it?"

Erasmus says, "A city of this size, there is so much rubbish, to burn it would darken the sky for days. But sewers are not for rubbish. They're for urine and feces."

"Your people go underground to piss and shit?"

"No, no. There are latrines throughout the city. Each sits atop a shaft leading into—"

"I don't give a shit," Ingirid says. "How does this help us?"

"Iron rusts," Erasmus says. "You see, I knew that when they built the tower, they tried a new cement mixture thought to be stronger. Ground iron was added, which did make it stronger, but the cistern leaked, slowly, for decades, a problem that was known but ignored, for what could be done but excavate the entire site? No, that wouldn't do. So, the ground around this pit grew damp."

"Which set the iron to rust."

"Yes, which made the walls of this dungeon weak in spots. Find the right one, and you can dig away the cement and let the bricks fall using little more than your fingernails."

"So you dug a tunnel," Rúnr says.

"I dug a tunnel."

"But wouldn't they have fixed the problem, or at least walled up what you dug?" Ingirid asks.

"They did." Erasmus points to the wall near Garmr.

Rúnr gets to his feet, and he and Ingirid inspect the area, finding the stone here solid.

"But they didn't correct the problem everywhere," Erasmus says. He gets to his feet and indicates the wall behind where he was sitting. "Go ahead. Try it."

Ingirid goes first, digging with her fingernails. Chunks of the wall come away. "It'll take days to dig through this with our hands," she says.

"Try this," Garmr says. From his belt, he produces four short knives.

"How?" Rúnr asks. "They took all my weapons."

"Yes, they were very thorough in their search." Ingirid says.

"I'm a sneaky one," is Garmr's only answer.

"If all we needed to do was get into here and then dig our way out, what did we need all the mystery for? What did we need him for?" Ingirid points at Erasmus.

Garmr strokes his beard.

"You didn't know," Erasmus says. "That I escaped, yes, but you didn't know how."

"I did not," Garmr says.

Ingirid says, "You don't know everything after all, do you?"

"Why the knives, then?" Rúnr says. "If you didn't know, why bring knives?"

"It's always good to have knives, isn't it?" Garmr says. He passes the first to Ingirid, then turns his back to her to hand one to Erasmus.

Ingirid grips her weapon tightly. Takes a step toward Garmr's unprotected back. And bows her head and stops. And waits.

Garmr hands the last knife to Rúnr. Wordlessly, they get to work.

CHAPTER 62

Nothing Rúnr has ever known—not the feel of the shit-sludge between his naked toes, nor the rotting Ubbein-thing, nor even the endless nightmares of Yrsa trapped in the black—compares to the miasma of Miklagard's sewers. He would take a hundred of the worst battles he's known, would suffer the most horrific wounds, even slog through days more of this mess, if he could do it all without the stench.

"I thought you said these sewers were no longer used," Ingirid manages to say, choking on every other word.

They've taken turns retching until there's nothing left in any of their guts, still needing to pause now and then for one or more of their bodies to convulse and heave. What little light there is—and from where, Rúnr has no idea—gives their faces each a deathly pale and forces them to keep within arm's reach.

"Must have—*urp*—crossed into the—*hugh, hungh*—new sewers," Erasmus says. "Or there was a . . . *uck*, overflow."

"Map," Garmr says.

Erasmus catches up to him and says, "What?"

"The map—you still have it?"

"Yes, yes," Erasmus says as if he'd forgotten it existed. He takes off his tunic and plucks the stitching until he can separate the map, as shit-covered and damp as they are. Garmr takes it and points out the crisscrossing lines on the city side of the map. Rúnr can barely tell the difference between a drawn line and a crease.

"This way," Garmr says. He hands the map to Rúnr, the first time it's been held by anyone other than Erasmus or Garmr.

The vellum feels old, as if it might come apart in wads if he holds it too tightly. When he offers it to Erasmus, Garmr grabs the merchant and pulls him ahead, leaving the map in Rúnr's hands.

"Lucky you," Ingirid says, moving past him to catch up.

Rúnr tries folding the map, but it will not go the way the folds want, and he nearly shreds it in frustration, finally crushing it into a mockery of a square before high stepping through the muck so he won't be left behind.

"Smell that?" Garmr says.

"Don't want to," Rúnr replies. He spits, but it only seems to make the taste stronger in his mouth. His mouth salivates. His belly constricts, forcing him to lurch forward, hand to his mouth. As with the last few times, nothing comes out, however. Just spasms and gagging.

"Fresh air," Ingirid says.

"This way," Garmr repeats, picking up their pace.

Soon Rúnr smells it too. Then he sees it: moonlight. How long have they been in this excrement and stench? Somehow, he finds the strength to pick up his pace and take the lead until he finds himself standing beneath a ring of open circles, the night sky above.

"I can reach it," Rúnr says, getting his fingers to the edge of one of the holes.

"But you can't fit through it," Ingirid says. "Boost me up."

Rúnr motions Garmr over, and the two of them lift Ingirid. Armed and armored, she would never fit, but dressed in rags, she's able to maneuver her way through and out.

"It's marble," she calls down. "Like a . . ."

"It's a latrine," Erasmus says.

"Fuck," is the only word Rúnr can find.

"I'll have to break it to make room," Ingirid says. "Wait." She disappears from view.

"We're in one of the old quarters," Erasmus continues. "No ceiling for the latrine means they're either rebuilding or letting it fall to waste."

Garmr begins laughing, loud and hard. "Fall to waste!" He motions at the shit-sludge around their legs.

"I—" Erasmus shakes his head.

"Come now, that's the funniest thing he's said all this time."

Rúnr finds himself smiling a bit.

"Fall to waste," Garmr repeats, hands on his knees.

"What in Freyja's name are you doing down there?" Ingirid says. She's reappeared at a different hole.

"Erasmus is making jokes," Garmr says, getting ahold of his humor.

"What? I—forget it."

"Can you get us out?" Rúnr asks.

"Back away," she says. "I'm going to open this hole bigger."

The three move back as she lifts a slab of marble over her head with both hands and smashes it down on the latrine, dropping chunks into the pit that send splashes of piss and feces all over them. Soon, the hole is large enough for even Garmr, allowing them to climb up one at a time. The latrine, seemingly under reconstruction, stands atop a hill overlooking a city the breadth of the world itself, to Rúnr's mind. White marble, clean brick, polished stone, and such painted colors make up the landscape like a forest among the mountains of such buildings he's never dreamed, all of it reflecting the crescent moon as if it were full. And the vibrancy, it's as if he's seeing Asgard itself. Or Valhalla.

This is what we've come to burn, he thinks despondently, the task seemingly impossible, for there cannot be enough fire in all the world to consume a city this large.

Then he sees the stadium—recognizable as a hyper-sized version of ruins he'd seen on the Saxon Isles—then the palace—surely a place for gods—and then the red temple. Almost black at night, with a roof taller and rounder than Rúnr could ever imagine possible, there is no mistaking it; this is his destination. The stench of the sewer is forgotten. Their mission and the fleet no longer matter. Somewhere he hears a small girl's voice.

Papa . . .

"Not yet," Garmr says, his mouth close to Rúnr's ear.

Rúnr doesn't take his eyes from his goal. "Why not?"

"You'll never see the inside now."

"It's night," Ingirid says. "What better time?"

"The city guard will be on alert with rumors of our capture and the possibility of others coming," Erasmus says. "During the day, we can enter without suspicion with the other worshippers."

"We?" Rúnr says, always imagining himself alone entering the red temple.

He spins, his axe suddenly in his hand once more, and takes off the merchant's head. His backswing splits Ingirid's skull. He dodges a meaty fist from Garmr, yanking his weapon free. One more dodge and he removes Garmr's hand. Then his other arm at the elbow. Then Rúnr opens his captain's chest with three fast hacks. Blood falls from the sky. Fire burns within his veins. His crew lie dead around him, but not so dead after all. They rise in the order they fell, eyes boiling in their sockets. Garmr's heart pumps outside his chest. Ingirid's tongue, split like a serpent's, licks both halves of her lips. Erasmus picks up his own head and throws it. Rúnr moves aside and watches it tumble down the hill before turning back to face the risen dead . . .

The crew stand watching him. Unharmed. His own empty hands clench air.

"Not having thoughts of going on your own, are you?" Garmr asks, knowingly.

"Just . . . wondering," Rúnr says. "How could men have built all this?"

"Maybe they had women to help," Ingirid says.

Erasmus says, "I've not heard of women architects, but—"

"Shut up, Map Man. What's our play here, Garmr?"

"There's a man we must meet," their captain says. "Let's not kill him, if you please."

Down the hill, the opposite way from the red temple, Garmr leads them into the city proper through paved streets and narrow alleys as if he's walked these ways a hundred times. All the walls seem three times the height of Helvig's mead hall in Skyjavík, as if it's a city of walls so high that one street's prizes, or secrets, cannot be seen from any other. Like a labyrinth meant to keep fools and prisoners ever trapped.

Such division must mean they're a focused people, like those of the North, though Rúnr suspects it's a focus for different ends. In the North, it's work and duty and song. For these people, whatever their focus has been, it will soon be war.

"How can he know his way so easy?" Ingirid asks.

"He studied the map," Rúnr offers.

Ingirid grunts in a way that makes Rúnr wonder about their captain. Not distrust him, exactly, but not trust him either, for he's certainly a man keeping many truths away from the crew. Not that it will matter soon. Come morning, Rúnr will enter the red temple and meet the Painted Fenn. He will end the man's life and free Yrsa from the black. Should Rúnr die there as well, the crew's fate will no longer be his concern. Should he live, he'll fulfill his oath to Ingirid, and together they'll kill their captain and his hidden truths. And then, back to Skyjavík to face Ubbein and Leif and avenge Torstyn. There is still much work to be done.

"This one," Garmr says, indicating a door across a street. He waits, looking in each direction multiple times before hurrying to the door and knocking three times, then three more.

The door is opened by a tall man with coppery skin wearing a many-colored scarf. "You smell," the man says in their language.

"You're ugly," Garmr replies.

They embrace and Garmr motions for the others to enter. The home is long and thin, like its owner's face, and far larger than any house Rúnr has ever been inside, as if everything in this city must be bigger than necessary to keep up with appearance and egos. The walls are plastered stone, and the air inside is cool.

"Wait there," the man says. "In fact, strip. I don't want those . . . rags in my house."

"Do you have clothes for us?" Ingirid asks.

"I have everything you need." He leaves toward the back of the house.

Garmr twirls his fingers, indicating they should do as asked. Erasmus hesitates. Ingirid doesn't, stripping off her rags to stand naked, her legs covered in shit to her knees, unabashed. Erasmus, on the other hand, seems to withdraw into himself as he makes every effort not to look at her nakedness.

"Afraid you might like this instead?" she says, squeezing one of her tits.

Garmr laughs and rips off his clothing, dropping it in a pile on top of Ingirid's. Rúnr does the same. They are crew, and though they've not stood so bare together like this, their bodies are not unfamiliar to each other, especially Ingirid's to his, and he finds he needs to keep his eyes averted to avoid his own body's desires becoming evident.

"In this," their host says, returning with a large clay vase.

Rúnr collects their clothes and deposits them, noting the way their host looks each of them up and down approvingly. When the vase is full, the man puts it outside, then closes the door warily, checking to be sure no one is watching out there.

"This way," the man says, leading them deeper into the house.

"My friend, Nikos Lampros," Garmr says. "And these are Erasmus, Ingirid, and Rúnr."

Nikos says, "A pleasure, certainly," without looking back at them.

"Who is he?" Ingirid asks.

"Ask me yourself," Nikos says, bringing them to a curtained doorway.

"Who are you?"

"I am Nikos Lampros."

"He's funny."

"Nikos and I are old, old friends," Garmr says.

"You have many old friends," Ingirid says. "Do we need to meet all of them before this city burns?"

"I'm not *that* old," Nikos says, not hiding his gaze when it falls to her breasts or below.

"Are we safe here, Nikos?" Garmr asks.

"As safe as anywhere. The White Fortress fell seven nights ago."

"The flames of its demise must have lighted the night sky enough for all the gods to see," Garmr says. He sniffs the air as if able to smell the smoke of it.

"Then surely warnings have been sent to this city," Ingirid says.

"I told you," says Garmr. "We're the tip of the sword, but not the only sword. Other crews have disabled the signal fires between there and here. This city is unaware of the fleet as it approaches."

How many such crews Rúnr wonders. What he asks is, "How soon?"

Erasmus shifts uncomfortably.

"Tomorrow," Garmr says. "Miklagard will burn before nightfall."

"I must admit," Nikos says, "I didn't think you would make it happen, but I'm glad I trusted you."

"Maybe next time you'll not doubt."

"I wonder if there will be a next time for you and me. It's a long history my family has with the Empire. A long history I'm abandoning for you."

"A history of being used and betrayed."

Nikos nods thoughtfully. "My ancestor Callinicus, who invented warfire and brought it to the Empire, would be pleased, even as I'm sad to forfeit my place in this city."

"Your fires will dim and cool if you stay," Garmr says. "Again, don't doubt me, and they will ignite the world for centuries more."

Nikos's eyes flash in the house's candlelight. "A prophecy?"

"Have I ever failed a promise to you?"

"Of course not. Everything you asked for is through here, down the stairs. When you're finished, leave nothing behind. As promised, the carts wait out the back. Remember, this house must burn when the fleet comes."

"I swear it."

Nikos and Garmr embrace once more, no mind given to the captain's nudity, it seems. Nikos then kisses Garmr on each cheek before grabbing Erasmus by the face to do the same, and then Ingirid. When he gets to Rúnr, he leans forward almost gently and kisses him on the lips. Rúnr, as if frozen by a god's hand, allows the kiss before being freed to pull back.

"What is this?" Rúnr demands.

"He does taste of death," Nikos says, then he laughs even louder than Garmr's booming guffaws. "And shit, like the rest of you. Farewell, Garmr. I'll see you again."

Garmr bows and they watch Nikos return to the front door and exit as if it were not his home at all.

"There's much you've not told us about who you are," Ingirid says.

"There is," Garmr says.

"Who named you for Hel's hound?" she asks.

After a thoughtful pause, Garmr says, "We earn our names. Come, let's gather what's waiting for us." He goes through the curtain. Erasmus follows.

"You and I," Ingirid says to Rúnr, at barely a whisper.

He nods, confirming their pact, but what if . . .

It's the first time he's allowed himself to consider such a thing: What if Garmr came by his name rightly? The man knows more than a man should. There's something *more* about him in all ways.

Odin is not the only god who walks among mortals.

"Say it," Ingirid says.

"You and I."

Ingirid goes through the curtain, and Rúnr follows. Inside is a small room with stairs at the far end. Again, Ingirid goes first. The storeroom below is narrow, with a basin against one wall and chests lining the other. The back wall is bare save for a small door.

"A bath?" Erasmus says, peering into the basin.

Ingirid says, "You knew about the sewers?"

"I prepare, just in case," Garmr says. He wastes no time shoving past Erasmus and submerging himself in the bath.

Ingirid, meanwhile, opens a chest, then two more. "Weapons," she says.

"Clothes are in this one," Erasmus says.

Garmr leans from the bath and points at another chest. "Armor in there, then."

They take turns bathing and dressing in what Rúnr takes for the clothes of the city, lightweight and poor cushioning underneath armor. But the leather and iron-plated armor pieces he finds are each quilted inside for comfort. A good system, one he'll keep in mind. Garmr has already emptied one of the weapons chests, finding a large warsword to replace the one taken when they were imprisoned. Ingirid, too, finds a pair of swords that come close to what she lost, plus a bow and arrows. And Erasmus chooses a sword and shield. To these, they each add multiple knives.

"Take the spears and whatever else looks useful," Garmr says. "There are wagons waiting for us out that door."

No one argues as they continue to arm themselves, with Ingirid rummaging through the second weapons chest. Rúnr, seeing nothing to catch his eye from the first, joins her, hefting swords and maces and hammers aside until, at the bottom, he finds the unbelievable.

"How can this be?" he says, lifting his own axe from the chest, disbelief and then acceptance mingling. Why not again? From the axe's two, now three, reappearances to the dead children who healed him to the black-and-red kite that seems to lead him when direction is needed, why remain skeptical? The gods are helping him to either victory or death. Either way, he's sailing their whale-road. Might as well take the wind how it comes.

"Looks Saxon," Erasmus says. "Like the one you had."

"It *is* the one I had."

Garmr comes closer. "You're certain?" His tone betrays both surprise and fear.

Rúnr touches each rune, each grain of the handle, each bloodstain, thinking the simplest thing. The most focused thing, perhaps, he has ever thought. A single idea over and over.

Vengeance is near, Little Bear. Vengeance is near.

"I'm certain," he says.

CHAPTER 63

The small door leads to open-air stairs back up to an alley where four narrow pushcarts wait, each laden with a large barrel atop a bed of hay. Under Garmr's orders, they've donned robes over their armor and arms and are taking turns bringing additional weapons out to the carts as night sails closer to dawn. With an armload of arrows on his way out, Rúnr squeezes aside to make room for Ingirid coming back in. She stops so they're practically face-to-face.

"Four carts," she says, her whisper husky and tense.

"I counted."

"Four barrels."

"Not five," he says, having noted this as well.

She nods. No need to explain. Garmr let her brother die, by manipulation or by withholding information or by callous indifference. It matters little to her which, Rúnr knows.

They part. She goes back into the storeroom while Rúnr drops the arrows into his cart. Garmr hasn't told them what's in the barrels, but he surely knows. He's known far more this whole time than he's let on. For a moment Rúnr feels the kind of fire Ingirid must, the kind of fire that would consume him if he thought too much about Leif or the Painted Fenn. So he keeps his mind—all its scattered geese—focused as best he can on the red temple and Yrsa. Being so close, he fears he might go mad if he does otherwise.

When he returns to the storeroom, Garmr is picking his teeth with a slender knife.

"It's time," their captain says. "The map, please."

Rúnr hands it over. Garmr unfolds it, grinning ruefully at the mess Rúnr has made of its creases, while Erasmus flinches at the same mess.

"Two watchtowers," their captain says, pointing at the map's northeast quarter, then at an area to the towers' west. "And the city's north harbor. The fleet is already burning the northern farms and lands and burgs. Ingirid and Rúnr, you each must remove the watchers from one of the towers so there will be no warning of the fleet's coming. Erasmus and I will disable the ships in the harbor. Then, when it's time, you two set your towers ablaze."

"The towers are stone," Erasmus says.

"When will we know it's time?" Ingirid asks.

"When you see smoke rising from the harbor, set your barrel inside the tower and give it flame, but don't be near when you do. What's inside will do the rest. The chaos we make will be seen by the gods and all the people of the North, and in that chaos the fleet will sail round the promontory to the south harbor, where the gates will be opened and the Rus will enter the city. When we've set all our fires," Garmr says, pointing this time to a spot just south of the north harbor, "we meet here."

Rúnr notes the route to the watchtowers. He notes the red temple's location. A simple turn at one intersection will divert him from the rendezvous to his fate. The plan set, Garmr returns the map to Rúnr, who tries to refold it. Erasmus relieves him of the task, quickly reducing the map to a small square that Rúnr is then able to stow easily.

"Who is opening those gates?" Ingirid asks.

"Other crews, as I've said. This has been well planned since long before you heard of it, Ingirid. No, don't look at me like that. This is Rurik's secret from you as much as it was ever mine."

Silence between the four of them for a time. Rúnr finds the quiet both comforting and distressing. He closes his eyes at intervals, willing himself to feel the god trance breathing behind his eyes—to know it's coming so that he can do what he wants to do: abandon his crew and go to the red temple.

But he feels nothing of it, and so he waits, trying to rein in the many directions of his thoughts, back to the moment, to the plan, to harbors, and to the watchtowers. To the barrels in the carts.

"What's in the barrels?" he asks.

"Miklagard's advantage turned to our own," Garmr says. "Warfire, as Nikos said, called Greek fire by the Empire's adversaries, is thick like seal oil and can burn the sea itself. It can turn a single ship into a fleet-destroying menace. It is what's given the Empire its mastery of the seas these past two centuries, and it will destroy the Rus fleet in moments if even two or three of the ships in this city's harbors are equipped with it. But luck is with us. The bulk of the Empire's fleet is away, warring with the Arabs, and what floats in the north harbor is their only defense. And fewer than a fistful of those ships have the warfire on board."

"All this you know," Ingirid says. "All this and more you learn somehow, but only reveal . . ." She shakes her head. Goes quiet, fists trembling.

Rúnr wants to go to her. He wants to back away from her, from all of them. Their fight is not his. Not anymore. Indecision fills him, the opposite of how a Northman should feel. He stands quiet, disgusted with himself.

"Nikos has adjusted the recipe for us," Garmr says as if there'd been no interruption. "Set the hay around the barrel alight and the warfire within will do more than burn on water. It will explode like Thor's lightning destroying a tree. Come, it's time."

The four return to the alley and their carts. The sky is lightening from purple to blue. Already, the city sounds awake and bustling.

"When we see smoke from the harbor," Rúnr says.

Garmr says, "Aye, smoke from the harbor."

"Is that all?" Ingirid says. "Can we get to it now?"

Garmr turns to Erasmus, who's been quiet much of the night. "You've not tried to flee yet."

Erasmus rolls his shoulders. "Where would I go?"

"Hide among your people," Ingirid says offhandedly as she test-lifts her cart's handles.

"These aren't my people anymore. Besides, what good will hiding do when the Rus come?"

"No good at all," says Garmr. "Let's make our way together until we reach the cistern, then we part into pairs."

He receives nods as confirmation, and they set out into the city. For all its grandeur, of height and color and stone, it's the people who capture Rúnr's attention most, how they go about their mornings with an almost lazy, yet somehow efficient, pace. These are a tall people, darker of skin though of a different tone than Rúnr himself, dressed in mostly loose clothing, draping scarves and hanging cloth like ill-fitted robes but of a lighter material and far more varied in color. Such contrast to the North and its drab palettes with clothing and decoration mimicking the colors of tree trunks and various shades of dirt—with some brighter colors displayed on shields and helms and ships. Here, however, everyone sports at least two brilliant or intense colors of flowers, fish, or autumn leaves. Painted faces, more subtle than the war paints of the North, appear common on women but not so much the men.

In comparison, Rúnr feels short and thick. The robe over his armor is heavier than what the locals wear, making it cumbersome and hot with the morning sun already raising the temperature to summer heat. And where is the breeze that should flow through a city on the sea? Where are the trees and grasses? All these flowering colors on the buildings, but where are the flowers?

His mind flits to Berthe and her purple flowers, then to Velaug.

"Can't fight in this," Ingirid complains, pulling at her robe and wiping her brow.

"The point is not to wield our weapons," Garmr counters, his voice low so that their language does not garner attention. "At least not until it's time. You look good like this," he adds. "Maybe you should paint your face like the ladies here do."

"The only paint on my face is going to be your blood if you suggest it again," she says.

"So many people," Erasmus says. "I'd forgotten."

"Do your job," Ingirid says.

"The cistern," Garmr says.

"I lived not far from here," says Erasmus. "The Jewish Quarter is that way."

"Don't go getting any ideas about warning them," Ingirid says.

"I told you, these are no longer my people."

"We'll see each other again," Garmr says. "In victory or in Valhalla."

Ingirid repeats it, though without their captain's vigor in her words. Erasmus nods, then turns to Rúnr. He looks as if he might say something. He licks his lips. Nothing more.

"This way," Ingirid says to Rúnr.

The crew parts without further words. Ingirid and Rúnr push their carts north and east, the map playing through his mind as if he can see a tiny version of himself walking its ways, climbing the folds, marking the words and symbols as if they're actually etched on the city streets.

"You're not going to quit us now, are you?" Ingirid asks.

They pass an intersection. If Rúnr turns here, he'll find himself at the red temple in two more turns. If he waits, it's a straight way to what looked like a plaza on the map surrounding the temple. They do not slow, and the next street offers a quick glimpse of a red dome high in the morning sky. Then it's lost behind more stone walls.

Are you ready for me, Odin?

But the god trance isn't coming. He must wait.

"I'll fulfill my oath," he says.

"Both of them."

To this he doesn't reply.

They soon come to another intersection. Rúnr knows it from the map. At the next crossing, Rúnr and Ingirid are to part, their watchtower targets waiting. He's certain there are words he should speak to her, but he doesn't know what they are. His mind, his focus, is restless. He wants to be there, at his watchtower, already. Or back with Garmr and Erasmus to ask more questions. Or in the invasion, the war, so that the god trance can come, can take him, and when he wakes, he can seek the Painted Fenn lying dead on the floor of the red temple.

"Why do you continue?" Ingirid asks.

"What do you mean?"

"Your oath to Garmr is no more than a whisper on the wind as far as I care anymore. You've done your job for the Rus. For Freyja's sake, they don't even know you. Why not just go? So long as you return for what you promised me, I won't stop you."

He wills that feeling of the rising god trance to find him, but it doesn't. "It's not time," he tells her.

"How do you know?"

"My fate is plain, told to me plain."

"No seeress has ever spoken a prophecy plain."

He almost defends Velaug in a childish way. *Yes too, she does*, his voice whines in his head, mocking his own nostalgia. Or is it something else he's mocking? Old love? Current lust? Faith and trust?

He deserves all the mocking, and Ingirid deserves to give it to him. But fate is fate, and he *does* know. Just like he *will* know when the third god trance approaches.

"Maybe," he says. "But numbers are numbers, as I told you. Three times the god trance will find me. Only after the third will I meet vengeance in the red temple."

"Three times," she says. "You will become Berserkr when the fleet arrives, then?"

"I must assume."

They reach the intersection of their parting and stop. Ingirid says, "I would leave the warfire and go find the red temple, if I were you."

Rúnr thinks this is not true. If she were one to do so, she would be one to take her vengeance at the first opportunity, yet here he stands with her, at a crossroads, and her knife does not seek Garmr's heart yet, nor his.

Around them, the people of Miklagard glide this way and that, paying no mind to the invaders. Just two laborers hauling their goods, Rúnr thinks, ignored by those who will soon die.

"Do you think this is the faraway land across the sea where you die?" he asks, the words coming unexpected.

"If it is, then it's also the land where Garmr dies."

"And you swore to this mission knowing you could be coming to your death. Why place your head within a hungry wolf's jaws?" Another question Rúnr hadn't intended to ask. What is he after? What can knowing her answer do for him? He doesn't know, but he needs, with a sure hunger, to hear it.

"Are you a man who fears his own death?" she asks.

"No."

"You hesitate."

"I considered my answer before speaking it."

"What do you fear, then?"

An easy answer for Rúnr. "Dying before finding the man who killed my daughter."

"And if you die fighting him—say you kill him as well—that'll be acceptable?"

He's being led into a trap of words, but he doesn't allow himself to think long on his answer. "Yes."

"And what then of the man who killed your brother? Won't he be free from facing vengeance?"

"I would like to be the one to kill Leif, but I believe he'll pay his blood price one day."

"We all die one day."

Like a rabbit who can't avoid taking the bait in the snare, he says, "I said I'm not afraid."

"Not talking about you," Ingirid says. "This Painted Fenn will die one day, whether by your hand or by another's or by time and old age, if it comes to that. Does it matter in the end, then, whose hand it is?"

The trap is sprung. She's asking to understand her own role in vengeance. Garmr is one target for her, but like the watchtowers, she has two: Rúnr must die as well for her to face her own death at peace.

And why not? He did kill her brother, though he has no memory of either intending to do so or of doing so. No excuse can be found in this fact, however. The gods never withheld punishment against Loki when his mischief came from too much drink.

"It must matter," he says. "Both the manner of the killing and the purpose in it must matter."

"Why must it?"

He wonders if she's playing with him now. "Why would you ask? Why question the gods and fate?"

"You're angry."

"I'm certain of my fate and not afraid of what comes after it."

"Are you certain you won't go to the red temple now?" she asks.

Rúnr looks down the way, imagining the temple tempting like a dancing girl who has not yet taken off her clothes.

He says, "It's not time."

"Then I'll see you again."

"Is that a threat?"

She gives that crooked grin and pushes her cart north and west, leaving Rúnr still looking in the direction of the red temple, willing himself to feel the god trance. He looks to the sky—it's bright and cloudless and hot and both more and less blue than the one he remembers in Skyjavík—and tells himself he need only be patient until the god trance, and the red tower, calls. But as he glances down the road Ingirid has taken, he finds patience in short supply.

CHAPTER 64

The watchtower is all angles and pale stone, like a mountain made square, flanking a great wall three times Ingirid's height. To her right, a long way down, she can see the tower Rúnr is tasked with destroying, built into the wall the same as this one. To the west is the harbor—Erasmus and Garmr's task there. It seemed such an easy plan when it was traced on a map, but now, facing the real thing, she feels doubt ice her confidence.

Why? They've succeeded against impossible odds in battle. They've found their way across the entire world just to stand here. Why think she might fail now?

Because I have failed.

A group of men passes dangerously close to her, one tapping casual fingers on the warfire barrel. Their words are foreign, but that one's tone, and the way he walks, is so much like Ingimar she half expects him to turn to her with his face and tell her to stop being such a *girl*, like all those other maidens and wives and crones who couldn't fight off a swarm of mosquitos. Not like *her*. Not like *his* sister.

The expectation is so real that the group of men are long gone before she realizes she's still standing in the street, exposed, wasting time that she'll need to complete the mission. For her chieftain, Rurik. Not for Garmr.

Say it again, to be sure, Ingirid.

"Fuck these Christians," she says, pushing hard to get the cart moving again. All around her, the city is alive like no city of the North. The smells are sharper. The colors brighter and more varied. The people—so many people! Which adds a layer of pungent sweat to every other aroma, like radishes offered by an unwashed hand stinking of labor. And the sea . . . What sea has she ever smelled so sharp and insistent?

Above, gulls swoop and laugh as if knowing what she brings and enjoying the anticipation.

Looking around, seeing that no one is taking note of her, she pushes the cart to the tower's wide wooden door. Unlocked. The Empire might as well be inviting this invasion. She opens the door slowly and waits for a shout of surprise. When none comes, she pushes the cart inside, then backs away. No one asked Garmr how quickly the barrel will ignite. Stupid. She exits the tower and seeks a place from which she has a clear line of sight to light the hay with fire from an arrow at a safe distance. Just as she finds the spot across the way between a building and a tree, a voice calls. She turns. Two men in flowing robes approach with smiles. Whatever they're saying, it's clear they mean to speak with her. Ingirid smiles big and nods enthusiastically at whatever they're saying. The one seems suspicious. The other is looking over her shoulder into the tower. They exchange words. Ingirid's hands grip knives beneath her robe.

A flurry of hands and more smiles tell her the first man is asking if she needs help with the cart or the barrel. She gives her best *I'm-just-a-girl* smile—the kind she's seen thralls give to their masters when they would clearly rather strangle the man than fetch his dinner or mend his trousers—and shrug and points up the tower.

The men, smiles growing bigger, enter the tower and beckon her inside. She follows willingly and points at the barrel, her head bowed, eyes looking up at them seductively. It works. The idiots start trying to figure how to get the barrel down off the cart. They discuss leverage, it seems, their voices sure to bring attention from the soldiers keeping watch above.

Kill them now, Ingimar's voice tells her.

Just a moment more, she tells her dead brother.

The men turn fully so their backs are to her.

See? she tells Ingimar.

He's silent inside her head. She pulls her knives and slices them down, allowing only a gurgle from the nice one as they both fall. She waits for Ingimar's approval, but it doesn't come. He's done with her for now, it seems. She listens for the soldiers above but hears nothing. Luck is with her.

She leaves the bodies where they lie and goes to the ladder that leads up to the next level and listens, again hearing nothing. So she climbs. The first platform is empty. The second is the same, save for a pile of feces and piss, creating a cloud of stench, in the corner. The third will be the top, she can see by the light coming from above. Still no sound of watchers atop the tower. She climbs slowly, trying to keep the ladder from announcing her approach.

She expects one or two watchers. She finds four. Two are awake and sitting lazily at the parapets looking out to sea, and two are sleeping in dirty bedrolls.

No time for knives, Ingimar tells her.

She nearly falls from the ladder in surprise.

Either help or fuck off, she screams inside her own head.

I am helping.

She pulls herself up off the ladder and draws swords. *Fuck off.*

She can be stealthy when she needs to be, and now is such a time. She maneuvers between the sleeping men, catching a look at the sea as she does. It's a gorgeous blue, both the same and different from the sea's blue in the North.

A glance east, to Rúnr's tower, betrays no hint of trouble or violence. She sees no watchers but also no Rúnr. She has to trust he'll do his job, and that the gods won't give his death to some Christian who hasn't earned it.

She readies her swords, swings them simultaneously. Two cuts. Two heads fall. Blood sprays. Using her own momentum, she spins and chooses a target, plunging both blades into a sleeping man's chest. The other wakes and shouts. She's too far to stop his voice, but she's too fast to give him time to grab a weapon. Two slices open his chest and belly. Wild-eyed, he tries to keep his insides from the outside, a futile exercise. He manages something that sounds like *bitch* in her language before falling face-first into his own blood and entrails.

Five heartbeats and the whole thing is over. She inhales deeply, enjoying the smell of the sea. With watchers like this, these Christians do not deserve their empire. She looks west at the harbors, able from this height to get a good view of the ships moored—it's less than half capacity—ugly wide things seemingly made of no imagination, suitable for war, for ramming, or maybe for carrying more horses than should ever be on a ship, but not for sailing. Not true, fast, purposeful sailing.

No, these people don't deserve what they have or what they've built. The Rus will see to it that this message is well delivered.

A last look east again shows a tower with no activity at its top. Back south, she can see the red temple, its crowning dome round like the sun itself. A fitting place for Rúnr to find his vengeance. And, with a little luck, for Garmr to appear and fall to her with Rúnr's help. And then for Rúnr himself to taste her blade.

Odd that as she thinks of taste, and of Garmr's death, she should know a sweet flavor on her tongue. But when she thinks of Rúnr's death, that sweetness becomes a tasteless ash instead. An omen, perhaps? Of fire. Of this city burning, certainly, so that the gods of the North can delight in its pyre even from Asgard's distance.

She climbs down the ladders and retrieves a bow, arrows, and stone and tinder from the cart. Then she leaves the tower and crosses the street to the spot she's picked out, where she can see the barrel through the tower's open door.

I did good, she tells Ingimar, but he's not speaking to her at the moment.

She prepares her spot to make a small fire and waits, hoping no one sees the blood or bodies before it's time.

CHAPTER 65

Rúnr leaves the bodies atop the watchtower and looks out over the water, where bone-colored sea walls extend like a giant snake slinking into the surf. It's peaceful up here, with a warm breeze. A place he could sit the way he used to in the hot springs, but thinking of the springs brings the wolf-thing to mind. He turns his back on the sea to find the red temple rising above the city, its domed roof like a massive brick breast. It pulls him, of that there's no doubt, but it's not the pull of the god trance.

If it were, I would go, he thinks, and the little doubt he harbors that he might abandon Ingirid and her people's mission drains like the blood dripping slowly from the watchers he's slaughtered.

He climbs down the ladder to ground level and checks on the cart that he's left just outside the tower's door. The streets are growing crowded as the morning ages on, and he's now sweaty and splattered with blood and his beard is like a forest compared to the bare-faced or thin-bearded men of this city. Someone will soon take notice.

The cart feels heavier now. A trick of his mind and muscles, surely. Careful not to swear, not to speak at all, so that none of the passersby hear his Northern words, Rúnr pushes the cart toward the tower. Death surrounds him. It's in the smiling faces of these Christians, unaware of what's coming. It's matted onto these cobblestone streets, where the blood will flow like creeks overrunning dams. It's in the sky that'll soon be choked with smoke and ash. It's the rotting jaw of a young boy carrying a basket of grain, his teeth falling out like acorns dropping. It's the sloughing flesh of a young woman passing by with her friends, diseased meat and muscle discharging a viscous goop, then all of it shedding like a snake does its skin.

He closes his eyes and finds memory: the wolf-thing, boiling eyeballs, the risen dead. The past, the now, the fate of his future—the killing he'll need to do to meet the Painted Fenn, followed by a return North to face Leif, and all the others whose blood he'll need to spill along the way—there's no escaping death. The stench of it clings to him like a babe to its mother.

Erasmus will not survive. Garmr is meant for death. Ingirid—she'll kill Rúnr one day. Maybe not today, maybe not tomorrow, but it will come, and if it comes too soon, if it comes before he's completed his vengeance, he'll have to stop her. To kill her.

Better never to see her again, then. Yes, he'll ignite the barrel and go to the red temple. Either the god trance will find him there, or he'll find the god trance. He'll never see his companions again. Never see his crew again.

Never have to draw blood with Ingirid.

"Do you hear that, Fate?" he says to the sky, no longer caring if he's heard. "I'm here, and I'll not wait on you any longer. Open your arms to me or have them opened by force."

The slightest whistle of wind is the only answer. It's enough. He positions the cart inside the open door and, wanting to see the sea again, climbs once more to the top, startling a raven that's begun feeding on the bodies. It squawks angrily, then takes flight.

It's nearing midday. The sun is large and seemingly angry for the way it throws down its heat on the city. Off with the robe. It's the only relief available as he stares at the sea, wondering at how much warmer the waters must be here than in the North. Do whales swim this sail road? Do cod bathe beneath its waves ready to make a salty meal?

A bird calls, sharp and insistent. Below, circling the sea wall, a red-bodied kite. Impossible to be the same kite that's appeared to him before. Impossible for such a bird to fly this far. But it's the same bird, he knows, and it soars high and to the north, bringing his attention to storm clouds far distant, above the lands across a narrow strait where the Empire continues to sprawl. Except it's not storm clouds at all. It's smoke, black and violent.

Rúnr looks west. The harbor remains quiet. Or are those people hurrying about their duties, so far away they look like beetles skittering, actually charging this way and that in chaos?

The kite rises fast and high and glides back to the south and west, to the red temple. Rúnr wastes little time debating his next actions. The kite has led him true thus far, why not farther? Down the ladder he goes and tries to set the fire with anxious fingers. What's the harm in detonating his barrel too soon? Garmr's life? Erasmus's? The latter he would mourn.

Thunder shakes the city. Shouting follows. Rúnr steps outside. Smoke rises from the harbor. Hurriedly, he gets back to his task. Another boom and quaking of the ground. Ingirid's watchtower, then. The hay won't catch. Rúnr, growing angry, nearly drops his tools. Finally, he makes a flame. Carefully, he coaxes it into a fire. Sets the hay alight. Flees the tower.

Outside is turmoil, people running without mind for safety. The old and the young being trampled. The kite returns, then flies south, toward the red temple. Rúnr follows, shoving and stamping. The next explosion nearly throws him flat.

He turns. The watchtower burns like no stone he's ever seen. A belch of black smoke rises and spreads so thick that for a moment he fears it will swallow him. Then the city comes alive around him like a nest of snakes battered by boys with sticks. The fleeing dead, their hair and flesh afire, scream and bounce off each other, spreading more fire. They fall, writhing, and setting homes and shops ablaze. Bells ring. Rúnr pays no mind to the frantic Christians racing and falling and crying. He pushes his way through those who will soon be corpse and ash when the Rus come. And he grins as he follows the roads like well-worn hunting paths through a dense forest until the red temple rises before him, its door thrown wide in welcome as if it knows why he's come and is a glad participant in his fate.

CHAPTER 66

The temple is magnificent, like something of an ancient age, or of the Aesir themselves. Marble and red stone. Glass in all the colors of the world's flowers. Windows impossibly high. It would not, Rúnr thinks as he looks about at the wide hall and rising dome and brightly painted statues and decorative medallions each the width of the moon in the night sky, be an unsuited hall to serve Odin as Valhalla itself.

He stands in the center, like being within the full depths of the ocean, watching chaos unfold. All around him, Christians slam into each other in terror. They huddle together as if their arms can protect their children from what's coming. They cower alone. None fight, and as many enter the temple as flee it. When a group of four shout at him, and later when a pair of armored soldiers approach him, he dispatches them with bored detachment. These are a soft people, protected by the vastness of their empire more than its strength. The Rus will make short work of them, which makes this temple all the more impressive, for it's truly a work of inspired hands and minds.

No matter. He waits, knowing the Painted Fenn will come. Must come. The kite's presence says it is so. Fate demands it is true. Yet still he waits while the air within the temple begins to smell of smoke, his attention returning to the statues that surround him. Scores of them, mostly women, in colors bright as the sun itself, strong and knowing. Like the Valkyries.

They are Christian women, of course, but Rúnr feels their eyes on him like the eyes of vengeance demanding he break through his impotence and do what needs be done.

But how? Where is the Painted Fenn so that he may take the blood price that is owed?

And then he knows. He feels what's absent within him, what he has not wanted to feel: There's no god trance coming.

"There must be," he says to the statues who look on mute.

He searches the crowd for pale Northern features. He rushes from one cluster of cowards to another seeking the familiar face, the one with Jörmungandr inscribed upon it, temple to jaw. He finds what he knows he'll find: His fate is not here, not within this red temple. Not within this city.

A bird's scream cuts through the clash and clamor. High above, the red-bodied kite screeches from pillar to pillar, demanding Rúnr do . . . something?

"What, bird?" he shouts. "What would you have me do?"

Bells high up in the temple's dome begin ringing, their sound an assault on everyone within, drowning all other noise. The bird flies low and then out, leaving Rúnr, hands over his ears, alone with Christians in their temple to their hanged, or nailed or whatever, god. He wants to tear it down around his beard. He wants to spill enough of their blood to drown the statues high up that, even now, seem to watch him, mocking his failure.

All this way you've come, they laugh. *All this way for what?*

He screams—no words, just pain and anger until his chest constricts and his breath wheezes and his desire for blood and victory is gone. Until he's empty, flaccid like sails in the calm after a storm.

Dragging his axe as if it weighs a hundred stones, he staggers from the red temple into a city aflame. Christians flee, Christians weep, Christians point at him and shout. Soldiers appear, come at him with spear and sword and pike. Half-heartedly, he parries.

Without vigor, he counters. Around him rages the largest battle he's ever seen. The city burns. Smoke crawls like a hungry bear. The half-dead, the maimed, the screaming burned are everywhere. And all who come at him are left dead or disfigured.

"Are none of you worthy?" he growls. There's no point anymore. No reason to keep going, keep hunting, keep killing. His fate is a lie. There's no red temple. No vengeance. No Valhalla for Yrsa. Somewhere in all this must be a warrior who can free him.

He pushes into the smoke, no longer caring if he fights soldier or farmer, Christian or Rus. He leaves the dead in his wake, faces slashed from skulls, groins split, chests caved, until he emerges into a clear square. Here, the kite sits on a rooftop.

"Take me to my death, bird," Rúnr says.

It cocks its head.

"Take me to my death or go find a fire for your feathers."

The bird hop-hops around the roof, then takes flight. Rúnr follows until he finds three Christian soldiers hacking a Rus to pieces.

"Thank you, bird," Rúnr says, though the kite is gone.

Three is a good number. The three winters without summer of Fimbulvetr. The three roots of Yggdrasill. The three sons of Borr who created the world: Odin and his brothers, Vili and Vé. Yes, three is a very good number.

Rúnr holds his axe strong and sounds his battle cry. The three turn to face him and—

Rúnr falters. He doubts. His axe lowers. Three times the god trance was supposed to come to him, yet the third remains distant. As does his vengeance and his fate. Was Velaug wrong? Could the gods have erred?

The first of the soldiers jabs a spear at Rúnr. Instinct forces him to roll aside even as his will to win evaporates. This is battle, and he won't allow himself to be butchered like a lame hog. He'll fight and earn his death and his journey to meet Yrsa in the black.

CHAPTER 67

Garmr laughs as he stomps a Christian's face over and over until it's little more than gruel. What a glorious day! He bares his teeth and shouts his joy. Four enemies flee. Two others come at him hesitantly. He makes quick work of them before seeking higher ground. The city burns. The war rages. But how does it go? He needs to see, to know he has done his Lady's bidding well.

He finds a hill—the city is built upon them, rolling here and there like comfortable waves—and climbs to a small temple, old and fallen with disuse. From here, he beholds the entire east of the city to the sea where the fleet has moored, nearly two hundred ships. The Rus have taken the south harbor while the north harbor and the north and east seawalls burn a line of flame like a dragon's tongue. The palace rises like a warning finger, seemingly untouched, but battle is manic around it. The stadium is being overrun. But when he looks west, he sees new Christians, disciplined soldiers, forming a line. He sees them holding against the Rus, even driving them back in places.

This is not how it's supposed to go. His Lady's vision was shown to him as plain as Erasmus's map. The red temple should be burning, yet it stands as an ally to the palace. The crew he brought should be making a stand between the temple and the stadium, but they're not to be found. The Berserkr should be breaking the Christian wall and will, but he's absent. Missing. All this way from

Uppsala, Garmr could feel him, the way charging horses can be felt in the earth from a fleet's length away, like an earthquake rising, but he feels nothing of that tremor now.

"What have I done wrong, my lady?" he asks.

When there's no answer, he knows his fault. He's let his faith falter. He breathes deep, filling his chest with warsmoke, holding it until it coughs from his lungs. Then he sees Erasmus nearing the stadium, outnumbered and backtracking, trying to keep the enemy from his flanks. Garmr could reach him, but he doesn't move. He has no need for the crew beyond this siege, no command from his Lady one way or the other about their fate beyond today, so he watches as Erasmus fights courageously and well. Until he stumbles.

Garmr takes two steps—an instinct, no more—before stopping himself. He must trust in his Lady.

Erasmus narrowly avoids being decapitated. In obvious pain, he backs up against a wall and steadies himself. He defends well, but his strength is fading. When the soldiers press, it's all Erasmus can do to keep his feet. Garmr knows the look of a man making his final peace with the coming Valkyries.

Look what I've done with this foreigner, he thinks. *I've made a true warrior from soft hands!*

And then Ingirid is there, a whirling rage. A Northern storm.

I've done well for you, my lady.

But not well enough. Until he sees the Berserkr in action, until he witnesses Odin's approval through his champion, he cannot know he has succeeded. And yet he's certain his time in this fight is complete. He's a watcher now, the way these Christian generals command their armies from afar. It's not the way he prefers, but he's loyal to his Lady and Her vision, so he waits and he watches.

CHAPTER 68

Ingirid guts the last soldier, spilling his insides, testicles to intestines, onto the street. He falls to trembling knees, no longer a threat. She doesn't bother finishing him.

"Can you walk?" she asks Erasmus.

He nods weakly, leaning on a wall.

"Can you run?"

"He was there," Erasmus says. He points to a hilltop.

"I saw him," Ingirid says. She doesn't need another reason to hate Garmr, so she doesn't dwell on the way he watched them fight, close enough to help without coming to their aid.

"He left."

"We'll find him."

Ingirid helps Erasmus to his feet. She will find Garmr, wherever he goes. He's too large and blond to hide among any population, even the Rus. She just hopes she crosses his path before he winds his way back to Rurik to whisper more lies and poor counsel. But first . . .

"We have to find Rúnr," she says.

Erasmus steadies himself, refusing to lean on her. It's almost impossible to reconcile this man with the merchant she first met less than a season ago. Though old enough to be her father, he's a strong warrior now, and an honorable man. The merchant, she would have left to die. But Erasmus is crew, and today he has proven himself.

"The red temple," he says.

Ingirid agrees. For good or ill, that's where Rúnr will be.

"If he's Berserkr?" Erasmus asks, the very question Ingirid was considering.

"We keep our distance until he isn't," she says.

They move north, the smoke thicker and thinner at times. Luck is with them as they don't encounter enemies along the way, despite their slow going and their lack of effort at stealth. The Rus seem to be gaining a hold here, and the farther they go, the more Erasmus seems to regain his strength.

It's enough that Ingirid begins to wonder if she needs Rúnr after all. Could Erasmus be the one to help her kill Garmr?

Possibly, but he'll not aid her revenge against Rúnr. The men are too close. There's no need to ask.

"I see it," Erasmus says.

Ingirid looks up to find the red temple's dome rising above the smoke, still a distance away, but at least they're going in the right direction. They hurry until they come to a clearing surrounded by four trees at the corners.

"This way," she says, angling for the temple.

Before they cross halfway, a score of Christian soldiers emerge. They don't hesitate, surrounding Ingirid and Erasmus.

"Not good," Erasmus says.

"We've survived worse," she replies, but it feels like a lie, the kind a mother tells a dying child.

The soldiers come smartly, in threes and fours, not one at a time. Ingirid is quickly cut off from Erasmus. The sound of battle is not glorious now as she parries and slashes, her swords cutting faster than they ever have, but it's not enough. She slices through a man's kneecap. Pierces another's forearm. And for those two successes, she suffers the pain of three spear points and a sword slash across her side. Somehow, she gets a glimpse of Erasmus, again down on a knee. The soldiers press in. The war may still be won, but the tip of the sword that began the war, she thinks, is about to be broken.

She's imagined her death before. Cut down by a heavy axe, her killer taking nine steps, then falling like Thor after he slays Jörmungandr.

Run through by a spear, her final act to behead her killer.

Cut down by a hail of arrows while taking one more life with her ebbing strength.

But this, seeing Erasmus down, shows her a death she's never considered. She turns, exposing her back, fighting to reach Erasmus so that they may die together. Pain erupts in her side, but on she goes. More pain, this time across her ribs, but she doesn't falter or fall, ordering her legs to carry her to her crewmate's side.

CHAPTER 69

The three lie dead before Rúnr. He kicks one. Spits on another. When he wishes victory, he finds defeat. When he wishes defeat, he finds victory. It's as if the gods are toying with him, entertaining themselves with his failures.

And then he turns a corner and finds Ingirid and Erasmus outnumbered and near defeat and thinks the gods must be delivering him to his end. So he'll make it an ending worthy of song and legend. The fatigue gripping his muscles and bones slips off like a cloak dropped when the rain ceases as he shoves into the fray, cutting down four soldiers from behind before they realize their ranks have been penetrated. By then, he's to Ingirid's side.

"Nice of you," she says, then coughs. Blood covers her lips. "To help."

Rúnr knocks a sword aside with his axe, then swings high. The soldier ducks low, but Ingirid stabs quickly, her blade piercing the man's ribs. Rúnr finishes him. Six remaining soldiers back off to regroup.

"What about you, Map Man?" Rúnr says.

"He's a Northman," Ingirid says.

Erasmus gets unsteadily to his feet. "I can fight," he says, though his pain is evident.

Rúnr respects his determination. *We were a fine crew once*, he thinks, before banishing the distraction.

"Go right," Ingirid says. "Fold them in toward us."

She nods at Erasmus. He returns the gesture. Rúnr sets himself to the side and in front of his companions. The soldiers adjust, as expected. They'll come at an angle, expecting to overload the center.

"Come on, you bastards," Rúnr shouts, knowing his role.

Three of the soldiers come but don't fully commit to the assault. Rúnr can only wound one before they back away once more.

"Shit," Ingirid says.

Rúnr follows her eye. A dozen more soldiers march into view, followed by three on armored horseback.

"I always figured I would die back here someday," Erasmus says.

Rúnr's confidence evaporates like mist in the sun. His axe, no longer an extension of his arm, is now a burdensome weight. An anchor. Where, moments ago, he was willing to forfeit his life, now standing with his crew, that is the last thing he wants. If this temple isn't the one he seeks, then the red temple of his fate is still out there.

"Fucking Garmr," Ingirid says.

"One more of us wouldn't make a difference," says Erasmus.

"Difference or no, his fate should be ours."

"Have you seen him?" asks Rúnr.

"Not since he fled."

"Fled?" Garmr may be more or less than he seems, but Rúnr would never have thought the man a coward.

"He saw us but didn't come to help." Erasmus points to an empty hilltop.

"And now he's gone," Ingirid says. "So let's kill these fuckers and go find our captain and tell him what we think of him."

Rúnr finds this plan acceptable. If Garmr walked away without aiding his crewmates, then he's a betrayer. All the more reason to survive this fight and fulfill his oath to Ingirid. But as the soldiers line up to charge, even more arrive to bolster their numbers.

Rúnr tries to stand fierce, but his axe is heavy, and his muscles are slack with fatigue. His breathing becomes labored. It even becomes difficult to lift his eyes to measure the enemy.

"Now would be good," Ingirid says.

"For what?" Rúnr asks, his voice sluggish.

"For the god trance, you idiot Berserkr."

"God trance?" he says as he touches his bear's tooth, and for a moment he doesn't know of what she speaks.

Then thunder rumbles inside his skull like a thousand horses on the charge. He screams from the pain of it and his vision tightens to a point and his muscles clench and convulse and the thunder becomes a war drum of purpose.

Finally!

Rúnr raises his axe and, having lost his shield, bites the blade and Thor's lightning rips through him and he has time to say only two words before the Berserkr comes.

"Get away!"

CHAPTER 70

The Berserkr arrives like a sea beast bursting up from the depths, and Garmr is glad to see it. He left the hilltop when Ingirid and Erasmus saw him watching and now regards the war from a rooftop, relief filling him like a cool drink. He'd begun to doubt, and that doubt had turned to a sour tingling in his teeth. His Lady was not pleased with his lack of faith.

But now, with the wedge of the Christian army pushing through the city, regaining ground, the Berserkr faces that wedge without fear, without humanity, killing like a scythe cuts through barely. Already, he's felled three horsemen and nearly two fistfuls of soldiers, and he shows no sign of slowing.

In the first moments when the god trance took him, Ingirid barely managed to evade his axe, to Garmr's great amusement. Where the shield-maiden and merchant went after that, he doesn't know or care. He's content to watch the blood and murder below.

Despite the carnage, the Christians continue to throw themselves at the Berserkr, outnumbering him the way ants outnumber a frog, and so they continue to fall, and their wedge continues to dull, and their lines continue to weaken. What beautiful butchery!

When the flow of Christians from the west slows, the Rus finally come from the east in two lines, steady streams that grow quickly into two rivers each more than a hundred strong. Here it is now,

Christians on one side, Rus on the other, and the Berserkr in the middle. The war for Miklagard will be won right here.

It is time, my pet.

Garmr starts at his Lady's voice.

Time to make war on all the people who do not know my name.

He's loath to look away from the Berserkr, such grace in that one's murderous hands, but he's a good servant to his Lady. He sniffs the smoke-choked air and asks, "Which way, my lady?"

The wind shifts, bringing the smell of roasting meat from the west.

"West," he says, seeing the next war laid out before him as if written upon an unfurling scroll. The Christian disease is spreading, having infected the Saxon Isles, and is now seeking anchor in the North. Pushback is needed. He closes his eyes and waits to see the plan.

At first there's nothing. Then, snakes. A corpse. A name. Ragnar Lothbrók, the great Danish hero. Dead. The future, then. Word of vengeance will spread. His sons will take up the sword against their father's killer, the king of . . .

Northumbria.

Yes, Northumbria. For vengeance, that's it. The way of all things. The circle. But not simple vengeance. No, assassination alone won't do for Garmr and his Lady. He'll wait until the hero is dead and then seek out his sons and convince them war is the way. It won't be difficult. Waiting is no obstacle for Garmr, not with his lifespan, one of the benefits of serving his Lady.

He opens his eyes and climbs down from the rooftop. Two soldiers come his way, bloodied and well-armed. Though this war, the war he started, is no longer his, Garmr will not turn his back on what killing presents itself. He stands and wields his warsword and waits to add more death to the count of his Lady's glory.

CHAPTER 71

Rúnr doesn't know when he returned to himself. He remembers fire burning inside his flesh. And now he's here, pressed against a wall as Rus run the streets shouting of victory, trampling countless dead, most of them Christians.

Most of them dead by Rúnr's hand.

The Berserkr's hand, he thinks, as if there's a difference. And yet in thinking of the difference, he feels hope. Until he remembers Ingirid once more. He was going to her aid when the god trance came. He was almost there, nearly close enough to touch her.

Ingimar's cold body consumes one of the many frayed threads of his thousand-thought mind. Cold certainty shivers his spine as he seeks her face among the dead. When he tries to stand on his own, however, his legs tremble and he must use the wall for support once more.

"Did you hear?" a wiry Rus warrior says, pausing to speak with Rúnr, joy afire on his face. "The Berserkr was here. Look at what he did!"

Rúnr's belly twists. He manages to turn aside before he vomits, surprised to see his axe on the ground near his feet. The Rus makes a face and returns to the victory sprint like a drop of water finding its way back into the rush of a river.

"No more, Odin," Rúnr says, spitting what's left in his mouth.

Do I mean of this war or of the god trance? he wonders, his mind conjuring an image of Ingirid broken like a tree limb after a storm.

"If I hurt her too . . ."

Three times.

He can barely keep up with the way his thoughts jump, but they all come together now. This was the third god trance. He takes up his axe and stands, unsteady no more. As the Rus go, he seeks the branded face of the Fenn, but there's a gnawing inside his mind. There will be no vengeance this day.

"There must be," he tells the city, its smoke and heat and stench. "There must be!"

"Rúnr!"

Ingirid comes, pushing against the flow of the Rus, and the relief he feels is like a cooling wave. At her side limps Erasmus. It's not lost on Rúnr that his concern until now has been for her alone, and for this he feels shame. Erasmus is a friend. It would be tragic to kill him as he did Ingimar.

"You're alive," she says when they reach him. She's bleeding openly from her scalp, and there are wounds across her arms and blood soaking much of her armor and clothing.

"It's more surprising you are, I think," he says.

Whatever concern was on her face vanishes in a blink. "Wouldn't want to break our pact," she says, cold as a seeress reciting prophecy.

"We should go," Erasmus says. His face is a mask of pain.

Rúnr asks where, though he's not truly interested in the answer. One direction is as good as another to the directionless, and he feels more lost than a floundering ship.

Ingirid grabs his arm. "I said, did you find him, the Painted Fenn?"

"No," Rúnr says, the word costing as much as all the blood he's lost.

"But the god trance, three times, right? Maybe we should go back."

Three times, Rúnr thinks, *on your journey as you seek the killer in the red house, the Temple of the Hanged God. There, Yrsa will have her vengeance.*

He's done something wrong. Thought it wrong or made a mistake. Something. Going back is not the solution. He can't even imagine doing so. Trying to think it—to conjure a version of himself that reenters the temple and finds the Painted Fenn—is as impossible as thinking of meeting Odin Allfather and looking into his eye. No, going back is not the solution, he knows in his bones.

"He's not here," Rúnr says.

"He must be," Ingirid says.

"I came all this way, and he's not here."

"I thought—when you said the Hanged God, I thought it fit," Erasmus says.

"You were wrong. I was wrong. I have nothing."

Ingirid comes closer, within knife's reach, if she wishes it. Rúnr doesn't stop her.

"Then we keep searching," she says, coughing as the smoke thickens. "As we pledged."

It reminds Rúnr of the black. "We need to get out of this smoke."

Erasmus looks around. "This way."

"You know where we are?"

"I know where we can get a better view of things. Maybe where we can see enough to find Garmr."

Ingirid eyes Rúnr. "I swore to find your man first."

Like finding a single fish in the sea, Rúnr thinks. "Just get us away from this cursed smoke," he says.

Erasmus leads them south, toward the harbors the Rus did not burn. Everything else, however, is aflame, the smoke at times so thick the sun is absent and Rúnr must grip Ingirid's hand and Erasmus must keep hold of his shoulder.

"I can see nothing in this," Rúnr says when they stop to catch their breath in the doorway of a butcher's lodge.

Ingirid says nothing. Her head still bleeds, but heads bleed, that flesh taking a long time to clot. It's her arm that concerns Rúnr. He makes them wait while he dresses the wound, a vicious gash across her shoulder and down her bicep, with dirty bandages made from the robes of the dead that lie about as if flowers planted for ambiance. In moments, the wrap is soaked through. He's amazed she can still use the arm, but it holds one of her swords without trembling.

"The fleet," he says. "They must have brought healers."

She looks as if she'll refuse, then simply nods in agreement.

"I think this way," Erasmus says.

He leads them on again until the smoke thins, and they begin climbing a hill that sits apart from the sounds of the spear-din. The three grip their weapons, each knowing how vulnerable they are. A legion of the Empire's soldiers could wait at the top, or just a single man, like Garmr, and they'd be in a poor position either way. Rúnr considers such a reunion with their captain. Not a happy one, for surely Garmr—who has known more than he should all along—knows of Ingirid's vendetta against him.

"He's a user," Ingirid says, as if she's pondering the same thoughts as Rúnr. She's keeping pace but beginning to limp. "He comes praying to give service, but he uses all those around him."

"To what end?" Erasmus asks.

"To the end his name hints at."

"You're not suggesting he is his name," Rúnr says.

"He's more than just a man," Ingirid says. "Or less than one, perhaps."

"You're saying he is Garmr, Hel's hound?"

"Is it so impossible?" Erasmus asks.

"Now you believe in all the gods?"

"Look at me."

"What's that supposed to mean?"

"Whatever I am, this time with you has let me see the people of the world anew, as if from a height. Like this." Erasmus spreads his hands over the city. "Is the red tower out there, Rúnr? The true red tower, the one of your prophecy?"

The question makes Rúnr uncomfortable. *Because I'm afraid I don't know the answer.*

"Of course it's out there," Ingirid says. "It's his fate."

"Then why not a god's servant walking the land with us? Doesn't Odin walk the lands at times?"

"He's a priest now too," Ingirid says, forcing a laugh.

"I don't care who Garmr is," Rúnr says, though he considers, briefly, the possibility that a servant of Hel might be able to free Yrsa if the Painted Fenn cannot be found. "Let's get moving."

Ingirid, with a burst of speed, takes the lead now, a guide no longer needed. They're going up until they reach the top. And so they go, and soon Rúnr can see a column rising from the hill as if part of a temple, though it's broken at the top. It reminds him of a tree, which makes him think of the North, which makes him see the grandeur of this place as less a testament to people and more a mockery of nature. All the trees they must have cut down to the roots to make this city, only to then build stone trees like the column above, twice the height and girth of what the world has provided. It's offensive, and he's satisfied that the city burns for it, even as he imagines what will be left when this war is over and the fires are doused and the smoke is gone and all that is left is blackened remains of people and animals and buildings.

And they deserve it, he thinks, for teasing him with their red temple.

"Slow," Ingirid says. "Quiet."

No other words are needed. The three spread out and crawl the remaining height of the hill. Rúnr finds a marble slab and sets himself behind it, spying carefully the hilltop. There are no legions. There is no Garmr.

"It's clear," Ingirid calls.

The three converge near the column. It has a square base and is covered with carved reliefs of battle scenes and victory parades. Once, Rúnr thinks, a totem might have sat atop the column. On the far side of it, four soldiers lie dead, their wounds telling of a huge sword.

"This is where he watched us from," Erasmus says.

Ingirid winces, impossible to tell from which wound, and spits. "Where did he go?"

"He's gone from Miklagard," Rúnr says.

"How can you know?"

He shrugs, not knowing how he knows. He just does. "The same way I know the Painted Fenn isn't here. He never was." Saying it aloud brings both relief and pain to Rúnr.

No one speaks for a time. Below, out past the burning city, a dozen Rus ships float menacingly, a portion of the fleet. The largest of them flies a trident embroidered on its sail.

"Rurik is there," Ingirid says, indicating the ships.

She sits beside the column, leaning against it as if they're taking a break from a pleasant spring hike. Which brings to Rúnr's mind a long-ago day when he showed Yrsa's chubby little hands how to plant carrots, the dirt cool between his fingers.

"You'll keep seeking the red temple, then?" Erasmus asks.

Seeking every red temple ever built, yes.

"I will," he says.

"We will," Ingirid says. She takes a heavy breath. "And you?"

Erasmus looks away from the burning city. "I've considered resuming my life as a merchant or starting a new one as a farmer or a fishmonger," he says. "I've considered staying and fighting with the Rus, taking my revenge the same as you."

"But you're not going to," Rúnr says.

"No, I'm not going to."

He doesn't speak of the violent circle they talked about all those weeks ago, of needing to find a different path that breaks free of that circle, but Rúnr knows that's what he's thinking.

"Not quite one of us after all, then?" Ingirid asks.

"Maybe not quite."

Rúnr waits for her to take offense, but she smiles.

"Where will you go?" she asks.

"I was a poet once." He thinks for a moment. "I think the North could use more poetry, don't you?"

"Then maybe we'll cross paths again."

He touches Ingirid on the shoulder and Rúnr on the arm. "I would welcome that." He nods and descends the western slope of the hill, away from the thickness of battle, and is soon lost to view.

In the silence after his leaving, it occurs to Rúnr that the sounds of war are lessened up here. It's almost peaceful. He turns to Ingirid to tell her this, but her eyes are closed. Her flesh is ashen and her chest rises and falls with breath, but erratically. His own breath snags in his throat. His heart thunders like a hundred horses galloping. She must be taken to the fleet, to her people.

He kneels and lifts her. She's warm and limp. There's no time for plans or routes. Only haste. Only prayers that the gods will have mercy and let Ingirid live.

CHAPTER 72

Miklagard burns. That's enough for Ingirid, she's decided. Whatever raiding is to be done, whatever ransom is to be extorted from the Empire to make the Rus go away, it can be left for Rurik now that he's come all the way from Lake Ilmen.

She's not surprised. How could the chieftain sit out such a raid as this? No, not surprised at all. Angry, though—yes, there's some of that. One of the thralls tending to the injured and the dying in this tent told her she's been here for a night and most of a day, and Rurik has not come. She's been awake since midday, and Rurik has not come. She's been told by those who lie around her, the ones who can still speak, that the initial invasion was more successful than anyone imagined. That the destruction and the spoils are beyond measure, and Rurik still has not come.

And Rúnr? That thrall said he's been by her side most of the time she slept, so where is he now that she's awake?

"You appear ready to fight."

She turns toward the familiar voice as if she'd conjured him. "Rúnr," she says. His name feels good on her lips, and for that she's ashamed. "You appear ready to quit the fight."

"This one is no longer my fight."

She sits up. Everything hurts. "I'm surprised you've stayed this long."

"So am I."

She believes him. If their positions, their oaths, were reversed, would she stay with the one promised to kill her?

Long enough to slip a knife between his ribs, Ingimar offers inside her head.

"I have to see Rurik," she says.

"I'll stand with you." There is iron his words.

"You don't have to."

He doesn't move, doesn't speak, but his dedication fills her with more strength than any of the medicines and poultices the healers have given her. The gods have quite the sense of humor, it seems, keeping the two of them together like this.

"Did you bring my swords and armor?" she asks.

Now, he lets free a grin. "Of course."

She tries to stand but stumbles. Rúnr grabs her like he's collecting a cripple.

"I can do it," she says, pushing him away. The pain is great, but it is also nothing compared to what she must do, what she must tell Rurik about Garmr.

And me, sister, Ingimar purrs.

"Swords, then," she says when she can stand without swaying. She will not go unarmed before her chieftain during war.

Rúnr gathers her gear and soon she is dressed as she should be. Her arm is bandaged and aches some, her leg feels like it was smashed by a warhammer, but she will manage. He offers his arm. Though she is proud, she's not foolish. She leans upon him and soon they're outside. It's almost evening. The smell of fire and death is on the wind. A strong wind, the kind that speaks of storms.

"Where are we, exactly?" she asks.

"A half day's sail northwest of Miklagard, up a narrow inlet the Christians call the Golden Horn. They're putting up quite the fight for their city, so your chieftain brought his part of the fleet around to squeeze them."

A smart plan, a very Rurik plan, Ingirid thinks as they cross the camp, what might have once been a fishing outpost, to a gathering on the beach. A war council. Standing two heads above everyone is Rurik, probably upon a bench to attain such height.

The gathered warriors make way for Ingirid and Rúnr. Familiar faces. Scarred and scabbed faces. They speak words of support and of condolence for Ingimar. Word has spread. Her brother seems more popular in death than in life.

When she stands before Rurik himself, the warriors go quiet.

The chieftain stands upon a barrel looking down thoughtfully as if unsure what attitude to take with her. His sharp cheeks are as she remembers. His straw-colored beard seems longer. His eyes are as piercing as ever. A handsome man, two fistfuls of winters her elder. A man born to be looked up at, or so he seems to think of himself.

She should wait. She should show deference. She should follow custom.

She touches her maimed ear, then her sword belt. She spreads her arms wide. "We've burned Miklagard for you, Chieftain!"

The warriors clamor and cheer. Rúnr, at her side, stands silent.

"So you have," Rurik says. He sounds amused. "Will you introduce your companion?"

"My *crew*." She makes this point well, holding Rurik's eye, only to find she suddenly misses her brother and Erasmus nearly to the point of tears. She swallows the knot in her throat and offers Rúnr's given name, nothing more.

"The Oppland Berserkr." Rurik has eyes only for Ingirid. "I thought he was a myth, but Garmr has proven himself once again, it seems. And where is he, my friend Garmr?"

Sucking a dragon's teat, probably, Ingimar growls.

"Fled, like a coward," Ingirid says.

At this, Rurik's countenance shifts. His eyebrows come together. His lips pucker as if tasting berries gone sour. "This is a serious accusation."

She wants to explain. She wants to call on Rúnr to corroborate what they know of their former captain. But her temper and her words get the better of her. "This is your worry, the truth of that man who abandoned his crew? What of my brother, your loyal warrior, Ingimar? Where are your questions of him? You let Garmr whisper his plan into your ear like a girl being seduced out of her dress. My brother was killed fulfilling that plan. He died for you."

Those surrounding them shift awkwardly while Ingirid regains her composure.

Rurik nods compassionately. "Ingimar will be missed." He then stands up straighter and speaks as if giving orders. "We'll find Garmr."

"Sure as Odin has one eye, I will," Ingirid says.

"Garmr is our friend. He is not to be hunted. He's to be welcomed as a hero of this siege."

Coward! Ingimar shouts.

Ingirid forces herself to remain measured. "This is your order, then? To ignore my accusation against him, ignore his role in my brother's death? To choose him over me?"

"Over you?" Rurik bites down hard on whatever words he was going to say next. "Clear the council!"

The gathered warriors do not delay. Within moments, it is Rurik and Ingirid and Rúnr and no others.

"Afraid to stand before me alone?" the chieftain says.

"There's no man alive I fear," Ingirid says, slowly, as if each word is a dagger thrown.

Rurik climbs down from the barrel but does not come closer. He eyes Rúnr. "Will you honor her chieftain even if she won't?"

"It's okay," Ingirid says.

Rúnr says nothing. He looks out to the sea a moment, then turns to go.

"This is your answer to me, then?" Rurik asks when Rúnr is gone.

Ingirid stands before him as tall as she can. The beach swims a little beneath her, the sky swirls a little above her. Her injuries require more rest, but they're not her concern. Not now. "I will hunt Garmr to the place where Jörmungandr slumbers if I have to," she says. "I will kill him there. I will say to his bones that I do this for Ingimar, son of Osmond, and for my chieftain and for all the Rus, for *he* is the betrayer. This is my answer."

The way Rurik's eyes flash from anger to fear to devious consideration gives Ingirid pause, but she cannot back down. She will not.

"This is not the question I meant for you to answer," he says. There's no time for her to reply before he adds, "I asked before you left—will you stay? I would make a good husband."

I told you he was serious, Ingimar says.

"You will make a good husband," Ingirid says, knowing on this she must be respectful. Men's egos can only handle so much. "But I am not one for marriage."

"You've not tried."

"I won't."

"What can I do to change your mind?"

He could order it, she knows. Have her confined to his tent. Have her made his, with all the trappings of a full marriage ceremony. Despite her popularity, he is chieftain. She must tread carefully, but she must also do what's right for her crew and her brother. "Declare Garmr a betrayer," she says.

He seems taken aback. He seems to truly consider it. Will she agree to his proposal if he agrees to hers? She's suddenly afraid.

"Go," Rurik, chieftain of the Rus, says.

She sees the unspoken in his eyes—*But if you go, don't come back.*

"May your song be sung until all restraints are broken and Fenrir comes free to face Odin Allfather during Ragnarök." It is the best honor she can offer him, for her past and for her people.

When he says no more, she quits the beach and goes in search of Rúnr.

CHAPTER 73

She comes from the beach, somehow both triumphant and defeated. She lumbers and limps, each movement clearly pained. Rúnr thinks maybe he'll insist they wait a day or two so she can rest further, but the closer she gets, the more he's certain they'll be riding into the night to be gone from this place.

What he doesn't know is if they'll be riding together or not.

"Where did you get these?" she asks of the two horses he is feeding apples to.

"A blacksmith," Rúnr says.

"In trade for what?"

"Your name was all it took, and the mention that you would be leaving, possibly against your chieftain's wishes."

He waits for her to ask more, but she doesn't. She chooses what the blacksmith said was the faster of the two horses, a bay mare. He could tell her the packs the blacksmith also provided are full of provisions, including more apples, and even some stolen imperial coin, but he doesn't.

"The way from here," he says, "is inland that way, I've been told." He points toward where the sun will set. "A crossroad then gives choice to anywhere, any land reachable by foot or horse."

Ingirid nods. She's gathering her strength to mount the horse, Rúnr can tell. He starts toward her to help, but she shakes her head. He holds, thinking of Erasmus, wondering if she would let him help. Then, as she gets atop of the horse, he thinks of Ingimar ribbing her for the less than graceful way she manages it. This brings a smile that he tries to keep hidden so she doesn't think he's laughing at her.

Then his thoughts of her brother turn darker, and he has to force his mind not to reconstruct the draugr version of Ingimar. But that detour only makes him think of the black mist. The dream. Last night, the black was blacker, and Yrsa was somehow less within it. She was there, of course, but she seemed further away, as if she were back in the North waiting for him, while the black beast of that place seemed closer.

And he is no closer to meeting his fate in whatever red temple Velaug or her prophecy intended. Which makes him want to gallop now across all of the lands they've traversed, back to the North to ask the seeress—to demand to know where she went wrong for him. Why she didn't warn him of Leif's betrayal and Torstyn's death. Of the false red towers. Of his crew, five reduced to two. And the foreboding feeling that it will someday be fewer still.

"What did you think of Rurik?" Ingirid asks.

The question catches Rúnr off guard. It's not like her to care what others think. He mounts his horse. "He seems like a good chieftain."

She grunts and turns her horse toward the road but doesn't get her moving yet. She seems to want him to say more.

Unsure what, he asks, "Did he ask you to stay?"

"Did he ask me to marry him, you mean?"

"I shouldn't have asked."

"No, you shouldn't have," she says.

She guides her horse in the direction Rúnr had indicated, leaving him to mount up hastily. He catches up and they ride silently for a time, until the sun almost touches the horizon, blinding them to what's ahead. At the top of a rise, the road splits into three. West, southwest, and northwest. Ingirid halts them and Rúnr turns so that the sun is at his back. Behind them, the Rus army and fleet are dark against the rising night. To the southeast, the fires of Miklagard keep the sky red and bright.

Ingirid comes up beside him. Again, she seems to want him to say something. This time he does not.

"You could have left me," she says.

She could mean at the Rus camp, in the tent for the injured warriors, but he thinks she means atop that hill after Erasmus left.

"You'd be dead," he says.

"If I live, I'll kill you one day."

Their pact. His burden—what he's done. He would make amends if he could, but how does one make amends for death? All he can do is repay what he owes when it's time. He'll not begrudge her for this.

"One day," he says. "Not today."

A column of smoke, black as tar, belches skyward.

"I no longer want to see this land," she says. She seems small. Not short or light of weight. The facts of her body haven't changed, but she's always carried herself larger. Stronger. More important. Now, however, she seems . . . defeated?

No, that's not it. It's not defeat he sees in her. It's loss. Suffering. He should ask. He should tell her he understands such things. But he doesn't. He produces Erasmus's map from inside his tunic.

"Kept it?" she says.

He shrugs. "After Garmr, then?"

"We have a deal. Your vengeance first."

"It may take a while."

She shrugs. Making fun, maybe. Rúnr opens the map. Seeks a line that seems promising, a feeling to tell him which way to travel. A bird calls. A red-bodied kite swoops low, then flies along the road that angles northwest.

"What about north?" he says.

"Choose any direction away from this place," Ingirid says. "I'll follow."

A threat. A promise. A moment of hope and even encouragement.

"So you can kill me after I've killed him?" he says, part-humor and part-defense.

She smiles that crooked smile. "To make sure no one else kills you first."

PART THREE

"Avenge us and avenge thee, we shall . . . if we live after thee."

—*The Saga of Burnt Njáll*

CHAPTER 74

Home. He expected it to feel . . . different.

Maybe Rúnr expected himself to feel different. The trees, birch and oak and aspen and rowan, now display their reds and yellows and golds along the road that leads into Skyjavík nestled between the mountains. Yet it feels like only days since he left.

Since I was driven away in exile by my brother's murderer.

"Big town," Ingirid says, a hand over her eyes to cut the glare from the afternoon sun.

It used to be, to Rúnr, but no longer. Not compared to other places they've been. The sound of an approaching horse and wagon interrupts any reply he may have had, forcing him and Ingirid off the road into fallen leaves and autumn mud. They watch the wagon pass as the wind that has been harassing them since this morning howls like a hundred wolves. They should go, but Rúnr can't get his boots moving. What waits ahead?

A welcome?

A traitor?

Forgiveness?

For no crime I've committed, he thinks, but that doesn't ease his mind. Justified or not, he was exiled for six years, and his return in just a few months will prompt a call for the law. Whether Jarl Helvig knows the truth of Torstyn's death or not, he'll be forced to face those calls.

And the law says an exile returned early must face the executioner's axe.

He looks at Ingirid who seems deep in thought. She tugs at her scarred ear. He wonders if she's reconsidering their pact. They've heard news of many things on their way north—including the end of the Rus invasion, the fleet driven finally from Miklagard after almost two months due to a combination of ransoms paid and violent summer storms—but no rumors of Garmr, no sightings of a huge blond warrior who prefers a warsword the size of a small tree. Surely coming here takes them further from her goal. Surely, she must be anxious to kill her brother's killer.

But for that, he's standing right here in the mud beside her. He turns, exposing his back. It's not the first time he's done so since they left Miklagard, but she's not seemed to notice, nor does she now. Instead of stabbing him in the back, she steps onto the road, and they move on and soon they're nearing Skyjavík proper. Ahead, people are moving in groups toward the mead hall. Ingirid shivers and rubs her hands over her arms.

"It'll only get colder as winter comes," Rúnr says, though he doubts they'll be here that long.

"Too much time in the south," she says. "Makes even a little chill feel like Fimbulvetr."

He laughs, just a little. She's not wrong; besides, who is he to judge when a woman is hot or cold?

"Who waits for us?" Ingirid asks. She's asked it two or even three times a day since they crossed the Skagerrak from the land of the Danes, seeking new details in his answers. Calling out discrepancies. Asking clarification.

It annoyed him at first, but he's held nothing back of his history, save for his relationship with the seeress—*Why do I still keep this secret to my chest?*—and her inquiries have helped them plan for this day.

"No one," he says. "Leif must have told of my death. He must have claimed it as his own doing. There's no other way he could explain Torstyn missing." He looks up the South Mountain to where the ravine gouges its shadow. Where his brother lies deep and forgotten.

"Friends?"

"I had few."

"Your mother?"

"Adopted mother."

"Is she an ally?"

The conversation is routine. She's asked this a dozen times. He's answered it the same just as many.

"She barely saw me when I lived here," he says. "She, I think, wouldn't recognize me if I filled her cup with mead."

"But your father, the jarl?"

"Helvig will know me."

She doesn't answer. Her silences are as varied as other people's words. This one speaks of her doubt.

"When I stand before him in the mead hall," he says, "he'll know me long before I announce myself."

"This is it, then? We go to the mead hall?"

This is the part they've debated for days. Do they go unannounced to the seeress and try to avoid being recognized, or do they go to the mead hall and let the jarl look upon him and accuse Leif of betrayal?

Each answer leaves more questions, more doubts for Rúnr about how long Ingirid will put up with his quest before she insists on taking the blood price she's owed. And these doubts lead to questions he doesn't ask aloud. Has he come home to seek a new prophecy from the seeress, or has he come to lie upon the ground next to his daughter and beg her forgiveness for his failures? Has he come to take the vengeance he can from the enemy he knows how to find, or has he come simply to keep Ingirid waiting?

"Rúnr?"

"The mead hall," he says, almost without thinking. Which makes it feel like the right decision. As much as he wants to see Velaug—the seeress, he corrects—as much as he wants to demand to know where the red temple hides, if there even is such a place, he knows he cannot put aside his confrontation of Leif now that he's back in Skyjavík. That one treachery must be addressed, Torstyn's murder must be avenged. And maybe that's the key. Maybe that's the first step toward finding the red temple and freeing Yrsa so that she may see Valhalla.

Ingirid asks, "This man who killed your brother, can you beat him in the Circle?"

He tries to convince himself she asks out of concern, but they've not lain together since before they arrived in Miklagard, before he failed to find the red temple of his prophecy and she failed to put Garmr to her swords. This is a business arrangement now. And despite the occasional look she gives, that hints at the way things used to be, he has tried to be at peace with how things are now. It's not been easy.

"In the Circle, I will beat him."

She nods and rubs her arms again. There was a time Rúnr would have seen this kind of behavior as weakness. Those of the North take pride in battling the cold without complaint. It's how they show the gods they're worthy of the boons they ask for. But Rúnr no longer feels like a man of the North.

Because I'm not.

The hard truth of an exile, but that's only part of it. The world is too large and even having seen only a small part of it in a short time makes him realize that he can't allow his past to define how his future will go. And, though he'll never admit it aloud, each failure to find his fate on this journey has sliced away some of his faith in the gods.

Maybe it's sliced away their faith in him. Maybe that's why Yrsa seems to be drifting further away in his dreams even as he comes closer and closer to where she lies. And these thoughts bring him to another: What of the god trance? He had his three of the prophecy, and yet no red temple. Will there be another god trance if he needs it, or will it remain dormant until he's found his fate?

"Let's get this done already," Ingirid says.

Rúnr pulls his hood low and leads Ingirid toward the mead hall. Around them, familiar faces pass without even a glance in his direction. Sifgrid and her father, the smith, pass close enough for Rúnr to smell the hearth and coal thick about them. Hrodny, Thyri's maidservant, crosses a street before him. It's as if he's not here at all.

"Seems too easy," Ingirid says. "I don't like it."

Neither does he, but why shouldn't it be easy? Who searches the faces of strangers for dead men? "This way," he tells her.

The road rises and then splits. Ahead, the mead hall stands like a child's joke. Once, it seemed so large and strong it could host an army. Compared to what Rúnr has seen, however, it's barely a horse stable. He looks up the road the other way. To go in that direction and turn one way, then two others, will bring them to his house. The other way will bring them to the seeress. Rúnr has thrown himself into battle easier than he takes the next steps forward, toward the mead hall.

"There's someone following us," Ingirid says.

Rúnr doesn't play the fool by looking back, but he slows his steps enough to hear better, and sure enough he notes the sound of boots matching their pace.

"Right," Ingirid says, indicating the direction she'll swing, at the same time Rúnr says, "Left."

They're of a mind, a fact that brings Rúnr confidence. But this isn't a Christian village. These aren't just farmers and merchants. These are Northerners. And scores of them against two, if it comes to that, can only end one way, especially if the god trance will no longer find him.

Rúnr feels Ingirid tense for the moment they'll act. He prepares himself, ready to shed blood in his homeland.

"Rúnr," a voice hisses.

He has less than a breath to decide what to do. Is it the voice of friend or foe? Of relieved recognition or indignant surprise? A mistake now will be their end.

"Hold," he tells Ingirid. They turn together.

Brondulf, the cattle-butcher, stands wary, hand on his sword beneath his cloak. "Is it you?"

"That depends on what you do next," Rúnr says.

"Come with me, quickly."

Rúnr doesn't allow himself to overthink. He follows Brondulf, and Ingirid follows him, off the road and toward the harbor before taking them to a barn. Rúnr knows the place well. Long ago, he and Velaug used to come here together when no one was watching. A memory that feels more distant than Miklagard itself.

Brondulf doesn't take them inside but rather aligns their backs to the barn so that he has them cornered.

"Did you kill Torstyn?" Brondulf asks, hand still on his sword, though it remains undrawn.

"That you're asking seems a good sign you'll take my answer as honesty," Rúnr says.

"I don't know about that, but the credibility of Leif Bjornson is lessened this past summer, at least for some of us. Give your answer."

"I did no harm to my brother, your friend."

"But Leif did, then, you'll say."

Ingirid taps Rúnr's leg with her hand. What he speaks now may hold consequences later, she's telling him. He knows it well enough.

"I'll say what I have to say when it's time," Rúnr says.

"When will that time be?"

A sound from nearby says they're not alone.

Brondulf says to the night, "Join us."

From the trees and the shadows and other places where Rúnr had not thought people could hide come four others, including Brondulf's wife, Ljufu. All armed. All grave of countenance.

"What do you think?" the butcher asks his wife.

Ljufu looks over Ingirid while barely paying Rúnr any mind.

"Are you looking for my steel or my tits?" Ingirid says.

"Who is she?" Ljufu asks.

"She's trustworthy," Rúnr says.

Ingirid snaps, "Talk to me, not about me."

"I like this one," Ljufu says, though Rúnr isn't certain she's honest in this.

"Means a lot to me," Ingirid says.

"All right," Brondulf says. He looks about, less than alarmed but far from calm. "You better come with us."

The swords and axes around them say it'll be no easy battle to decline the offer.

Ingirid raises an eyebrow deferring the decision to Rúnr. Though he's reluctant to delay his visit to the mead hall, he knows Brondulf as a good friend and an honest and honorable man.

What say you, Torstyn? Rúnr wonders, seeks his brother's voice for advice, but if his brother replies, his words are lost in the ravine, unable to climb free.

"We'll go," Rúnr says.

"Send word to the others we're coming," Brondulf orders. "Tell them no one goes to the mead hall yet."

Two of the newcomers take off at a jog, evening the odds quite a bit. Ingirid tilts her head, a question: *Better odds now; shall we fight?*

Rúnr shakes his head. "What others?"

When he gets no answer, Ingirid says, "Where are we going?"

Brondulf, with Ljufu by his side, simply says, "Somewhere even more dangerous now that you're here."

CHAPTER 75

The mead hall is full. The ale—Thyri hears from her bower in the rousing cheers and slamming waves of laughter and the many, many voices—flows fast and strong. She calls over a thrall and says she's changed her mind about which dress she'll wear for the feast tonight.

The thrall, a new girl purchased this past summer, is quick enough helping Thyri disrobe but slow to prepare the new dress. This leaves Thyri standing naked before her bed for longer than she's accustomed. It's been a long time since anyone wanted to see her bare body like this in bright firelight. Her husband has other attentions and attractions to focus on. She begins to cover herself with her hands, then stops.

She's the jarl's wife, not some modest maiden. She's the jarl's wife and she could have her choice of young, strong men in her bed. Her husband no longer cares, nor would he notice a man striding the hallway between his room and hers, for his attention is only ever on the many young women who hurry that hallway into his bed.

"Oh, just let me do it," she snaps, pulling the threads from the girl's hand, taking pleasure in the way her fingernail rakes the girl's hand and the way the girl winces in pain.

"My lady," the girl says and backs away.

"Well, don't just stand there useless. Do up the back."

The girl gets to work, but the pulling and tugging makes it difficult for Thyri to get the front of the dress to fall properly.

"I swear to—where is Hrodny?"

For such a loyal maidservant, Hrodny is away far too often these days. There's cause, of course, and good cause at that. It was Thyri's idea, after all, to keep a closer ear to the goings-on of Skyjavík. A jarl is only as safe as the disloyal in his lands, she knows. Loyalty is stagnant, like a standing pool of mosquitos, while disloyalty is like those mosquitos in flight all summer, taking small bellies of blood. But if they all fed at once from a single vein . . .

"Here I am, my lady," Hrodny says, hustling into the bower. "You can go, Dagna."

The young thrall bows her head and leaves quickly, more attentive to Hrodny's orders than to Thyri's own, it seems. Not a good development.

"I thought you were going to teach her."

"She's smarter than she is adept, my lady," Hrodny says.

"Well, the next time I have a child who needs learning, I'll call for her."

Hrodny remains silent at this. A wise choice. Even as she speaks the words, Thyri feels her stomach tighten and shrivel. No mention of a child, hers or not, can go without her seeing the face of her son. Some days, she can't even come out from her bower to sit beside the jarl, as she's meant to do, for seeing the children in the mead hall, eyes eager and bright like her Torstyn's used to be, sends her mind to dark, dark places.

"My lady," Hrodny says, producing a cloth.

Thyri takes it and dabs her eyes while Hrodny sets to dressing her properly.

"Will it be a good feast, do you think?" Thyri asks, almost absently.

"This is why I've come, my lady. I have news." Hrodny lowers her voice. "Very big news."

Thyri finds herself more affected that Hrodny came only because of the news—*She should be attending me at all times; she's my maidservant!*—than she is at the ominous way Hrodny mentions this news.

"Big enough to keep my husband's prick out of some other girl's cunt tonight?"

"It's Rúnr, my lady. I saw him outside just now."

"Rúnr," Thyri says, rolling the name on her tongue as if she's never heard it before.

"Your son."

"That traitorous bastard is no son of mine!"

Thyri is shocked at the volume and venom of her own voice so that she needs to sit. She puts out a hand and finds her bed and falls onto it. Hrodny sits beside her and takes her hand.

"My lady, what would you have me do?"

"Do?" Thyri says. The sounds of the mead hall seem very far away now.

"About the return of—your son's brother?"

"He's dead. Leif killed him for k—for betraying my son."

"Apologies, my lady, but I saw him. He was cloaked and trying not to be known, but that black beard and those dark eyes—there can be no doubt."

"No, Leif told it plain, what he did. That's not a thing to misjudge or misspeak."

Hrodny squeezes her hand. "He could have lied."

"Why would Leif lie?"

"He is the jarl's Hersir."

"He's always been the jarl's Hersir."

"My lady," Hrodny says.

Thyri looks at her. They've known each other a long time. Words are not always necessary between them. Leif is a quiet, dour man, like Rúnr in many ways. The opposite of Torstyn, who was like the fire at the heart of the mead hall, bringing joy and warmth and smiles to everyone around. But Leif is also thorough and not given to storytelling. He is honorable and honest. If he said he killed Rúnr, then Rúnr is dead.

Unless . . .

"It can't be a mistake," Thyri says.

"No, my lady."

"Tell me, what might compel a man like Leif to lie?"

"An oath. A stronger oath than honor in speaking the truth."

There are only two oaths she can imagine prompting a man like Leif to dissemble on such a momentous matter: an oath to the jarl or an oath to the gods. But which could justify letting her son's killer live?

Thyri sucks her teeth. Breathes purposefully, willing both her heart and her lungs to slow their racing. "If he lied about killing Rúnr, what about . . ."

She can't finish. The pain of hoping is too much.

"If he lied about that," Hrodny says, "there are surely other lies he's told."

"Torstyn," Thyri says, almost wails, trying desperately not to let her voice carry. Change is coming, she can feel it the same as she can feel winter's grip tightening on these autumn evenings, and it would not do to let on what she knows.

"My lady," Hrodny begins.

Thyri pulls her hand free and silences her maidservant with a gesture. She places her palms over her heart. Feels the thumping inside her slow and become steady once more, like the waves of the fjord on a calm day. Ideas spin in her mind like the warp and weft of her loom. Now, in this moment, she feels more herself than she has in years. Smarter. Stronger. More beautiful. She stands and smooths the front of her dress. She feels like a jarl's wife again.

How nice is that!

"Tell no one of this, Hrodny," she says. "Not even my husband. But go find the returned exile, wherever he's hiding. Follow him. When he starts on his way to the mead hall, hurry to my side."

"You think he'll come here tonight?"

Thyri has never been more certain of anything in her life. "It's the Autumn Reaping Feast tonight. He'll come, and one way or another I'll attend to the needs of my son, be they in Midgard or—" She has to collect her voice. "Or in Valhalla."

"Of course, my lady." Hrodny leaves quickly.

Thyri examines herself in the dress once more, then calls for the young thrall. "I feel like jewels tonight, girl. Over there. Choose me something that sparkles like the stars."

CHAPTER 76

Brondulf's home is narrow and long and smells of meat, though not in an unpleasant way. Through a curtain at the far end is where Rúnr and Ingirid are brought, into the butchering space. It's a place of serious business, where Brondulf, Torstyn, and Rúnr were allowed as boys to watch Brondulf's father work, but never to play. Torstyn and Rúnr avoided it whenever possible, preferring swords and hunts and the butchery of warfare.

To Rúnr, it's the same as he remembers, with a large boiling pot off-center between three thick-slabbed tables stained with decades of blood and blade marks, some cuts of mutton covering one of the tables. The coppery scent of blood is thick in this humid room, like a summer night after a battle quiets.

"You can't be walking around like this," Brondulf says.

"People barely looked at me when they thought I was alive," Rúnr says.

"Three people came running when they recognized you. Andhrímnir knows how many more saw your beard and are already whispering of the exile's return."

Rúnr finds this surprising, especially as he took note of no alarm on their way through Skyjavík. Ingirid says nothing, but Rúnr knows that face she makes. She's thinking. Considering when to speak, to act, to attack.

"I must ask," Brondulf says. "Is the lie of your death a design between you and Leif?"

"I come to expose Leif's lie, and his murder of Torstyn."

"You think to stand before the jarl and simply speak your truth and have it believed?"

Hearing Brondulf say it so plainly pours doubt on Rúnr. He hadn't expected it all to be easy, of course, but somehow, he had thought it might be simple: reveal himself alive before the jarl, accuse Leif, kill the bastard, and then go see the seeress and demand to know where the fuck the red temple is.

"I did think something like that," he admits.

Ingirid shifts her weight and taps a finger against a hunk of mutton. Ljufu watches her with distrust.

"Leif told quite the story," Ljufu says. "Betrayals all around, from Gellir to you to Torstyn. A cabal. Eilif supported him, though the talking tree seemed less than happy to be doing so."

"He didn't leave out his own heroics, of course," Brondulf adds. "Your father took the story as Forseti's own words. Strong as stone."

"Will Rúnr standing alive and true before the jarl sway the matter?" Ingirid asks.

"He's a fair jarl," Ljufu says.

Brondulf slams a hand on a butcher's board. "Fair doesn't mean a cursed thing, not when his judgment is based on lies. For all we know, he's complicit in all of it. This is why we're here. This is why we're doing all this, Ljufu."

"I don't disagree with you, husband, or with what we do," she says. "I never have. But I know what I know of Skyjavík. Our people prefer a strong jarl."

"We swore, you and I."

Husband and wife face each other without speaking, though Rúnr is certain they're communicating in the same way warriors do without words in battle. The same way Ingirid is telling him right now that they should leave the butchery and go do what they came to do before the surprise of his arrival is spoiled.

"Leif must be exposed," Rúnr says, feeling the same vigor now that he felt when he saw the red temple in Miklagard, thinking he was *that* close to his fate.

"He remains Hersir still," Ljufu says, as if that is the end of the matter.

Ingirid begins pacing the small space. "We've come to reveal a truth. Are you our allies in this?"

"This one suits you," Ljufu says.

"As if he gets to choose," Ingirid says.

Rúnr hides a smile.

"We're your allies, Rúnr," Brondulf says. "And we're not the only ones."

"Then we go see Jarl Helvig now," Rúnr says.

At this both Brondulf and Ljufu cease moving. It's as if each is frozen in an icicle. Slowly, wife turns to husband and tilts her head.

"He doesn't know," Ljufu says.

Rúnr's belly rises, then drops away like a ship bouncing over a sudden wave. "What don't I know?"

Brondulf puts a hand on Rúnr's shoulder. "You ask this in truth and honesty, don't you?"

The butchery is suddenly cold. "How else could I mean such a question?"

"It's not him anymore, is it?" says Ingirid.

"What's not him?"

Brondulf lowers his head and his voice. "Helvig was removed from the jarl's chair a month after your supposed death."

Rúnr's legs are weak. He leans against a table. No one comes to his aid. Good. He squeezes the table's wood, feeling splinters. Pain. Truth. And he wants more of each.

"Is he dead? Was it a Challenge? Ubbein?"

"There was no Challenge," Brondulf says. "Leif came down from the South Mountain with a story of betrayal. He spent the spring speaking against Helvig's bad judgment and rotten blood. Eilif supported him, which was enough to begin whispers and talk of a new jarl, though Ubbein himself remained silent on the matter."

"Positioning himself," Ingirid says. "Gathering allies."

"In the north and the east," says Ljufu.

"Fenns," Rúnr says.

"Fenns," Brondulf repeats gravely. "The turn of his friend seemed to drain Helvig of energy, until it began to drain him of . . . himself."

"What does that mean?" Helvig was raw strength, arms of iron, hands like clubs, resolve to match a dog's loyalty.

"The destination for our summer raids was still debated as spring approached summer, with Helvig on his chair unable to be swayed, or maybe just unable to decide. Finally, Ubbein came to the mead hall to demand a decision. As he spoke, Helvig seemed to age years in moments. Our jarl stood and pointed as if to make a declaration. The left side of his face began to droop like melting candle wax. His left arm dropped to his side, weak and useless. His words slurred like he'd had too much mead. Then he fell. We feared him dead, but it was worse, as if he'd died yet still lived."

This description runs a chill from Rúnr's boots up his spine. "Dead but alive?"

"Not like that," Brondulf says. "Not a draugr." He whispers the last word.

"He was no longer himself." Ljufu shrugs. "There wasn't even a choice to be forced," Ljufu says.

Ingirid says, "Ubbein simply filled the mead hall with his name, is that it?"

Rúnr can almost see it happening. In the absence of a strong jarl, the people of Skyjavík would seek one. They began chanting

Ubbein's name, and without pushback, without Helvig able to demonstrate his wisdom and vigor, Skyjavík took a new jarl right then.

"Helvig was given a choice, quietly, later that night," Brondulf says. "Accept Ubbein and stand aside from the chair and live."

"Or face Ubbein in the Circle," Rúnr finishes.

"Those of us who care for Helvig took him away to his former daughter's home, to Jarl Harald of the Hordalands."

"Berthe's father."

Brondulf and Ljufu lock eyes with each other. "Jarl Harald welcomed Helvig," Brondulf says.

"We've been preparing to remove Ubbein since then," Ljufu adds.

"Why?" Ingirid asks.

"Because I knew it was a lie," says Brondulf. "The betrayal. You and Torstyn against each other? It couldn't have happened that way. Never."

"In the Hordalands, Helvig could gather support and strength once more," Ljufu says.

"We didn't come for this," Ingirid says.

Rúnr grabs her arm. "He's my father. My jarl."

"Looks like Ubbein is your jarl."

"Fuck Ubbein!"

Brondulf and Ljufu shush him at once. Rúnr grabs a piece of meat and throws it against the wall.

"What? Is Ubbein such a jarl that he punishes words? Is he so corrupt he can't allow disapproval or dissent? Is this what Skyjavík has become?" His defense of the city surprises Rúnr. Though it's his home, has he ever felt he belonged here? Has he missed it at all since he left?

Brondulf puts himself between Ljufu and Rúnr, a warning. "Why did you return?" he asks.

"I—for . . ." Rúnr can find no words. He can find no purpose. He feels like he did in Miklagard when that red temple proved false: adrift. Lost. Ready to lie down and be done.

"Vengeance," Ingirid says.

"Against Leif?"

"I didn't even know about Helvig," Rúnr mutters.

"You know now. Will you stand with us?"

"To do what, usurp the usurper?"

"This isn't our fight, Rúnr," Ingirid says.

"It's certainly not yours," Ljufu says. "So why don't you be quiet about it?"

"Tell me again." Ingirid places a hand on her sword.

Ljufu, unarmed, doesn't flinch. "Ubbein does not deserve to sit upon that chair."

"I couldn't give any less of a fuck about Ubbein."

"Who else is with you?" Rúnr asks.

Brondulf eases his wife away from Ingirid. "Enough people that we have voice."

"Face down the Hersir," Ingirid says. "Let that be your contribution to their little revolution. You and I have other matters to attend."

"More important than an undeserving jarl?" Ljufu asks.

"The world is full of undeserving jarls and well-deserving corpses. Rúnr and I are sworn to each other and to our own goals. That's enough."

Sworn to each other. The phrase strikes Rúnr odd, like a blow to the tip of his elbow, a pain that doesn't match the severity of the injury.

"You're afraid," Ljufu says.

"Not of any man in this freezing fucking town."

"Ingirid," Rúnr says. "He's my father."

"Another revenge, then?" Ingirid says. She holds up three fingers on one hand and a single digit on the other. "The balance is off."

Rúnr nods to acknowledge this. The memory of Erasmus's words comes to Rúnr: *When does the cycle of violence end?*

Rúnr's response was: *When there are none left to kill.*

"I'm not saying it's our fight," he says, "but it is partly mine."

"You're not about to tell me to leave while you address this," Ingirid says.

"I know better than that." He has more to say—to ask her for patience, just a little, but she speaks first.

"Fuck it. At least it's something to do," she says with a shrug.

The four stand in silence a moment.

"We should go see Helvig," Rúnr says. "Berthe's father will welcome us, I think." His words sound confident, but he doesn't believe them.

Brondulf and Ljufu look at each other. Ljufu shakes her head a bit, in the negative. Brondulf lowers his eyes, just a moment, then repeats her motion, negating her negation.

"He's my friend," Brondulf says of Rúnr.

Ljufu sighs.

"Thank you," Rúnr says.

Ingirid rolls her eyes.

Ljufu says, "Very well. Come on."

She puts her shoulder to one of the tables and pushes it against the wall. Brondulf then gets on his knees and pulls at a floor plank, revealing a handle and a door to a cellar below, a secret Rúnr never knew was here.

Brondulf goes first down a short ladder. "It's okay," he says.

"I heard," comes a woman's gruff reply.

Ljufu indicates Rúnr and Ingirid should go next. Curious, Rúnr descends into a wide but shallow cellar, deep enough for Ingirid to stand but he must hunch. In the center, surrounded by hanging beef, is a withered old man, thin as a rope, left side of his face slack, asleep, or maybe dead, on a cushion of hay and blankets. Kneeling beside him, hooded head down, is the woman who spoke, a caregiver by her clothes, holding his hand.

"What is this?" Rúnr says as Ingirid comes down the ladder, followed by Ljufu.

The caregiver says, "Do you not recognize your father?"

"This is not my—" Rúnr stops speaking. Not because he recognizes Helvig, somehow aged a hundred years in the span of months, for it is Helvig lying there, but because he knows the woman's voice.

She removes her hood to reveal bright coppery hair and blue eyes. Had he a shield in his hand, Rúnr would drop it. Tonight, it seems, is surely a night for the dead to walk the Opplands.

"Berthe?" he says.

"Berthe," Ingirid repeats. "Your dead wife?"

"Ex-wife," Berthe says. "You look good for a dead man too, ex-husband."

Rúnr blinks. He should say something. He should drive back her wit with his own, but for no reason he can fathom, for the first time in longer than he can remember, he begins to laugh. Truly laugh. Hearty and loud, tears filling his eyes, until his cheeks and chest and belly all hurt. All the while Berthe and Ingirid stare, while the others look on curiously, which only makes him laugh all the harder.

CHAPTER 77

Thyri goes to Ubbein's room. He's standing beside the bed, shirt off, his back mostly to her, a thrall, fully naked, on her knees before him, tugging at the draws of his trousers. Thyri watches this a moment, amused at the girl's inability to release the jarl's cock. She feels strong watching the girl's eagerness, knowing it's not for herself or her own enjoyment.

I never had to perform like that with Helvig, she thinks.

With Ubbein, however, she has. It's what he likes, after all, and how else could she have proven her value to him, wrinkled as she is, soft and past her birthing years? Enthusiasm covers all such things with a fine veneer, at least for a time, like painting the rotted wood of a door frame. It may not last forever, but it makes the entrance pretty for a while.

And she feels pretty now too. A long time since that. She slides her hands from her breasts to her waist to her ass. Nothing in this dress or these jewels would turn a young man's head from a young woman with her mouth pleasingly agape, but it's enough, she thinks, if it's the young man's wife wearing them.

"Husband," she says, tender, nonthreatening. Certainly not a hint of surprise or betrayal.

Ubbein turns his head with the same nonchalance while the girl jumps to her feet and covers her chest.

"Come to help?" he asks pleasantly. "This one is having some trouble getting what she wants."

"That's the pain of thralls—they don't get what they want very often, do they? Free women give and get as they please, however."

Ubbein laughs and tells the thrall to leave. She searches for her dress, but he slaps her ass and repeats the order more sternly. The girl does as she's ordered, shuffling past Thyri.

"That one's cute," she says to her husband.

"Dumb as a spoon," he replies. "Have you come to my room to enjoy my husbandly duties?" He thrums his fingers on his muscular stomach.

"Your duties are more often than not attending to non-husbandly events." Again, she makes sure not to allow a hint of emotion, other than perhaps playfulness, to infect her words. Ubbein is a wolf, tightly wound to attack, but able to be calmed for a nap just as readily.

"Time is short because of the feast," he says, sitting on the bed. "But we've got time to explore your desires, wife."

Thyri doesn't miss the emphasis on *wife*. Not derision, exactly. Ubbein is not a cruel man. It's more smug, like a reminder of station. Of the deal she made to keep her place as jarl's wife. Lend her popularity to him through marriage to ease the transition. And she is popular in Skyjavík, but that is at best a blanket against the cold, not a shield. Eventually, he'll take a wife more fitting his age and desire for legitimate children.

None of which matters to Thyri anymore. Rúnr's return has set the future into motion, like one of the heralds of Ragnarök. The next harbinger will come at the feast before all those gathered. But there can be no room for error or surprise. She has a plan, and it must go as she thinks it down the line.

"Shut up and listen a moment," she says.

Ubbein's attitude changes in a blink. Though he still sits, he's tense, almost threatening. "I don't think you've ever spoken to me like this."

"Because you're usually smart enough to know when to listen."

He looks past her, out the door.

"She'll come back and take it in her tight little ass if you want when we're done here," Thyri says. "But I need you to hear me first."

She could keep going, say what needs to be said now without giving him a chance to interrupt or order her away, but she wants him to hear her words because he's listening, not just because she's spoken them quickly enough.

He narrows his eyes at her. She stands straight, hands at her sides. No fidgeting. No fear. Like she stood when she and Helvig were wed.

"What is it you want me to hear?" he asks.

An exhale is all she allows of her relief. "You must call for a voice of support."

"From who?"

"Everyone."

He stands. A voice of support is a powerful tool for a jarl, but one fraught with danger. If he calls for it and doesn't receive it, he'll be known right then to be less powerful than previously thought.

If he does receive it, however, his hold on the jarl's chair will be stronger than ever.

That's her play. Make him believe the support is inevitable. Make him speak every man and woman's name. That's how she'll find the truth.

That's how she'll end this pact with him.

"You were right when you came to me in secret and told me I could wrest the chair from your husband by calling for a voice of support," he says. "You were right that taking you as my wife would ensure I could sit upon the chair without bloodshed, though I still doubt sometimes it was wise to let Helvig live. A favor for a favor, however, right? You asked his life, and I spared it. And now, as you promised, there's not a word in Skyjavík of me that says I'm an unfair jarl. I am, again as you promised, more popular than any jarl we've known in generations. On all these points, I concede you were right."

But . . . Thyri thinks, fear taking hold beneath the expensive belly of her dress. And with that fear comes something unexpected: She misses Helvig.

"But," Ubbein says, "why should I take such a risk now?"

"As you say, my advice was good. Better even than the nonsense a seeress gives, perhaps. You trusted me then. Trust me now."

"The feast is ready to begin. I'm expected to—"

"If there was time to spew your juices down a girl's throat, there's time to find the words to call for a voice of support."

"One is quicker than the other."

"Something I know as your wife."

"Watch it, woman!" Ubbein snaps. "Jarl's wife is the only protection you have, and that can be lost with a few words tonight."

Thyri has overstepped, she knows. She turns her palms out and bows her head. "Forgive me, husband," she says. She can afford no more spite or bravado. "I speak out of care for you. I am the jarl's wife, your wife, and that duty I take seriously."

"Until you see a stronger jarl to marry."

She refuses to show that the blow lands. Refuses to react at all. "If you don't want to meet a stronger jarl, Ubbein, go out there now. Put on your shirt and go out there and call for the voice right now."

"What danger do you fear? Speak it plain."

"There's nothing plain to speak. I feel what I feel and I know what I know."

"No better than the seeress after all."

Thyri steels herself the way Helvig used to before boarding a ship to go raiding. "Nevertheless," she says, "now is the time. Make the call, and then when you've heard it—for you *will* hear it loud and strong—then call on your Hersir directly."

Ubbein pulls on his shirt. "Leif? Is there a plot? Is my faith in Helvig's man as poor as my faith in his wife?"

"You have no fear from Leif," Thyri says.

"Then why call on him? Such a call is never done. The voice of support is from all, not from individuals."

"And so yours will be greater than any voice ever spoken before. Honesty and loyalty you must ask of him. You must make him say both."

Ubbein wanders the room, snatching up belt, knife, boots, bracelets, and more. He finishes dressing methodically.

"What are you up to, wife?" he says. "Tell me."

She has him, but she may still lose him. He's a man who does not trust well, so she must hide her plans for Leif in plain sight. "After Leif," she says, "call on Eilif. Call on the lawspeaker, the smith, and every fisherman whose name you know. Call on me. When I'm the last, when we've all spoken our oaths—honesty and loyalty—you will have saved your chair. If you want to remain married to the jarl's wife, do it now."

"Is that a threat?" he asks, though he shows no piece of fear.

"It's advice, husband. It's good advice, I swear it. And when the night is done, I'll come to your bed and show you all the things these young girls don't know how to do."

He stands before her, taller than Helvig, his chin above her head. He looks down on her and she up at him. He runs a hand down her arm then across her belly. Thyri sucks in her gut and tightens her core.

"Nice dress," he says.

"Thank you," she says.

"It's better than most women are buried in."

The threat is not lost on her: *Betray me, and you'll die tonight.*

"It's better than most women throw on the floor beside your bed," she says.

He smiles, just a little. "Honesty and loyalty," he says.

"These I swear on Odin's eye," she tells him. "And I will say so when called upon."

He leaves the room shouting for a servant to bring him ale. Only when he's gone does Thyri exhale, the breath barely from her lungs when Hrodny appears.

"My lady, they come," the maidservant says, firelight dancing in her eyes so that Thyri could swear she sees her son Torstyn in there calling her toward vengeance.

CHAPTER 78

Bringing Helvig from the cellar takes time.

"If it is this man Helvig," Ingirid says.

Rúnr waits with her in the quiet, empty market. The sun has gone. The people of Skyjavík are all—or nearly all—in the mead hall for the Reaping Feast. The quiet is unsettling for him, as if that quality alone makes this place feel less his home than it could be.

"What reason have they to lie?" Rúnr asks.

"What lies haven't been told to reach for power? Look at me, Rúnr." He does. "Is it him?"

The introduction in the cellar was brief. Geirny and others came, and Berthe insisted Rúnr and Ingirid wait outside while the conspirators discuss their plans. So Rúnr and Ingirid wait. It seems hours, though it's been mere moments, as if Rúnr has lost all concept of time. Of life and death. Of truth and lies. Were the gods themselves to ride the Bifröst into this market and declare they themselves don't exist, Rúnr would accept it because why not?

If Berthe could be dead and now alive, if all of Skyjavík could know him as dead while he stands here outside the butchery, if Helvig could be both a man and a shadow of what a man should be, why not the gods cease to exist while clearly existing?

A dangerous insult, he thinks. Followed by: *If Berthe can live, why not Yrsa?*

But that's foolishness. He buried her himself. And yet . . .

His fingers touch the axe. Reality speaks through its cold steel. The gods are not here. Yrsa will never again take breath. He's here for a purpose, and he'll make that purpose true no matter what else comes his way.

"It's Helvig." Saying it makes it true, in the way the seeress speaks fate and makes it real for the listener.

Berthe comes from the butchery, followed by Ljufu.

"I didn't expect to see you again," Berthe says.

Rúnr replies, "Nor I you."

Silence follows until Ingirid says, "So is the old man climbing the ladder?"

Her tone is purposefully combative. Rúnr knows he should diffuse the fight Ingirid is aiming to begin, but he doesn't.

Because I know the reason why.

At first, he thought it was jealousy, but that's a flippant reason, a girl's impulse. Ingirid is a shield-maiden, like Berthe. She's protective, like Ljufu. This is about his bond with her, their oath. Her most important resource for her own vengeance and not allowing it to get distracted.

"He doesn't walk anymore," Ljufu says, projecting her most motherly tone, seeking likely to chide Ingirid into silence.

"He can't speak or do much of anything other than lie there and be recognized," Berthe says.

"Strong choice for jarl," says Ingirid.

This time, Rúnr does interject. "What do you plan with him? As you say, he can't stand as jarl, so why is he here? I thought he went to the Hordalands after Ubbein took the chair. And how are you here, Berthe?"

"He's here to remind Skyjavík of their oath," Ljufu says.

"Have they sworn to Ubbein?" asks Ingirid.

"They have," says Berthe. "I have not."

"So what can an oath to Helvig matter if new oaths have been sworn?"

"If you can't understand," Ljufu says, "you don't belong here."

"I don't understand," Rúnr says. "Do I not belong?"

"You asked the questions, I'll answer as you do," says Berthe. "Helvig can't stand as jarl. He won't have to."

"Who will?"

Berthe stands tall and straight, as if defying anyone to contradict her. "I will."

Rúnr says nothing. He can think of no reason Berthe wouldn't be a strong and wise jarl. She was always the better part of their marriage, confident and courageous. He loved her for these qualities, even if he never felt as united, as purposeful, as he did with Ingirid before her brother's death. But Berthe as jarl—part of him begins to yearn for it, as if seeing that come to pass will somehow challenge, maybe even vanquish the remaining pain of her public call for divorce. If pain is even the correct word for it. Regret? Maudlinness?

"That's some hairy balls there," Ingirid says.

"You don't think a woman can be jarl?" Ljufu asks.

"Anyone can be jarl, but I've never heard songs of Berthe, wife of Rúnr."

"And who has heard songs of Ingirid, whore of Rúnr?"

Rúnr and Berthe get between the women, back to back, speaking words of calm, entreating a truce.

"Whatever fool's plan you like," Ingirid says. "This isn't going to end well for anyone involved, Rúnr."

"We've planned Helvig's return for this night, for the Reaping Feast, for weeks," Berthe says. "And now you arrive in time to enter the mead hall with us. This is the gods granting approval for all we've planned."

"Or it's happenstance," Ingirid says. "Luck."

Ljufu says, "Luck is the gods' favor."

The butchery's door opens. Geirny comes out and says Helvig has been brought from the cellar and will exit the building in a moment. He then returns inside.

"Why did you come?" Berthe asks Rúnr.

"For Leif," he says. "For vengeance."

"Torstyn?"

"Yes, and to see—to speak with the seeress."

Berthe bobs her head knowingly. "Velaug."

"She'll be there tonight," Ljufu says. "To witness."

The door opens once more and Helvig is brought outside on a litter, with Geirny and Brondulf on one side, and two men Rúnr recognizes on the other, though their names he doesn't recall. One is a fisherman, he thinks. The other is maybe a goat farmer or one of the poulterers.

"We must make haste to the mead hall," Brondulf says. "The feast has already begun."

Helvig, barely more than a straw-stuffed effigy of himself, slides his hand to Brondulf's. The former jarl then raises his head, barely. The shock in those gathered is palpable to Rúnr.

"Father," Rúnr says, going to the man and offering his hand.

Helvig takes it, his head falling back. He shakes his head as if to say, *Do not call me that yet.* He works his mouth for some moments before he can make sound.

"Answer," Helvig says, his voice tattered and weak. All gathered know what he asks.

"You've heard Leif's lies," Rúnr says. "I'll tell the truth, Father, for I'm your son. As much as Torstyn, I am your son. And I am Torstyn's brother in faith and in love more than any blood could command." Since the day of his adoption, Rúnr has not said so aloud, not so plainly and heartfelt.

Half of Helvig's face sags slack, a look of pain in the one eye that sees Rúnr.

"Eilif and Gellir came while I was tied to the punishment chair to take satisfaction in my blood. Leif came to my rescue and then escorted me over the South Mountain to begin my exile."

"Gellir was found there according to Leif's story, much the same so far," Geirny says.

"Mine differs when Leif took me to the deep ravine and told me of his fading allegiance to you, Helvig. He said you were weak and that Ubbein would rise as jarl and that the only way he could be loyal to you was to stand with Ubbein and convince him not to kill you when he became jarl."

"That same excuse," Brondulf says. "They might have even spoken of it together."

"Who?" Rúnr asks.

"Thyri said the same of her abandonment of Helvig and her support of Ubbein."

"She's the jarl's wife still," Ljufu says.

"Ubbein's wife?" The shock of the news wanes quickly but not completely. There was never any secret to Thyri's disapproval of Rúnr's place in her family. He'd always thought her loyal to Helvig, however. Always thought theirs was a real love. He looks on his adoptive father's face for a reaction, but it's like before—barely a sign the man is alive.

"It is so," Brondulf says. "We must move."

It's slow going with Helvig on the litter, but they manage a steady pace, and while they walk, Rúnr continues his story though he's unsure if Helvig hears.

"Leif attacked me," Rúnr says. "He sought to drive me into the ravine, but Torstyn came. I don't know which god whispered my need to him, but he came. He fought strong and glorious to defend me, and when it was clear Leif would win, he threw himself in the way of a killing blow meant for me."

"My son did this for a criminal?" Helvig blurts, the words slurred.

Geirny nearly loses his grip on the litter in surprise. Berthe places a hand on Helvig's forehead.

"Easy, Father," she whispers.

"I'm sorry to say it," Rúnr says. "I'm sorry to have seen it and survived it, and to know the reason for it. He told me. He said—" Rúnr has to stop. He has to swallow hard to find his words again. He has to wipe the back of his hand across his eyes. "He said, *find him*. He saved me so I could avenge my daughter, your granddaughter." Rúnr looks at Berthe. Holds her eye, and she his. "So I could avenge our Little Bear."

Helvig reaches for Rúnr's hand. The old man's flesh is soft, like leather worn almost all the way through.

"Find him, son," he says, then lapses back into silence, his arm falling limp.

It's like Rúnr has removed all his armor, for the weightlessness of his chest and shoulders. He can breathe now with an ease he hasn't known since Yrsa's death.

"I'll find him," he tells his father.

"Find him?" Berthe repeats, seemingly dazed.

"The Painted Fenn," Rúnr says. "I heard the prophecy from our own seeress. I was to travel, to endure the god trance three times, and then find a red temple, and within its walls meet our daughter's killer."

"Our daughter's—you've not been to our home?"

"I have not since I returned," Rúnr says. He bows his head in shame. "But I will. And I'll seek our daughter's killer until my last day."

"Then your last day was nearly a year ago, you stupid donkey's taint!"

"What do you—"

"He's dead," Berthe says. "I left Skyjavík and went north to the Fennvold. Where did you think I went?"

"I—" Rúnr doesn't remember how to make more words.

"I went in the storms and the blizzards. I froze but did not quit." She holds up her left hand, revealing two fingers lost. "Not even when I had to cut these off to keep the icebite from taking my whole hand. Not even when I reached the Fenn's village and saw the numbers there. No, unlike you, who became a shell of empty, useless moping, I did not quit. I hunted him like a wolf stalking a hare, his painted face easy to recognize. I caught him alone by the water. He tried to beg, mewling about his blamelessness before I even said a word. I cut his lips from his face. I cut his fingers from his hands. I cut his testicles from his cock and shoved them into his lipless mouth. And only then did I tell him why. Only then did I do him the favor of cutting out his heart and eating it while he watched!"

"You killed him," Rúnr says, feeling suddenly so small, so weak. So wasteful and broken. He drops to a knee. Then lower. "You killed him?"

Berthe looms over him. "The killer of our daughter is long dead."

CHAPTER 79

Rúnr has become silent, marching alongside Ingirid as if an empty shell, like his father. She understands, at least a little. Berthe's revelation has cut her own verve in half. Surely it has sliced Rúnr's to near nothing.

"You're certain it was him, the man Rúnr seeks?" Ingirid asks her.

"I fought the invaders, driving them away from our mead hall, and returned to our house to be sure all was well. When I neared, the Painted Fenn was fleeing, frightened as a mouse in a room full of cats. I knew why. My husband, the Berserkr. A terrifying sight. And I took comfort in that, for surely our Yrsa was safe, protected by Odin's unbeatable champion. Out of arrogance for our victory, I let the Fenn flee. Had I known what he'd done . . ." Berthe exhales heavily. "Had I known, I would have given chase then."

For the first time in the short while Ingirid has known Berthe, the would-be jarl seems fragile.

What would I do if I learned Garmr has been dead for months?

"You couldn't have known," Ingirid offers. The words seem to flutter away like embers from a dying fire.

She eyes Helvig. The few words he's spoken—or perhaps what he's heard from Rúnr—appear to have sapped what was left of his strength. The way his chest moves with his breath, erratic and shaky, she doesn't think he's long for this life.

Berthe stops, forcing them all to halt. She stamps her feet one at a time. Bares her teeth. Rolls her shoulders. She's stern and compact with arms like a man and hair like the fires of Ragnarök. She looks like a warrior preparing for battle, which makes Ingirid's blood flow the same. They have much in common, she thinks.

Then Berthe turns her attention to Rúnr with a surprisingly kind eye. "You've done well enough," she says, her voice almost tender. She takes her ex-husband's hand and squeezes it. "For her, you've done well enough."

There's no desire in their touch. It's a comfort and nothing more, Ingirid knows. The past between Berthe and Rúnr is dead, like their daughter. And yet . . .

And yet, if she doesn't let go of his hand, I'll cut it off!

The violence of the thought surprises Ingirid. She's never been a jealous person. A man or woman who wants another pair of tits other than hers is welcome to them. Jealousy is a weakness, one she doesn't allow. So what is this?

You know what it is because you've been feeling it a long time, Ingimar's voice tells her.

That's a lie, she protests.

But this feeling, small and petty, comes every time Berthe gets near Rúnr. It comes every time he mentions his fate, his prophecy, his seeress. His Velaug. And though that woman hasn't yet shown her face tonight, Ingirid knows the jealousy she feels for Berthe is merely preparation for what will come with Velaug.

You're afraid, Ingimar insists.

Lie!

But the lie is the denial. She is afraid. Of losing Rúnr—a fact she's been trying to avoid since Miklagard. She tells herself it's because she's afraid of losing her pursuit of Garmr, but that's the lie. A circle of denial and lies. She thinks of Erasmus. He would have advice for her, though she'd probably not heed it.

She waits, expecting her brother to have something more to say, but it's silent in her mind—save for the fear. This time of finding herself in Valhalla one day and her brother not there, as Yrsa is not feasting there now.

But surely Rúnr's daughter is in Valhalla now. The Painted Fenn is dead. Berthe says so.

Could she be wrong?

One look at the woman says she's not mistaken about the Painted Fenn's death. What does this mean? Should Ingirid quit this place? That was the pact she and Rúnr made—the death of the Painted Fenn first, the hunt for Garmr next.

So why are you still here?

Now Ingimar speaks! When he does, she wants him silent. When he doesn't, she misses his voice.

"You were there," Rúnr says to Berthe, "when they brought Helvig to the Hordalands?"

"I spent the winter in the Fennvold," Berthe says. "After I killed the Painted Fenn, the snows and storms grew worse, too much to travel, so I found a wolf's den. There were three inside and I made them my meat for the winter and their home mine until the thaw. I saw no reason to return to Skyjavík, so I went to my father's hall. Not many weeks later, Brondulf and Ljufu arrived with Helvig and told me of your death." She offers a mirthless chuckle. "Together we planned these next steps with my father's support and returned to Skyjavík in secret a sennight ago. We've been preparing since, gathering support. Almost half of the warriors in the mead hall tonight disapprove of Ubbein's taking Helvig's chair and wife." She separates from Rúnr and stands alone as if wanting to do something but unsure what.

Ingirid moves to Rúnr's side. "Your daughter is avenged," she says. "We can go and seek Garmr."

He looks at her as if he doesn't know her. "We're almost there." He points. The mead hall stands before them, full of the sounds of a feast.

You should go.

Ingimar is right. She doesn't need Rúnr. She can find another warrior to help her hunt Garmr. She can convince a shipload of warriors. Rúnr is nothing. A beaten man, at best.

Then why do you stay?

She doesn't want to answer her brother. Doesn't want to hear herself think the words, even as she knows she must: to recommit, to pay what's owed.

To me.

Yes, she thinks. *What's owed to you, brother.*

And now she's imagining it to come. She and Rúnr, on other roads, in other lands, far from her home and his, chasing rumors together, a crew of two, nights spent like they were before the Berserkr took her brother.

Finding Garmr, Ingimar says.

Yes, finding Garmr at last and killing their former captain.

And then what? Ingimar asks.

And then I kill Rúnr, as promised.

CHAPTER 80

Berthe lives. The Painted Fenn is dead. Yrsa is avenged.

Rúnr should be pleased, but he can't find that happiness in any of it.

Yrsa is avenged? How does he still dream of her, then?

Is it because Berthe took his vengeance? Is that why his Little Bear is faded within the dream?

But Berthe killed the Painted Fenn before he ever went to the Fennvold, before he fought Ubbein and was declared an exile. Before Leif killed Torstyn.

Before Velaug spoke her prophecy and my fate.

He's aware of Ingirid at his side. He's aware of Berthe and Brondulf and Helvig and others around him. He's aware of the mead hall standing before them. All of it feeling like little more than wind and shadow, mattering nothing to the truth of fate.

Or the lie of it.

There's a commotion. Someone bumps him. Someone pulls on his arm. He turns. Ingirid is shouting, her mouth and eyes wide, but there's no sound. She punches him in the chest.

His hearing returns like air to a drowning man. He gulps and gapes and the world spins into action around him. Brondulf is arguing with an armed man at the mead hall's entrance. Berthe and Ingirid hold swords. Geirny is barely keeping Helvig's litter straight with only three men holding the corners.

"Enough of this," Berthe says. "You know me, Rangvald."

"I know what I've been told," Rangvald, Skyjavík's best carpenter now armed and armored as if for battle, says. "You're not allowed inside without permission."

"Permission? Since when is permission needed to enter the mead hall? This is the people's hall!"

"I'm sorry," Rangvald says. "Orders."

"The lady is right." Ingirid says. "Enough of this."

She draws her sword and runs it through Rangvald's ribs. He cries out. Rúnr watches him crumple, feeling nothing. Not the rush of the shield-roar in his ears, nor the fire of battle-blood in his muscles. Not the tightening that precedes the god trance. Rangvald dies to no recognition or retaliation.

"What did you do?" Brondulf says. "We need to speak to the people, not cut them down."

"So speak," Ingirid says.

"You're insane," Ljufu complains.

Ingirid shrugs.

"Rúnr, you need to control her."

This brings Rúnr back to himself. Whatever the truth is, it will begin to reveal itself inside the mead hall. For this, and the suggestion that any man could control Ingirid, he can't help a small grin. "Not likely," he says.

"We're not lost," Berthe says. "Look. Listen."

Inside the mead hall, the people press toward the fire, their backs to the door, shouting but not for violence. Ubbein is standing before the jarl's chair, its crimson paint all but faded now, calling names and pointing at each person he's called in turn.

"He knows we're coming," Brondulf says.

Ljufu grabs her husband's arm. "We need to abandon the plan. It can't work if he knows, not if he's taking oaths of support as we enter."

"We're not abandoning anything," Berthe says. "This is happening. Flee if you want to, but I'll remember when I'm jarl."

"You sound like Ubbein," Brondulf says.

"But I'm not him, am I?"

Brondulf doesn't answer. Geirny, however, says plainly, "You are not."

Rúnr repeats, "You are not."

Even Ingirid says it. The spear-din is twisting strong in their blood, now, contagious to Rúnr.

"You are not," says Brondulf.

Berthe says, "We go in now, as we planned."

She enters. No one stops her. Rúnr follows, passing into the mead hall's warmth like going through a wave. Together, they make room for Helvig on his litter. Ljufu comes to assist, as does Ingirid. Brondulf and Geirny lead Helvig in to mutters and drowned shouts for attention. Ubbein is too strong, the crowd near the fire too loud, for any who do not see the litter to be aware it's coming.

"Sifgrid and Sverre," Ubbein calls.

"The smith's daughter," someone yells.

The shout is taken up by others until Sifgrid and Sverre approach the fire and say their names. Rúnr spies over and under and through, seeking faces in the hall. Friends. Allies. There—the one face he needs to see!

"I swear honesty and loyalty for all times," Sverre declares, "to Jarl Ubbein!"

Rúnr abandons his task and begins pushing into the crowd, toward the corner where Velaug stands—where answers await. As if feeling him, she turns, her blue eyes visible from here.

"Rúnr," Berthe says. "I need you."

He ignores her and keeps pushing. Someone grabs his arm. He pulls free, looking back to speak horrible words only to find it's Ingirid.

"Let's do what we came to do," she says.

"I am," he tells her.

Again, he tries to go. Again, she grabs him, her grip like iron.

"The seeress can wait," she says.

"Your bullshit vengeance can wait," he says, voicing all the rancor he'd intended for Berthe.

Ingirid will not let go. "But yours can't. It's right here in this hall, so you might as well finish the hunt."

He can't pull free, but he can avoid her eyes. Her truth. Because she knows him. She knows that he's nothing without his vengeance and hopes to die achieving it so that he doesn't have to pursue Garmr with her.

She knows all this, he can feel through her hand on his forearm, so he looks the other way, but Velaug is no longer there.

"She can fucking wait, Rúnr," Ingirid says.

He lets his arm fall slack. She releases him.

"And now, my Hersir," Ubbein calls. "Leif Bjornson, will you speak your oath of honesty and loyalty to this jarl in all your words and deeds?"

Those in the mead hall seem to all take a breath as Leif steps to the fire, his face taking the light of the flames so that it's as if the gods are showing Rúnr's way. Yes, Velaug can wait.

"I am Leif Bjornson," Leif says, confident and proud, like when he killed Torstyn.

Together, Rúnr and Ingirid make their way to the fire, but Berthe has made it there first.

"Hear me, Jarl Ubbein," she shouts before Leif can speak his oath.

So much happens next, all at once, while Rúnr claws his way to the fire, all the motion around him slow, as if the hall is underwater.

Berthe calls her claim on behalf of Helvig while Ubbein denounces the interruption and demands Leif speak his oath.

Berthe repeats her words.

Someone shrieks, demanding Leif speak his oath.

Another voice calls for it.

Ubbein orders it. Next to him sits Thyri, wild-eyed and frantic like a cornered wolf.

Ingirid spills through the crowd to Berthe's side, pulling Rúnr with her at the same time Brondulf leads the litter to the fire. Someone says Helvig's name.

"The rightful jarl of Skyjavík," Brondulf declares.

"The coward you once let speak for you," Ubbein says. "I am jarl, by voice of support, as you all hear tonight. Say it, Leif!"

Geirny shouts Helvig's name, Eilif shouts Ubbein's, while some voices call for Leif's oath. Many hold their breath and wait. None seem to notice Rúnr.

Leif chooses a place not too close to Berthe and shouts, "I swear loyalty now and for all time."

Berthe draws her sword.

"Wait," Rúnr says, afraid she'll rob him again of his right to vengeance.

But she points the sword at Rúnr. "See the truth, people of Skyjavík."

Leif finishes at the same time. "I swear honesty now and for all time, to Jarl Ubbein!"

"Liar," Thyri cries out, rising from her chair.

Berthe says, "See Rúnr Njalson, unlawfully declared exile. See your Berserkr, forgiven by his jarl, my father-in-law Helvig."

Leif turns, seeing Rúnr, and for the first time Rúnr sees fear in the Hersir's face as the mead hall erupts into chaos.

CHAPTER 81

Thyri grips her knife. Her husband is shouting. Berthe—*Berthe? What draugr's barrow has she been hiding in?*—draws her sword. Helvig is . . . She can barely look at him lying there, dead if not for the rise and fall of his chest. Were he snoring, she could imagine him asleep beside her when she was his wife.

Helpless. As he always was.

As I made him.

No, no. As he made himself.

"See the truth, people of Skyjavík," Berthe says.

But Thyri already knows the truth. Rúnr lives, so Leif lied. And for that, the Hersir will die tonight. Maybe Ubbein and Rúnr will meet their ends as well, if the gods will it, but Leif's fate is hers.

"I swear honesty now and for all time, to Jarl Ubbein!" Leif says.

"Liar," Thyri shouts, standing, her knife gripped hard.

"See Rúnr Njalson," Berthe says, "unlawfully declared exile. See your Berserkr, forgiven by his jarl, my father-in-law Helvig."

The mead hall becomes like an anthill stomped by a bear. Ubbein is pointing this way and that, mute, helpless. Just like Helvig.

Maybe it's the chair. Maybe sitting in the thing even just once dries up a man's scrotum and drains his penis until it's as flaccid as a wet rope.

Rúnr's name is now on the lips of everyone in the hall as Thyri's adopted son—*Yes, my adopted son, which makes you a brother killer,*

Rúnr, like Hodr killing Baldr, but oh so much worse, for Hodr was tricked and you chose your murder—comes to face Leif across the fire. The Hersir's deception is revealed to all those gathered. It's being spoken by every tongue in the hall, some of those tongues questioning Ubbein's complicity as well.

"For whatever part you did or didn't play," she says to her husband.

She slashes at him with her knife, then flings herself at Leif. Never mind the shout for guards. Never mind the fire, which she hurtles through. Never mind she's no match for Leif as a warrior. His back is to her, and she leaps onto him, driving her knife down, feeling it bite flesh. Chortling in his ear.

"For Torstyn, you fuck!"

Hands grab her, pull and gouge and punch her, but she will not let go, not even when a biting pain rises in her back, her ribs, her gut. A burning pain. A cold pain.

"For Torstyn," she says, her mouth full of blood as she stabs and slashes until her strength ebbs and she feels herself falling. No matter. She's done her duty as mother and as jarl's wife. She's done her duty and will die content.

"Torstyn."

CHAPTER 82

Thyri, hair on fire, flies through the air.

Helvig gulps loudly, then heaves as if expelling what remains of his life.

Leif, eyes on Rúnr, reaches over his shoulder with a dagger to stab Thyri over and over before she's ripped from him and thrown down. Eilif emerges from the crowd and runs her through with his sword. She is dying with Torstyn's name on her lips, never seeing that Leif still stands, her attack causing only scratches to his neck and shoulders.

Ubbein shouts about the law and how weapons aren't allowed in the mead hall, just as castrated by the law as Helvig was when he sat in the jarl's chair.

Berthe and Ingirid pull at Rúnr, demanding opposing directions as he remains rooted to the spot, taking in the chaos around them, his eyes eventually falling on Helvig. The former jarl lies still upon his litter, his convulsions having passed, as has his life, one of his hands reaches toward Rúnr, its fingers open as if waiting for his sword.

Brondulf, seeing his lord dead, lets go of the litter. Geirny and the others do the same. Helvig falls like so much unneeded wheat, forgotten at least for the moment.

Berthe is pulled away. Ingirid shouts something. Neither matters. Leif faces Rúnr. All else is distant thunder from an even more distant storm.

"I Challenge you, Leif," Rúnr says loudly. "For the murder of my brother, Torstyn Helvigson, I Challenge you to the Circle."

"Silence," Ubbein cries.

Eilif comes for Rúnr but is held back by the crowd.

"You killed Torstyn," Leif says.

"So you told us," Brondulf counters.

"As you told us you killed Rúnr for it," Ljufu adds.

Rúnr says, "Yet here I stand, well alive."

"A Challenge," Ubbein says, trying to regain control of his hall. "A Challenge has been rightly spoken."

Leif turns slightly. "My lord?"

"You claimed his death, yet here he stands."

"I—" Leif's eyes find Helvig's litter, discarded on the floor by the fire. His stoicism shatters. His eyes dart this way and that. "Torstyn betrayed me."

"Torstyn saved me," Rúnr says.

Brondulf and Geirny flank Leif.

"The Challenge will be met in the Circle," Ubbein says. "When the sun is high tomorrow."

Leif waits for no more. He throws an elbow into Brondulf's temple and dashes through the crowd. Rúnr gives chase but is met by Eilif. The people part. This fight will happen here, now.

"Stop," Ubbein orders.

Rúnr is aware of Berthe climbing to the jarl's chair, sword in hand. "I Challenge you, Ubbein, for this chair."

"I told you I would kill you," Eilif says to Rúnr.

Rúnr draws his axe and slashes low, having no patience for this fight. Leif is nearing the door. If he makes it outside, he'll be gone, by boat or by horse, before Rúnr can catch up. Eilif, tall but fast, steps casually away. On an open field, he would avoid the strike easily, but the hall is crowded, and Ingirid is near. She throws her shoulder into Eilif's back, knocking him toward Rúnr. The tall man tries to compensate with a quick stab of his sword. Rúnr anticipates and parries easily. He has no time for Eilif and simply clubs the man in the chest with the butt end of his axe and then pushes toward the door, skirting around a clutch of armed warriors separating Berthe and Ubbein. When he reaches the exit, he yanks a spear from a warrior's hand, then looks back in time to witness Ingirid slashing open Eilif's bowels and neck with her swords.

Outside, he spies Leif fleeing toward the North Mountain, which offers more than a score of trails over its peak. He makes a powerful throw with the spear, narrowly missing the Hersir, but causing him to alter course to the road that winds toward Velaug's house. Yes, of course it will end there. Forget prophecy, forget fate. The seeress spoke the words to send Rúnr east. Now he'll slay Leif before her house so that her flowers may drink his blood and thrive.

"Leif," he shouts.

The Hersir looks back, no longer the fearless, unbeatable warrior of Rúnr's youth. And though he's a murderer, the sight of him in flight saddens Rúnr. He wants an honorable fight. A public redemption.

I want Yrsa and Torstyn, he thinks, but since when have his wants been rewarded?

Ahead, Leif stumbles. To regain his balance without falling, he's forced to turn and take another road away from Velaug's house. A familiar road. One Rúnr would prefer not to tread, but he can't let Leif go. He digs in and runs with all his strength and speed toward his own house, rounding the final curve to finally stop dead at what stands before him.

The house he remembers is gone. In its place stands Rúnr's fate.

Have you been home? he remembers Berthe asking, her eyes sad. He thought nothing of it at the time, but he understands now, for the land of his home, of his former self—son, husband, brother, father—has been plowed flat. And upon that flattened land a new building is being erected, tall and adorned with totems of the gods.

With a partially completed roof painted red as a kidney torn fresh from the dead.

And where once Yrsa lay beneath the earth, where Rúnr buried and reburied his axe not so long ago, Odin stands, a carved tableau of the Allfather's sacrifice to himself by hanging upon the branches of Yggdrasill.

As Leif flees inside, Rúnr looks up and laughs. He laughs so hard his belly hurts and tears flow. He laughs and cries until he's nearly driven to his knees. Then he stands tall and looks up.

"You must find this all so amusing," he accuses.

Three times his own height, the Allfather glares mute as Rúnr follows Leif into the red temple.

CHAPTER 83

The temple is much like the one in Uppsala, though almost mockingly so for its diminished size. The moment Rúnr steps inside, however, he feels Odin with him, like the coming of the god trance yet different, as if Odin is watching closely, still deciding whether or not to lay his hands, his gift, upon his champion.

And watching is what the Allfather is doing, with many more than one eye, for the temple's hall holds seven more totems, four of them, the ones at the corners, are each Odin. One slaying Ymir and building Midgard from his flesh. One giving his eye for knowledge. One seated with his ravens, Huginn and Muninn, upon his shoulders. And one locked in battle with Fenrir amidst the fires of Ragnarök.

The other three totems depict Thor and Freyja and Tyr, each vigilant and grim.

"You should have stayed gone," Leif says, facing Rúnr across the temple's great hall, lit by a dozen sconced torches, countless candles, and a brazier at the center between them. He holds his sword steady. Whatever fear, whatever panic he'd known in the mead hall is gone now. "Should have remained dead."

"You should have remained loyal," Rúnr says.

"I have been loyal," Leif growls. For a moment, his eyes are wild, then he finds control, that coolness Rúnr remembers in him returning. In the next breath, his face emaciates, his eyes blacken and ooze, his flesh rots and sloughs away.

To the draugr-Leif, Rúnr says, "Your jarl, your friend, lies dead on the mead hall floor."

In a blink, Leif is whole once more. He bows his head without looking away. "Your father lies dead."

"Both of them." Saying it, surprisingly, brings no pain. No regret. The time for such things is gone. Vengeance is an action of the past and the present, and Rúnr—his first vengeance stolen by Berthe—is ready to finish the past and present. He's ready for the future.

What future? There's only more vengeance waiting.

No, he tries to argue, but the truth is as obvious as Leif's intentions. Ingirid will find Garmr, and when their former captain is dead, she'll slay Rúnr. His violent circle will finally be broken.

Won't you be pleased, Erasmus?

Leif holds his sword casually and looks to the sky. Rúnr can't help a glance as well. At the red roof above.

"The red temple," he says, naming the obvious. "It was you."

Leif narrows his eyes. "What do you accuse me of?"

"My vengeance for Yrsa comes in a red temple, and here we are."

"For Yrsa?" Leif lowers his sword, confusion and horror plain on his face. "I wasn't there. No one was there but you and the Fenns. Now come, boy. Let's see if Odin favors you still."

"Fuck Odin and his god trances."

Leif advances, fast for a graybeard, his sword slicing close enough to hack off half of Rúnr's black beard were he not quick as well. Two more slashes and Rúnr is backed against Odin's legs, the All-father's eye glaring and unimpressed. Leif's next attack is a feint and a stab. The point of his sword sticks into Odin's wooden groin where Rúnr's head was a moment ago. A feint of his own followed by a quick jab with his axe gives Rúnr the advantage. Leif is forced to leave his sword stuck in the totem like Odin's own cross-hilted phallus.

The Hersir snatches a torch from its sconce. Axe versus torch, a good match for Rúnr, but Leif is canny and experienced, and the fight turns quickly again when Leif throws his torch like a spear. Rúnr ducks, but Leif uses the time to pull free his sword. The next seconds are a relentless clash of iron. And heat. Only peripherally does Rúnr become aware that the thrown torch has set the totem of Freyja ablaze behind him. Leif, however, has already found a way to turn the moment to his benefit, his quick feet and quicker sword pressing Rúnr backward, deeper into the temple's hall, the door at Leif's back, until Rúnr knocks into the brazier, toppling it and spreading flames like spilled ale.

Against these flames, Rúnr feels something coming. Something different. Something that makes him think again of the Painted Fenn and the vengeance stolen from him. He thinks inexplicably of Ingimar and of the Raumsdair Berserkr.

Leif feints one way, comes the other. Rúnr parries. Tries to flank Leif but is thwarted. He goes straightaway. Again, the Hersir is prepared. The flames climb to Freyja's hair. Leif slashes twice, the second jarring Rúnr's axe so that his hand goes almost numb, the ringing rising to his elbow. Then his shoulder. Rising still, to his neck, his skull.

It comes.

But it's not the god trance. The tightness in his bones is there, as is the pressure behind his eyes, and the way his vision begins to funnel, but this is different. It's not Odin's breath nor Thor's lightning. As the flames climb from Freyja to the ceiling like salamanders, as Rúnr grips the bear's tooth around his neck, he knows it is something new overtaking him.

"You should have died on that mountain," Leif says.

He comes fast and true, faster than Rúnr can counter. Smoke fills the temple, choking, making it difficult to breathe. Pain flares in Rúnr's ribs. He cannot find Leif. He can barely see. Barely think. If the Hersir stays, he'll slice Rúnr to pieces. If he's fled, then Rúnr will burn.

"All this way just to die here, Allfather?" More pain ignites in Rúnr's shoulder, his hip, his ribs from Leif's relentless blade.

The burning roof begins to crack, pieces of it falling, narrowly missing him. Very well. If it must be smoke and flame, if it must be sword and failure, then that's how it must be.

"I'm sorry brother," he says, raising his axe and closing his eyes and waiting for what must come.

CHAPTER 84

"Papa."

Rúnr blinks the smoke away only to discover there is no smoke. He's in the black. Yrsa is with him, smaller than he remembers. The beast he's heard before in the black approaches. Taking form the closer it gets until it becomes a black bear. At the sight of Rúnr it rears to the height of two men.

Rúnr knows this bear well.

"You must kill the brute," Yrsa says. "You must kill the beast."

Rúnr's hands are empty. He reaches for his axe but finds it's not on his belt.

"When the beast is gone," his daughter says, "I will feast in the great hall."

This she's told him before, but Berthe has already slain the Painted Fenn. That vengeance is done.

"It's not done," Yrsa says.

Again, he remembers Ingimar. He remembers the Raumsdair Berserkr. He remembers Leif's words: *No one was there but—*

"You," Yrsa says.

"Me?"

Yrsa smiles.

The bear roars. Its teeth are knives. Its claws are daggers. It strikes.

There's no pain in this place. Only need. To stab. To hurt. To kill. Rúnr's first blow, a mighty punch, barely ruffles the bear's fur. His second, after ducking below a sweeping paw, draws the tiniest drop of blood. There can be no defeating this beast in such a manner.

Yrsa sets herself between the bear and Rúnr.

"No," Rúnr shouts, determined to take the bear's next strike.

It lands square on his shoulder, spinning him, throwing him down.

Unafraid, Yrsa stands before the bear.

"You must kill the beast," she says.

"It's too strong."

She shakes her head, tears rolling down her cheeks. The black turns, twists, becoming a shade. Red, like the temple. Like fire. Like blood.

The bear swats her down. She lands across Rúnr's lap, still smiling though her throat is wide open to the bone. Her blood soaks his hands.

"Yrsa," he cries.

Memory comes like an avalanche. The sounds of the raid. The need to protect his family. The Painted Fenn. The pressure behind his eyes. The stone man. The shadow-hag. Ingimar. Yrsa in his lap. The axe.

It's there, in her hands, painted with her blood. As it was that night.

"The beast killed me," she says.

Understanding comes now with the power of the bear's attack. The brute. The beast. The Berserkr.

Me.

"I killed you," Rúnr whispers, remembering it all. The god trance taking him as the Painted Fenn struck. The Berserkr's attacks a whirling rage, driving back the enemy but, like with Ingimar, cutting down all who came too close. Even his brave Little Bear.

"Free me, Papa. Kill the beast. Free yourself."

Rúnr weeps tears of blood that fall and drench his daughter. "How?" he asks, the pain in his chest worse than if the bear were to rip him open and spread his ribs to chew the marrow.

His dead daughter's hand touches his. He understands. The god trance is a gift. To use. To refuse. But how?

"Kill the beast," Yrsa says. She fades until she becomes smoke, and then like nothing at all.

In her place, the axe remains. Rúnr stands and wields it against the beast. It comes, roaring and hungry. He swings once, twice. Two paws fall. He chops the axe down into the beast's skull. It howls in pain and then fades as Yrsa did.

And then he's in the temple once more, the roof burning above him. Leif lies at his feet, both hands dismembered, and his skull split open. From somewhere Rúnr hears his name.

"Rúnr," Ingirid shouts. "This way."

Though he can't see her through the smoke, he can follow her voice. He can escape. If he wants to.

Movement draws his eye. There, his Little Bear, barely a shadow next to Odin giving his eye for knowledge. Above, the burning beams creak and begin to crack.

If we hear death coming, Rúnr remembers telling Yrsa, *we'll grab my axe together so the Valkyries can find us.*

All he has to do is hold out the axe and let her grip it, her hand next to his, and they'll go to Valhalla together. But as he looks upon the axe, he knows he cannot. Whatever its strange runes offer—power, perhaps, or a curse—it's no longer part of his fate. He lets it fall from his hand.

"I've fulfilled two oaths, Little Bear. I still owe one."

"It's okay, Papa." Yrsa smiles at her father. "The Valkyries come."

Rúnr knows they do. He pulls the black bear's tooth from around his neck and drops it beside the axe.

The burning beam above him snaps and falls.

CHAPTER 85

Ingirid has never seen such smoke, not even when Miklagard burned. She's surprised that trees remain standing in the Opplands for the size of this pyre burning on Skyjavík's beach. The honor granted here for Helvig is intended for the gods themselves to see, and surely, they must.

Beside her, Rúnr grunts. It sounds like approval, but she's not sure she knows him well enough anymore.

"Are you coming?" she asks.

He looks back toward the mead hall. Or maybe to something beyond it. They spent the night together, after the brief battle in the hall and the burning of the temple. After the deaths of Leif and Helvig. After Berthe cut down Ubbein in the makeshift Circle that formed in the mead hall. Ingirid wishes she'd been there to see that.

It was a good night, the two of them together. He told her what he discovered about the god trance and his daughter's death. She was angry at first, that he could do such a thing. Then she was sad for him. Then . . . she could not understand, exactly, because who could understand living with such knowledge, but maybe she could accept.

After they spoke, they gave in to their passions like they used to. Before. Maybe the start, or restart, of something. Maybe the end.

"I don't think so," he says.

"She's down there, your seeress, performing the funeral."

"I'll wait at her house."

That nagging jealousy rises. She tries to be reasonable. "Are you angry with her?"

"Maybe. I'll see what she says."

Ingirid thinks he should be angry. She wants him to be angry.

He turns and goes without saying goodbye. This doesn't make her angry. It just makes her a little lonely. Then again, she realizes, she was a little lonely with him last night. As if the man she used to know was not fully present.

She turns back to the pyre, its smoke touching the setting sun. The funeral nears its end when she approaches the beach's sand and stones.

"You might like it here," she says to the autumn air, thinking her words might somehow find Erasmus, wherever he roams. It's a place for people who enjoy farms and fishing and families and foundations. If she ever meets him again, she'll tell him to try this place, Rúnr's home, as his own.

On the beach, the seeress speaks her final words and takes her leave of the scene, soon to meet Rúnr at her home. For a moment, Ingirid is tempted to go, but the gods watch seeresses, and she doesn't want to be seen by the Aesir, just in case Garmr is what his name says.

"You're leaving."

Ingirid laughs at herself, having allowed not just one person to approach without noting them, but the jarl with full entourage.

All the more reason this is not a place for me, she thinks. *Comfort leads to complacency.*

"We've made no secret of it," Ingirid says, nudging the pack at her feet.

Jarl Berthe nods knowingly. Her retinue is large, her support growing by the moment now that those few who supported Ubbein and still live have been shown the way out of Skyjavík.

The two women eye each other a moment. Berthe's left arm is bandaged, and there's a wound on her neck below her ear, same side as Ingirid's maimed ear. Berthe stands tall and strong, but she's tired, Ingirid can see, in need of rest. It's the kind of thing a woman can see in another woman, but most men won't ever notice. The kind of thing Ingirid won't betray.

"Can we speak alone?" she asks, showing the proper respect for a jarl.

Berthe dismisses her attendants. When they're alone, Berthe's shoulders relax. She bows her head briefly. "I would have made Rúnr my Hersir," she says.

Ingirid speaks the truth they both know, "He wouldn't have accepted."

"No, but my offer would have been for him to decline, so I could ask you after."

"Me?"

"The old ways are fucked, I think," Berthe says. "What your Rus have done in Miklagard, what Ragnar Lothbrók did in Francia, and the havoc he spreads now across the Saxon Isles, things are changing."

I bet that blond bastard can be found within that havoc, Ingimar whispers.

It's a fine idea, one worth pursuing.

"If I can be jarl," Berthe continues, "why not change who can be Hersir. Or even what a Hersir can do."

It's a good point, though to what end, Ingirid is unsure—it's not like men will step aside and women will sit on all the jarls' chairs. One thing she does know is that whatever jealousy she felt for Berthe is dead, which may not be the same as admitting she likes Rúnr's ex-wife yet, but she likes her as jarl. She likes the idea of change, even if she's not ready to embrace such changes herself.

"I can't be that," Ingirid says.

"I know. You'll leave to seek your revenge."

"I will." Ingirid imagines the disappointment Erasmus would show in her decision, and this both heartens her and fills her with melancholy. "You keep making changes, though. Just remember if you defeat all the men, there'll be nothing left to change."

"I don't suspect the world will run short of old men clinging to old ways in my lifetime."

The two women are silent for a time. The pyre burns like Surtr's sword cleaving Midgard.

"I thought he'd come for his father," Berthe says. "To say goodbye."

Ingirid is uncertain if she means goodbye to Helvig upon the pyre, or goodbye to her. Either way, it's not her place to answer for Rúnr's decisions.

"He watched from afar for a time," she says.

Berthe looks off in the direction Rúnr went. "And then went to her."

Ingirid shrugs.

"You go there now?" the jarl asks.

A good question. There are oaths to be reckoned, and blood.

Blood, Ingimar's voice says. *For me.*

"I go there now," Ingirid says.

"He was never mine, you know," Berthe says. "He'll never be yours either."

"We have a pact," Ingirid says. "An oath."

"So did we."

"You broke that, not him."

Berthe sighs. If she seemed tired moments ago, she's exhausted now. "I speak as your friend," she says.

"Is that what we are?"

"Until you betray me, or him, yes, I think so."

It's a fair accord. "I think so too."

"As your friend, then, just know that he belongs to himself."

Ingirid bites back a spiteful reply and thinks on this a moment. He's not the same man she met, that's certain. Is he still the man who can help her find and kill Garmr? If he's no longer the Berserkr, as he told her he suspects, is he useful to her at all?

"And we are two women making changes in the world," Ingirid says at length.

Berthe nods respectfully. "We are that."

Berthe turns to go, but Ingirid speaks.

"May I make a suggestion for your first full night as jarl?"

"Of course," Berthe says over her shoulder.

"Leave the feast early. Get some rest."

Berthe smiles. "You'll make a good Hersir."

Enough, Ingimar says. *It's time for blood.*

"Someday, maybe," Ingirid says.

"Someday," Berthe says.

Soon she's gone and Ingirid is alone on the small hill. She stays until the people have left the beach and Helvig's pyre has begun to wane. Finally, with the sun dipped below the mountains, she hefts her pack and makes her way to the seeress's home.

CHAPTER 86

Rúnr paces Velaug's home, his boots walking familiar floors, his nose inhaling familiar scents, his memories recalling familiar moments. But these moments tell like someone else's life stuck inside his mind, so he turns his thoughts to other memories. More recent ones. Like last night with Ingirid. Like his conversation with Berthe this morning.

"Will you be a good jarl?" he asked her.

She laughed, but not for long. Her smile faded. Her eyes narrowed. She drew a knife and touched its point to his chest. "I think of our daughter often," she said softly.

Rúnr's throat became a fist, a knot that refused to loosen. He fought tears, knowing then that he had to leave. Staying here confused him. It clouded his Little Bear in his mind.

"I think you do too," Berthe continued. "It was unfair of me to accuse you of otherwise. Do you remember how she liked sunsets?"

The tears came. Yrsa never stopped asking questions, Rúnr remembered.

Where does the sun go at night?

Does the sun ever sleep?

How do you know? Can we ask the seeress to be sure?

"She feasts in Valhalla," he said, his voice broken.

"I'm certain of it." She withdrew the knife and gripped his wrist with her free hand and turned his hand over and drew the blade across his palm, tracing the scar left from his visits to the seeress. "Bleed for her," she said, all the rage of all the gods in her voice.

It took everything Rúnr had not to flinch. She cut him again, crossways. This time, he couldn't help a grimace. And tears.

"Yrsa's killer truly is gone, isn't it?" she asked, her anger lessened, though maybe not the condemnation for him.

He shook his head. He didn't know then, and he doesn't know now.

"You owe no blood price," she told him.

"You'll be a good jarl," he managed to say.

She did not look back when she left.

The memory drains him so that he stops pacing and sits in the chair in Velaug's house, the one for those seeking prophecy. It's uncomfortable, hard and unforgiving. Like a jarl's chair. Like fate. Rúnr can't help a laugh at that.

"Humor is rare in this house," Velaug says.

Rúnr, startled, gets clumsily to his feet. "It wasn't always," he says.

There, the twitch of a smile, though it's gone so quickly he can't be certain he even saw it. For a moment he wonders if the Velaug he remembers is still in there, then he lets the thought go.

"I thought you'd attend your father's funeral," she says.

"You don't know everything, then." He tries to say it playfully, but it comes out flat. Maybe even accusatory.

"I know you think one father's funeral is enough."

To this, he nods. It's exactly what he thinks.

"I've come." He pauses. What has he come to do? To ask? To tell? To accuse?

"All who come here have questions. Most have more than one. Ask yours."

Though he respects her role, this persona, he decides he hates it. Finds it insulting to the young woman he once loved. And for that, he finds that he no longer wants to see that young woman in this seeress anymore. He wants answers from the gods, and he sees no reason to think he'll get them here.

"Never mind," he says. "I wish you well."

He makes it as far as the door.

"Rúnr," Velaug says.

Without looking at her, he says with all the venom he is capable of producing, "Did you know where the red temple would be found?"

"Sit in the chair."

"I don't want—"

"Sit in the chair."

He does, avoiding her eyes.

"They call me seeress," she says, "but I see nothing but what is before me. I hear nothing but what the gods whisper in my mind, and that, I must tell you, is not a language any mortal can speak. I tell what I am given to tell. Nothing more. Nothing less."

"You didn't know the red temple would be built here?"

"Not until it was being built."

"You didn't know what I—" He chokes on his own words.

She places a hand on his shoulder. "I suspected from the time it happened, but I did not know."

"You suspected?" He shrugs. Her hand falls aside.

"Would you have wanted me to tell you my thoughts?"

He wants to scream yes, but that would be a lie. He wouldn't have accepted her words as truth, not then. He needed to learn it the way he did. But to have to go all the way to Miklagard to earn that moment? And all the death between then and now?

What would he have done, he wonders, had he known from the start? Would he have let Eilif or Leif kill him? Would he have taken his own life? Could he have ever accepted, like he does now? Would he have exchanged his time with Garmr and Erasmus and Ingirid and Ingimar to know sooner? Would Ingimar have to die?

And what of all the Fenns and Christians and more he's killed? His oath to kill Garmr?

The gods must be insane, he thinks, *to demand such things of us while still expecting veneration.*

"And we must be insane to give it," Velaug says, finishing the thought.

"You do know my mind, then?"

"I know you, Rúnr. Sometimes, knowing the person is enough."

Which makes him think of the endless cycle of violence Erasmus spoke of. Which is the only real question left, he decides. The cycle, and his role in it.

"The god trance," he says, "the beast, is it gone?"

Velaug looks him up and down. "You carry an axe, but not the same one. You wear no bear's tooth."

"But am I—me and nothing more?"

"You have always been you and nothing more. But," she adds when he's about to protest, "who you were was much more complicated than who you are now."

It seems a straightforward answer, but he knows better. "Will the god trance take me again, or not?"

"No."

Rúnr closes his eyes and sees in that darkness a bright hall. And there sits Yrsa, his Little Bear, at a fine table surrounded by the best of men and women, brave warriors all.

"Unless you ask for it," Velaug says.

Rúnr's stomach twists as his eyes open. "Odin doesn't heed demands from his champion."

"He doesn't, but sometimes he answers those he favors."

"And he still favors me?"

For the briefest moment, her eyes pale, but like the smile he thought he saw earlier, that too is gone quickly. "Odin always favors the brave, and who is braver than a Berserkr?"

"Anyone," Rúnr says. "Maybe everyone."

Velaug kneels and places her hands over his ears, her palms warm. "Do you hear?" she asks, her voice as if far away.

Inside his skull, the sounds of the sea, soft and rolling, calm and beckoning.

"The harbor," he says. "The fjord. The sea. The . . . No, wait."

It's not the ebb and flow of the sea, he hears. It's his own blood in his veins, tiny rivers of thunder and violence, currents that keep him walking, talking, breathing, fighting, fucking, eating, sleeping.

Velaug removes her hands. "Do you hear it now?"

"No."

"If you want to hear your blood, place your hands over your ears. If you don't want to, if you want the peace of the wind and the sea and the frogs and the kites, don't cover them."

"I think—" he stops mid-sentence. Kites, she said. "A red-bodied kite."

Velaug stands, offering her hands. He takes them and gets to his feet.

"I help when I can," she says.

The number of questions flooding Rúnr's mind is almost too much, a hundredfold more varied and intense than the usual scattered streams that make up his thoughts. But he asks none of them. He knows she won't answer.

"If you choose it," she says, "you are free."

"If *you* choose it, you can be free. You can be Velaug, daughter of Olga," he says, not for himself or for the two of them but for *herself.*

She smiles politely. "I'm the seeress, promised to the gods. And you're promised to Ingirid of the Rus."

"A blood oath, not a marriage."

"What difference is one pact from another?" Velaug says.

The circle, as in all things. As Erasmus pointed out. Live, die, and another will do the same after, endlessly until Ragnarök. And then again until the next ending to bring a beginning. And then again. Forever.

Prophecy.

Fate.

Oath.

Rúnr misses his friend Erasmus. Maybe they'll meet again. Maybe the hunt for Garmr will bring him and Ingirid the merchant's way. Maybe . . .

"Tell me my fate, seeress," he says.

Velaug comes closer to him than she's been in years. Her breasts press into his sternum. Her breath is of cinnamon and onion and mint. She places her palms on his shoulders, her toes to his toes. He waits for her eyes to become ice, but they remain blue as the sky.

"No," she says.

"No?"

"Knowing your fate won't help you or make you happy, but I'll tell you this. Yrsa dines in Valhalla. One day, you will too."

"Is that a promise?"

"It's what I know of you, Rúnr Njalson. It doesn't take a seeress to know you'll die a warrior's death. Be satisfied with that."

He almost asks if he'll see her again, but he no longer wants to know what will come. Maybe he'll return this way one day. Maybe he won't. That's enough for him now.

Velaug smiles, for real this time. Like when they were young. He leaves her house, making certain not to touch the bloodstained doorpost.

Outside, Ingirid kneels beside a tuft of purple flowers.

"Learn anything about your fate?" she says, standing, a flower in her hand.

"It's not here," Rúnr says.

"Nor with me."

"What—my oath?"

"You're no longer the man who seeks blood or vengeance," Ingirid says. "And that's okay. I like who you are now, but that's not who I need where I'm going. When you're ready for adventure, I'll see you again."

He almost protests, but a small voice in his head—a voice not unlike Yrsa's—tells him she's right.

"Is that a threat?" he asks.

She gives that crooked grin and drops the flower and walks away, leaving Rúnr with no direction to go.

No, not no direction, he thinks. *Any direction I want.*

He picks up the flower and goes the opposite way and doesn't look back until the moon is high and the seeress's house is long gone from sight.

EPILOGUE

The farmer shoos two goats from his barley rows with a stick. It's a good crop. Hearty. Growing well here where little else prefers, but not so abundant that he can sacrifice any to his goats. He tosses a few carrots, tempting the goats further away and turns back to the barley, the glint of steel catching his eye. He squints into the late-day sun, watching as a warband comes over the rise.

Two dozen, armored, mounted, riding with purpose. Too many, and too well equipped, to be bandits. And what could his little farm offer anyway?

The farmer moves to the edge of his lands, hoping to keep the horses from trampling his barley. They pull up a ship's length away. It's a hot afternoon. He wipes sweat from his brow. Clenches the stick. Just in case.

A forked-bearded man, clearly the leader, climbs down from his horse, followed by three others. Each removes their helm. The farmer tenses, expecting a familiar face, but sees none he recognizes.

Somewhere, a wolf howls a sad verse.

The leader inclines his head as if awaiting an invitation. The farmer doesn't offer one. The leader comes forward anyway.

"We're looking for someone," he says, a hint of humor in his voice, as if he expects the farmer to know what he means. To be in on the joke.

The farmer finds no humor in the situation. He swallows hard and waits. Just in case. But nothing rises within him. "What would you have me do about it?" he asks.

"Maybe you know the man we seek."

"Maybe I don't."

The leader comes closer. He's tall and thick-shouldered with the countenance of a king.

"We've ridden many days with the permission of the jarl in search of her husband."

"The jarl isn't married."

"Ex-husband, then."

The farmer pokes at the ground with his stick.

The leader's eyes narrow. "We were told the Oppland Berserkr lives out here."

The farmer sighs. "The Oppland Berserkr—"

"Don't say he's a myth. We know better."

The farmer points at the barley. He points at the goats and the tiny cottage. "Does this look like a Berserkr's home?"

The leader motions to the others. The three who've dismounted return to the warband and prompt a man from his horse. The man is shuffled forward. Unfamiliar face but familiar markings on his arms and shield. A Fenn.

"Tell him," the leader says.

"I've seen the Berserkr," the Fenn says. "It's real."

"And does he look like me?" the farmer asks.

The Fenn stutters, looks to the leader, to the sky, the ground.

"I've seen the Berserkr's body," the farmer says.

The leader steps on the first row of barley. "Where?"

"In the temple to Odin that burned more than a year ago. He fought for the jarl, as did I."

"You were there?"

The farmer nods.

The leader seems to chew on his own tongue. Spits blood. Licks his lips. "Do you remember Ragnar Lothbrók?"

"All know the stories of Ragnar Lothbrók."

"Then you've heard of his death, executed by a cowardly Saxon king who cast him into a pit of serpents?"

"I did not know this."

"I am Hvitserk, Ragnar's second son."

"You have my sympathies for your father. He was a great hero."

Hvitserk bows his head briefly, as if remembering. "My brothers and I are gathering an army to raid the Saxons. Invade their lands like never before."

The farmer nods, understanding. "For vengeance," he says.

Hvitserk's eyes flash fire. "Yes! For vengeance!"

"The Berserkr is dead."

"You look strong."

"I'm a farmer."

"We've all been farmers, friend. We'll all be farmers again when the Saxons are slaughtered and we have our choice of their green lands."

The farmer forces a smile. "I'm not a warrior any longer."

Hvitserk appraises him up and down. "Jarl Berthe has pledged a hundred men," Hvitserk says. "We have room for a hundred and one."

The farmer looks past Hvitserk at the warband. They seem formidable. Opplanders there, and Fenns, Swedes, Danes, Jutes. A true army of the North. He wonders if *she* is among this army, somewhere. If she'll sail with them across the sea to fight the Saxons. If she'll fall in battle.

Something stirs within him. Fear? Hope?

He looks to the cloudless sky and imagines her cutting through Saxon after Saxon, her crooked smile the last thing each sees.

She'll not die before she's had her vengeance, he's certain.

As certain as he is that one day she'll find him, wherever he may be.

Easier if he stays here and waits.

"I'm just a farmer," he says.

Hvitserk signals and the others climb their mounts while he stays, chewing his tongue, eyeing the farmer. "We sail from Skyjavík in three days," he says.

The farmer says, "May you find strong winds and calm waves."

Hvitserk spits, then climbs his own mount, and soon the warband is riding for Skyjavík and the farmer is chasing the goats from his barley. Somewhere, a wolf howls and a bird *chirrups*. Maybe a kite.

ACKNOWLEDGMENTS

At the end of 2020, working from home during the COVID-19 pandemic, I wrote the acknowledgments section for *The Hidden Empire*, my final Rafael Ward book, and one thing I noted was: "I'm working on a Viking ghost story."

Well, this ain't exactly a ghost story you're reading. But it's also not *not* a ghost story. In any case, the Viking Book, as I've spent the last few years calling it, has gone through some changes, including time period, geography covered, and even point of view, which I switched from first to third person at about the 60K-word mark of the first draft (what in the name of Hel was I thinking?).

Whatever I did, things went right eventually, but not without the input, help, and support of so many people. I'm going to name some of them here. I'm going to forget to name some of them here, and for that I apologize.

Thank you first, and always . . .

Colleen, my love, best friend, and occasional sparring partner.

Our children, Coraline and Rowan. And our cat, Wednesday (because the kids asked me to include her).

Next, my heartfelt thanks to my agent, Kimberly Fernando, for her endless enthusiasm and confidence, and for giving me and this book the one shot we needed. To Evan Phail, my editor, for challenging me to make every bit of this book as great as it can be, and also to keep checking my sources. Ugh, real work—am I right?

And to all the fine people at Diversion Books who worked their butts off to help make this book into, well . . . this book.

Thank you to Melissa Seyler, a never-ending source of support and belief in me. Dan Schall, Michelle Tooker, Bright Kelly, Susan Alloway; so much of this book rounded into shape because of your feedback, advice, questions, and suggestions. Jessie Bacho, Jenn Fleetwood, Abigail Michelini; I couldn't have gotten here without our writing time together and you three propping me up whenever I started losing momentum. Eric Smith; always willing to answer a question, give a recommendation, or help me decide on a book title—dude, look: it's freakin' *Valhalla Burning*!

One last note. Some of the places and events in this book are real, such as the siege of Constantinople in June 860 by the Rus', and I did a ton of research in order to write a book that shares a fairly accurate view of Norse life and customs. But this is a work of fiction and fantasy. I invented a good deal of the details, filling blanks where the facts are thin, or where the story needed a nudge in a different direction. So, just to clarify, all inaccuracies are my own, mostly on purpose.